Peeces of Eight

Peeces of Eight

Based on characters created and immortalised
by Robert Louis Stevenson

A.J. Rimini

The Pentland Press Limited
Edinburgh • Cambridge • Durham • USA

First published in 1999 by
The Pentland Press Ltd.
1 Hutton Close
South Church
Bishop Auckland
Durham

British Library Cataloguing in Publication Data.
A Catalogue record for this book is available
from the British Library.

ISBN 1 85821 691 5

Typeset by CBS, Martlesham Heath, Ipswich, Suffolk
Printed and bound by Antony Rowe Ltd., Chippenham

For my wife, Janet.
A Treasure Beyond Calculation!

"I think you will eventually get to where you want to go,
but it'll take you longer than you think!"

Words that were spoken to me by my wife when I first
started writing – Thirty-One Years ago!

The Understatement for: 1968!

CONTENTS

ACKNOWLEDGEMENTS xi

FOREWORD xiii

PROLOGUE 1
Soundings From Long John!

BOOK ONE

PEECE I 11
A Call to the Colours!

I	Beware the Press!	13
II	HMS *Agony*!	17
III	Ordinary Seaman Silver RN!	21
IV	Death of a Swab!	25
V	Birth of a Buccaneer!	30

PEECE II 35
The Gathering!

VI	Long John Silver Esq. – Gentleman o' Fortune!	37
VII	Blackbeard's Gunner!	42
VIII	Mister William Bones – Mate!	48
IX	Cold Steel – Hot Blood!	52
X	Flint – Flower of the Freebooters!	58

PEECE III 69
Flint's Flock!

XI	Messrs Pew and Black Dog!	71
XII	Ben Gunn and Co!	79
XIII	Flint's Flying Forty!	88
XIV	Flash Dan!	93
XV	Escape from Porto Bello!	99

PEECE IV 107
On the Account!

VI	Pop Goes the Weasel!	109
XVII	Making Purchase!	117
XVIII	Clapping Aboard!	128
XIX	Serpents, Sharks and Silver Bars!	140
XX	Nanny Town!	151

BOOK TWO

PEECE V 165
Disaster and Deliverance!

XXI The Flying Dutchman! 167
XXII The Battle of Lowether's Folly – Dry Blows! 181
XXIII Wooden Ships – Iron Men! 195
XXIV Minus Five Toes! 206
XXV Sanctuary in Savannah! 212

PEECE VI 221
Of Savage Seas and Men!

XXVI Flint's New Quarter-Master! 223
XXVII The Sacking of Sarasota! 230
XXVIII Treasure – Yellow Jack – and a Tempest! 244
XXIX Cannibals! 254
XXX A French Coward and a Courageous Carib! 262

PEECE VII
Mutiny! 271

XXXI Blind Pew's Duel! 273
XXXII Port Tack! 281
XXIII A Cripple Grapples Four! 289
XXXIV Devils Never Die! 295
XXXV Fifteen Men! 304

PEECE VIII Skeleton Island!		313
XXXVI	Marooned!	315
XXXVII	Flint's Last Fling!	322
XXXVIII	Billy Bowls Out!	332
XXXIX	Walrus Goes West!	346
XL	The Quest for Flint's Fist!	358
GLOSSARY		365
SOME VERY GOOD BOOKS		377

ACKNOWLEDGEMENTS

I would like to express my appreciation for the encouragement given to me by the late Gordon McKenzie, a one time Executive Editor of the *Daily Mail*, who tried so hard on my behalf to promote *Peeces of Eight.*

My daughter, Diane, deserves a mention for all the time she spent in doing various things for me, regarding this book, on her computer. She inherited her mother's brains along with my good looks!!

And to Stacy Keach, for his comments, suggestions and for taking time out from a very hectic work schedule to write an excellent 'Foreword'.

Finally, my most profound thanks to my sister, Freda, without whose help and support, *Peeces of Eight* would never have been launched!

I'd also like to extend my gratitude to R.L. Stevenson and Robert Newton for giving us *Treasure Island* and 'Long John Silver'. A further list of acknowledgements can be found at the back of this book!

FOREWORD

Peeces of Eight is a great read. A grand romantic, swashbuckler of a book that just gets better with each chapter. An unforgettable tale of yesteryear with a superb gallery of characters, combined with terrific action and battle scenes so vivid, I almost started coughing because of all the powder smoke swirling between decks.

In this fore-runner to *Treasure Island*, the language and texture of it is so tight, and such great fun to read, it sweeps the reader along at a heart racing pace from one adventure to the next.

Although Stevenson created Black Dog, Blind Pew, Billy Bones and Flint, Al Rimini was the one who blew the full breath of life into them, especially Captain Flint. He rises up in the story like an ogre, larger than life and twice as terrible as the bloodiest buccaneer ever to have appeared either in fact or fiction. I just hope he doesn't cause the kids to have nightmares. However, I deem it an honour and a privilege to surface briefly in the story and get 'bumped off' by him!

Long John Silver truly emerges as a full-bodied incarnation of the original. Well, perhaps not so 'full bodied'! In fact I'm convinced that he *is* the original and R.L.S. followed A.J.R.! Given time, *Peeces of Eight* might well rank alongside *Treasure Island* for pure story telling and high adventure. Aside from being a canny historian, Al Rimini really does have an ancient, nautical savvy that is remarkable.

It's hard to pin point a favourite chapter. All great stuff. I really take a hankering to those sea-fights and tales of battle, murder and sudden death. I found the introduction of the women, funny, colourful and romantic. The whole thing is like a return to a big 'birthday party for pirates'. I loved the scene with the ghost-ship, very eerie and evocative – a sure-fire winner for suspense. The description of the Seminoles is some of Al's most poetic rendering. Also, Long John's amputation sequence conjures up fantastic scenes, culminating in the death of Old McGinty. Another memorable scene is when they storm Sarasota and discover the treasure. I could almost feel that gold trickling through my own fingers.

It's a terrific saga full of life, colour and adventure; of eloquent descriptions and interesting facts and characters pertaining to their time. Long John's first meeting with Israel Hands and Billy Bones. Then his encounter with the shadowy, mysterious figure of Jim Flint. A great whale of a swashbuckling section.

I knew it was just a matter of time before someone would pick up this story. I'm proud to say I was a small part of the process and it's a pleasure knowing you – not only as a friend, but also as a fellow artist. What more can I say? Terrific action and suspense. Snakes, crocodiles, storms, sea-fights, cannibals, battle, murder and mutiny – it's all here. You really put the reader right in there along with the characters, Al. It was a joy to read and I couldn't put it down.

STACY KEACH

PROLOGUE

SOUNDINGS FROM LONG JOHN!

Robert Louis Stevenson – by the Powers what a Scribe! Barring Defoe, Ballantyne and a precious few others his match were never seen – you may lay to that! He was a Master story teller, him that created me. And he immortalised hisself when he penned us Pirates into the pages of *TREASURE ISLAND*!

But he's dead now. Dead and under hatches in far off Samoa where he has laid a-top o' Mount Vaea for these past Hundred Years.

The Captain, I calls him that out of respect, was dogged by ill-health for all the forty and four years he held the Helm, but he weren't the one to complain or holler for 'Quarter' and 'Strike his Colours' – not him! When illness had him close-hauled with his bows facing a lee-shore, he clawed off from the very teeth o' destruction. It was a double go of Grog for all hands and Stand-By to Come-About! Why, with hardly a shot left in his locker he repelled boarders against lung fever in San Francisco on the Californ'y Coast. Fanny, his lady-love, was the one who nursed him back from beyond the Bar. Dragged him feet first out from under Davy Jones's lock, in a manner o' speaking, same as my Negress done for me after a broadside from the Royal Navy lost me my leg off Palm Key. Death's final cannonade caught the Captain unawares as he stood talking gaily along with his mess-mates on the veranda of his house at Vailima. Thundering apoplexy chopped him down like that much pork, the same as did for Billy Bones the Mate – you mind Billy?

Now the pity of it were this: What with writing other classics such as *Kidnapped* and *The Amazing Case of Doctor Jekyll and Mister Hyde* after he finished *Treasure Island*, he never found time to tell the tale of Ben Gunn and Black Dog, Blind Pew and Billy Bones; of Morgan, Merry, Israel Hands, Job Anderson and Me, and how we all came together and went 'On the Account' a-buccaneering under Jim Flint in the *Walrus* as I've seen scuppers under in purple gore and fit to sink with Gold. By thunder, but there was some powder burnt aboard that old War-Horse of the Waves – so there was!

So here be a sorry plight: Crew intact and Ship intact, but both in irons. Any Fo'c'sle Hand worth his salt can steer a course, but who's to set one? What with the Captain gone below there were none to take over the helm, so it looked to be as if the Spanish Main had seen the last of us. To be sure, we were snug enough on this lee-side o' literature with plenty of grog, tobaccy and fresh rations, but Buccaneers weren't born to eat dainty and laze around for all their days. It just ain't in our character not to have t' repel boarders an' organise killing parties in quest for plunder. But here we were with no 'ope of hoisting the Jolly Roger ever again – or so we supposed.

It was a little before the 'First Bell' of the Middle Watch on New Year's Morning, way back in '77, that this stranger first clapped aboard our realm of fantasy. With not so much as by-your-leave he sat down opposite me alongside the mess-deck table, then poured hisself a brandy from my own bottle, so he did, calm as you please. Took a good gill too – sink him for a land-locked lubber!

'Well if this don't top the stiffest yard-arm to nothing,' thinks I. 'This swab is either bolder than brass, an escaped Bedlamite or a fool!' Even Old Flint hisself wouldn't o' dared broach Long John's bottle without asking permission – you may lay to that!

"John Silver," says he, taking out this battered, rusty baccy-tin. "I have had my weather-eye on you and your Gang, ever since I began scribing for a pass-time ten years ago."

"And who might you be, if I may make so bold?" I asked, wondering if Ben Gunn, him being on watch, had gone to sleep under the poop again.

"Why, John," replied the Stranger surprised, looking up from rolling tobaccy in a piece of paper. "I'm your New Author, just come aboard, so summon the Crew if you please and lively – for what I have to say to you shall be said to all."

'Thunder,' thought I, 'and here's promotion!'

New Author indeed! Just let this lubber try lording it over Flint's old buccaneers and a mighty rebellious Crew he'd have of it, to be sure. Anyhow, I done as he bid me and piped: 'All Hands.' Up they came from below, drunk as ever and chanting the old favourite in celebration o' the New Year. Tom Morgan was leading the singing, same as all Welshmen will anywhere given half a chance to warble their tonsils.

"Fifteen Men on the Dead Man's chest!"

And the whole Crew bore chorus:

"Yo-ho-ho and a bottle of rum!
Drink and the Devil had done . . ."

Morgan broke off abruptly on seeing the stranger and reached for his hanger: "Avast there!" he cried. "Who be this swab? He ain't one of us, look you!"

"Avast yourself, Tom Morgan!" returned our New Author. "And easy with your insults. Trifle with me and I'll summon someone who will batten down your hatch in a brace of shakes."

"Name the dog!" snarled Morgan. "Barring Long John, Billy Bones and Israel Hands, there's none can match me with a cutlass – mark you that!"

"No?" Our New Author smiled and raised a fore-finger. "Listen," said he, cocking his head to larboard and his grin grew even wider.

Now I confess to feeling a mite jittery. This stranger were too cock-sure o' hisself by a long sea mile t'be bluffing. I knew something was in the wind, but there weren't one amongst us prepared for the voice that came ringing through the Ship from astern – a voice that had been silent since that distant, main-hot day in Savannah.

"Darby M'Graw! Darby M'Graw! Fetch aft the rum, Darby!"

"It's Flint!" cried George Merry, cringing into a corner.

"Aye, Flint as ever was!" confirmed our New Author. "Come for to take command of his old ship-mates aboard *Walrus* once again!"

Sick weren't the word to describe the look on all their faces.

As Darby hurried to the rum locker, fumbling for his keys with his own foxy features the colour of a Marine's pipe-clayed cross belt, Morgan's eyes bulged from his head like a pair o' musket balls. Blind Pew gripped Black Dog's hand and began biting his finger-nails. Billy Bones and Job Anderson were both wedged in the bulk-head doorway, same as two corks in a single bottle. And as for Israel Hands; why, sink me for an old sinner, fainted clean away he did, like a country maid getting her very first kiss! For my part I was bad shook, to be sure, not that I were afeared o' Flint, mind! But the thought of facing his old, battered blue mug again fair set my stump to tingling. We were all in a right clove-hitch, you can lay to it. Even Sir Francis, the ship's cat, took refuge in the nearest rat-hole under a flag-o'-truce!

"If Flint finds out it was me as dug up his blunt back on Skeleton Island, then I'm as good as pork, I am!" wailed Ben Gunn from where he was hiding under the mess-deck table.

"Flint will only know what I choose to tell him," replied our New Author. "From now on I am holding the helm. This Ship's Company will go where I steer and do as I direct. Every man-jack aboard, whether he be Flint or fo'c'sle hand, will do nothing or say nothing until I gives the word. In short, you

"Gentlemen of Fortune" now have a New Author, namely – ME!"

A full broadside from a First-Rate-Ship-o'-the-Line couldn't have shook 'em more. At first they just gawked at him as he sat puffing on his paper-pipe, then they all began squalling at once. Our New Author gave Billy Bones the nod and flicked his ash into the sand filled butt beside the cracker barrel.

"Avast!" roared the Mate, striking the barrel with his belaying-pin. "Silence between decks! If you've ought to say then elect your spokesman, according to Council Rules, an' let him pipe-up! Otherwise – lay to!"

Merry, it were, who stepped forward. Always had a lot to say did George.

"You!" he said, pointing at the Stranger. "There ain't an established scribe the length and breadth o' the Seven Seas, wot's alive t'day, as can hold a cross-nibbed quill in the lee of Cap'n Stevenson's shadow. Yet you – you as never had so much as your blessed birth published, comes creepin' aboard this 'ere Ship, unlooked for like a pirate at prayers, all set to step into the sea-boots of one o' the greatest story tellers as ever was! Split my sides, but we'd need to be full-seas-over, one an' all, to sail along o' the likes of you – that's wot I say!"

"I don't profess to be anywhere near R.L.S.'s mark, but with all of you and *Treasure Island* to guide me, perhaps I can gainfully employ this laid-up crew while writing a Dedication to my Dear Wife – a treasure worth more to me than all the gold and silver plate that lies sinking into the silt of the Seven Seas!" said the Stranger, blowing a cloud of smoke towards the deck-head.

"Ah, now I declare that be a nice sentiment," I replied, thinking of my own woolly-headed Missus – her to whom I owed so much and who was more precious than a brace o' barrels brim-full with Sparks and Margaritas.

"At the same time it would be a Tribute to R.L.S. – him and one other," continued our New Author, pausing to swig *my* Brandy.

"And who might that be?" I asked, shifting my timber leg so's to pour myself another drink before our would-be-benefactor turned the blessed bottle into a 'Dead Marine'.

"Robert Newton!" said he.

"Bobby! By the Powers, but didn't he do me proud." I cried. "Played me to perfection, so he did, from Peek to Keel!"

"All the Actors in Walt Disney's Classic did every one of you proud," replied our New Author suddenly looking melancholy. "Sad to think that so many of them have crossed-the-bar now. Drink sent Robert Newton nose-diving down to Davy Jones. But it was the most pitiful of Fates that put poor Bobby Driscoll under hatches – him who played Young Hawkins."

"Aye, drugs it were as placed Jim in a pauper's grave before he ever reached the Peek o' Manhood," I said sadly shaking my head. "Drink and drugs have done for many a younker – rich and poor alike."

"Well, God rest them," continued our New Author. "*Treasure Island* will serve for their Monument. People, young and old, will still be watching it for as long as the World lasts."

"I never 'ad much of a part," grumbled Black Dog. "There again, I never 'ad much o' nothin', not I."

"What of me!" snapped Blind Pew. "I came alongside at the very start and was trampled below in a brace of shakes. ME! Me that's worth any ten of you shirking skulks!"

"Why, sink you for a lubber, Pew," growled Billy Bones. "You was only the Bosun, yet there was I under hatches afore the first shot were fired – and me the Mate!"

"An' Flint were only a printed word on the blessed story-paper," cackled Ben Gunn. "Only a name were that genteel."

"Thanky to Cap'n Stevenson for that," breathed Merry with relief.

"Aye, to be sure," I replied. "'Twould have gone hard for the likes o' us had Flint surfaced on *Treasure Island*. But if our New Author has his way, Flint'll be more'n just a name on this voyage – you can lay to it! He'll walk and he'll talk an' breath blue fire fathoms worse than Blackbeard. He will direct broadsides and carve with his cutlass the same as ever he done, by thunder!"

Ben Gunn came cringing around the table and tugged apprehensively at the Stranger's sleeve. "Tell me, matey," said he, wriggling like a lugworm on a Fisherman's Hook, "if we was to Sign Articles along o' you – you wouldn't go and blab to Old Flint about me, now would you? You'd not peach on poor Ben as being the one who lifted his Blunt. Wot's overboard is overboard and far astern, says you, and right you are, says I."

"Wrong you are, Benjamin Gunn," returned the Stranger. "*Treasure Island* lies far in the future – it hasn't happened yet. *Peeces of Eight* will end where *Treasure Island* begins."

"Fancy, an' there were me all in a clove-hitch over nought," chuckled the former Maroon.

"*Peeces of Eight*?" queried Job Anderson. "Would that be the name of this new venture you're so keen to recruit us for?"

"Pressed, I calls it, t' judge by his soundings so far," grumbled Morgan.

"Shiver my sides, Tom Morgan!" I said with some annoyance. "You always was a wooden-headed lubber as couldn't tell sugar from salt! Why, here be this New Author willing to put hisself under the Black Jack, and risk swinging to give us another go at the Spanish Main, an' all you do is gripe! By the Powers, Tom, you ain't got the h'invention of a cockroach! Are we to hang in stays here 'til blessed Judgement Day or cut loose with a chance to exchange the bilge in our hold for GOLD!"

"GOLD?" cried the Crew. "The Stranger fer Cap'n! Three cheers for our Noo Author!" And loud did they vapour.

I thought a slight mention o' their favourite metal would help matters along a bit and sway 'em to change their toon. But there were some who had to be convinced further. Billy was caution itself. He were never the one to poke his head-piece out a gun-Port, unless he was cock-sure o' not getting it blowed off – not Billy!

"Now see here, Barbecue," began the Mate. "All these ideas of booty an' buccaneering is heady stuff, to be sure, but what do our New Cap'n know of such things? What do'e know of the 'Main' and the 'Dry Tortugas'; of broadsides and sea-fights; of cold steel and hot, red blood? There now, tell me that, by thunder!"

"I have read fairly extensively on the subject," said our New Author, looking a mite peaky around the gills. "There are some very good books . . ."

"BOOKS?" exploded Bones. "Books is all bilge! Books is for sea-lawyers an' them infernal doctor swabs! There's none gets rich reading books and precious few as wot writes 'em!"

"You're ****ing right there," muttered our New Author under his breath.

"Listen, Sonny," said Black Dog, bending close and making him cringe as the foul rum fumes fanned his face. "You seem to be a likeable lad as ever I clapped eyes on, but Bill's in the right of it. What do you know of seafaring men and sailing ships?"

"Ever been b'fore the mast, matey?" leered Pew. "Ever heard the wind howling through the rigging in the dead of night like a Lament for Lost Souls or seen waves bearing down upon 'e bigger than the blasted ship, eh?"

"Indeed I have," replied our New Author brightening. "I was once in a typhoon in the South China Sea. I also had the honour and good fortune to serve aboard HMS *Victory* as a member of Her Majesty's Royal Marines."

"MARINES?" shrieked Pew.

"Boarding Parties!" roared Billy Bones clawing for his cutlass.

"We'll all swing and sun-dry on Execution Dock, we will!" wailed Ben Gunn wringing his hands and falling upon his knees.

"Belay this bilge!" I cried. "All this talk ain't worth a Buckled Doit! First and last we're only the h'invention of one man's imagination what's found a berth in the mind of another. Outside o' *Treasure Island* we don't exist. None of us be for real, nor ever was."

"Not so, Mister Silver," replied the Stranger smugly. "There are, in fact, two of your Company who actually lived. Yes indeed, R.L.S. took poetic licence and borrowed them both from the pages of history."

"And who's to say so?" demanded Billy Bones gruffly.

"BOOKS!"

Billy had no answer to that. He just puffed through his nose all fierce like, glaring at our New Author – who glared back.

"Well now, as to this piece o' news," said I, "seeing as Cap'n Stevenson kept me on deck mostly in *Treasure Island*, I reckon I must have cut quite a character in real life – you may lay to it."

"Wrong again, Mister Silver," says our Host. "Israel Hands was Edward Teach's 'Sailing-Master' and Benjamin Gunn ran a tavern on the Rio Pungo."

"Hands sailed along o' Blackbeard, did he? And Old Ben were a Buccaneer's Pot-Man?" I cried. "By the Powers – if this don't beat all!"

Israel hooked his thumbs into his belt and took to strutting about as if he were a blessed Rear Admiral o' the White, while Ben danced a jig around the mess-deck, clapping his hands and proclaiming to one and all: "I'm real! I'm real, I am!"

They became so full o' themselves that Billy had to lay 'em both alongside the lug with his belaying-pin to put 'em back in their proper place.

"Here's the way of it, my lads," said our New Author. "As you remember in *Treasure Island*, it was young Jim Hawkins who told the tale. Now I propose to have Long John tell this story – your story."

"I'm all for that," growled Billy Bones. "I ain't much use with the quill along o' the printed word nor ever was."

"I'll go bail for Barbecue," said Job Anderson. "He can spout like a book when so minded, can Long John."

"It will be a rum cruise with fair shares for all," continued our New Author. "Flint'll be Flint; Pew gets his glims back; Black Dog'll have a full crew of fingers on his left hand; Billy will be a picture of rare beauty without that cutlass cut on his cheek; and if Long John cares to look beneath the table, he'll find himself with ten toes!"

"Thunder!" gasped I, for so it were.

"Shrivel my Soul!" cried Pew. "I can see all the lovely carnage, along of the clash of cutlasses and the roar of cannon – clear as clear, I do!"

"If you're to Cap'n this 'ere Crew, what might you be called?" asked the Mate of our New Author.

"Just call me Captain A.J."

"Cap'n A.J.?" queried Hands. "That ain't much of a name, now is it!"

"No," replied he, "it ain't. But there again, perhaps I'll turn out to be not much of a writer – so it won't matter will it?"

"One point that needs a mention, Cap'n," I remarked. "My time at sea from when I was press-ganged into the Royal Navy, until my final fling along o' Jim

Flint, covers nigh on thirty years."

"It 'ud make a weighty Tome, to be sure," voiced Billy Bones, rasping a hand over his unshaven jaws.

"*Peeces of Eight* will consist of two parts – Book One and Book Two," said Captain A.J., thoughtfully rolling another paper-pipe. "No other way of doing it in regards to the continuity of the story-telling."

"Beggin' your pardon, Sir!" said George Merry tipping his forelock in salute. "Since ye've already written one blood-soaked story an' failed to catch the tide with it, in a manner o' speaking, how do'e reckon to fare any better with this un?"

"The saga of *Big Harpe – Little Harpe* was rather too raw for the delicate British palate. This one will be different. I intend to have Long John write it in the same vein as Robert Louis Stevenson would have done. I'll go easy on the gore and not mention the seedier, more sordid side of piracy on the high seas. Long John's narrative will be a book that can be read by anybody aged from eight to eighty – just a good, old fashioned adventure story," explained the Captain.

"Happen ye reckon t'be shipping aboard with a bunch o' blessed choir-boys?" bellowed Billy Bones. "Flint's old Crew never went easy on blood-letting, any more'n they do on rum."

"I'll keep a firm hand on the tiller, with your help, of course, Mister Mate," replied Captain A.J. He suddenly stood up and raised his glass, grinning around at the Ship's Company. "Here's to Luck, my Lads!"

"Here's to Luck!" chorused the Crew and drained out their double-grog in one go.

So there you have it, Mess-Mates. You can lay-to and hang in stays where you are or step aboard the pitching gun-deck of a privateer and come away with Long John, for a tale of battle, murder and sudden death on the Spanish Main.

"Why, hark you at the time," said Morgan cocking an ear. "Six-bells, so it is! If we don't budge soon, mates, we'll miss the turn of the morning tide!"

"To Quarters!" comes the Captain's cry. "All Hands on Deck!"

FIFTEEN MEN!

Fifteen men on the dead man's chest –
Yo-ho-ho and a bottle of rum!
Drink and the Devil had done for the rest –
Yo-ho-ho and a bottle of rum!

R.L.S.

Corpses by the score afloat in the tank –
Yo-ho-ho and a bottle of rum!
Some by the yard and some by the plank –
Yo-ho-ho and a bottle of rum!
They was a brave and hearty crowd –
Yo-ho-ho and a bottle of rum!
But one and all now in his shroud –
Yo-ho-ho and a bottle of rum!
Sewn in a hammock for a winding sheet –
Yo-ho-ho and a bottle of rum!
With a twelve pound ball resting at their feet –
Yo-ho-ho and a bottle of rum!
Jonah's Toss without terror or groans –
Yo-ho-ho and a bottle of rum!
Then down and down to Davy Jones –
Yo-ho-ho and a bottle of rum!
And all for gold and silver plate –
Yo-ho-ho and a bottle of rum!
Doubloons and Moidores and Pieces of Eight –
Yo-ho-ho and a bottle of rum!

A.J.R. *for* R.L.S.

BOOK 1

PEECE ONE

A CALL TO THE COLOURS!

CHAPTER I

BEWARE THE PRESS!

There be a saying that covers my commitments as snug as a scabbard do a sword: 'He who Ships with the Devil, must Sail with the Devil!' But it weren't from my own free choosing – you may lay to that! From first to last I had no vote in the matter, and by the time I were master of my own destiny once more, too much bitterness and blood-stained water swirled in my wake for me to go about and sail an honest course.

We are all as God made us, so Chaplain 'ud say, but that ain't the way of it when you be poor born – no, by thunder! Not by a long sea mile! In my day many an honest, so-called free man, leading a law-abiding life at one tick of the clock, got a crack on the head from a handspike the next and woke up under the deck pumps aboard a Man-o'-War – courtesy of the Press-Gang. Such was my lot, ship-mates, and me only a few points short o' my eighteenth year.

Thinking of the merry milk-maid I went hand-in-hand with, naval Head-Hunters were the last I thought to encounter guiding the plow behind Big Ben, such as I was doing at the time I got took. To be sure, we lived a good five miles from the coast, you see, so I reckon it truly was an ill wind as blowed them mess o' swabs my way on that gusty, March afternoon in the year o' little grace, 1719.

He was a fine looking Lieutenant, him who clambered over the gate and approached me. He wore a smart, cocked hat, fore-an'-aft, and a square breasted, blue tailed coat a-gleam with brass buttons. His white knee-breeches and silk stockings were spotless, but his silver buckled shoes were soon a sorry sight. All caked in the rich soil o' West Sussex they was after he'd tramped across the fresh turned furrows to where I was at. For my part, I were too busy admiring his fine tuck to notice much else. Had I cast me weather-eye to all quarters, I'd have spied the six burly Seamen a-sneaking up on me over the field from astern. But there was nobody to bawl me a warning of: 'Beware the Press!'

Old Ben whinnied a greeting to his horse tied at the gate.

"Good day to you, plow-man – if but a windy one," smiled the Lieutenant pleasantly. "Now tell me, my fine fellow, since leaving Shoreham I seem to have lost me bearings a bit. How now do I get back onto the Portsmouth Road?"

I never got so far as to give him a reply. The last I remember was of Big Ben swishing his tail and twitching his ears, then a blinding orange flash blocked out the world as I fell face foremost into a furrow. I mind as if it were yesterday, the fresh, rich smell of the newly turned earth in kissing the land of my boyhood goodbye for many a long, weary year.

Now it don't do to dwell on that which be remembered mainly for its pain, fear and hardship. Thinking on the wrongs as were done me, poisoned me to my very keel. Aye, poisoned even my Soul with a black bitterness that gnawed it away like worms in wood leaving me cold, hard and empty – afeared o' neither God, Man nor Devil! To be sure, I recalls little of my first few months in the Royal Navy, like snatches o' a bad dream befitting a nightmare. But some things become burned in a man's memory, branded in his brain as it were, in a manner o' speaking.

I didn't wake up under the deck pumps of a Man-o'-War, but in the dark confines of a closed cart – bouncing along in the company of five others. On reaching Portsmouth Harbour we were transferred into the pitch black bilges of a Frigate. Now I ain't a boastful man, but I were the pick o' that bunch – you may lay to it. Young, strong and tall I was, topping near six foot with a ruddy, beefy face and blond curly hair as 'ud do credit to a babe. They were older men, mostly, but none the less a-feared save for two drunken draymen. However, within hours of us being hauled a-fore the Officer o' the Watch, each on 'em, due to his own foolish mouth and fiery temper, were paraded briefly before the Captain. The Charges were read and the whole Crew mustered aft to witness punishment and it was terrible t' see. After being preached to from the 'Articles of War', each defaulter, in his turn, took a go at the grating. The 'Cat' came out the red, baize bag and the Bosun's Mates soon had its nine tails flaying their bare backs. Two dozen each they endured, screaming to the last lash. Such were my initiation into the ranks o' the Royal Navy.

"Keep yer eyes down, sonny," was the whispered advice to me from one seasoned Old Salt who was soon to take me under his wing, as the saying is. Being just a poor, country boy, I never dreamed there was so much brutality attached to keeping a Nation – 'Free!'

Due to my Dear Mother's insistence I had a good education in a country 'Free' or 'Charity' school, as it were, in my younger days and excepting for the officers and several Seamen o' rank, I were the only one on the lower-deck as could read, write and do arithumytic. I could recite blessed passages from the Bible too, so I could, my Catychism and a few o' the Psalms. Sad to say such knowledge of so gentle a nature went by the board long ago. One part o' 'Proverbs' I remember, now as then, were this:

> There are three things which are too wonderful
> for me, yea, four which I know not:
> The way of an eagle in the air;
> the way of a serpent upon a rock;
> the way of a ship in the midst of the sea
> and the way of a man with a maid.

I knowed nothing by way o' these Articles, 'cepting the feelings I had for my own sweet lass whom I never were t'meet more. But the way of a ship in the midst of the sea I was soon to fathom, for we sailed on the ebb-tide the following day.

A brisk breeze were blowing, not hard but gusty. A minor draught, to be sure; but picture yourself stood on a one inch rope, what we calls a horse, swaying fifty feet above a pitching gun-deck with only a yard-arm b'tween you and a free fall into Eternity. Add to this the effort o' clamping numbed elbows over the wet, slippery spar and fumbling with frozed fingers to untie the gasket cords and unfurl the sail, while all the time being tossed from starboard to larboard and from stem to stern as the ship rolls and plows her way through a six foot swell. And I tell ye, matey, when umpteen square feet o' canvas catches the wind it do so with a crack and shudder as can jolt you into 'Jonah's Toss' and down to Davy Jones quicker'n a secret circulating among washer-women!

Such was the fate o' one of our new members. A tinker he were by trade, as I recall, always lamenting the hardship his loss 'ud cause his crippled missus and her with five small children. Not too crippled b' the sound of it! Us untrained hands were wedged between AB Master-Mariners and we took our orders from them. He were far out on the main-yard, all but one from the end.

"'Old 'ard me 'arty luffs!" cried a Leading Hand as our mains'l unfurled.

But the tinker heard him too late. As our flapping canvas caught the wind the whole yard-arm swung to starboard on slack braces. The tinker gave a strangled cry of mortal terror and plunged backwards off his perch into the briny far below, hitting the sea's swell with an 'orrid 'smack!'

He never surfaced in this world. Small odds if he had, since he weren't no swimmer, and we couldn't about-ship nor lower a long boat to pick him up nohow. So for fair or foul, his troubles were over – ours were just beginning and a right rough time we had of it too!

The Bosun's Mates, along o' their 'starters', soon had us raw ODs scurrying like rats to all points of the compass. We stowed cordage and cheesed down ropes onto the spotless decks – doing all the hundred and one minor tasks that make everything run 'Ship-Shape-and-Bristol-Fashion' aboard a Frigate o' the Royal Navy. Even them among us as had the intelligence of a turnip soon realised they were condemned to a Living Hell – imprisoned within reeking wooden walls on the High Seas.

Him as died quick was the lucky one, I reckon!

CHAPTER II

HMS AGONY!

HMS *Agamemnon* were not a happy ship. To be sure, no such Crew existed in 'The Turnip Man's' navy, you may lay to it! In the Fo'c'sle and among the lower-deck she was known as 'Rolling Aggie'. I had my own private name for her: 'The *Agony*'. Aye, and much did she cause me, both in mind and body. By the Powers but the Royal Navy cost me dear, all articles listed alow and aloft!

She were a fast 'Fifth-Rater', frigates being built for speed more'n fire-power. Their duty, for the main, was the carrying o' messages and despatches between Squadrons. They were the work-horses of the Fleet and never took station in a line of battle. But that ain't t'say we burnt no powder or met cannon-balls a-coming the wrong way. We collected more'n our fair share o' foreign scrap-iron – you may lay to that, by thunder!

The *Agony* was 700 tuns burthen, cost around £12,000 pounds to build and carried 32 guns. Her armament consisted of: Twenty six 12-pounders as stood thirteen a-side o' the main gun-deck; four 6-pounders, two a-side on the quarter-deck; and two 6-pounders, one either side of the Fo'c'sle. Years later she would have a brace o' large bored Carronades mounted on the Fo'c'sle, but they weren't invented in my day, you see. Pintled to the gunnels on the Poop-Deck were two 3-pounder brass swivels. These, so I learned later, belonged to the Captain, a private purchase on his part, not standard issue.

Our allotted complement of men, referred to by our 'Betters' as The People, was about two hundred. But life in the Royal Navy not being a bed o' roses, most Crews were always fathoms under strength. We were around twenty and five short, I reckon. Apart from us New Recruits, the Ordinary and Able-Bodied Seamen, the Ship's Crew were comprised of the following: Captain; Cap'n's Clerk; Sailing Master and two Mates; two Lieutenants; six Midshipmen; Boatswain and two Mates plus one Yeoman; Carpenter; Sailmaker; Chaplain; Master-At-Arms; Gunsmith; Surgeon and two Mates, 'Loblolly Boys' were the name given t'these assistant butchers; Gunner plus one Mate with eleven

Quarter-Gunners and one Yeoman; six Quarter-Masters and their Mates; and finally, the Purser and his Steward.

I owed much to this last cove, seeing it were me as took over his duties after our second action, on account of an argyment he had with a Double Headed Angel that chopped him clean athwart-ships.

Thems of us fresh aboard were assigned to either the port or starboard watch and joined various Messes to make up the numbers. All Gunners were trained Seamen, the same as all Seamen did a gunnery course. In time of engagement some hands whose duty it were t'sail and steer the ship, might find 'emselves helping to serve the guns if heavy casualties occurred among the Crews. It took seven, strong Seamen to operate a Long Twelve, and five to manage a Six Pounder. On a First-Rate-Ship o'-the-Line, where the 'Big Teeth' lived, Crews of thirteen and fifteen men were mustered to manhandle monsters as fired 32- and 42-pound balls.

Our mess, port side aft, was no more'n a detachable table, slung by ropes from the deck-head and set between the guns with benches either side to sit upon. In time of action when we 'Cleared', they were stowed away in the hold. The Gun-Deck was our 'ome. 'Twas here we ate, slept, lived and fought – aye, and died too, by thunder! When we slung up our hammocks athwart-ship, we had fourteen inches space per man. But it were not as cramped as it sounds, being as we was arrayed in alternate Watches. The two ratings on either side o' me belonged to the starboard watch, so when I were a-bed, they were top-side on duty – and vice-versa, so 't was quite roomy, you see. Just about the only blessed concession we got in regards to the Rules and Regulations in the RN!

As to the Rations – BILGE! Uneatable they was, but eat 'em we did. Aye, either that or starve! Seeing it were me as did the clerking for Mister Bunce, the Purser, I knowed the rightful amount due each man down to the last crumb. Officially, each Rating was supposed to receive a weekly ration of: 4lbs o' salt beef; 2lbs o' salt pork; 2 pints o' dried peas; 3 pints o' oatmeal; ½ lb o' butter and a pound o' cheese. There was also a daily issue of bread, known as 'ship's biscuit', and a gallon of beer – flat and sour, mostly. In my day in the RN, 'Up Spirits' was piped twice, but that were back in the 1720s. A measure of half a pint o' neat rum per man was issued at Noon; then at 6 p.m. he received another half pint. Ship's Boys only drew a quarter pint at each issue.

Now I reckon it be high time I 'Cleared Lower Decks' and explained the term 'Grog!' It wasn't until 1740, long after I'd left the navy, that Admiral Ned Vernon ordered a quart of water to be mixed along o' the daily rum-issue to cut down on drunkenness. Mind you, mess-mates, only a complete lubber 'ud get full-seas-over so he couldn't do his duty. Any as did, soon sobered up under three dozen lashes at the gratings! But to return t' the subject. It was because of the Admiral's nick-name, 'Old Grog', on account of a grogram cloak he always wore, that rum was later referred to as 'Grog'.

At messing time each man ate from a communal dixie, using only his fingers. Plates, knives, forks and spoons were Ward-Room luxuries. Some old sea-dogs of long standing boasted of having horn or tin spoons, but thems were few and far between. Our usual fare was what we called 'Skillygolee', a sort of gruel made up from crushed biscuit, oatmeal and lumps o' fatty, boiled beef or pork. It smelt like pig-swill and probably tasted worse! Salt was all we had by way o' seasoning, that and maybe a little cinnamon or a pinch of pepper if we were a-serving 'Farmer George' in the East or West Indies.

There was Worms in the Water, Weevils in the Biscuit and black-headed Maggots in the Cheese – brave creatures all an' tasty! The water stank, stale and scummy, it were. The bread broke your teeth. And as for the cheese – I've seen AB Master Mariners carving buttons from a block. Buttons and Ornaments, mind, because they reckoned it to be stronger and better than blessed bone. An' to top the stiffest yard to nothing, I've seen barrels o' salted meat whose markings showed the contents to be close on Six Years Old, shiver my sides!

The h'officers didn't eat the same bilge as us, mark you, deary me no! Up for'ard, in what were called 'The Manger', was all manner o' livestock; calves, sheep, pigs and a goat to provide milk for the gentry's tea or coffee. There were also crates containing chickens, ducks and geese. Those swabs who lived aft, ate dainty, feeding on fresh fish, onions, carrots an' roasted turnips and potatoes, all washed down with the finest wines and cognac – rot their livers!

No standard uniform existed in the Navy during my day, either for the Ward-Room gentry or Lower-Deck. Officers pleased 'emselves. We wore what we stood up in. Clothing could be bought from the Purser's store, known as: 'Slops', but that swab's prices started at the Cross-Trees and went aloft clear past the Peek! After six months of hard saving, you could purchase such items as:

Canvass suites: 5/-
Blew suites: 5/-
Blew shirts: 3/6d
Cotton waistcoat: 3/-
Yarn stockings 3/-
Neats-leather shoons: 3/6d
Monmouth caps of coarse yarn: 2/6d
Red caps: 1/1d and Blew neckcloths: 5d

The People were filthy dirty and stank. By the powers, a pig-pen 'ud smell like a rose-garden compared to my mess-mates. It were no fault of theirs, mind. Only officers washed and boasted clean linen. Once a week we sometimes took a turn under the deck pumps – clothes and all – but only in the summer-time. Cold, salt water did little to shift our second skin of grime, grease and tar. Besides, the muck helped keep us warm in winter, so it did. The whole ship stank to her very timbers. Oh, she were scrubbed, swabbed and Holy-Stoned daily, to be sure. No mates, her stench was of hemp and tar; of fear and sweat; and of decaying Souls o' living dead men treated worse than swine!

CHAPTER III

ORDINARY SEAMEN SILVER RN!

My mess-mates were a rum crowd, game for anything. Gaunt and thin with a hungry, hollow-eyed, haunted look. Some were dubbed 'Shell-Backs', on account o' their hides being horribly scarred by repeated floggings for minor offences. One such man was our Number four, Shell-Back Bates. By the powers, but he were a brisk hand when it comed to giving the officers a sly poke in their pride. I mind one time. 'Closed-Up' ready to engage a pair of French Privateers, we was, when Bates gets down on his knees alongside the gun like he was praying.

"What's this?" says Grumble Guns the Gunnery Officer. "At prayers with the enemy bearing down upon us! Are you afraid, then?"

"Afraid? Not I, Sir!" bawled Bates. "I wus jus' a-prayin' that the Froggies' shot may be distrib'ted along o' the same proportion as the Prize Money! The greatest part among the h'officers!"

We all roared with laughter, but the jibe cost our Loader dear. Two dozen lashes for insolence, but none of the swabs could put Shell-Back Bates down for very long. Took a full go of grape-shot to send 'im below and tack 'Amen' on the end o' his name.

Many of our People bore other marks about their bodies. Deep, ugly gashes, blue and purple. Hideous, some of the wounds were. Made me wonder how a man could survive such injury. When I volunteered my ignorance as to what caused these terrible scars, afore I smelt powder smoke and saw the blood fly for the first time:

"Flizzings, sonny! Flizzings! 'Tis when the shot comes inboard, splinters fly," explained my mess-mate. "Aye, 'tis the d—d flizzings as do us the most damage."

"What about the cannon-balls?" I asked

"Can'bulls? Can'bulls?" repeated he, laughing. "We mind 'em no more 'n carpet bowls, my son. Can'bulls on'y killee, lad, but oak darts kin cripple ye most cruel. That's why the gun-carriages be beech wood. Thems don't smash an' splinter s'easy, see."

There were a thousand things to learn from starboard to larboard, stem to stern, alow and aloft: knots, splices, tackles and terms. Everything aboard ship had a name and served for a particular purpose. Us new ODs got to know 'em all an' many a hard lesson were hammered into us – usually by a Bosun's Mate aided along o' his d—d starter! We learnt how to handle the helm with a head sea running – box hauling and what not. How to tack. Sailing full and by; and what to do when the wind veers so's to keep her close on course. One mistake at the helm in heavy weather could cost you the ship, aye, and your life too – by thunder!

Under the Master-At-Arms we were taught the management of muskets and pistols. I became a dab-hand with both; and another art I mastered came in most handy later on in my career – how to cut and carve my way out o' trouble with a cutlass!

Then there was gun drill, gun drill, and more blessed gun drill! I mind yet, mostly in haunted dreams after too much rum, the shrill voice of the Gunnery Officer coming as clear as clear across the years:

"Silence!" was the very first order and all Crews gave attention to take notice o' what were said.

"Cast loose your guns!"

"Level your guns."

"Take out your tompions!"

"Run out your guns! Move, blast your eyes!"

"Prime!"

"Point your guns!"

"Fire!"

"Spunge your guns!"

"Load with cartridge! By Grenville's blood, you'll have to come about and look livelier than this!"

And so it were, day after day; week in, week out; month by month; fair weather or foul. Our Gun Crews became so expert we could load, lay and fire two rounds every three minutes. But still it weren't good enough for the likes o' Grumble Guns – rot 'im! Cheated by Purser, beaten and bullied by Petty Officers, Jack Tar's lot was not a happy one and he was far from 'JOLLY!' Discipline was the spur that drove us! Survival was our Secret God! An' Lord Fear our Task Master!

My wages as an OD were 19 shillings a month, paid in the form of a 'Ticket', which the Purser exchanged for cash at way below its true value. That be after the swabs had docked 6d. for the Hospital at Greenwich; 4d. to the Chaplain as payment for the saving of our Souls; and another 4d. to the Surgeon for releasing 'em which were often the case, likely as not, when one of our People got laid under his knife!

"Young Silver! Hark'e well t' wot I tell ye. Speak soft an' look obligin', and when so ordered, act lively. Do as ye be bid by yer betters wi'out grumble or mischief, an' barrin' splinters or can'bulls a-comin' of your way durin' time o' action, ye might survive t'be paid off one bright day. Mind wot I say now. Obedience first an' last be the watch-word aboard this 'ere ship!"

Such was the advice of Jem Huggit, the seasoned Old Salt who befriended me, him as died yelling encouragement to the rest of us from where he lay amid his own red ruin – both legs crushed by a dismounted cannon. By the powers, but the double-shotted guns of a rogue Dutchman cost us dear that day.

We patrolled the Channel for months on end, standing off an' on the French Coast like a blessed Bum-Boat. Every few months we put into Portsmouth for provisions, but us 'Pressed Men' were never allowed to set foot ashore. Two ODs tried swimming for their freedom and were shot down like dogs by a pair o' hawk-eyed marine sentinels. Just as the Crew were bracing 'emselves for another cruel, cold winter afloat on Channel Patrol a despatch from the Admiralty sent us beating-up down Channel, bound for the West Indies.

In beating our way down-channel or 'tacking,' as the term is, that means zig-zagging against the wind, I saw the Needles off the Isle of Wight, rearing up from the sea like a row o' ragged, broken teeth. They were framed against a back-drop of pitching, white-capped waves and an over-cast sky of low scudding clouds. This was to be my last glimpse of Old England for thirty long, battered, blood-soaked years.

Pirates were a plague in the Caribbee and commerce near strangled. Talk of Buccaneers such as 'Blackbeard', Howell Davies and Calico Jack set conversations buzzing between decks. And there was another whose Pennant was rapidly rising to flutter from the highest Peek o' Piracy, a name that were spoke of in awe – 'JIM FLINT!'

During the two years we helped keep the trade routes open, I became a fully fledged AB, worth £1 4s. a month, less deductions! The Purser got a new Steward, but he still retained my services to do most o' the donkey-work. I was cheaper, you see.

Heat and short rations set tempers on a hair-trigger. Then scurvy started to rear its ugly head among the ship's company and topping the stiffest yard-arm to that – we run out o' rum! Discipline were harsh and disobedience brought quick reprisal. Floggings, beatings and buckets of abuse became commonplace during our daily routine.

I were free of it, mostly, on account of my duties along o' the Purser. But for the rest of the crew, a black look given too quick or an order obeyed too slow, had the Bosun's Mates laying about 'em with their cursed 'Starters' in a brace of shakes. These instruments of ill-office were lengths o' stout rope, around eighteen inches long, with a Turk's-Head knot spliced in one end. It were a blasted 'Starter' that started me down the Road of No Return, in a manner o' speaking.

But read on, Ship-Mate – read on!

CHAPTER IV

DEATH OF A SWAB!

We were anchored on the Lee-side of a small island in the Bahamas, for to 'water ship'. Seven Bells had just struck o' the Fore-Noon Watch, (half past eleven to you landlubbers) and it were hotter than Hades. The breeze had dropped off and the pitch in the seams was sticking to my pumps as I carried the Ration Book for'ard to the Galley for the Cook's attention. Five barrels o' meat had turned putrid and stank so abominably that even the blessed maggots were waving white flags!

A working party, stripped to the waist, were sweating and straining over one of the Long Twelves, trying to chock it up so's to change a cracked truck. The Bosun's Mate in charge was a surly, evil-faced swab named Finch. Bullying was his sport and cruelty his delight. 'Flogger' Finch he were known as, for he laid on the lash with a will. Almost level with 'em, I were, when one of the hands, a sickly, skinny, elderly fellow with a hacking cough, suddenly collapsed across his iron crow. He were panting and wheezing, his face a horrible colour.

"Avast! Bear up, you shirkin' lubber!" snarled Finch.

"Your pardon, Sir," gasped the hand, "but I feels all a queerity."

"A queerity, is it?" cried Finch, bellowing like a branded bull. "Common lazyness I calls it! Well, here be a sure cure fer yer queerity, m'lad!" And he struck with his 'Starter', catching the man across his kidneys.

Under a flurry of blows, the rating writhed and screamed. Suddenly he gasped, gagged and rolling up his eyeballs, passed out cold, so he did.

"He be looking mortal white around the cutwater, Mister Finch."

With a start I realised the speaker were ME!

"Is 'e now," replied Flogger, his voice soft as a serpent's hiss. He straightened up and stared at me with mad, hot eyes. "We-e-ll, we-e-ll," purred he. "Assist'nt Dep'ty Steward Silver, com'd to give us the benefit o' his brains. Not only can 'e read an' write an' do 'rithumytic, but 'e can tell sick swabs from malingerin' scum! Or maybe I is mistook an' 'tis Surgeon Silver now, eh?"

"He looks mortal bad, Sir," repeated I lamely, wishing I had passed to leeward and left well alone.

Whether it was jealousy because of my book learning or the 'square-number' I had in working for the Purser, Finch hated the very marrow in my bones. The glances he'd given me in the past were sour enough to blister varnish on a binacle.

"Wot be wrong wid yer mouth, Surgeon Silver?" he hissed, pushing his leering face close to mine.

"W-why, why nothing, Sir," I stammered, puzzled by his question.

Finch swung his 'Starter' and the heavy, Turk's Head knot smashed into my lips, splitting 'em open alow and aloft.

"There be now, my book suckin' buck!" cried he and roared with laughter as the blood poured down my chin.

I staggered back, my head buzzing from the blow. But then blind anger over-rode my reason and flooded through me like fire. Before I knowed what I was at, my fist repaid him in kind and with bonus too, since I felt his front teeth snap beneath my knuckles. Finch fell as if pole-axed, striking his head a glancing blow on the cannon's cascabel afore he hit the deck.

"Yew fool, Jack!" cried a burly AB. "Yew'll go t' the gratings fer this mawn's madness, sure as sin!"

"T'ree dozen if'n ye collect a stroke!" added someone else.

"An' if Flogger 'as an 'and in swinging the cat ag'in yer, he'll 'ave yer back t' the very bone by God!" exclaimed a third.

"Finch won't be a-swinging the cat at no more floggings," replied a fourth Rating quietly from where he knelt alongside the Mate, "'appen he swings it from hell. He's slipped his moorings, he has, mates. Dead as bilge he be. Hit his head on the pomiglion. See here," he said and pointed to a red smear on the knob of the cannon's breech.

Despite the heat I grew cold, my mind numb.

"All's up wiv yew, Jack. Yew'll fathom the long an' the short on it now, along o' 'im whose 'ead yew broke," said the burly AB.

"'Tis Jonah's Toss fer ye, shipmate," voiced the third man.

"Aye," agreed his companion. "Straight down t' Davy Jones, bound stem to stem wi' Flogger's foul face afore yer deadlights fer all Eternity!"

"Here comes the 'Bullocks!' Trust 'em to smell blood!" said the Rating crouched beside the body.

He got to his feet and hastily moved clear of the corpse as a Sergeant of Marines arrived with a Corporal and half a dozen men, their red coats darkly stained with sweat. Sunlight flashed on the long bayonets fixed to their fire-locks as they came off the high port and levelled their pieces to cover us.

The Sergeant pushed his black, lacquered shako further up on his forehead and scowled down at the two men sprawled beside the gun. Him who had fainted moaned and started to stir. But there was no such life left in Finch. His very pose told one and all he wouldn't sail under his own wind again this side o' Judgement Day. He lay on his back, one leg buckled beneath t'other, one arm outflung, his glassy glims fixed and staring with his head resting in a red pool that slowly crept across the deck. I stood mesmerised by the macabre pattern his blood were making on the planks along of each roll o' the ship.

"And which of you jolly Jack Tars lent a hand in this piece of knavery?" enquired the Sergeant, his dark eyes flashing from face to face.

Finally they rested on me.

"Well, Sailor? Come on, pipe up!" he ordered. "You a-didn't trip over each other's toes a-dancing to the Hornpipe, I'll stake me stripes!"

Guffaws and sniggers came from various quarters of the crowd that had gathered fore and aft of the gun.

"Belay there!" bawled the Corporal. "Shurrup!"

Nervously, still clutching the Rations Book, I wiped the back of my hand across my bloodied mouth before answering. "It were a mishap, Sargn't – only a mishap. He struck the pomiglion . . ." My voice faded into a croaking whisper.

"A mishap?" queried the Sergeant, peering at me as if I were moonstruck. "Two smashed hatches, one Rating stunned and a Petty Officer laying dead as a damp cartridge at the very feet of you, him with his head stove in, an' you calls it a mishap? I calls it Murder, my lad! And since you're a Seaman an' him a Petty O, an' seeing as how the crime was committed on the High Seas aboard one of his Majestie's Ships – that makes it Murder most Foul, it do!"

I don't rightly recall what my reply was, but I remember the Sergeant, a tall man and straight as a rammer, had to cock an ear to catch my mumblings. Perhaps it was the stricken look on my face that softened his eyes and filled 'em with pity – a rarity among Sergeants o' the Marines, you may lay to that!

"Don't you realise what you've a-done, lad?" said he. "Don't you know the High Price you've got to pay for the a-doing of it!"

My brain felt swollen between my ears. I thought my head were about to burst like a blessed Grenadoe and I could give no answer.

The gaping Seamen suddenly stiffened into statues and the Marines snapped to attention as their Captain appeared with the Duty Officer, followed by the Purser, the Master-At-Arms and four, gawky, gangling Midshipmen – mere boys just launched into their Teens.

"What outrage has been committed here?" demanded the Duty Lieutenant.

"Murder, I'm afraid, Sir!" replied the Sergeant saluting.

"Who is responsible?" snapped the Captain of Marines.

"Not Silver, surely?" cried Mister Bunce the Purser, on seeing me.

"I fear so, Sir!" confirmed the Senior NCO.

"Dash me buttons!" exclaimed Mister Bunce aghast. "'Pon my soul! Young John Silver a Murtherer and Mutineer? Wellesay!"

"Take him below and clap him in irons – under armed guard!" ordered the Lieutenant. "I must report this to the Captain, immediately!"

Murder? Mutiny? My mind was in a whirl as, wedged between a double file of four Marines, the Corporal marched me away. I were taken down aft in the main hold, searched, manacled and bundled into a cell no bigger 'n a cubby-hole. The Marine detailed to stand guard cursed his own misfortune and mentioned me in Flying Colours – Blue mostly!

"Fish-Food!" he snarled. "Ye ken that, ye dab-toed swab! Ye an' that Bosun's Mate! Dead men both! Had ye attack'd a Listed Officer, ye'd ha' danced the Yard-Arm-Jig. But when they bury the pair o' ye, lash'd face-t'-face, ye'll still be blowin' bubbles when the fishes comes ta feed!"

I cursed him for a cross-eyed son of a Scotch porridge planter, whose rightful place were here beside the bilge along of other rats. He in turn made a few more pleasantries about 'live-bait' and 'bubble-blowing' before giving me the grace of silence.

Eerie, it was, being entombed down there in the depths of the Hold. Like being buried alive, which in fact I were. The ship remained at anchor, rolling on a slight swell. The only sounds were of her creaking timbers, the soft slap of bilge-water, together with the squeak of scurrying rats, and the chink of my manacles and gyves if I so much as moved a muscle. Sometimes the Sentry coughed or shuffled to get comfortable and on one occasion, most satisfying to me, he dropped his musket on his foot with a string o' pickled oaths. Fresh air never got this far below decks and the stench from the oily scum of the bilges, spliced with tar, turpentine, hemp and hot dampness, made the rank air a point short of being poison. Excepting for a faint glimmer o' light coming through the narrow grill in my cell door from the Sentry's lanthorn, I were in darkness – alone and depressed with only my own miserable thoughts for company.

It didn't last, mind. I soon had a ship-mate alongside when Flogger Finch's stiffening corpse were carried in by two Seamen and dumped at my feet like so much junk.

"Cap'n's orders, Silver! Your Court-Martial convenes at Eight Bells this afternoon!" snapped the Crusher and slammed the door, shooting the bolt home like the clap o' Doom.

Eight Bells – four of the clock – start of the evening or dog-watch. But where would I be when Eight Bells tolled at the end of it? My Guard was changed for a better breed of man. Cut me a quid from a plug o' pigtail tobaccy, bless 'im. Shortly after, the ship's rhythm told me she had weighed anchor and was under way.

In referring to the evening watch instead of the first and second dog-watch, let me explain. Split Dog Watches were only introduced after the Mutinies at Spithead and The Nore as occurred on Easter Morning in 1797 – a far cry from my day. The signal for all hands to refuse all orders and down tools, until better conditions were met with, was the Striking of 5 Bells or 6:30 p.m. They climbed the fore-shrouds o' their ships and gave three 'Huzzas'. Shipboard life improved afterwards, to some small degree, but not before Dick Parker danced the Yard-Arm-Jig along of twenty-eight other Mutineers.

The Royal Navy is the only sea-faring nation in the world that has the Evening Watch divided into two: First Dog, 4:00 p.m. to 6:00 p.m. Second Dog. 6:00 p.m. to 8:00 p.m. 'Tis said that their Lordships at the Admiralty changed the Bells so's to break up the rotation of Watches – by way of a change; and also to Commemorate this Major RN Mutiny. But I'd bet my 'ticket' it were because they preferred to forget it. I reckon no seagoing Officer could bear to hear the striking of Five Bells in the evening without a sense o' dread ever afterwards!

From those dark days back to mine.

To this same blessed moment on the clock, I still can't fathom what came over me. The nearest I can batten it down to is t'say I were Reborn. Aye, mates, Reborn although I were as good as condemned to die as made no difference. Captain Sloane – we called him 'Sludge' – were a hard man to serve under and harder still on thems as crossed 'im. Hard and cruel, he were, like the sea he sailed upon and the Senior Service he'd spent all his life in – boy and man.

One moment I was Able Seaman Silver, afraid and alone, sick with fear from thinking on the death I were soon to endure, drowning like a dog tied to a dead man, then a black bitterness surged through my veins and swept all terror away. From that time to this, I've never been a-feared of God, Man, Devil nor Death. I ain't too keen on creepy-crawlies, mind!

The sheer injustice of it all, mates, that be what done it, I reckon. Had I lived like a well trained Lubber, eaten bilge, taken blows, spoken soft and obeyed orders all these years, just to be led like a Lamb to the Slaughter? No, by thunder! I resolved, then and there, to go below like a Lion, swearing blue-fire and a-cursing of them who were to do me down. By the powers, this Ship's Company 'ud long remember the day that Able Seaman John Samuel Silver went to his Maker – one an' all!

Only 'The Fates' could fathom or foresee the Death of a Rating in the Royal Navy giving Birth to a Buccaneer!

CHAPTER V

BIRTH OF A BUCCANEER!

A Corporal and three, it were, that came for me. They removed my irons and along o' him as was already on sentry go, I were marched topside. It amused me that it took Five Marines – Marines mind! – to deliver one sorry Seaman into the Hands of Justice and I chuckled all the way up. The Bullocks eyed me in some alarm, thinking no doubt that I were a ripe Candidate for Bedlam. Well, maybe I was a little mad at that!

The ship was making slow headway under her fore and jib-sails, cruising among numerous small islands that made navigation tricky. Eight Bells sounded my 'Death Knell', in a manner o' speaking, as me and my 'Guard of Honour' emerged from the aft hatchway onto the Quarter-Deck and into dazzling sunlight. After my eyeballs stopped burning I took in the scene of this, the Last Act of my Life, and a right Royal Show it looked to be sure.

The burnished bayonets of the Marines formed a hollow square of steel around the Quarter-Deck, their ranks extending up both sets of steps onto the Poop. Lined along the quarter rails they appeared like painted stanchion posts themselves in their bright, red coats, muskets at the shoulder and their black hats a gleaming contrast to the white of their pipe-clayed crossbelts. Seamen sat along the yard-arms, clung to the ratlings on the shrouds and stood packed in the waist. Behind a table, set below the Poop, sat the Captain between his First and Second Lieutenants.

Standing in line behind 'em were the Captain of Marines, the Master-At-Arms, the Surgeon, the Chaplain, six Midshipmen and the Purser – Mister Bunce. The Sergeant flanked the Sailing Master, who was stationed alongside the Helmsman at the wheel.

"Prisna an' hes-cort, 'alt!" bawled the Corporal, crashing to attention and slapping the stock of his musket in salute six feet from the table.

"Top o' the a'ternoon to 'e, Cap'n Sludge!" cried I in a voice that rang clear to one and all. "Still a-wearing your silly hat athwart-ships, I see! You should wear it fore-an'-aft, Sir, like normal idiots!"

Gasps and suppressed sniggers came from the Ratings on deck, but the shrouds and yard-arms rang out with wild peals of reckless laughter. Cap'n Sloane's eyes bulged from his bloated face 'til I thought they'd fly from their sockets like a pair o' musket balls.

"Sergeant Parker!" shrieked he. "Ensure your men fire upon anyone seen smiling – inclusive of each other!"

"Aye, aye, Sir!" replied the stripey, known among his men as 'Knuckles'. "You 'erd your Captain! An' woe to him as goes ag'in his dooty!'

Grimaces replaced the grins on the Marines' faces, as if they were puppets pulled by a single string.

"Right you are, Cap'n Sludge!" I hollered, touching my forelock in mock salute. "Kill all hands, alow and aloft, and see how this old bilge bucket sails with only six Snotties fer Crew!"

That done it, that did!

I were seized by two Bullocks and a canvas wedge was rammed in my mouth and tied with my own neck-cloth, while the Captain raged in his seat, thumping the table-top with both fists like a demented monkey.

The Corporal whispered to the Sergeant; the Sergeant whispered to his Officer; the Officer had words with the Captain, who spoke to his Surgeon. There was much muttering and nodding of heads. No hard guess to fathom their findings. I were being classified as cookoo. Aye, mates – mad!

My Court-Martial, that malignance o' Military Justice, same as Civil only with more trimmings, was a rushed affair – a mere formality. And to top it all, I reckon the Captain was miffed over missing his afternoon Tea!

Witnesses were called, but none spoke against me. Mister Bunce gave a glorious account o' my credit, more for his own needs than mine, being as I was so handy. But all in vain. My fate was signed and sealed. The Captain read from the Articles of War, concluding with: "John Samuel Silver, you have been found guilty of murder aboard His Majesty's Ship *Agamemnon*. You are therefore compelled to suffer death as designated by their Lordships of the Admiralty. Were I to award you a lesser ill, would be to neglect my Orders and fail both King and Country. Bosun, do your duty!"

I were about turned by them as held me close and beheld Finch, who had been brought up from below. He looked grey and stiff, and his odour was a little high. As his former mess mates bound us together, face to face, by means of wrapping a haliard line around our bodies like a blessed serpent, the Chaplain mumbled prayers for those buried at sea. When all was ready we were hoisted onto strong shoulders.

The Captain and his Officers removed their hats.

"Able-Seaman John Samuel Silver," said he, "you are dismissed the ship! May God have mercy on your afflicted Soul!"

It was just the gentlemanly way of saying: "Chuck the swab overboard."

Then the drums of the Marines began to roll.

I caught a glimpse of the Hands mustered along the Main-Yard, their silhouettes showing sharp against the Fore-Sail like a line of black crows a-waiting on pickings.

"TWO-SIX!" cried the Bosun. "TOGETHER – HEAVE!"

Ship, sky and sea became a whirling blur as I was given 'Jonah's Toss'. I hit the oggin with Finch top-side o' me, his weight forcing me down deep. Even as we smacked into the water, I felt my bonds go slack. The old haliard line, hard used and rotten, parted near my shoulders. I had my arms free in a brace of shakes and floundered my way back up to the surface. Gurgling for air, I ripped the gag from my mouth. Moments later, Flogger Finch popped up alongside me.

The *Agamemnon* were some distance away now, the Hands cramming on all canvas since she had nought but the open sea before her. No one would have seen us, nohow, even had they been looking, what with the gathering dusk and the sea's swell. I remember thinking: 'That's the last I'll ever see of the *Agony*, an' good riddance,' but I were wrong, mates. I was destined to meet her again, years later, and once more she cost me dear.

Me and my mate Finch were quite buoyant, to be sure. Bobbing along on the swell like a pair o' over-sized birds, we were. Our pitch-stained, greasy canvas clothing, being a fair ways waterproof already, had pockets of air trapped in it, you see; also, although the Bosun's Mate were only so much jetsam in the form o' dead-meat, the air and gasses in his body helped keep him afloat and such close company. Lucky for me that were the way of it. I had my legs free by this time, but I was still anchored to the swab by the line being tangled around my left foot.

Now apart from him not being very ornamental, my worry was that if he took a sudden nose-dive down to Davy Jones's Locker, I'd be hauled below along with him. True, the rope was rotten and might give way again, but two miracles in one go was a flimsy main-stay for a mortal such as I to hang his life on. But a miracle it were, mates, as freed me from Finch. Aye, and in such a manner as 'ud cause most men's brains to shrivel! I suppose some of you would put it down to God and Providence; well 'Amen' and so be it. But I reckon 'twere the Devil who delivered me that day – him along o' two Disciples!

Finch were floating face up, rolling on the swell only a few feet off from me, while I, in between taking deep breaths, struggled and tore at the line tangled around my ankle 'til me finger nails was broke and bleeding. Mind well my words, mess-mates. If you venture forth into sunny climes and go for a wallow in warm, tropical waters, be sure there's no blood about your body; either that or have a Corpse close by to Barter in exchange for your Life – and you may lay to it!

I'd just surfaced to get my wind. Taking a breather, I were, while treading water. The sun was perched on the horizon and shining far to westward. Less than half a league to starboard I could see the palm fringed, sandy beaches of three small islands – the last in the chain where we had watered ship that morning. At first I thought it was a pair of black sticks cutting a 'V' shaped swathe through the water t'wards me. How two sticks came to be travelling at a rapid rate o' knots, I didn't have time to fathom, for they suddenly veered to port and showed their true colours. The black, triangular shaped dorsal fins proclaimed them Pirates from the deep, the worst kind as ever was – Tiger Sharks! This brace o' Buccaneers fought under only one flag, the 'Red' one, neither asking nor giving Quarter!

A-feared? Not I, mates! And to make good my Boast, I'll explain why. Since my re-birth in that dark hole aboard the *Agony*, when I resolved to meet Death in a calm manner, fighting to the bitter end if only armed with words, my look-out on Living be this: You Win or you Lose – Live or Die! If you win, then the Fates cast you adrift again into the Mainstream of Life for more mishap and mischief. If you lose, why, then you goes to where both Good and Wicked cease to Worry! Coming from a man before the mast, that ain't too bad a Philosophy – now is it?

Well, I'd cheated Davy Jones, yet here I were facing a Fate fathoms worse than 'bubble-blowing'. Now there be some 'Sea-lawyers' as would tell you all sharks circles their prey afore coming in for the kill. These same blabber-mouths'll say that sea-wolves have to turn on their side to take a bite o' what they fancies. Here's the true way of it, mates.

They came in fast, the both of 'em, side-by-side. One pass was all they made, sweeping by port and starboard of the mate and me. Then, with a sudden swirl o' water, they turned and streaked into the attack. But it was Finch they clapped aboard. What took the wind out of my sails was the fact they brushed past me as if I were a drifting lump o' log-wood. Yet it were me as was bleeding. Finch had drained dry hours ago.

The larger of the two monsters had a chunk out of his fin, as if a small round-shot had clipped it leaving a half-moon nick in the curve. Its black, dome-shaped head reared from the surface, its jaws agape and extended – agleam with row upon row of large, triangular teeth. A moment before that terrible maw closed on the Mate, amidships, its eyes went milky-white and the impact carried Finch clear of the water.

A thunderous jolt near tore my left leg loose o' my hip socket, shades of what was to come years later, and I were dragged through the sea, shorewards, as if on a blessed 'Nantucket Sleigh Ride'. Anchored to Finch by that death-line, I was swept along, my headpiece just alow of the surface, and near to drowning. The rope went slack, sudden like, and I gulped in a lungful of God's Air – mercy be!

I broke surface in time to see the second shark seize his share. With great jaws locked upon a limb he battled ag'in the bigger bully, him o' the clipped fin. For perhaps three ticks of the clock they fought above their domain and together tore Flogger Finch asunder. Shaking him like two terriers with a rat, they fell back in a welter of pink foam and dragged his remains down into the depths. An ever widening red stain on the surface of the sea was all that marked his passing, mates.

Now I reckoned when them man-eaters finished argufying over dinner, they'd be casting their weather-eye in my direction for dessert, so I lost little time in striking out for the islands. Breast stroke, being the easiest and least tiring, soon brought me close in where I felt the tug o' the inshore current. I cast a few glances astern, expecting to see them tell-tale pennants a-pursuing of me, but the sea remained empty. It were with no little sense of relief that I staggered up the beach and dropped to my knees in the soft. white sand – gasping.

I don't rightly remember how long I remained on all fours, my mind in a whirl over what had befallen me in the last hour. Wearily I stood up, feeling light-headed, hungry, thirsty and weak as a kitten. I scanned the sea, but there was no sign of *Agamemnon* nor anything else.

My first collected thoughts were for water, so I turned and started for the tree-line. I hadn't taken six paces when a score or more shadowy figures emerged from the shelter o' the palms.

'Thunder!' thought I. 'Here I be, having killed my first man, eyeball to eyeball; cheated RN Justice; daddled Davy Jones and escaped from a pair of the most ferocious fishes in the sea, only to be devoured by a pack o' heathen Cannibals.'

This were turning out to be one of 'them' days!

Well then, so be it an' let her rip! I'd do my best to defy these Sons of Satan and break a few teeth b'fore they sank into me after I were served up on a spit to provide 'em with a Barbecue!

PEECE TWO

THE GATHERING!

CHAPTER VI

LONG JOHN SILVER ESQ. –

GENTLEMAN O' FORTUNE!

The sun was only a few points short of sinking into the sea as these Savages stepped out onto the sand and came striding down the beach towards me all in a cluster. There in the twilight I saw 'em to be White Men, but of such a rum collection that I began to doubt my deliverance.

From first to last, each man was a walking Arsenal on his own. Between 'em they could have armed a couple of Companies in a Royal Regiment o' Foot – shiver my sides! Cutlasses, Rapiers, Swords and Sabres swung from wide, leather baldrics looped over their shoulders or were tucked into colourful sashes wrapped and knotted about their waists. All carried Pistols, a pair mainly, but some had as many as three brace slung about them. Apart from Pikes, Pole-Axes, Hatchets and a few Halberds, at least one in four carried a Musket or Musketoon – what some calls a Carbine.

As for dress . . . why, they ranged from Rags to Riches with items o' clothing representing a score of countries: French pantaloons of velvet; Spanish knee-breeches of silk; glossy, Dutch leathers; open knee'd ducks of English 'Jack Tars', such as I were wearing; and the fringed, buckskin breeks of the Colonials in the Americas. Some had their heads bound in coloured scarves; others sported Tricorne Hats or wide brimmed Sombreros. One wore a necklace of silver; another boasted earrings of red gold. A few had shoes or sea-boots and looked reasonably clean, but the main of 'em went bare of foot and were filthy dirty.

They stopped, forming a half-circle around me some few yards off, and weighed up my worth with hard, unfriendly eyes. Seeing as I had nought to lose, except my life, I took a brash course and spoke accordingly.

"Well here be a pretty parcel o' Pirates as ever came athwart my hawse!" cried I, grinning. "You can't 'Make nor Mend' now, my lads, for I has you surrounded, single-handed, and arrest ye, one an' all, in the name o' Farmer George – Rot 'im!"

A stunned silence greeted my bravado. Then every man-jack of 'em bellowed a broadside of laughter, some bending themselves double with mirth. One of their number, resplendent in a suit of velvet maroon, complete with a matching, gold laced hat, a great red sash and black sea-boots that reached to his thighs, stepped forward grinning, his left hand resting lightly on the pommel of his finely chased, long rapier.

"Bold words, friend, if friend you prove to be," says he. "Aye, bold words well spoke, I'll lay you that. But methinks 'tis you who will have to strike his colours and ask for quarter. So you claim to be a King's man, eh? What might your name be and from whence come you?"

"John Silver – Seaman; late o' His Majesty's Ship *Agamemnon*; logged as: DD, but still very able!" I replied and then gave the main soundings of my story, securing with: "So after I'd fed Flogger to the sharks, I bit a chunk from the fin o' the biggest one, t'show I weren't to be trifled with, and bade the pair of 'em to tow me ashore, sharp like, under pain o' me punching their teeth down their gullet – an' here I be!"

Mine host in the maroon coat showed much good nature, as did most of 'em. But one surly brute, dark and dago-looking, with shoulders like a bull, gave vent to a string of oaths, hot enough to pop chestnuts!

"You don't appear t'be a d—d Dagon to me!" snarled he, hooking his huge thumbs into a wide, brass-buckled belt that supported a cutlass, a dirk, a hatchet and two brace of pistols. "And as to your galley yarn about killing parties an' getting Jonah's Toss to be towed here by a pair o' Sea Wolves – why, think you 'tis a bunch of buffoons you be aspeakin' to, boozed-up and brain-less!"

"Belay such bitter talk, John Taylor, and dampen down your temper, man. This poor castaway ain't a-crossing of us," retorted my maroon coated colleague, whom I took to be the leader, and right I was.

"Now since I command this Company," continued he, "I vote he be given the chance to sign our 'Articles' and come 'On the Account' with us. What say you, Brothers?"

"Be ye an 'Artist'?" enquired a bearded ruffian, bristling with pistols same as the Almanack Man do with darts.

When I replied that I were no candidate for Master Rembrandt's brush, they roared with laughter yet again. It was explained to me that by 'Artist', they meant Specialist, such as Carpenter, Boatswain, Sailing-Master, Mate or Gunner.

"Shiver my sides!" cried I. "If it floats upon the blessed sea, I can sail it! And I'll lay any piece that eats powder and ball for breakfast. Aye, and hit the mark more'n most swabbers as calls 'emselves Gunners!'

"Talk's cheap!" snapped Taylor. "But small odds it. We'll be trying the temper of your blade soon enough, m'brave buck, then we'll see how Pistol

Proof you be."

"Thankee," I replied, returning his arrogant stare, measure for measure. "An' speaking o' blades; maybe you'd oblige me a lend of your'n to cut this 'ere cable away from my foot as bound me to Flogger Finch."

It were him o' the pistols as drew his knife and done me service, remarking that: "The line be tight tangled, lads. Tied by one as knows knots sure 'nough."

"A tatty rope don't prove nuthin'," growled Taylor.

Just at that moment a Buccaneer yelled: "TIBURONS!" and everybody's head turned to follow his pointing finger.

Cruising close in-shore, swimming back and forth like a pair o' guards marching a beat, were the same brace of dorsals I had boasted about as someone soon verified. "Look t'the for'ard fin, mates! There be a bite out-a it, same as Long John said he'd done, by blazes!"

A gasp of surprise and their awe-struck faces swung back to gawk at me. Many a poor Picaroon in that unholy gathering, not being over in ballast with brains, gazed at me as if I were Old Nick, hisself.

"That Barbecues your grumble about galley yarns, Taylor!" bawled a voice from the back.

The First Mate, for such was he, swung round, his bearded, brutal face livid, his hand clamped to a pistol butt. He was about to snarl a reply when a musket flared and bellowed. The shot sounded like a thunderbolt and rolled on far out to sea. A white cloud of smoke engulfed half the company on one side and the splash of a striking bullet showed between the fins. Lazily, both killers veered towards the sanctuary of the open ocean and were soon lost to sight.

"Avast!" cried the Captain. "What fool fired his Fuzee with a King's ship cruising these same waters not an hour since? 'Tis you, Thomas Armstrong! By Neptune's Beard, 'twill go hard on you if all hands have to close-up and trade dry blows with the Royal Navy for your folly – and you yourself an RN Deserter!" He turned, slapped me on the back and offered his hand. "Glad to have you aboard, Long John Silver, and right welcome. There's more to you than most men can match, I'll stake a dozen Doubloons any day. And if you don't prove a credit to this crew, then my name ain't Edward England!"

That be how I joined the Brethren o' the Coast, mates, and came to go 'On the Account' under the great Captain England. He had a fine Sloop anchored snug and safe in a hidden creek, while ashore the Pirate camp was the cosiest berth I'd been in for many a long year.

After a complete shift o' rigging, taken from the common chest, under the care of the Quarter-Master, I sat down beside the cook-fire to the finest fare I'd tasted since leaving home and loved ones. There were sweet potatoes, yams, plantains, venison, beef, pork and goat all skewered on steel ramrods and interspaced with pieces of apple, pineapple, peach and alligator-pear. I never knowed such food existed in all the world like I tasted that night. There was turtle soup with its flesh broiled in it too. Pure nectar. No Lord in Parlyment ever dined better, shiver my sides. And none of it above six hours old. A far cry from the Naval bilge hoarded for six years!

The Buccaneers done Long John proud that night, such as they'd Christened me. There was several 'Johns' in the Company, but none to match my six-foot. They made me a present of a cutlass, a gully and a pair of pistols, plain and brass-bound, to be sure, but a joy to the touch. We sat smoking and talking, like jolly companions every one, yarning far into the early hours. I had my first fill of 'Rumfustian', a potent mixture o' Gin, Beer, Rum and Sherry – heavily spiced. Strong waters ever did agree with me, one of my minor bad habits. But needless to say, mates, I 'threw out my ballast' before morning and awoke with Thor's Hammer housed inside my skull.

From the Bahamas we sailed our Sloop to the Main of Africa, seeing as the RN were making the waters in the Caribbean too warm for the likes of us. We laid aboard and plundered prizes from Madagascar to Mauritius and on to the Malabar Coast. Between the River Gambia and the Castle at Cape Corso, where so many mess-mates were hanged like dogs to shrivel and sun-dry in future years, we took no fewer than Nine Sail.

'Twas off the Malabar Coast we clapped aboard the *Viceroy of the Indies* out o' Goa and I got a share of the Great Mogal's diamonds. Aye, mates, forty-two small sparks were my cut, apart from the blunt. One fool only got a single spark. A beauty, it were, about the size of a musket-ball.

The Quarter-Master, whose duty it was to work out Fair-Shares for all, reckoned it were equal to the value of forty-two others. He was wrong. I later learned that a Diamond such as this was worth a great deal more But the oaf what got it, thinking hisself to be dutch-traded, puts it in a mortar and beats it into forty-three crumbs, telling us he now had a better Share than any. I seen simpletons with more sense, so I have!

We met other 'Rovers' during this time and among our Company, word filtered down to us that another Buccaneer was raising Cain way out in the Dutch East Indies. Ranging from the Malayas to Java, the terror o' the South China Sea was the *Naiad*, and the mere mention of her Captain's name evoked fear throughout the Far East. Aye, ye've guessed it, mates – JIM FLINT!

Ours was a wicked world, full o' dark deeds done in the Devil's name for the profit of them as served him. Aye, wicked ways to be sure; but who's to blame? There now, tell me that! Who dragged me off from ploughing an honest furrow and cast me adrift from all I held dear? LAWS! Laws as was made by high born, infernal society swabs in Parlyment for their own ends! There's wickedness for you. The Gentry were never Press-Ganged. Laws that governed them were a far cry from those that controlled the Peasantry – you may lay to that! Might is Right! Well, what stands good for them, stands good for me!

To my mind, the daftest song that ever came to be sung in the Royal Navy in the 1740s was 'Rule Britannia'. You recall the words? 'Rule Britannia, Britannia rules the waves – Britons never, never shall be slaves!' So be it, but don't sing it to those such as I who were Pressed into Service – by thunder!

Now for all the wrongs done in this tired old world and for all my own black bitterness, I still reckon that to lay an honest course through Life be best. If some of you Younkers are figuring to go 'A-Roving' or to 'Take to the High Toby', think well on these words: any gutter scum can be a Buccaneer an' most of 'em are, but it takes a tougher breed of man to live fair and square, and help people instead of doing them down. The most precious Treasure a body can hold in its coffers is a Clear Conscience, Contentment and Peace of Mind. Believe me, shipmates, those articles be worth more'n all the Gold that lies sinking into the silt beneath the Seven Seas!

I've a black conscience, I have, that clouds my mind and gives me bad dreams at night. I've lied and cheated, plundered and pillaged, dabbled in double-dealings and dealt out death! Only in self-defence, mind! I'm a saving soul, really, at heart. Live an' let live – that's my motto!!! If a cutlass slash or a cannon ball don't do for me first, and I don't end my days dangling in chains on Execution Dock, where will I be thirty years from now? An old, rum-soaked hulk, living with some degree o' comfort in this world, to be sure, but with no chance of any in the next. When Gabriel blows his Horn and Saint Peter summons me up from below to stand in Final Judgement of HIM, by the powers it'll be a black day for old Long John – so it will!

For all my earlier brave talk, thoughts o' the gallows and the gibbet fair gives me the vapours, especially when I be far gone in rum. But that Call from the Great Creator is what I dreads most. My only hope is to live forever and not go to my own place like what it says in the Bible, for I knows full well where that'll be!

But look here! This won't do! Me spouting off like a pious Chaplain holding a Sermon on the Poop! Stand-by to go about; helm hard-a-lee and on with the blessed Story!

CHAPTER VII

BLACKBEARD'S GUNNER!

Edward England was a brave man. Aye, 'Ned' had the courage of a Lion at close-quarters, but his fault lay in being too generous with those he took prisoner. It be one thing to spare a man's life, yet to give a Crew their blessed boat back or set 'em safe ashore near habitation – well, that do top the stiffest yard-arm to nothing! Ned's kindness to captives proved near fatal for us on several hair-raising occasions like when John Company ships or R.N. Frigates came beating-up in our wake in a brace of shakes. 'Twas only because we kept a light pair of heels that we out-run 'em. After one such incident, in which we came within a cat's whisker of losing the ship and our lives, the Crew held Council and deposed Ned from command. At his own request, we put him ashore on the Island of his choice – which was Mauritius. Three others decided to join him on this green jewel set in the Indian Ocean, east of Madagascar.

John Taylor was elected Captain. Under England I had graduated from Quarter to Master Gunner and now I was made Sailing-Master. On occasion, when the opposition grew too hot and I weren't needed at the helm, I laid a long twelve and swung a match to help rupture our victim's rigging a bit smart. He was a shark, was Taylor. Tough and ruthless, but a Seaman second to none. And shrewd – a Jew money lender 'ud get hisself daddled in dealing along o' him! He suited the Crew, mind. The safety of our necks was top priority in his book, not niceties!

By the time, Taylor brought the *Cassandra* home safe to Porto Bello and surrendered to the Spanish Governor, along of an 'Act of Grace', I had four 'Sheet Anchors' in my favour. Firstly, a nickname as was known the length o' the West Indies – few were the Harbour Bars that hadn't heard discussions on the Merits of Ned England's Gunner, 'Long John'. Secondly, a reputation for hardness and honesty – the latter being as rare as a Bishop among the Brethren of the Coast. Thirdly, a Letter of Credit to the tune of Nine Hundred Pound, all safely banked in Boston. And lastly, I had me a pet – the pride of my heart!

A bottle-green Parrot from Surinam, she were, smart as paint and pretty as a picture. Now that old Bird knowed more sea-terms than most landed lubbers and she could swear blue fire fathoms worse than the roughest Rover I ever sailed with, barring Flint, and seeing as he dominated Tavern Talk, at the time, I named her after the Famous Buccaneer. Not exactly a Lady-like name, thinks you, but then she weren't exactly a Lady – swearing worse than stevedores do. Worth her weight in Margaritas, she was. Ashore or afloat I could lay my head down and be safe at night, for if anybody set foot within a mark of me, her shrill squawk of: "Avast! Avast!" aroused me double quick!

Edward England's former Crew dispersed. Some took ship in a Sloop owned by the South Sea Company; others berthed aboard various Traders. Most of 'em eventually clued-up with the King's Pardon; but the unlucky few who signed and sailed under Bart Roberts were doomed to swing and sun-dry years later at Corso Castle. As for Taylor, he sold his sword to the Spanish and commanded a Man o' War against his own country when the Peace of Utrecht came to a rupture. Wanted me to join him, but I drew the line at killing Englishmen in the service o' the Dons! I wanted to lay a new course and shake out a befitting berth, somewhere secure and profitable for me and my feathered Buccaneer.

Porto Bello was a natural harbour, land-locked on three sides. Two Forts dominated the narrow entrance and guarded the town sprawled around the long bay. Old style Spanish Colonial houses with white-washed adobe walls and roofed in red tejas, some of them dating back to Drake's Day, lay jumbled together on the steep hillsides. A few streets were only a degree or so from being sheer. Yellow Jack and other diseases were rife. Adding to people's misery were thousands o' tiny, biting insects called Moskitos that whined in your ear all through the night!

All manner of people used the Port, but only one Spanish Merchantman a year was allowed in to trade. High profits were to be had in the Smuggling Game. The main hazard was that Captains caught 'Freebooting' normally got their ears cut off, while their Crews were committed to Slavery in the Mines – sometimes for life.

The Natives were a gay lot to look at, mixed Breeds, mostly, consisting of Negroes, Indians, Cholos and Sambos. The Negroes and Indians were easy going enough if treated fair; but the Cholos, half-breed Indians with Spanish blood – a treacherous crowd, them. It didn't take much to set their knives a-going! The Sambos were by far the best bunch, being a mixture of Negro and Indian parentage. They was friendly, good natured, always laughing and most obliging.

The Tavern where I took residence were nicely situated on a bluff to give a grand view of the Harbour. As was my custom after supper, which included such succulent luxuries as Oysters, Lobster and home-smoked Ham, I was sitting on the Balcony enjoying a pipe and a glass o' Hot Punch to ward off the agues that plague this part of the world, when a ragged looking Seaman wearing a red flannel night-cap limped over to me.

His clothing was well out at the elbows and he hisself was thin and emaciated, his ears sticking out from his blue-jowled, gaunt face like a pair o' cleats. My eyes fell to the pistol in his broad belt and the cutlass hanging on his left side. Both side-arms bore the 'Lion' mark of the East India Company, Naval Defence Force. The barker was as clean as the burnished brass on a Man o' War's tiller-bar and ready primed too, if I knowed ought of fire-locks. As to his hanger – there was a weapon as had seen a sight of times, judging by the battered brass guard with numerous dents and slash cuts as had been smoothed down around the curve of the cup.

"I ain't in the habit o' being a beggar," began he, more by way of a statement than apology, "but seeing as I'm near to floundering for want o' sustenance and you look to be well hauled an' all, maybe you could see fit to spare a fellow Englishman, wot's down on his luck, the price of a dram?"

"Pull up alongside, matey, and I'll go you one better," replied I. "Good nature being part of my nature, just order anything your 'art desires. I'll lay it's been a time since you last took ballast aboard b'the cut o' your jib!"

"Well now," said he, rubbing his hands and licking his lips as he parked hisself opposite. "I confess to bein' empty as a light Collier running North, I do. 'Taint every day an Old Hulk, such as me, gets an invite to heave-to and take on life's cargo b'the likes of your own good self. I thankee!"

I ordered a double go of Brandy for the both on us and sought to get better acquainted with my guest. He thought likewise, for he picked up his glass and held it aloft, poised in salute beneath the smoky lantern.

"Here's to luck, long life and a fair wind with it. Mister . . .?"

"Silver, such is my name – Long John to my mess-mates!"

His eyebrows shot up, creasing his forehead into furrows. "Well now, by thunder! I've heard you well spoke of from Salem to Surinam and clear across the Caribbee to the Coromandel Coast, so I have. We both o' us be Artists of the same kidney, seein' you was England's Gunner, while I. . ." He shrugged and left the sentence unfinished, tossing down his drink in one gulp.

"Being at the Seas yourself, who did you ship with, matey?" I asked, noting his unease.

He fidgeted with his empty glass, his eyes darting to all quarters like a rat in a cheese factory, then looked me straight in the glims and said: "BLACKBEARD!" He spat the word more'n spoke it. "I burnt powder under

Teach the Terrible, I did!"

"Blackbeard's Gunner?" gasped I. "By the powers – Israel Hands!"

"Israel Hands as ever was," replied he, rising. "Now I'll lay you won't want the likes o' me sitting alongside your table, partaking of your charity. 'Tis always the way on it when my name be spoke above board!"

Israel Hands were a name well known among the Brethren of the Coast, to be sure. A man who carried the Mark of Cain. For it was he who took 'the Turnip Man's Pardon' and 'Turned King's Evidence' against the survivors of Blackbeard's Crew after they came to dry blows with Lieutenant Maynard at the Battle of Pamlico Sound. Hands wandered an outcast for a while, then disappeared. Most thought he died a beggar-man, starving and alone in London Town.

"Avast, Mister Hands!" cried I as he made to leave. "Hang-fire and don't be a-going off at half-cock! I ain't such a swab as t'throw a life-line to a man one minute, then haul it back the same blessed moment! Sit you down!" I turned towards the bar and bawled: "Holloa, Sambo! Bring brandy and a supper for this Seaman - the same as was served me!"

"John Silver, you be a brisk hand and no mistake," said Blackbeard's former Gunner, putting hisself to anchor again and ogling the juicy dishes as were being laid before him by a grinning darky. "For if you ain't the saving o' me this day, I'll eat my hanger - aye, sheath an'all!"

My new found mess-mate broached those platters to in a brace of shakes, using both fork and fingers, as if expecting 'em to vaporise in a puff of smoke. Sweet 'tatoes, oysters, plantains, lobster and chunks of ham disappeared down his hatch, swilled into his belly-bilges with great gulps of Chicka.

"'Taint so much what a man does as goes ag'in the grain along o' his mates," said I, "but how he does it and for why. Gentlemen o' Fortune usually trusts little among 'emselves, to be sure, and neither forgives nor forgets those as sinks their own kind. A Buccaneer's business is his own affair, that's what I say, and I never judge or condemn a fellow Rover on the say so of others – 'specially tavern-talk from Sea-Lawyers and boosy Old Seamen."

"Oh, it be right enough," admitted Hands, matter of factly. "But there's none as knows the true way on it." He swallowed a brace of oysters, took a swig of beer and continued. "Blackbeard were a mad prankster. Aye, an' a d—d dangerous one. His high jinx near killed me, so the swab did. Deliberately wrecked the *Queen Anne's Revenge* in Topsail Inlet. A fine Flag-Ship she were too, an' us all having to crowd aboard a Sloop," he said with a sad shake of his head. "Another clotpoll caper was when he took half a dozen o' us down into the hold and had the hatches closed. "Come," says he, "let us make a Hell of our own, and try how long we can bear it!'"

Hands paused to feed his face, cracking a lobster-claw with his strong white teeth. "Them's his exact words," resumed he. "Then Teach lit three stink pots. Stuffycation all but done fer the lot o' us. I were breathin' out sulphur fumes for days a'terwards."

I puffed smoke at the rafters. "Why didn't the Crew depose 'im and elect a new Cap'n, according to the Fo'c'sle rules of most Rovers?" I asked, then took a sip of brandy.

"Depose, Teach?" guffawed Hands and near choked on his grub. "We none of us had the bottle, Long John. One an' all walked in mortal terror o' the man. He were big as a barn door, strong as a brace o' bulls and ten times more dangerous!" The former Gunner gulped beer to clear his gullet and carried on. "Me'n Blackbeard came to a final rupture when he invited me and the Master down to his cabin for a dram. He were dangerous drunk a-fore we went below. Well I thought to watch out for m'self, so I did, but I thought too slow, by thunder! Teach were too sly. One moment he were laughin' and tellin' a joke; the next he blows out the glim, pulls a pair o' pops from his sash, crosses his hands under the table and lets fly. Put a blasted ball through my leg and left me lame for life – the black-hearted swab!"

"Shiver my sides, Israel," I replied as he fell to attacking his food again. "Had Teach done that on me, I'd have shown him the colour of his own insides, so I would!"

"Ah, John, John, you never knowed Blackbeard," said Hands between mouthfuls. "He were the Devil in disguise. I never see him Bested by Seven – Seven at one go, mark you! It took five and twenty great wounds to bring him by the board an' five o' those were from shot. Maynard hisself, it were, as finally downed him and only then by firing a ball point-blank into his black heart!"

Hands hove-to long enough to swill down the last of the ham with the last of his beer. "Now thems who survived swore an oath on the Blessed Book that a'ter Blackbeard was decapitated and his corpse thrown overboard, he swam around the ship three times and shook his fist afore sinking from sight into Okerecock Inlet. Galley yarn or no, I for one don't doubt it. If any man 'ud be defiant in death, it 'ud be Teach!"

"Makes me flesh creep just thinking on it," I murmured.

"As fer those other swabs," said Hands firing up his pipe, "they left me high and dry in Bath Town, beggin' for bread. Not one sided along o' me or raised objection when Teach sailed off with my Cut. If it were all above board for 'em to cheat me along o' saving their own miserable necks, then according to my Articles, I were well justified in peachin' on them to save mine!" Hands puffed out a cloud of smoke and pushed the empty platters away. "By the powers! I ain't tasted such dainty rations since Maynard sailed his Sloop into Bath Town with Blackbeard's head-piece swinging from the bowsprit!" concluded he.

CHAPTER VIII

MR WILLIAM BONES – MATE!

“Well none could fault you on that verdict, nohow,” admitted I after hearing Hands’s tale of woe. “But see here, Israel; where was you at all these years? Talk was you’d slipped-your-moorings in London Town a long time since.”

“Not I,” replied Hands, coiling his tongue in his cheek, while giving that sly, guilty grin I were to know and see so often. “Not I,” he repeated and took a gulp of brandy, then continued his intriguing tale. “For a two year term I sought my bread at sea, wielding an honest harpoon ag’in the Mighty Leviathan. A’rter that I spent a season as a ‘Slitter’ in the d—d Fishery at New-Found-Land. Aye, under paid, under fed and near froze t’death an’ all, by thunder! From carvin’ fish guts and freezin’, I took ship to the Coromandel Coast and fried, sweating out my soul in a French Factory at Pandicherry.

“One day an East Indiaman anchored in the Road and I enrolled in the Bombay Buccaneers as a Quarter Gunner. But I had to take French Leave a bit lively, along o’ the Second Officer making a mockery of my buckled leg. Chucked the swab overboard, I did, and he got took by a Tiburon. I’ve sailed on most things as ’ud float since then: Traders; Slavers and wot not, ’til here I be, out o’ salts and short on Luck along of clappin’ me weather-eye on you, Long John. That’s my story!”

Now all the time that Israel were talking I noticed this Stranger at the bar, taking more’n just a casual interest in me and my mess-mate. He was a heavy, strong, nut-brown man, around forty and five, I’d say, with a face already marked by the purple tinge and broken veins of a hard drinker. A tarred pigtail jutted out from beneath his tricorne hat like a jib-boom. Under the broad flaps of his soiled, blue coat I caught the dull twinkle of light glinting on chased silver pistol butts. Leather breeks were stuffed into sea-boots, turned down at the knee, and at his left side he wore a great curved cutlass.

The Stranger drank his rum out slowly, all the time with his dark eyes locked on mine. Gruffly he called for a refill and came over, moving with a lurching sea-walk that showed he weren't much use at hoofing it ashore.

"Top o' the evening to ye, John Silver," says he. "Ah, an' Mister Hands has come alongside too, I see. Well, well, I calls it right matey all round, I do!" He passed to port of Israel, and sat down to starboard o' me with his back to the balustrade, facing the bar-room with what I thought to be a wary eye.

"How would you be knowing my name?" snapped Hands. "'Specially seeing as I don't know yours!"

"Bones! Mister William Bones – Mate! And if I ain't bad mistook, ye'll both be very much for my Service afore this hour's out – and you may lay to that, my Bold Blades!" scowled he, snorting through his fleshy, broken veined nose.

"I've heard mention of a Billy Bones, him as use to sail along o' the elusive Cap'n Flint who . . ." A first-rate oath cut me short.

"Use to?" echoed Bones. "Thunder, I still do! I'm Flint's First Mate, I am! Me'n him 'ave sailed between wind and water right from when he first hoisted 'Old Roger', aboard the *Hastings*!"

"Flint ain't been heard of these past two year gone!" growled Hands with a look as sullen as winter. "There's them as claim he's under hatches – secured by Davy Jones's Lock. Went down off Cape Horn with All Hands, aboard the *Naiad*, so 'tis said."

"That was a rumour as were started by Flint hisself," explained Bones. "A Crew reputed dead ain't looked for, see! Ah, he's a man with a headpiece on his shoulders is Jim Flint! Now where do you suppose his old Crew's at? Why they is all paid-off and set up as Gentlemen in Ernest – one an' all. Living like Lords in Parlyment, they be. And for the two years you spoke of, Israel Hands, we was plundering prizes in the Great South Sea. Aye, from Acapulco clear across Polynesia and on up to Penang, by thunder!"

"I've been 'at the seas' since turning twenty," stated I, "and never once met with Flint's ship nor drank a dram with any Rover as sailed along of him. Now I calls that a mite odd, I do."

"I calls it good planning from a man with common sense enough for sixty! The Captain has his own bases! Secret, snug berths! Why, he's even got a whole town at his beck-an'-call!" snapped Bones with a snort.

"How many Rover Crews retires intact, rolling in guineas, and lives to a ripe old age?" continued the Mate. "How long did Bonnet last or Low, or 'Calico Jack'? Aye, Rackham – him who cowered in the hold, drunk in company with his Crew. They got clapped aboard and left the fighting to a brace of Bonney Strumpets!"

"Aye," agreed Hands. "Mary Reid and Ann Bonney. A pistol proof pair of brisk lasses as ever was."

"And look to Kidd," continued Bones. "The great Captain Kidd! I see him turned off at Wapping Old Stairs with these same deadlights. Reeling drunk in a black draped cart, he was, when the rope broke and the hangman had to give him a second go at choking! And what did he amount to, mates? A tarred corpse chinking in chains, hanging at Tally Point – an' him with a Letter of Marque from blasted Royalty, by thunder! Why, you both know, Blackbeard hisself lasted no longer than half a blessed Dog-Watch!"

"Where's Flint at now?" I asked.

"And how comed you knowed our names?" demanded Hands yet again.

"The Captain's close by, hove-to aboard a Lugger," replied the Mate and drained his drink. "As to knowing your markers – well, we has ears and eyes in every Port worthy of the name."

"If Flint be such a Flyer, why don't he retire too?" enquired I, for there were a few points I couldn't quite fathom concerning the doings of Messrs Bones and Flint.

"Likewise yourself," added Hands.

"Reasons of his own!" came Bones's blunt reply. "An' what goes for the Captain, goes for me! Now your sea-chest, Mister Silver, were placed safe aboard the Barca-Longa berthed below, not an hour since, along o' that Parrot you put such high score by."

"Thunder!" exclaimed I, feeling sour that such liberties had been taken with my traps. "Supposing I don't choose to sign Flint's Articles and goes my own way?"

"Why then, it'll be a long haul for Israel Hands and Long John, with a short shuffle into the mines at the end o' it! Less you'd prefer entering the Spanish Service such as Taylor?" replied Bones. "For the Snow that sailed in at sunset, brought news of a rupture between England and Spain. We be at War, mates! At this same moment there be details o' Dago Infantry rounding up all Englishmen who ain't got the correct Papers!"

"You took your blasted time to tell us that!" snapped Hands.

"Best we budge then, afore they comes a-calling here," said I.

Billy Bones suddenly stiffened, his fleshy nostrils flaring as his face went stoney. "Belay the last pipe," said he. "We be boarded!"

The bar had filled up somewhat since supper time with Seamen and Merchants of all nationalities. Most were in the pay of Spain; some, along of ourselves, weren't. There were those engaged in low conversation, while smoking and drinking. Others laughed uproariously, trying to make free with the Serving Wenches, giving sauce to them as they moved between the crowded tables bearing pots of ale. More'n one encounter ended with a sharp slap and a drunken peal o' laughter.

Gaiety and good humour dropped off when a Capitan led a dozen, dirty looking Soldados into the bar, each armed with a bayoneted musket held at the high port. The Capitan gazed around him with distaste, tapping long, slender finger-tips on the pommel of his fine sword. He barked out a harsh command and bedlam broke loose as the Soldados began herding everybody against the far wall. There were cries and curses from those who didn't budge fast enough, when a clout from a musket butt caught 'em alongside the lug-'ole.

We three seated on the balcony in shadow, Billy having blown out the glim, never moved.

CHAPTER IX

COLD STEEL – HOT BLOOD!

"Stand-by to repel boarders!" hissed Billy Bones fiercely. "I fancy we'll have to raise Cain and carve our way through this mess o' stinking swabs. Have ye a barker handy?" he asked, glancing at me.

When I replied, "No," he slipped me one of his smart Brescian Snap-haunces, heavy and handsomely inlaid with silver. The Capitan, spying us still seated, came striding over, his glossy black boots twinkling in the light. Behind him waddled a fat Sargento carrying a sabre, with four scruffy Soldados in tow.

"So!" spat the Capitan, stamping his feet apart and placing elegant, well manicured hands on lean hips. "*Tres* Engleesh *perros*! You wi-illa alla placa your we-epons on ze table, yes?"

"NO!" roared Billy and jumping up, fired his pistol point-blank at the Capitan's breast, so close that the muzzle-blast set his coat smouldering.

A white shroud of powder smoke swirled about the Spaniard. He staggered back under the impact of the ball, then lunged forward and gripped the side of our table to keep from falling.

Without further ado, me'n Hands pistoled a Soldado each, shooting 'em down like dogs. Billy transferred his barker to his left hand, holding it by the barrel to use as a bludgeon, and drew his cutlass just in time to parry a murderous slash from the Sargento's short sabre. A mighty underhand swipe in retaliation brought the Sargento's weapon clattering onto the table-top, smashing a glass. The fat man shrieked, seizing his stomach in both hands, and with the inner redness of his belly dribbling between his fingers he stumbled forward, crashed through the balustrade and fell screaming into space where the sea awaited him far below.

We had created more confusion in that there Tavern than a pork chop thrown into a crowded Synagogue! Men cursing, women screeching, they all stampeded for the narrow passage in a heaving mass, turning over tables and chairs in the mad scramble to get clear. Several Soldados caught up in the rush, whether by accident or design, fired their muskets into the ceiling, showering everybody with bits o' plaster which bolstered the panic no end. Adding to the chaos was the powder smoke from the discharged arms, rolling around the bar-room like a thick, white fog.

Hands, Billy and me were now hard pressed with our backs to the broken balustrade. It were cutlasses and pistol butts against the bayonets and musket stocks o' seven Soldados. Me'n Israel were tackling two apiece; Billy was fighting three! Being crowded so close on all sides, the Dagos couldn't bring their Fire-Locks to proper play for fear o' hitting their own. Wreathed in smoke like phantoms in a fog, I could see two others battling the remaining three soldiers within the bar.

Me'n Hands were one side of the table, Billy was on t'other with the dying Capitano between us. I see it all clear now as I did then. The Spaniard, his life blood spattering the white, scrubbed table-top, suddenly seized the dead Sargento's sabre and along o' the last breath in his body dealt Billy a mighty blow across the right cheek, laying the flesh open to the bone, disfiguring the man who had killed him. Billy uttered a fearful oath and sprang back with the red blood pouring down his coat. The Mate swung up his great cutlass, ready to strike, but the Don were already dead. He lay slumped across the table, the sabre still gripped in his lifeless hand.

The surviving Dagos suddenly fled into the smoke, dodging around our two unknown allies who came striding over to us, kicking aside the broken furniture as lay in their path.

"All's up with us, mates!" cried one cheerfully, grinning fit to split while shaking blood from a gashed hand.

"There be a score or more o' the swabbers just arrived outboard!" added the taller of the two. "Much hurt, matey?" he asked, peering at Billy's dripping cheek.

"I'll live," growled the Mate, sheathing his hanger as I handed back the borrowed pistol. "Who might you both be?"

"I'm Job Anderson," replied the tall seaman. "This here's my ship-mate, 'Gypsy' Fuller!"

Shouted commands in Spanish came clearly through the smoke, putting the dampers on further introductions. Billy returned his pops to his pockets and growled at the four of us: "There be but one way to go and 'tis straight down," said he, peering over the broken balustrade. "When yer jump, spread wide. I don't want the imprint of a sea-boot in my brain!"

Then he was gone, the skirts of his blue coat billowing out behind him like a galley sail. We four gazed in horror at his descending figure, watching it grow smaller and smaller.

"Thunder!" cried Hands. "Must be close t' fourteen fathoms straight down to the briny! The fall will probably do for 'im as sure as Spanish steel!"

"Just as well, mates," replied Gypsy Fuller still grinning. "I can't swim a blessed stroke nohow!"

And he too launched hisself into space. I saw the white splash of spray where Billy hit the water far below, but being in the shadow of the bluff, I couldn't tell whether he had survived.

Anderson, Hands and me exchanged sick glances and mortal white we three looked, to be sure. A musket suddenly flared and bellowed beyond the smoke, spitting a tongue o' flame at us, and a ball hummed between me'n the Gunner. Shadowy figures appeared, flitting among the shattered furniture and filling the bar like avenging Spectres rising up from Hades. No time for second thoughts. Hands jumped straight out; Anderson leapt to his left, while I sprang to the right and not a moment too soon. Above us a thunderous volley reduced the remains o' the balustrade stanchions to kindling.

The wind sang past my ears, snatching away my fine hat. The skirts of my coat streamed about my head, tugging at my armpits. As I fought to keep an even keel I saw Hands below me, his arms also a-going like windmills to help maintain his balance. A great spout of spray came up to meet me where he took the plunge. Then I whooshed into the water with a mighty splash and the world went black. Down and down I went. I heard a rush of water on my left, where Anderson hit. My feet touched firm sand and I shot upwards, popping to the surface like a cork with my clothes ballooning about me. Billy was being hauled dripping into a fishing boat. Anderson and Hands were towing a spluttering Gypsy Fuller between them. Surprising the number of Seamen as couldn't swim in my day!

As I drew alongside them the sea around us erupted into little splashes of spray. 'Twas then we heard the reports of muskets chasing the shots home. Shooting at us from above, so the swabs were. Away from the bluff we was now bathed in bright moonlight – sitting ducks one and all.

The Barca-Longa swung round, presenting her bows to the bluff, and I caught the words *EL COMADREJA* painted in white script. Coming level with her we had three boat-hooks thrust down to us by several figures leaning over the bulwarks. Shots splintered the ship's side and one man, clapping a hand to his head, toppled feet over forelock into the sea.

"Damnation seize my soul!" roared a terrible voice as I flopped onto the deck, gasping like a stranded fish.

A great shadowy figure bounded past me to the bows and crouched over a long, vicious looking Swivel-Gun. Moments later smoke and flame belched from the serpent-headed muzzle and a parcel of musket balls hurled skywards to scatter among them as lined the balcony. Five of the swabs took a nose dive to Davy Jones and the rest retreated to safer regions.

Several of the Crew were all a pully-hauly, hoisting the lug-sails. The Helmsman put the tiller-bar hard-a-lee and we sailed smartly out of further harm's way, slap-bang between two forts dominating the Harbour mouth. No cannon fire came. Too little time had passed for them to have been informed o' the rupture taking place ashore, I reckon, and being so small I doubt they could see us anyway. Clouds were now crossing the moon at a rapid rate and all became darker, adding much to our safety. The black figure silhouetted in the bows left the smoking Swivel and strode aft to where I still lay panting and wheezing upon the deck.

"Holloa, Long John Silver, just dropped in like. Dinna hang a leg there, m' Bonnie Laddie," said he helping me up. "Away below to a dry shift o' rigging. Mister Bones! When ye've berthed our new boarders and seen to bodily comforts, report ye aft!"

"Aye, aye, Sir!" replied the Mate.

Before I could say a word the shadowy stranger with a sombrero pulled low over his eyes, stepped across the hatch coaming and disappeared below. Apart from him sounding Scottish, all I could tell of him at this point was he were bigger and broader and taller than me. Far to seaward, lightning flickered amid low growls o' thunder. Storms in the Tropics are apt to be savage and they comes quick with little warning.

"No harm to us," remarked Billy Bones at my elbow, eyeing the approaching tempest. "Betime 'Hunraken' rides over our rigging we'll be safe at anchor in a snug berth. Follow me!"

He led the four of us below to a cosy cabin with double bunks set ag'in the bulkhead. A lanthorn hung from a centre beam above a small table. On three of the bunks were neat piles of clean, dry clothing; at the foot o' the fourth stood my Sea-Chest and on the bed itself, my bird's cage – empty!

"Where be my Parrot at?" I demanded, feeling a hot flush of anger.

"Ah," breathed Billy, grinning and causing fresh blood to ooze from his gaping cheek. "I reckon Cap'n Flint'll be supping along o' her name-sake."

"Flint!" exclaimed Job Anderson. "Not Flint the Buccaneer?"

"No! CAPTAIN Flint – Freebooter and 'SIR' to the likes o' you!" snapped the Mate. "Hear me now! When you speaks o' the Cap'n – speak civil! Cross 'im but once and you'll go where many a better Seaman's gone these last eight years! An' you may lay to that, my Buck!"

"I thought he were dead?" said Gypsy Fuller looking ill at ease.

"Devils never die!" retorted Bones.

"How soon do we meet Fl . . . – the Cap'n?" asked Hands hastily.

"You has already! 'Twere 'im as slew them Spanish Musqueteers with the Swivel and helped Long John off the deck. He'll send his Steward for'ard to fetch you when he's so minded."

With that the Mate departed, leaving the door open so's the air could circulate. I produced a key and unlocked my Sea-Chest. Nought were missing. We changed our wet clothes and looked to the cleaning of our weapons while we waited. Salt water plays havoc with cold steel if left unattended.

My main concern was that during the fight a bayonet had pierced the thick, left cuff on my coat-sleeve and since my Letter o' Credit were hidden there, wrapped in oilskin, and seeing there were too many strangers present to risk removing it, trusting soul that I be, I had to just ponder what damage Spanish steel and salt water had done to my Receipt for Nine Hundred Pounds!

We was sitting beneath the lanthorn, grouped about the table discussing what were to come, when a small, foxy-faced fellow entered our cabin, his beady, bright eyes darting in all directions – missing nothing.

"Wot's your name?" asked Gypsy Fuller. "Reynard?"

"Darby M'Graw, mates – that's me!" grinned he. "Captain's compliments to'e gen'l'men and would yew be good enough to j'ine him aft for a friendly chin-wag, an' partake in a glass or two of punch-toddy."

Muffled commands sounded among the Crew top-side. Moments later they dropped anchor. The storm were now snapping hard on our heels, but apart from a slight swell we remained in tranquil waters. Darby M'Graw explained that high cliffs sheltered the cove we were in and dense jungle protected us from prying eyes. Thunder rumbled and crashed overhead and the rain came down in a deluge, it did, by the bucket!

"I see the old riggin' sits snug on noo yard-arms. I've a good glim fer size, me," remarked the Steward on the fit of our borrowed clothing. He chatted on as we followed him aft from the Fo'c'sle.

"Measured yew when yew all took the plunge. By the powers, wot a leap that were! 'Darby,' says J.F. to me as yew was all on the way down, 'Darby, jus' yew nip below and lay out a shift o' dry togs from the QM's Common Chest, for our noo Lodgers as Bill be bringing aboard double quick!' He's the one for organisation and having it Ship-Shape-an'-Bristol-Fashion, is J.F. Ah, here we be, mates."

Darby stopped before a heavy, solid looking door at the end of the narrow passage beside the companion way, and held up a restraining hand. So sharp did he halt that in the dim light from a single glim swinging amidships, we all bounced into each other. Gypsy Fuller swore when he lost balance and cracked his elbow bone ag'in the bulkhead.

"Shuuush!" hissed M'Graw, making more row than any of us. "Now listen, mates," said he. "J.F. drunk ain't the same as J.F. sober, see! Rum be his only Master - that an' Drugs! They be Man and Wife, Meat and Drink t'him! Once J.F. drowns hisself in his cups, it pays t' ease off a point or two. Try and leave, if yew can, but don't be brash. Not as yew'll feel over-bold when he gives yew a grin. Stand-by for a shock as like a full broadside from a 'Three Decker' when he does that on yew, mess-mates. Bill, the First Mate, him it was as told me to give yew all fair caution. Mind now, be warned!"

I were still trying to fathom the inner meaning of all this Double-Dutch talk when Darby removed his hat, tucked it under his left arm and rapped hard on the door. I felt my tarred pig-tail twitch as a cultured voice, yet sounding somewhat coarse and broken, said:

"Enter!"

CHAPTER X

FLINT – FLOWER OF THE FREEBOOTERS!

Darby ducked beneath the low lintel and stepping smartly to one side, held the door open while we filed through like four condemned Felons fresh to New-Gate. "The 'Ands be here, Sir!" announced he, sticking his pointed nose in the air like he was a Flunkey to Royalty.

"Belay the last pipe! Stand-by to go about!" screeched a familiar voice, making us all jump in our skins, and there was my old bird pecking at a bunch of grapes on the table.

"Thankee, Mister M'Graw," chuckled a shirted figure, his sleeves rolled up to the elbow, who was bent over a seated Billy Bones with his back to us. "Ye may dismiss!"

Darby disappeared in a twinkling, the door clicking shut behind him.

"Sit ye down, Gentlemen," said Flint, "and help yourselves to toddy. I'll no keep ye in stays but a moment," added our Host, turning back to Billy with a pair of surgical scissors in his hand.

I couldn't see his face, not clearly. The cabin were too gloomy. Only two glims gave off a smoky light. One lanthorn hung above the Mate, who sat receiving a final stitch in his cheek, and the other stood on the table beside a Surgeon's instrument case in company with a steaming silver bowl of Punch. Arrayed along the front of the table were three, square-shaped rum bottles and glasses of pure, cut crystal.

Silent as the grave we four were in placing ourselves in the chairs at the table and partaking of a much needed noggin o' Punch. When Israel Hands chinked a glass against the ladle, the rest of us glared at him as if he'd belched in Church before Bishop. 'Punch' were right! After the first gulp I felt fingers of fire spreading to all quarters down in my belly regions. Flint and the Devil were the only ones as knew what was in that brew, but the effect on a body was quite pleasant – both mellow and warming. When I got my wind back and my eyeballs stopped watering, I took stock o' the cabin.

A large, brass-bound chest with a humped lid lay at the foot of where the mizzen mast were stept and a colourful native hammock was slung between it and the bulkhead. Muskets stood racked around the mast, but when I saw what was suspended above 'em the blood ran cold in the very veins of me. Being in dire need of a bracer, I took another hasty gulp o' the Punch, for it were a human head as hung there, mates! Aye, a shrunken head and it didn't belong to no native neither. I reckoned him to have been a Dago, judging by his well trimmed, goatee beard. The hair had remained the same length as when he were alive. but everything else, barring the gold earrings, were in miniature – the whole face reduced in size to a little bit bigger than that o' a large grapefruit.

"Stab me!" exclaimed Flint, stepping back a pace to admire his handy-work. "That be as pretty a piece of embroidery as ever was done on any mon's chops by a professional saw-bones, by thunder! What think ye ta Bill's beauty now, ship-mates?"

Flint turned to us, the light falling full on his face, then he grinned. The shock of seeing a shrunken head was nothing to what his contained. All his front teeth, alow and aloft, were filed to needle points. James Flint had a mouth akin to a Heathen Man-Eater! Seeing our expressions, and we must have looked gob-smacked, the Big Buccaneer threw back his head and bellowed with laughter. Billy joined in the joke, wincing as the pack-thread pulled at his wound.

Flint returned the scissors to the case, snapping the lid shut, and re-hung the lanthorn, hooking it to a beam above the table before seating hisself in a high backed chair over which his coat, cutlass and hat were draped. Taking up a great silver goblet, he drank it down in one.

"Ahhh," sighed he, helping hisself to more punch, "that's some better. A mon can make do on Rum and Coca Leaves when all else fails him. Stow the instruments away, Bill, and bring ye 'The Book'; also break out pipes and tobacco for our guests, if ye'd be so obliging."

Bill were more'n obliging, near tripping over his own toes in his haste to please. He took a thick book from the chest, leather covered and bound in brass, and placed it before Flint. Looked much like a, Bible, except this Tome contained no Holy Scripture – you may lay to that! He opened the clasp and turned to a marked page, studying his own hand o' writ. Small and neat it was too. We each filled a long-stemmed, clay pipe from a Sandalwood bowl full o' dark, rich Virginy. The Mate fired a spill from the glim and lit Flint's pipe first, then his own, passing the taper to Hands who flunkeyed for us lesser mortals.

Now while Billy were playing Valet, book fetching and such, and us busy filling pipes and punch-glasses, I made a careful study of James Flint Esquire, unobserved as I thought. But this Prince of Picaroons, who was fast becoming a legend in his own lifetime, missed nothing.

From sea-boots to sombrero his wardrobe were black. A silk scarf was now tied about his head, the long ends trailing over his left shoulder. Large rings of pure gold hung from his ears. Pain, Grief and Heart-Ache were stamped in craggy lines across his broad, clean-shaven face. Watery blue eyes, pale and piercing, flashed from beneath thick, bushy black brows. Few could match his gaze without a flicker. His nose was what we called Nasee, bad broke by some bygone blow, and his mouth containing them terrible teeth was a mere gash in sallow skin. The thin lips were bloodless – tinged with blue. It was a face to inspire fear, were Flint's. His sleeves were rolled up to the elbow and his shirt open to the waist. On his chest and the thick, sinewy forearms were tattooed the indigo dots and lines of Carib culture. Hanging around his neck on a long, heavy chain was a large, gold medallion with strange, ancient runes marked on it.

One more point worthy o' mention were the scars on both wrists. The flesh was puckered an' purple, the mark of a man who had worn manacles for years – years by thunder! As to his age? He might have been anything from Forty and Five to Sixty!

Flint looked up, sudden like, and those pale blue orbs bored into mine. Made me feel dizzy, they did.

"So ho, John Silver!" says he, giving me a ghastly grin. "D'ye ken me enough, having taken stock of my measure, to sign mine 'Articles'? I reckon myself to be high in your esteem, seeing as ye named this old Surinam Polly after me." He chuckled and tickled my bird beneath her beak.

Now that Parrot didn't cotton to strangers normally, but she fluttered up to perch on the Freebooter's broad shoulder and sat there preening herself – happy as a babby in a bath.

"Animals and Children ever did take to me like pitch," said Flint and a misty look came into his eyes. Then it were gone, replaced by a flash o' blue fire. "To business!" snapped he. "See this here Tome," growled the Buccaneer, tapping the thick volume with a finger like a cudgel. "It be my 'Doomsday Book'-cum-Bible. All who sails under me has their names Logged and lives by what's wrote here. Failing that, then for him as defies me – DEATH!"

We all of us winced when he bellowed the word. Hands jumped in his skin so much he spilt part of his punch. Flint glared at each of us in turn for a moment and continued.

"I've berthed some aboard in the past who have tried to daddle me, along with the rest of a True Crew. But every last Man Jack of them went to Davy Jones in the Tank, some by the yard and some by the board and all to feed the fishes! No Company of mine ever fell together by the ears nor split the bear-skin between them neither. Aboard any Ship under my command, it's One for All and All for Flint – stab me if it isna!"

He drank his second half-pint o' Punch without pause and indicated to Billy for a refill. The Mate seized the goblet and had the ladle bailing booze as if afeared o' sinking.

"You be missing the main-stay, Cap'n," said Gypsy Fuller, swallowing hard and putting on a bold front. "We ain't none of us consented to sign along o' you yet."

"Ye have-na' been asked!" Flint's voice cracked like the cat and Fuller's face froze as if it were about to crack. "Long John and Israel Hands I know by reputation. They had an invite here and right welcome. Ye and yon ship-mate were unlooked for! If I dinna sign ye, then 'tis the mines for the brace o' ye! And may the Devil deliver ye – God won't!" Fuller and Anderson sat there looking like a pair of paupers condemned to the work-house. Sick wasn't the word for it!

"Me'n Gypsy be good Seamen both, Sir," returned Job Anderson hastily.

"Maybe ye are – maybe ye ain't! Perchance the pair o' ye could prove to be the biggest brace of lubbers as ever wore out boot leather between wind and water. We shall see," replied Flint reaching for his goblet.

"What might you be?" demanded Billy Bones gruffly, blowing smoke through his fleshy nose with a snort. "ODs, ABs or Artists? Come, pipe up!"

"Fore-top-man, Sir!" answered Fuller in a flash. "Few gets aloft as can match me!"

"I'm a Coxswain, full qualified," added Anderson touching his forelock in salute.

Flint grunted, downing half his drink. Then his glims flickered over our faces as he topped up his goblet with neat rum from one of the square bottles. Pure Jamaicy Tar it were, thick and black as Satan's Soul!

"I'll sound out my Articles," said the Buccaneer. "Ye either sign, if so minded, or seek ye your bread elsewhere. But first heed well my words. Any as makes his mark along of me, proving their Worth, will die rich men all – my word on that! I'll give ye Gold by the barrel! Enough Moidores and Doubloons to play Duck and Drake with. Ye have the choice: Live the life of a lubber and die a pauper or beat-up with me to roll in Rhino and go out with a bang! Farthings or a Fortune! Stab me if I lie, eh, Bill?"

"Aye, right you are, Cap'n! All as signs along o' you makes more noise in the world than most – eventually!"

Flint and the Mate roared with laughter. Fuller, Anderson and Hands all joined in, although they were as puzzled by the remark as I was. I managed a weak smile, but it ain't my manner to make merry over jokes I don't fathom. I had the feeling that my three ship-mates were laughing ag'in themselves, and right I was, but it took years to find out.

My reserve weren't lost on Flint. As he preached his Regulations, he studied my face after each Rule were read to see my reaction. But I could play the game as deep as he and gave him nothing by way of return, except a level, stoney stare.

The Main-Stays of his Articles were these:

The Captain's Word, first and last, in all Affairs of Moment, is Final.

*

Every Man has Equal Title to the Fresh Provisions, unless a Scarcity make it necessary, for the Good of All, to Vote Retrenchment.

*

All sharing of Plate, Jewels, Money, Clothes and all other Articles of a Prize, to be taken in Turn by List, under direction of the Quarter-Master.

*

If any Man shall Loose a Joint in Time of Engagement, he shall have 400 Peeces of Eight, if a Limb, 800, if an Eye, 1000, above his Lawful Share and Remain with the Company as long as he shall think Fit.

*

He that shall be found Guilty of Cowardice in Time of Engagement, shall – Suffer Death.

*

He that shall be found Guilty of taking up any Unlawful Weapon on board the Privateer, or any Prize, so as to Strike or Abuse his Fellow, shall Suffer Marooning, or as the Captain and Company Directs.

*

All Hands to keep their Peece, Pistols, Cutlash or any other Small-Arm, clean and Fit for Service.

*

No Petty-Coates aboard; No Person to Game with the Devil's Books or Dice for Money or any other Article; No Secrets to be Kept from the Company.

"I needs a Master capable of sailing a ship clear across the Doledrums and doon the Devil's throat, if so ordered," continued Flint. "Aye, and, back again, by thunder, without losing a stick, yard or shred o' canvas!"

His mad eyes were locked on mine.

"I can manage a ship as well as any an' better'n most, but I ain't no Artist when it comes to navigation, plotting courses and such. Figures and calculations were never a strong point with me, to be sure during my school-days," I replied somewhat sadly.

"I'll set the course, all ye has to do is sail it and get us there safe! What say ye, Long John Silver?" asked the Buccaneer in earnest, his pale blue orbs boring into mine.

For answer I leaned across the table, dipped a brightly plumed quill in the ink-pot and signed my name alongside that of 'Sailing-Master'. Israel Hands followed me, enrolling as 'Gunner'. Job Anderson's shaky hand blotched his tottery scrawl, drawing a first rate oath from Flint; and Gypsy Fuller made his mark:  I noticed that 'One Arm' Phineas McGinty was listed as 'Quarter-Master'. A good man, him, although nearing his Three-Score-Years-and-Ten. He was one of the 'Old Standers' who had sailed, as a younker, under 'Mighty Morgan' hisself!

"A Toast!" cried Flint, raising his goblet. "Here's to Luck, my Lads, and a short haul to the King of Prizes – GOLD!"

We all drank heartily, then Flint, thumping his goblet in time on the table, began to sing:

"Fifteen men on a dead man's chest –
Yo-ho-ho and a bottle of rum!
Drink and the Devil had done for the rest –
Yo-ho-ho and a bottle of rum."

Billy joined in the chorus, but by the end of the second verse we were all giving out lusty Yo-ho-ho's between each line. Darby M'Graw slipped in unheard and stood unseen to one side. When the sixth and final verse came to its bawdy close, he approached Flint, touching his forelock in salute amid our applause, and handed him my Letter o' Credit – the swab!

"See here, Jim Flint!" cried I, springing to my feet. "That be mine! What manner o' seamanly behaviour allows you to send this foxy-faced lubber to rifle a man's togs, while he be . . ."

"Avast, John Silver!" roared he in reply. "I dinna send Darby ta rob ye, but there be nay secrets aboard this 'ere boat! Ye have signed Articles and now, by thunder, ye'll abide by 'em!"

"There was me," began M'Graw, "drying all yewer wet togs, when I sees this 'ole in yewer coate cuff. Long John 'ud apprec'ate a neat bit of mendin', thinks me, and Darby's the cove to do it. That be how I found yewer Ticket and brung it to the Capt'in as in dooty bound. Dooty be first an' last in my book!" explained the Steward, standing there looking as pious as a Preacher in a Pulpit.

"'Taint much use now, is it," said I sadly viewing the paper. "Not with four holes in it and the blessed ink run every-which-way. I doubt if the Banker in

Boston will honour it now on my say-so."

"Old Jacob Myers will honour it on mine!" vowed Flint. "For I ken him as Banks for Lombard's, Boston being one of my secret retreats. I keeps an Account there myself, along of 'unforeseen expenses'." Flint and Bones eyed each other and sniggered, both enjoying the same secret joke.

The Big Buccaneer took a gulp of rum. "What paltry sum be ye in dread of losing, Long John?" he asked, giving me a steady gaze.

"Nine Hundred Pound," replied I and thought to myself: 'For no Secrets to be kept from the Company, this brace o' Worthies had their pockets brim-full between 'em!'

Israel Hands whistled. Anderson and Fuller gaped at me like I were Midas.

"Nine Hundred? Stab me!" exclaimed Flint with a sneer and lunged from his chair. Crossing to the great humped Chest, he flung open the lid and returned carrying two weighty bags of thick leather. As he dropped them on the table there came the chink of coins. Flint unfastened the drawstrings and pushed both bags over. "There! Feast yer deadlights on that!" cried he as Doubloons, Moidores, Ducatoons, Louis d'ors and Double Guineas spewed out all a-glitter. "Here be TEN THOUSAND, by thunder!"

Anderson let go an explosive oath; Fuller gasped the name of the Almighty; and Israel's eyes burned and bulged in his head 'til I thought they'd pop. My tongue flickered over dry lips and I felt my internals tingle as Flint slumped back in his chair. He reached for his goblet, but his fumbling fingers knocked it over. The black, thick rum splashed onto the Blunt and in the flickering lamp-light it looked like a pool of congealing blood. I wondered how much had been spilt to amass such a Fortune?

"Rum, Bill," croaked the Captain. "Give me rum and a wad, for I feel the need of a caulker."

The Mate took from the Chest a small parcel of compressed Coca leaves, steeped in lime juice – the essence of the bitter tasting shrub being Cocaine. Flint swallowed a mouthful of Neaters that Darby handed him, popped the drug into his terrible maw, then leaned back and closed his eyes, chewing the narcotic wad like a cow do her cud.

"Ahh," sighed he as a peaceful look crept over his face. "By thunder, if ever drugs saved a Mortal Man's mind from Immortal Horrors – it be mine!"

"Asking yewer pardon, Capt'in, but will that be all?" enquired M'Graw, rubbing his hands together in the greasy manner of a Jewish money lender. "Only Samson ain't had his rations yet and his three chickens be keepin' the Stand-by-Watch awake. Squalling worse than washer-women, they is."

"Aye, Darby, attend ye ta my Beauty and secure," replied Flint drowsily, his eyes still closed.

"Who might Samson be, Sir?" asked Anderson looking curious as the Steward sniggered and left. "Three chickens be a mighty mouthful at one go."

Flint's eyes snapped open. "All in good time, Coxswain," said he, giving us the benefit of his hideous grin. "All in good time."

"Thunder!" exclaimed Hands in an awed voice, gazing up in horror having just noticed what hung on the Mizzen above the muskets. "In God's name, Cap'n, what be that?"

Flint followed the Gunner's pointing finger and the stamp of Hell appeared on his face. "THAT?" spat he with a vehemence as sent Cap'n Flint fluttering onto the hammock strings along of a loud squawk. "That be a Grandee, Don Juan de Anton Enriquez – that was!"

The Buccaneer reached behind him and unhooked the grisly Trophy, dangling it before our eyes, while his own burned with a hate filled, inner fire. "Speak ye not of Gods to me, Mister Hands! Of Devils and Dagos, yes! For this dog was the damnedest as ever was! Master and part owner of a fine Merchantman, that were me when first I fell foul o' this Devil and became clapped aboard! We stood nay chance alongside his Three Decker! I kept his scum from my cabin for as long as I were able to swing m'blade, but when my Dear Wife, Nester, saw me fall with what she supposed was my death hurt, she jumped through the stern window holding our baby, Hamish, to her bosom. And ere they sleeps in the briny below – safe in Neptune's keeping!" Flint cheeked his cud of Coca Leaves, his eyes misty, his face horribly contorted by rage, and gulped rum.

Thunder crashed over head like a broadside and blue lightning split the sky asunder beyond the lead panelled window panes, filling the cabin with an eerie, bluish flicker. Flint's gruesome looking shadow fell across the bulkhead like an Ogre as he stood swaying, dribbling rum down his shirt.

"I near done for the Grandee," continued the Buccaneer, glaring down at the head where it lay between the bags of Gold. "When he entered the cabin I lunged up'ards and delivered him a woundy stab to his spine, along o' my dirk. Never did he walk another step! Crippled, he was, his legs limp and useless as a cut hawse! For Punishment he promised me a slow death back on his Plantation outside Nombre de Dios."

Flint suddenly fell to his knees, snarling and staring at the sewn up lips as if expecting a reply. "There ye shackled me to the water-pump bar, in place of the Donkey Beast, didn't ye, where I walked in circles for three years! Flayed and fed bilge by Day; freezing and sleeping on m'knees o' Nights, ye thought ta drive me mad! But I out-stayed ye! Your own over-seers undone ye, yer Dago Dog, when they caught a Carib Princess's son and chained him alongside me! Two hundred Warriors wiped out your soldiers and servants at cock-crow one morning! Fed 'em to the piranas and crocodiles, thems who didna die or flee! And ye, m'fine Grandee Buck! Abed and abandoned, begging God's Mercy from ME!"

A look of pure ecstasy came over the Captain's battered face. He slowly stood up and closed his eyes. "Ah, Carijo, Carijo. I owe ye my very Soul," he murmured. "Ye gave me back my sanity and a satisfaction as tasted sweeter than wine." His eyes opened, pale blue orbs flashing fire, and he gazed down at the Grandee's head with ferocious glee, reliving again a scene that was a Treasure locked secure in his demented mind.

"How ye pleaded when we dragged ye back into the jungle by the heels!" The ecstatic savagery in his voice, part snarl, part shriek, chilled the marrow in our bones. "How ye raved while I fed ye yer own living flesh for a week! And how ye screamed for the Virgin's Mercy before I tore the black heart from ye with these same two hands and devoured it like a starved dog!"

My skin crawled and I felt the sweat popping out o' my pores as his mad gaze engulfed me. "Adopted me into their Tribe, did them Caribs, then Carijo shrunk his head-piece which he presented to me along of my tattoos and pointed teeth."

"Oh, happy days," I muttered, speaking before thinking, but my sarcastic remark fell upon deaf ears.

Flint gasped for breath, swaying slightly, his eyes bulging, his lips blue and flecked with foam. A tongue of forked lightning ripped across the Heavens, followed by a great clap of thunder and the larboard casement crashed open under a windy gust.

"Hark ye ta God's Guns!" cried the Buccaneer, rolling his insane eyes at us. "Trying to do me doon, so's Davy Jones can clap aboard o' me! But I worship the waves covering ma Dear Nester an' oor Beloved Bairn, and I pays mine dues to Neptune! Rum! Rum and Gold for the 'Old Man'!"

Seizing a bag and a square bottle he lurched towards the casement, scattering coins in his wake, and threw both into the bay. By the look on the faces o' my mess-mates, I thought all three were about to weep.

"I defies YE!" roared Flint, shaking his fist at the Heavens. "May I be damned to sail the seas for all Eternity, same as the Dutchman do, for I'll spend it killing Dagos and a-cursing of Ye as Ye cursed Me and Mine!"

The sky exploded in dazzling, blue light and the noise were deafening. Flint staggered back, semi-blinded, and clutched the muskets around the mizzen for support with the wind howling about him. Billy were by his side in a brace o' shakes. Flint blinked at we four, still seated, as if seeing us for the first time.

"Who are ye? From whence come ye?" cried he and seizing his cutlass that hung on the chair-back, drew the broad blade hissing from its sheath. "Be ye for Battle?"

"Friends, Jim! Friends! Come for to help you kill the Dons!" bawled the Mate, clutching his hanger arm. To us he mouthed one word: "OUT!"

We needed no prompting. Hands, Fuller and me near became wedged in the narrow doorway. My old Parrot shot past as Anderson barged the three of us on through.

"By the living powers," gasped Hands, wiping his clammy brow. "Wot kind o' man must he be to throw Gold and good rum overboard – answer me that!"

"A moon-struck Devil!" snapped Anderson. "I thought he'd sink us all!"

"Aye, mates," agreed Fuller. "First and Last we've signed Articles along o' a Bedlamite! What say you, Long John, do we stay or split?"

"Split?" enquired I, cocking an eyebrow at all three. "Split to where? I ain't a-feared of Flint drunk or sober – sane or raving. Now I'm for me bunk and sweet dreams o' Gold."

"Amen to that," said Anderson and led the way for'ard.

As we followed the tall Coxswain back to our berths we could still hear Flint ranting and raving, screaming defiance at the storm.

Elsewhere, the rest of the ship was as silent as the Grave.

PEECE THREE

FLINT'S FLOCK!

CHAPTER XI

MESSRS PEW AND BLACK DOG!

Flint weren't seen above board for two days, but we heard him pacing the deck during the dark hours. Billy Bones said he was a-waiting for information on where some British Prisoners were bound and when.

"The sooner we gets a full Crew, the sharper we goes 'On the Account'," explained the Mate, sweeping the jungle covered shore-line with a spy-glass.

"This old bucket ain't big enough to go a-roving in!" retorted Hands as we lounged on the Fo'c'sle – drinking.

"Sink you for a lubber, Israel," growled Billy, glaring at the Gunner and snapping his glass shut. "Afore we sets about finding a seaworthy ship, we first has to muster a seaworthy Crew to man her."

Gypsy Fuller suddenly sprang to his feet: "Savages!" cried he, pointing astern, then grabbed at the pistol in his belt.

Two Piraguas came gliding towards us, each being paddled by a pair of Indians. Sitting amid-ships in the leading dug-out canoe was One Arm McGinty, Flint's Quarter-Master. Behind him, sat a Carib wearing white man's clothing.

Anderson, who had also drawn a pistol at Fuller's first cry, stood gaping. He gave a start and swore, slapping his arm, crushing a yellow Tabana fly that had just stung him.

"Put up yer barkers," said Billy. "Them Caribs be the Captain's kin."

Flint came up from below as the Piraguas drew alongside. McGinty and his companion clambered aboard along of their savage Crew, the Quarter-Master giving us a cheery: "Top o' the mawnin' to 'e, mates!"

Flint shook McGinty's hand, then made a great show of affection for his 'Blood-Brother' – Joe the Carib. This handsome half-caste Indian was the product of a Carib Princess and a former Coromantee Slave called Cudjoe, who now lived in Nanny Town in far off Jamaica and ruled a class of people there known as the Maroons.

"Joe were the one as was captured an' chained alongside the Cap'n," whispered Billy to me. "Carijo, that be his proper name, was the saving o' Flint and the Dons' downfall."

The Carib Chieftain wore a shirt and pantaloons, but no hat or boots. A baldric looped over his right shoulder supported a sheathed cutlass on his left hip. On the right was a cylindrical box of woven fibre that contained poisoned darts for the long blow-pipe he carried. Stuck in the broad belt around his waist was a Scottish dirk and a fine pair of silver mounted pistols.

The Caribs had pleasant, intelligent tattooed faces which were also painted with the red juice of the urucu berry. Their black hair was long and straight. Silky and shiny, it was, not coarse and woolly like Sambo's or the Negro. Each coppery skin bore the same weird patterns as were on Flint's body, tattooed in blue dye. They were all armed with blow-pipes and carried long bows that fired five-foot arrows.

After Flint had finished hugging Carijo, he shook hands laughing and spoke to 'em all in their own lingo. Quite a linguist were Flint, speaking fluent Spanish, French, Latin and Chinee too, I shouldn't wonder! Rum and tobaccy were ordered up for presents; and when they grinned their gratitude at the Buccaneer, every mouth displayed the same set o' them fearsome filed fangs.

A Council was held on the Fo'c'sle. Flint presented his plan for freeing the English captives and recruiting a Crew, then we were issued arms. Apart from his own hanger and dirk, all hands drew a brace of pistols, a musket, a powder flask, a bullet pouch and spare flints. According to Israel, who had assisted the Quarter-Master, the fish-hold had been converted into a magazine, and contained enough powder and arms to supply a King's ship.

When all was ready we divided into two 'Killing Parties' and took our places in the Piraguas, each man carrying enough 'jerked meat' and biscuit for three days. Flint commanded one canoe, Billy Bones the other. I was in Bill's boat, along o' Hands and Gypsy Fuller. Job Anderson acted as the Captain's Coxswain. Flint cut a fierce spectacle, along of his Carib Crew. The shrunken head hung on his chest, supported by a thong looped about his neck and passing through both the Grandee's lug-holes. Billy told us he always wore the Dago's napper in the manner of a medallion when embarked upon engagements.

"Tends to put the opposition off their stroke," explained the Mate. It sure put me off mine. As for poor Job, I seen happier men on the gallows!

We crossed the creek and paddled upstream with hardly any current to contest our headway. On entering the river, thick jungle closed us in on all sides – starboard, larboard and aloft. So dense was the foliage overhead, we never caught a glimpse of sun or sky. Eerie, it were, travelling along that tunnel o' vegetation in a gloomy, green twilight with the sluggish water, black as pitch, hiding all manner of unknown horrors. Billy named a few for the benefit of us lesser souls as didn't know of the dangers that lurked both in and out the water. A regular mine of information, were Bill, for a seafaring man.

There were shoals o' vicious little Pirana fishes as could strip the flesh from the bones of man or beast in a matter of moments, and Crocodiles weighing nigh on a ton with jaws capable o' crushing a canoe into tooth picks. Hunting these waters were also serpents longer than a yard-arm and thick as a man's thigh! None o' these delights were to be seen, mind, but the fact we knowed 'em to be lurking close by made their presence all the more hard felt. A mere mention of snakes terrified Hands.

"If I sees one, I'll slip me moorings," croaked the Gunner hoarsely. "Even worms gives me the vapours!"

"Ye'll die, right enough," assured Billy by way of comfort, "if one gets its coils about your body. Why, down on the Orinoco I see a serpent crush and swallow a bull, aye, horns an' all, by thunder!"

There was Beauty too, mark you, along o' the Beasts. At one point we passed a cluster of brightly coloured butterflies, hovering over huge water-lilies with wings the span of a man's hand. Morphos and Queens were what Billy called 'em. Sometimes brightly plumed birds flashed past us. Hidden from sight, high up in the trees, we could hear spider monkeys. One weird creature we did see was a surly-eyed, three-toed sloth.

Near sun-down we camped on a sand-bar and had supper. Fires were lit and Flint ensured every man rubbed some stinking mixture, provided by the Indians, on his exposed skin. Mosquitoes were a plague and near devoured us alive before this balm, reeking o' rotten flesh, gave us relief.

In the morning we pressed on, heading roughly south-sou'west. At noon we beached the canoes and met with a Carib war-party, twenty strong. We whites only numbered fourteen all told. Two of Flint's trusted hands had been left to guard the *Weasel.* The Indians appeared like Hell's Imps, what with their painted faces, pointed teeth and tattooes. Near naked they all was, like so many Sons of Adam. Some wore pieces of bone thrust through their ears and noses. For weapons they had bows, taller than me, that fired five-foot arrows. Many of them had blow-pipes, like Carijo carried, capable o' sending a plumed, poisoned dart into a mark no bigger than a baccy box from a distance of fifty paces. A few had spears that were hideously barbed with points of bone or fire-hardened wood.

Leaving the canoes, we struck out into the jungle, Flint's party leading, guided by Joe the Carib. The rest of the Indians were interspaced among us, the remainder bringing up astern, for if a man came adrift in that green sea his bones 'ud rot there. Our reeking balm gave protection from the myriads of insects, but bees clung to our clothes in clusters and leeches crawled beneath 'em to suck our Life's Blood. Israel Hands cut more capers than a Merry Andrew when three took a shine to his chest, but to pull them off would have left the heads in to mortify and cause ulcers the size of a crown piece.

QM McGinty 'cleared-lower-decks' afore we started and gave our Crew a stern lecture about snakes. "Apart from Rattlers, there be two huge pit vipers you has to watch out fer, mates. Both be aggressive creatures. The Bushmaster and the Fer-de-Lance will strike without warning. One bite from either o' them beauties an' ye'll stay here! Keep yer weather-eye on the bushes and trees too. Watch out fer the Greenpalm Viper as dwells there. Caution be the bye-word in this here jungle!"

"Yew mind the froggies too, 'Q'," reminded Darby McGraw. "Even thems be poisonous in these here parts!"

"Goodly brew to smear on tips of darts and arrows," grinned Joe the Carib.

Lesser things to worry about were the ticks and chiggers, mites that bored into the flesh and caused a body to itch as if infested with fleas. There were inch long Paraponera ants whose stings could lay a man out cold; and during a brief shower, Joe the Carib warned us about the Hura tree. The sap could cause blindness if the rain washed it down onto a man's face. Sometimes we encountered clouds of blackflies and mosquitoes. Diseases such as Yellow Jack, malaria and dysentery took a back seat in regards to the other perils this Green Hell had on offer.

We covered the three miles to the Camino Real by mid-afternoon. To me and most others it seemed like thirty. Jack ashore ain't much of a dab hand when it comes to hoofing it for any distance, you may lay to that! Billy were puffing and blowing, fit to pop. In dread o' treading on snakes, Israel Hands went through the undergrowth as if bare-foot on broken bottles. The Crew nick-named him 'Twinkle Toes'! Job Anderson kept tripping over his cutlass and anything else as came into contact along of his kipper feet, much to the amusement of the Indians. And I clewed up with blasted blisters – sea-boots not being the best o' hiking wear. Only Flint and the grizzled old Quarter-Master, a man close on seventy, seemed as fresh and fit as when we started. As for the Caribs, why, it were nothing more to them than a turn around the deck 'ud be for us!

The Royal Road, like most routes through the forest, was merely an animal track in the beginning. The Dons, during its two hundred years of hard use, had bricked it. Since the time of the Conquistadors, countless mule trains bringing Treasure from Panama to Nombre de Dios had kept the jungle at bay. In my day, Porto Bello was the main collection point where the Terra Firma Flota picked up the blunt en route for Old Spain, via Havana. In years long past, the Immortal Drake had preyed upon convoys using this same Royal Road, and according to Billy, quite near to where we was now at. By way of interest to the Young Reader, Drake was laid to his Final Rest in the waters off Porto Bello. Died of the Flux, he did. A befitting end really, considering he gave many a bad case of it to the Dons!

Our aim was to clapp aboard a Spanish Convoy transporting provisions to Panama, along of British Prisoners bound for the mines in South America. The spot chosen was ideal for ambush – 'Bush-Wacking' our American cousins call it – with thick foliage bordering both edges of the track. Flint acted sharp and soon sorted us into position. Billy's Party, reinforced by ten Caribs, were strung along the port side; Flint's took station to starboard, but further up. We had staggered fire positions to save from shooting into each other. And there we lay, mates, amid stifling heat with the buzz o' insects in our ears, sweating and tingling with excitement as we waited and watched.

Flint's information and timing were pure precision, like a forty shilling watch. "About an hour, Lads," said he and right he was, almost to the last blessed tick. His plan was simple: 'One Arm' McGinty was to kill the Rear Guard, the sound of his shot being the signal for attack. By then all the Convoy 'ud be between our two parties.

The Caribs heard 'em coming long before we did and gave signs for us to make ready. I cocked an ear to the jingling bells of the pack-mules carrying rations and the chink and rattle of chains; then the leading riders came into view through our green screen. Two Officers rode in the van. Behind them, flanked at regular intervals by scruffy Dago Infantry, came as sorry a looking bunch o' British Seamen as ever I clapped eyes on. Chained in twos by the wrist, they shuffled along like the Lost Tribe of Israel, staring bleakly at the stumbling footsteps o' the man in front. Here and there came a sharp whip-crack, followed by a cry of pain or a curse, depending on the bottle of him as was struck.

Flint's Plan were flawless, but there's always the unforeseen. There were us, all screwed up for the attack, when this clotpoll, a skinny, swarthy creature with pock-marked cheeks, ruptures our timing by punching a Dago in the eye after getting clouted with a quirt for dragging his stern. Other Guards rushed to the affray. The Officers dismounted, bringing the column to a premature halt, short of our Gang and only half covered by Flint's.

Billy cursed under his breath beside me as the offender was unmanacled from his mate and strung up by the wrists to the branch of a gnarled tree beside the trail. His shirt, mere ribbons anyway, was ripped off and the Spaniard whose left eye he had closed started to flay his sun-blackened body. Swearing oaths and curses as 'ud make a turn-key blanch in New-Gate, the Seaman writhed under the thin, short lash. Every time the Dago struck, he screamed his own insults in reply: "Perro Ingles! Perro Negro Ingles! Perro Negro!" (English Dog! Black English Dog! BLACK DOG!)

All eyes were on the flogging. Black Dog's mate stood back aways, close to our side of the road. The two Officers were on his left. I saw him take a slow, firm grip on the two foot o' chain hanging from his right wrist with the empty manacle attached to the end of it. I had him logged for a shark from the first, what with his large hooked nose and long, lank red hair that he wore loose. He suddenly exploded into action.

Swinging the manacle like a medieval mace and chain, he struck one Officer across the face sending him sprawling, then plucking a thin bladed dirk from the belt of the second, delivered him a mortal stab to his guts. Next instant he took off, crashing into the jungle not five paces from where we lay at the head of our line. A yell of alarm was followed by a shot, the bullet clipping branches above us. More shouting and three Soldados rushed after the fugitive.

"Take Hands and settle those three swabs," ordered Billy. "See if you can save that Judas haired Tartar. He seems worth his salt in a tiff!"

A shrill whistle sounded and Flint's Party descended on the column amidships. Billy took his own silver call between his teeth and blowing a reply full blast, led our group surging into the van – cutlass held high in one hand, pistol levelled in t'other.

"AT 'EM, ALL HANDS – ALL HANDS!" roared the Mate and shot a Dago dead.

I saw Flint, that grisly head-piece a-swinging on his tattooed torso, carving his way through the Spaniards like the demented Devil he were. Me and Israel waited no longer, but plunged in pursuit o' the hunters and their red-headed prey with the sound of cries, shots and the clash o' steel ringing in our ears. Hurrying to catch up and clapp aboard our quarry, we came within half the carrying distance of a musket ball of being hove-to ourselves. Hands saw 'em first. Standing in a group, they was, staring back towards the noise of the hurly-burly still faintly heard beyond the green wall.

Hands cried a warning as two of them presented their pieces in a brace o' shakes and disappeared in twin puffs of white smoke. I gave vent to an oath, dropped my musket and spun half ways round clutching a torn right arm. The Gunner's head was near broached by a bullet that clipped twigs alongside his lug. He returned fire and took cover behind a tree. I lay prone beside the trunk of a dead-fall. For Dagos they was damnable good shots!

"Be you hard hit, Long John?" enquired Israel, rolling a cautious eyeball around the trunk like a blessed Chameleon.

Afore I could reply the three Soldados, maybe thinking me mortal hurt, charged our position, vapouring to boost their courage. Dodging between the tall trees and ducking beneath vines they came through the clear spaces at the run, their long bayonets extended ready to do us grievous damage. Israel fired both pistols, right and left, dropping the middle man, but his mates came on. Cool and calm as a mill-pond, the Gunner cleared his cutlass and stepped forward – meeting 'em with a clash o' steel.

I struggled to sit up, propping my back against the log. Pain knifed through my arm and more warm blood soaked my shirt-sleeve to the cuff. Feeling sick and a mite light-headed, I were, as I pulled a pistol left handed, cocking it with difficulty. Israel was just holding his own ag'in the two Dagos lunging at him. I fired, missing 'em both by a long sea mile, but the ball made Hands hop!

With a startled yell one of 'em swung round and seeing me fumbling to draw my second barker, the lock having snagged on the carry-strap of my powder flask, he broke off and charged. I cleared, cocked and presented my piece, point-blank, as he loomed above me, his musket poised for the *coup-de-grâce*. I shut down on the trigger, but the blasted dog's head snapped without firing. Sparks was all I got for my efforts. Jungle damp priming powder in the pan looked like the final ruination of me.

Gaping down the black o' of my gun barrel the Dago's expression changed from frightened horror to evil glee and he paused, savouring his good fortune, gloating down at me with a sickly leer on his swarthy, greasy face. I hurled the barker at him, but he deflected it with ease. His musket rose a little higher in preparing for my death plunge. A mere point from casting loose my cable, he were, when his glims grew wide with surprise. He twitched, belched blood and fell full length on his mug – the triangular bayonet 'thunking!' into the log alongside o' me. Sticking from between his shoulder blades was the haft of a white handled dirk. Six paces or so beyond the body of the Late Departed stood the red-headed fugitive, his hand still extended from the force of throwing.

Israel finished wiping his cutlass clean on the third Spanish corpse, picked up his musket and strode over as the Stranger joined me.

"Here's a merry twist to the tale," says I thickly. "Seeing it were us who set out to save you."

"Aye," agreed Hands, grinning. "A nifty piece o' knife work as ever I see, by thunder!"

"Fair for a hasty, left-handed throw," stated the Stranger stepping nearer and never have I, afore or since, heard a voice so cruel and cold.

Seeing his face in close-up gave me another jolt. By the powers, but his mug 'ud make Apollyon appear a beauty by comparison, so it would! Pale, yellowy green eyes, slitted and evil looking like those of a mad wolf, glared at me from above high cheek bones. They say a man's Soul be reflected in his glims. If that be so, then this cove didn't have one! Above a thin, cruel mouth his great hooked nose smacked of the vulture.

"Whom have I to thank for saving my skin?" I asked, offering my hand.

The Stranger took it in a tallowy, vice-like claw, his manacle chain chinking. "A Bosun I be," said he. "But one an' all – they calls me, Pew!"

CHAPTER XII

BEN GUNN AND CO!

My bicep were bad torn, but the bullet had passed through the muscle and no damage was done to the bone. Praise be for that small mercy, for we had no Surgeon with us. While Israel bound it up using my left sleeve, Pew collected the muskets and any other articles of interest off the dead Dagos.

"Don't you want this here dirk?" asked Hands, pulling the knife free from the Spaniard's back and offering it to Pew.

A handsome tool it were too; good Toledo steel, thin bladed and double edged with an ivory hilt wrapped in a spiral o' silver wire.

"Not I," replied Pew. "Seamen such as me who sails closer to the wind than most, can't afford to risk their luck carrying white handled knives aboard ship."

"I don't hold with superstitious sea-talk. A man's luck depends upon hisself, I say. That there knife were lucky for me, by thunder! So if you ain't keen on owning it, I'll add it to my arsenal – aye, white handle an' all!" And so saying I slipped the blade into my sea-boot.

We returned to a right Royal welcome. Flint was gracing his triumph with captured Spanish booze, along o' all hands. Free of their shackles, the former Prisoners of War pranced about like ten year olds at Yuletide. Near forty pack-mules carried supplies for the garrison at Panama. Much of it was luxuries for the Officers: pickles, fine wines, tobacco steeped in rum, and six half-ankers of Hollander gin, Schnapps some calls it, each keg containing 8½ Gallons.

Not one Spaniard escaped. Our losses were slight; three killed and five wounded. But a Sail-Maker's Mate, suffering a bayonet thrust to his belly, slipped his moorings that same night. Flint's Caribs made a great coil out of the slain, cutting off the heads of friend and foe regardless. Some of the Seamen didn't go for former mess-mates being so mutilated, but they stood in awe of Flint and were afeared o' the savages. The dead didn't complain nohow. Imagine the panic if they had done, mind!

The Caribs had themselves a prisoner too. The Officer whom Pew bashed in the face with his manacle stood between two warriors, a rope around his neck, his arms pinioned behind him at the elbows, and stark naked. His brow was badly cut and blood dripped from his chin onto his chest. Spanish cruelty was well known to the Carib people. They had fought Spain alongside the French in times past and just thinking of his fate caused my flesh to creep. He who had flogged Matey was still standing, only now he stood transfixed to the tree – skewered amidships by a spear! A Carib Shaman or Medicine Man attended to my arm. Strange, it were, but for savages they knew a good deal about healing. The gash in my bicep was gently soaked in Copaiba oil, widely used on the Spanish Main for wounds, then it was bound in a soft, fibrous bark by way of a bandage.

"So ye be a Boatswain by trade," remarked Flint as he released Pew from the manacle, while Billy passed out Schnapps in horn cups. "I have a need for brisk hands, such as yourself. And what say ye, Perro Negro?" he asked, addressing him as still stood half naked showing the vivid, red weals on his swarthy skin. "Ye be a bold blade, true enough. By what tag are ye known in company?"

"Shrivel my soul, but here's a thought!" snapped Pew. "For close on a week you an' me have shared the Honourable Order of the Padlock and Chain, yet I knows not your name? Black Dog was all that Dago cur called you!"

"What's in a name? I changes mine along of every noo ship," returned the other with a sour look that disclosed stained, broken teeth. "Black Dog the Dago called me – Black Dog let it be!"

From that day forth and for ever after, he were known by no other handle. Once, years later, Pew referred to him as Humphrey! They became staunch mess-mates and among all our Crew, barring Billy Bones, Me and Flint – two o' the most feared!

"Come," said Flint. "Time for all hands to clear decks and get under-way. Mister Bones, assemble the mule train for travel. Mister McGinty, detail swabber parties to ditch yon Dago corpses amidst the trees. Lively, my lads! It lacks but Four Bells to sun-down and we've yet to travel near a league afore we can organisc a campo!"

Shouted commands rang out up and down the road as Flint's orders were applied. Soon we were once more tramping along a jungle trail. Following our Carib Guides we reached a camp-site beside a wide, sluggish river, its surface broken in the centre by a sand-bar. Bordering the opposite bank were tall reeds growing from marshy ground. The Caribs didn't seem happy about this. After jabbering to Flint they moved further down-stream where the water ran swifter, taking their hapless prisoner with 'em. We stayed put.

"Crocodiles is what they be afeared of," explained Flint. "Them reed swamps yonder run for miles, mostly, and 'tis there they like to be at, alongside slack-water. But I dinna reckon to get Muggers on this side of the river, not with fires a-going and sentinels posted."

The QM and Billy Bones, assisted by Pew, Black Dog, Job Anderson and Israel Hands, organised the bivouac areas. Me'n Gypsy Fuller took charge o' the mule party. They were watered, then picketed out in two lines. Much to do, there was, seeing as we now numbered over a hundred strong. Bowers were built from woven branches. Beds of split bamboo and soft ferns gave added comfort. Rations were issued and cook-fires soon flared among various groups. Our side of the river was open, like an enclosed meadow, walled by jungle, and the lush grass provided ample grazing.

I took charge o' cooking for the Captain's party. Most Seamen tend to be lubbers at playing pantry hand, but I likes to eat well, when possible, so I serves meself. Under Edward England I learnt the art of 'Barbecuing' meat from the Boucans in the West Indies. They were your original Boucaniers or Buccaneers as we be known nowdays. It came from a French word meaning Meat Hunter, and that's what they were 'til they turned their guns on bigger game – namely Spanish Treasure Ships!

Along o' Taylor, when plundering in the East Indies, the word was that Long John be a dab-hand with a skillet. Now I can prepare anything from Curried Cow to its West Indian counterpart – Salmagundi. Solomon Grundy we calls it, containing everything from fish and fowls to pork and plantains, plus enough spices and red peppers to make the grub hotter than a fish-wife's temper!

While preparing supper in that small Savannah beside a nameless stream, my second nick-name was bestowed upon me by Israel Hands. "This be a tasty brew, 'Barbecue'," said he, dipping his fingers in my gravy pot. Flint's Crew adopted it and it was in general use by the time I cooked geese of a different feather, to be sure!

Darkness falls fast in the Tropics and as was our custom we were seated around the fire, partaking of a pipe and a dram, when an outsider joined our circle, a rank Irelander – O'Brien by name. Flint was down-river on a visit to his Carib kin, leaving Billy in charge. The conversation was floating along calmly, until a chance remark by QM McGinty nearly caused a fatal rupture between Hands and O'Brien.

"Being a Master Gunner," began the Quarter-Master, "I've heard it said that Israel Hands never missed the mark when . . ."

"Israel Hands? 'Tis yerself is it!" exclaimed the Irelander. "Oi had me a brace o' mates as shipped along o' Blackbeard! Both on 'em hanged and set t' sun-dryin' on your say so! Begorrah, but a black day 'twill be for any as puts to sea an' sails 'longside a turn-coat!"

With a mighty oath Israel came to his feet, his hanger half drawn before Darby M'Graw seized his arm. "Avast yew, Gunner!" cried the little Steward, losing his hat in his haste to check the fight. "There'll be no blood-shed among mates! Them's J.F.'s articles mind!"

O'Brien had also leapt up, but Billy blocked him.

"Mates?" squawked Israel, his face working with wrath. "This swab ain't no mate o' mine! He ain't even in our Company, nor be he article bound! And I'll swing afore I swallers bilge from a blasted Irish bog-hopper! So I will, by thunder!"

"Listen you lubber!" growled Billy Bones, grabbing a fistful of the Irelander's shirt front and near lifting him off his feet. "Flint hisself accepted Hands and appointed him Gunner! Contest the Cap'n and you'll court disaster afore the Devil's ready to clapp aboard you! Guard yer tongue and keep your own council in future! Back to your berth!" Bill's push all but floored the Irelander and he stumbled away looking sicker than a Papist Priest holding an empty collection box.

"Some day, O'Brien," called Hands after him. "Some day I reckon I just might have to settle you!"

The shriek of mortal terror that suddenly split the night near settled the lot of us! Then the drumming started and a multitude of high, quavering yells came from the Carib encampment. Billy, One Arm McGinty and Darby M'Graw sat down quite unconcerned and set brands to their pipes.

"Ain't you worried what's going on, Bill?" asked Anderson, pale as putty and wide-eyed like the rest of us.

"I knows what's going on," replied the Mate gruffly.

"Aye, that we do," confirmed McGinty, giving a gappy grin.

"Yon Caribs," concluded M'Graw, "is cannibals, don't yew know, and they's about to cook their supper!"

"Let's go for a look-see," said Hands eagerly.

"If them savages catches the likes o' you a-spying on 'em, they might have a mind to boost their rations!" cackled the Quarter-Master and spat into the fire.

Groups of scared Seamen clustered together in the safety of their firesides, gazing down-river, but none ventured out. In the glow from the Carib camp we saw smoke and sparks spiralling upwards; then above the din of yells and drumming there came another series o' agonised shrieks. The Fiends were roasting their Papist prisoner ALIVE! More cruelty was never inflicted by Jew, Turk or Heathen.

Now I'd witnessed most oddities in the World by this time. I seen Fire-

Walkers on the Coromandel Coast and Indian Fakirs with skewers stuck in 'em – clean the way through. I once saw a West Indian Voodoo Witch Doctor curse a man to death, then bring him alive again to walk the earth as a dreaded Zombie – the Living Dead! But I'd never seen Cannibals cooking human pork! Curiosity having a strong pull on me, I stole off under the pretence o' paying the debt of nature. Cloaked in darkness I approached the Carib's camp from alongside the river and cautiously parted some bushy ferns. The sight as met my gaze near blasted the eyes from my head.

Between a brace of fires, set within the Carib circle, hot coals had been raked into a narrow trench. Above this bed of glowing charcoal was a spit, suspended on two forked branches, and lashed along it, his arms above his head, was the Spanish Officer. Making more noise than a Robbed Jew, he was, and who wouldn't! No mortal man could have endured such torture in silence. His skin were now bubbled over in huge, white blisters as he slowly roasted. The Savages howled and stamped, dancing about the fire, brandishing weapons and the newly shrunken heads of the late departed. But by far the most fiendish sight was Flint hisself.

There he stood, mates, naked to the waist in the light o' the flickering flames, his tattooed torso glistening with sweat as he slowly turned the spit. His battered, broken old face glowed, it did – a glowing mask of devilish glee. Never was there a more demented demon in human form as could call himself 'civilised'. And if ever a Mortal Soul were double-damned and hell-blasted – it were James Flint!

"Burn, ye Dago dog! Roast, ye Papist pig! I'll devour the black heart of ye afore moon-rise!" raved he.

Moving at a stumbling run, I threw out my ballast on the river-bank. I reached the sanctuary of our fire-side, pale and trembling – drenched in icy sweat.

"What ails thee, Long John?" asked Old McGinty. "'Tis whiter than the Holy Ghost, so you are, Lad! Ain't taken a chill, have you?"

"Maybe I ate something that didn't agree with the mixture in my guts," I mumbled by way of excuse.

"Or maybe something about to be eaten, eh John?" grinned the QM and handed me a go o' rum along of a wink.

I drank it out in one!

"What I don't fathom is how them savages shrink those nappers? Gets away from me clean, it do," said Israel hooking a fresh clay pipe from the fire with a bit of bent stick.

"'Tain't too involved when you understands the technique of it," replied the QM. "After chopping the head off, they slit it open from the back of the neck half way up to the pate, then skins it off the skull – nose, lips, ears an' all. Next they boils it, then smokes it, same as a kipper. The ears and nostrils be plugged with latex and oakum. The eyelids and lips is sewed up, along o' the slit in the nape o' the neck. Finally, they fills the head with hot sand several times over. When it's shrunk they pours in latex sap, put a wooden plug in the neck, and re-mould the features while the sap's still soft. And there you have it, Israel my lad," concluded the Quarter-Master. "A head half the size o' the original, face perfect, as in life, an' all in miniature 'cepting for the hair. It don't shrivel same as the flesh do."

"Fancy that now," said Hands in wonder. "An' they calls them savages h'ignorant!"

Well into the early hours, it was, before the Caribs finished their fiendish feast and silence settled over the forest. Although tired from a hard day's toil, sleep came slowly to most of us. My arm was stiff and played me up some. I dozed, cat-napping mostly, only to wake in fits and starts. Dreamed I did, too! There was me turning the spit with Flint balancing on it, as if walking on a tread-mill. Laughing at me, he was, his pointed teeth red with gore and munching a human thigh bone – shiver my sides!

Never did the sun rise more slowly than on that foggy, jungle morn.

A thin mist shrouded the river and clung to the tree-tops as the whistling call of monkeys stirred our camp from a fitful slumber. Several breakfast fires were already going when I opened my eyes and crawled stiffly from the bower. The smell of wood-smoke and hot meat hung heavy in the air, along of a musty dampness from the forest. Billy and Old Phineas McGinty were frying pork, while Darby heated water to shave Flint and prepare a hot punch.

"Here's Long John," greeted the Quarter-Master, rolling baked plantains from the ashes with a stick. "Sit you down, my son, and break your fast."

"There yew are, Barbecue," added Darby and handed me a horn cup containing a steaming mixture of rum, brandy and sugared water. "Jus' the caulker yew need t' repel a raw, chill mawnin' such as this. 'Tis the damp that do the damage t' a man's bones, don't yew know, an' gives 'im the ague."

The sun had all but sucked up the river mist when the flat, crack of a musket shot brought us to our feet.

"Stand to arms!" came a sentry's warning cry.

Flint came out his bower like a bullet, eyeballs rolling to all quarters. "All hands to battle stations!" he roared, looping a baldric belt over his shoulder. "Sub-Commanders close on me!"

Pulling two pistols from his bandolier, he raced for the river with the Grandee's dwarfed head thumping against his chest. We grabbed our weapons and followed him. Every man had previously been shown his fire-position in case of attack, so the camp was well defended from all points. Our main set-back was that we didn't have enough captured pieces to arm all hands.

My thoughts were on hostile savages or a Spanish patrol as I ran along with the rest, but it turned out to be neither. Caught on the sand-bar in mid-stream was a kind of Catamaran. Its twin floats were mere bundles of dried bulrushes, marled to bamboo poles set athwart the two hulls. Six men were aboard. They stood with raised hands, save for one who lay slumped against the crude steering oar – sore wounded by the look of him. It appeared that the starboard float of their cumbersome craft was coming adrift.

"Quarters, Señors!" cried a ragged, bearded, sun-burnt scarecrow in a high, quavering voice, his skinny upraised arms trembling like taut hawsers. "Don't shoot us down like pork for pity's sake! We surrenders, we does! You'll have no trouble from Ben Gunn and Co – I swears it!"

"Shiver my liver," murmured Billy. "Here's a courageous cove."

"Holloa!" bawled Flint through cupped hands. "Who are ye? From whence come ye and whence-for be ye bound?"

A puzzled expression appeared on all five faces.

"English?" enquired Ben Gunn.

"Well, we dinna be Chinee!" thundered Flint.

"Not in the Spanish Service, are you?" asked Gunn, looking shrewd.

"The only service we do for Dagos is cut throats – theirs!"

The castaways joined us in laughing at our Leader's rare humour. Jumping for joy, they was, clapping each other on the back. "We be saved, mates! Fellow Englishmen, look you!" rejoiced a squint-eyed Welshman.

"George Merry, very much at your Service, Sir!" hollered a third party. "Prisoners, newly escaped from the calaboose in Panama!"

"Aye, Sir, we were that!" confirmed the Welshman. "Berthed on a South Sea Trader when we got clapped aboard off Balboa!"

Ben Gunn suddenly pointed a trembling hand down-river. "Beware, mates!" screeched he. "Cannibals bearing in on you off your starboard beam."

Our second broadside o' mirth, on seeing the Caribs creeping cautiously towards us, really had the Fugitives foxed. They stood gaping, not knowing what to make of it. But then the savages started to act peculiar, shouting and waving their weapons, pointing at those on the raft.

"Reckon they's just seen their breakfast," sniggered Hands.

Flint's withering, icy gaze cut the Gunner cold.

"'Tain't them as have seen their rations, by thunder!" cried Billy seizing the Buccaneer's shoulder. "The reeds, Cap'n! Look to the far bank!"

Our attention swung to beyond the sand-bar. "CROCODILES!" came the cry from half a hundred throats. The sight we see sent a ripple o' fear through the Company like a windy chill. Coming out the swamp were a score of scaley, evil-eyed Monsters – mouths agape and hissing.

Now I seen Crocodiles a-basking on the mud-banks of the Hooghly in far off Calcutta; and I've seen 'em at Madagascar and on the Guinea Coast. Seven and eight footers, mostly, but thems were babbys alongside these brutes. Why, one twisted toothed giant must o' measured fifteen feet from stem to stern and weighed in at close to a Ton!

"Swim for yer lives, ye squalling swabs!" roared Flint. "Musqueteers to the fore!"

Squalling were right. As those with muskets took station, the five men stranded on the sand-bank performed like a bunch o' Bedlamites. By the powers, 'twere as good as the play to watch 'em panic. The Welshman ran from end to end of the small island, flapping his arms along of a blessed bird trying for a take off. Ben Gunn hopped about on spindly legs, wringing his hands and wailing worse than a Turk at Prayer Time; and George Merry were huddled between the other two on the Catamaran's bamboo deck, each a-pushing and pulling at each other so's not to be nearest the Crocs.

With a sudden burst of speed that caught us all by surprise, the reptiles rushed into the river. They can move fast on land, when so minded, despite their vast bulk and waddling gait. Self preservation being the first article of the Christian Faith, all five finally took Flint's advice and abandoned ship – along o' their wounded mate. Windmills in a gale couldn't rival the way their arms and legs were a-going. Blurred, they was, lost in a welter o' spray.

"FIRE!" roared Flint as the leading Reptiles swept around the bar, gliding fast through the water with scarcely a ripple.

The volley-fire caused execution sure enough – and how! Along of two creatures, their brains ruptured by eye-shots, I reckon, as turned belly up and sank like stones, one of the Seamen took a ball clean between the glims. He flung his arms in the air, rolled onto his back and went to the bottom amid a cluster o' pink bubbles.

"Begorrah, Oi got 'im, Oi did!" bawled O'Brien and threw his cap in the air to mark his triumph.

"You chuckle-headed Irish Lubber!" cried Billy. "Aim at the blasted muggers, not the men!"

For the main, our musket balls just bounced harmlessly off the crocs' horny, plated backs. Every man-jack joined in the shoot, including the Caribs who fired showers of arrows at their natural enemies. A few of the reptiles slipped beneath the surface. Others did a rapid about-ship and sought sanctuary in among the reed marshes. As we dragged the four survivors from the jaws of death, their abandoned ship-mate started to scream. Blood-curdling, it were, reminiscent of Barbecuing Spaniard. Half a dozen crocs had clapped aboard the Catamaran and were tearing the Tar to pieces. Amid the threshing tails and snapping teeth he clung to the steering oar as if it were his Mother, the whites of his eyes rolling upwards in his final agony.

Flint hisself delivered him. Raising his pistol he shot the doomed man amidships o' the fore'ed. Then using his second piece, he burst the brains of the twisted toothed brute, putting a bullet in the Black Cayman's eye with a left handed aim from a distance of twenty paces.

"There!" hissed Flint. "I reckon that retires ye from man-ewating!"

It was in my mind to ask him when he intended to retire from the same practice, but I bit me tongue just in time!

CHAPTER XIII

FLINT'S FLYING FORTY!

Since ambushing the Convoy we couldn't afford to hang in stays, whistling for a wind. None knew it better'n Flint. After breakfast he called a general council of all hands and put phase two of his Plan into the pot. A Master Orator were Flint. He played upon the two main weaknesses of mankind - Fear and Greed!

"We kinna afford to take time by the forelock, my Lads!" began he with the Seamen seated before him, some cleaning their guns, while others still munched on fried pork. "Ye ken who and what I am! Mayhap there's those among ye who dinna care to sail the course I set – so be it! But for the moment it be in the common interest of all that we hang together!"

"Aye, we'll hang t'gether, right enough, if we gets took!" bawled some wag from the back, amid a burst of laughter.

"Ah!" cried Flint. "There's the man for me with a sense o' humour! And he'll need it, by thunder! For when those Papist Pigs realise the rupture we've caused, they'll hunt us down like dogs from all points of the compass! Mark ye this! Those who get captured again will die a death fit to make Dante's Inferno appear as Paradise by comparison! Crucifixion or Gibbeted Alive at least, I shouldn't wonder!"

The sniggers ceased and a nervous murmur rippled among the men. Flint held up his hands for silence.

"Ye have all seen the plight of poor Mad Murdock, him as was rescued along of Ben Gunn, George Merry and Tom Morgan. There he sits, mates, mute until his dying day on account o' swearing at the Alcalde who had his tongue torn out! I tell ye, Lads, thee willna find a safe berth in all the Isthmus of Darien, unless ye care to live in company along o' my Carib brothers!"

There were no takers – you may lay to that!

"Show us the way, Cap'n Flint!" cried one man jumping up. "You set the course and I for one will follow!"

A great roar of approval greeted his words. Flint held most of 'em as putty in the palm of his hand. Once more he waved them to silence.

"With forty Bold Blades I intend to seize a ship that be berthed in the bay at Porto Bello. She's all set ready for sea with only half a dozen Dagos on watch between decks!"

"What do you propose to do about the Forts, my man?" enquired a haughty, cold looking cove – a captain hisself, I shouldn't wonder. "They will blow you out of the water before you clear the harbour mouth!"

"Not with the signal lanthorns I'll have hoisted on the boltsprit!" replied Flint. "I already ken the Colour Code for safe conduct as be laid down for the eighteenth! Once we slip through, we rendezvous with the rest o' ye aboard my Lugger!"

"And what of the honest, God fearing Seamen among this Company, such as myself – what becomes of us?" asked snooty-head, standing with his arms folded and his nose stuck in the air like a Lord in Parliament.

"Those who don't wish to sail along of me, can take the Fishery Boat and beat-up for where they will!" continued our Captain. "'Tis brisk hands I be wanting! Buccaneers pistol proof enough to take their share of the World's Wealth, protected by their own courage! Each and all will have his chance to choose! Hard labour and low wages in honest service, or power and prizes a-plenty on the Pirate Round with only cannon balls to contest ye and mayhap a sour look at choking if captured and transported back in chains to Execution Dock!"

Most of the Seamen vapoured, yelling and clashing weapons, as if a Prize had sailed into view already. Only a few Artists held check. Masters, Mates and a few ABs loyal to their Employers – married men, mostly.

Flint gave us the final polish to his Plan, then we struck camp. One Arm McGinty took charge of the party returning to the Lugger. Litters were fashioned for the wounded who had previously been carried on makeshift stretchers slung between a brace o' mules. When all was ready they moved off in company of the Caribs, taking some of our muskets with 'em. The Indians were to provide canoes to carry the hands back aboard the Barca-Longa. Before leaving the Savages presented Flint with a necklace o' crocodile teeth, the very same twisted tusks taken from the monster he had slain. His old friend and blood-brother, Joe the Carib, decided to accompany our Crew and sail the Great Water to see his Father, living in far off Jamaica.

"My Brudder," declared Carijo solemnly to Flint. "Wid you I come, for back I did no wish to went!"

Being wounded qualified me a place among McGinty's Crowd, not that I needed a litter, mind. But one jungle jaunt a-foot was enough for this Jack, so I decided to stick with Flint.

"Your pardon, Cap'n," said George Merry, while we stood watching the QM's departing column retreat into the trees, "but wot's to stop 'em cutting the throats of the Quarter-Master's Crew once on board ship and slipping their cable?"

"George has a point, Sir," piped Ben Gunn. "And here be another hitch what I heard with me own two lugs. 'This Flint,' says that snooty Sea-Lawyer, 'is more famous for High-Seas Robbery than Cromwell were for Rebellion. And I for one don't intend to wallow in his wake all the way to Execution Dock!' That's what he said, Sir, and there's a few amongst them as sided with him too!"

"Aye, Ben," replied Flint, "but only a few will return to an honest way, like a dog to its vomit. The bulk and the best of them has the glitter o' Gold in their glims. They'll come on the account, along o' me!"

"Suppose they was talked into a cut-an'-run caper," suggested Israel Hands. "Leave us High and Dry, now wouldn't it? 'Specially if we fails to clapp aboard this here ship at Porto Bello."

"If we fails at Porto Bello, we'll all end up as pork or be set to sun-drying on the dock!" snapped Billy Bones, blowing through his nose like a grampus.

"Faith, Bill, have Faith," grinned Flint. Turning back to Hands, he said: "Stab me, Gunner! How far, think ye, would they get? Packed tight as salt beef in a barrel of brine they'll be, with scarce two foot of freeboard in a calm sea – to say nought of swell or storm. And with only enough rations left to last a ten-man Crew a week, it wouldna stretch a day in the serving of sixty. They ain't that dumb, I reckon!"

None could fault him; none could match him; few, it were, as failed to follow him. The Flower of the Flock – that was Flint!

We called ourselves Flint's Flyers, on account we were to travel the thirty miles to Porto Bello in style – riding the mules along the Camino Real. But before we ever got started there were those of us who changed the title to Flint's Flying Forty!

Now I've seen a sight or two, I have, since being hauled off to sea, but for sheer comedy I never seen nothing as could compare to Flint's Flyers. Of the two horses that had belonged to the Officers, Flint had one and Billy the other as befitted their station.

"When he were a younker, the Cap'n rode with the Scots Greys under the Duke o' Marlborough," confided the Mate to me. "Aye, he fought as a Cornet along of the great John Churchill."

Spaniards only rode stallions. High strung and skittish, they were, but they made a man feel proud. Flint glowed, he did, as if about to charge the French Line at Ramillies. Those Chargers were the only mounts with saddles and bridles; the rest of us had to clamber aboard bareback using either a leather lead-strap or a rope hackmore for reins.

For an ex Officer of Horse, Flint sat a trifle heavy in the saddle and was somewhat rusty, but he could ride. Billy was in the same boat as me. The both of us being country born and bred, we managed to stay aboard and steer our creatures with some degree of accuracy. I played crafty and chose a docile old mare who had been saddle-broke at sometime or other, I reckon. She tended to drift off course, being blind in her starboard glim, but a pull on the port rein now and then kept her on an even keel. As to the others? Newmarket run amuck it were, shiver my sides!

"To Horse!" cried Flint, standing up in the stirrups, and near falling off when his blessed foot slipped.

"Mount aboard yer mules – all hands!" bawled Billy, clutching his reins in both fists like a coachman with a tearaway team of six.

Mules can carry loads close on three hundred pound in comfort, but most of 'em didn't take kindly to their human cargo. No sooner did our lads show a leg and mount than those over-sized Dobbins started cutting more capers than a shindig in an Irish pot-house. He-hawing, bucking, kicking, twisting and biting, they sent Flint's Flyers flying sure enough – aye, in all directions!

Black Dog came careering by me, hanging with both arms and legs wrapped around his nag's neck. Cheek to cheek, they was, like blessed Sweet'arts! George Merry boosted Ben Gunn aboard his burro amid much grunting and pushing, but somehow our new Ship's Carpenter got hisself sat facing aft. One mighty buck knocked George flat and sent Ben somersaulting over its head. Made more holler in mid-air than a troop of howler monkeys, did Ben. I saw Pew being dragged along behind his beast. Clinging to the halter rope, swearing fit to frighten the French, he were!

"Damn to him who ever lived to wear a halter, as 'Black Bart' 'ud say!" I gaily called out as Pew plowed past. The Bosun bared his teeth at me, half snarl, half sneer, the nearest he ever got to a grin.

"The larboard side, Man! Mount ye from the left!" screeched Flint to Morgan. "Dinna ye know even the basics for boarding a beastie?"

"All I knows, Cap'n, is they bites from one end and kicks from both, see!" retorted the Welshman, turning in endless circles with a curly haired grey. A gayer game of 'Ring-a-Ring-o'-Roses' you wouldn't look to find!

Job Anderson, Darby M'Graw and Israel Hands were three of the few who remained mounted, although their mules were trying hard to harmonise with their mates. Eventually, with nothing more damaging than slight hurts and contusions, to say nought o' dented pride, we got under way. Joe the Carib scouted ahead of the main column in case hostile company should come at us bow on. We followed at the rate of around three knots an hour, what with beasts bolting or refusing to budge – in between dumping their riders on the deck!

'Boil my blood!" exclaimed Flint to Billy, sweeping off his sombrero and slapping his thigh with it. "If a blasted Sergeant of Dragoons could clapp eyes on this, he'd fall on his sabre! Sink me if he wouldna!"

We covered twelve miles during the afternoon and camped off the Road beside a small stream as cut across it. Mid-morning on the following day found us in the vicinity of Porto Bello. What remained of the daylight hours were spent hidden in a Monastery, above the bay. It was destroyed in a raid by Morgan years ago. Having no further use for the mules, we left them browsing among the ruins.

In scanning the bay with his spy-glass, Flint discovered that a Man-o'-War and a boom of huge logs were now anchored between the two Forts guarding the harbour mouth. The Guard-Ship was a three decker of a hundred guns or more – the massive *Santa Anna*.

"Here be a twist in our tiller-ropes I didna reckon on," growled Flint. "We'll have to fathom the answer afore we budge, Lads. Plain sailing ain't on the chart – not now!"

Came the dark we set off in two groups. One party under Billy were to raise Cain within the town, to create a diversion, then cut the boom adrift. The other, led by Flint, were to secure and steal a 300-ton Privateer called the *Walrus*!

CHAPTER XIV

FLASH DAN!

Twenty strong, we sat huddled astride the timbers in deep shadow under the jetty with the rising tide creeping up our dangling legs. Close to midnight, it was, and all quiet save for the gurgling water swirling about the stanchions and the distant sound of drunken laughter from within the ship moored at the end of the jetty. When the wavelets were lapping the high water mark on the support posts, Flint signalled us forward. Cautiously, we crawled along the wide, centre beams until the measured tread of a pacing sentry brought us to a halt with baited breath. Flint motioned to Pew, pointed upwards, then ran a fore-finger across his throat.

Clamping a dagger between his strong, white teeth, which were small and curved like those of a stoat, the Bosun stealthily crept to the edge o' the jetty and peered above the planking. He eased hisself up. Half his body remained suspended in space for a moment, then slid from view. We heard a muffled scuffle, a stifled gasp and a musket clattered onto the boards above us.

"Thunder!" hissed Flint. "The Boatswain be making enough din to arouse the whole blasted town."

With our hearts hammering in our mouths, as the saying is, we listened to the rasping slither as a body were dragged to the jetty's edge and tumbled into the sea. To us, crouched below, the splash was amplified a thousand fold. Sounded like a breaching whale, so it did! Pew's head appeared, hanging upside down and framed by his lank red hair that he never wore queued.

"All clear, Cap'n," whispered he and we clambered top-side, sweating as if we'd just climbed Snowdon.

"There be more'n half a dozen swabs aboard, Sir," declared Black Dog. "At least a score, I reckon, judging by the row amidships."

"We'll join 'em and spike their merry-making," replied Flint grimly.

Dividing into four groups of five, we swarmed aboard the ship. Flint's party entered the gun-port of the starboard Bow-Chaser. A second Crew, led by Pew, climbed onto the Fo'c'sle. A third gang followed Israel, gaining the upper deck by way of the main-chains, stays and shrouds. I led the fourth bunch, slithering along the barrel of a Stern-Chaser into the Gun-Room. Up for'ard the Revellers started singing.

The pong as permeated the place stank of stale cooking oil, boiled fish and a smell that makes my guts roll to this day – garlic! Most Spaniards ain't up to much when it comes to house-keeping, you may lay to that! In the dim light of a smokey lanthorn, its glass brown as amber, we beheld six bodies in various states of repose. Four lay curled upon the bare deck like kennelled dogs. Another sat astride a bench, slumped across the mess-table; while a sixth was sprawled over it, flat on his back, arms dangling – snoring. Several empty black bottles showed they had been drinking Rack, Spanish Seamen preferring wine to spirits.

We trussed 'em up with cordage, hands and feet, afore they were proper awake. In answer to their mumbling protests, Black Dog snarled a curt: "*Silencio o muerte*!" in bad Spanish – 'Silence or death.' They got the gist of the message and lay like blessed lodgers in a grave-yard, watching our every move with wide, frightened eyes.

Leaving Morgan to guard 'em, I took Black Dog, George Merry and Gypsy Fuller to sound out the great main cabin – my responsibility being to secure all below the poop-deck. Pistols cocked in case of mishap, we crept up the companion way and paused before the door. The singing up for'ard suddenly stopped and I could hear my own heart thumping in the silence as settled throughout the ship. Flanked by Merry and Fuller with Black Dog close behind, I took a deep breath, then turned the handle, flung the door wide and darted through – my barkers aimed before me.

I've met some cool customers in my time, I have, but this cove as confronted us took First Prize hands down, by a long sea mile! He lounged in a high winged chair alongside a carved desk of redwood with one leg draped over the arm-rest, swinging free, and the other resting upon the desk-top. His crimson, damask waistcoat and matching pantaloons in rich velvet made him more suited to a drawing-room in some London Club, than aboard a captured British Privateer. Silk bows on his garters topped his stockings. Valenciennes lace adorned the wide cuffs on his ruffled shirt; a gold watch-chain looped his pockets; and his cravat boasted the biggest ruby brooch I ever clapped eyes on, encircled with diamonds. To crown his glory he wore a white wig, queued by a bonny red ribbon.

Disregarding the menacing black muzzles of our guns, he grinned, his smooth, middle-aged face bright with laughing blue eyes. Glass in hand, he raised it in salute. "*Salve! Aqua vitae!*" said he in Latin, then added in perfect Spanish. "Good cheer, señors! Are we under attack, what?"

"We ain't!" snapped I in reply. "But you be! No false moves, mind, or I'll blow your brains apart!"

"Thunder!" exclaimed Black Dog, his eyes glinting with greed. "Look at this 'ere Bauble on his halter-cloth, Long John!"

"Odds bodikins!" cried the crimson tippler. "You're British! A glass of brandy, Gentlemen, or would you prefer claret to cool your coppers – you all seem somewhat vexed."

"An' you'll be somewhat ventilated between the lug-'oles if you don't batten yer hatch an' hand them sparks over a bit lively!" sneered Black Dog pressing his pistol muzzle against the man's ear. The leering Bosun's Mate's mouth was on par to Flint's for beauty with a row o' teeth akin to pit-props in a disused colliery: one black, one broken and one missing! His breath were none too choice either.

"Forsooth! Would'st rob a man of his last memento from dear departed Mother?" replied the Dandy Buck; then slowly pushing the gun barrel aside, he stuck a forefinger down the bore. "Touché!" said he softly with a deep chuckle. "I suggest you sit down and rest your brains!"

Black Dog's leer changed to a scowl: "If I triggers this 'ere piece, you'll be missing a hand. Now . . ."

"My dear Sir," interrupted the Dandy. "If you triggers that piece we shall both be missing a hand and possibly our heads to boot! Know you nothing of small-arms?"

"Belay this tomfoolery, Black Dog! Time enough for trinkets later!" I snapped. Turning to the Dandy, I demanded: "Do you Cap'n this 'ere ship?"

"No, my good man, not I," replied he tossing down his drink. He stood up and extended a leg in a foppish, but most graceful bow. "Doctor Daniel Hunter, one time Lecturer at the Royal College of Surgeons and of late, Consultant to his Lordship the Right Honourable, Sir Robert Walpole – your humble servant, Gentlemen."

"A saw-bones! Why, you're just what the doctor ordered," sniggered Gypsy Fuller, grinning fit to split.

"Aye, an' one who's served Walpole – him as runs Parlyment, by thunder!" exclaimed Merry. "Now see here, Doctor. I've a spot o' back bother . . ."

"Avast you, George Merry! This ain't the place or time t'air your blasted aches and pains! Nip for'ard and inform Flint – all secured aft!" I ordered.

"Flint? Do you mean, James Flint, Esquire, that esteemed Gentleman of Fortune, is actually aboard this boat?" queried the Doctor as George slouched away mumbling to hisself.

"Ship!" corrected Black Dog. "This 'ere's a Ship!"

"Captain Flint as ever was," confirmed Fuller.

"In that case, should your Captain recruit me for the Services I can render his Crew, you Gentlemen might do well to reconsider before plundering my person," reminded the Doctor, eyeing Black Dog.

"You'll do as yer bid, 'Flash Dan', or go by the board!" snarled the Bosun's Mate, pouring hisself a full glass o' brandy.

"Truly," agreed the other. "But who is to say I shall do it well?" asked he, cocking an eyebrow. "Certainly not the patient who happens to lie beneath my knife. Perchance it maybe yourself, Mister Dog, then we shall hear how loud you can howl!"

The Bosun's Mate spluttered into his brandy and near choked.

"See here, Black Dog," says I, feeling my face flush with anger. "'Tis me as commands this gang and we'll both come to an ill office if the Cap'n clapps you aboard – a-boozing on dooty!"

"Blast my eyes if ever I needs to ask pardon of any man afore I takes a tipple!" cried he, raising his glass for a second gulp.

"Taste ye another drop and 'twill be a sight more than your glims as gets blasted, by thunder!" came a cold voice from astern of us.

We spun about to find Flint's vast bulk filling the narrow doorway. He held a Queen Anne pistol, its cannon-barrelled black O gaping straight at Black Dog's breast.

"Cap'n! I wus . . . we wus . . ." faltered the Bosun's Mate, his swarthy face turning a sickly shade o' grey.

For answer, Flint reached him in four strides. "Dog by name and Dog by nature!" grated he through his terrible, clenched teeth. The pistol swung in a short arc, smashing the brandy glass, then came back catching Black Dog alongside the chops. He staggered against the mizzen-mast, clutched the varnished trunk and slowly slid down it to sprawl senseless.

Flint rounded on me. "Next time ye act in my name, John Silver, and some swab defies ye, dinna argufy with 'em – KILL 'EM!" roared he, "CLEAR?"

"Aye, aye, Sir!" I replied, tipping my forelock in salute.

"And who might you be m' Bonny Buck?" asked the Captain, jabbing his gun muzzle at the Doctor.

'Flash Dan' introduced hisself along of another graceful bow. "I was to take appointment as personal Physician to my name-sake, Governor Hunter of New York, but the Dons, in finding a doctor of high standing in their midst, decided to transfer me to Trinidad and the service of Alcaldes Benette Alfonso del Manzano," explained he.

"Better than on a slave-gang working the mines," returned Flint. He drew the doctor aside and after a brief chin-wag, they shook hands.

"I have often heard the saying that 'two heads are better than one'," remarked

Flash Dan with a smile, tilting the shrunken napper on Flint's chest, "but upon my life, Captain, I never thought to meet the living proof of such a fable. However, I feel your friend is somewhat past my professional skill!"

Flint clapped Flash Dan on the back and we were all laughing when Pew and Israel entered, followed by Ben Gunn.

"All prisoners secured in the gun-room, Sir. Fifteen all told," reported the Bosun, then balked when he spied his Mate sprawled below the mizzen. "Shrivel my soul!" exploded he, his yellow eyes flashing. "What swab cut Black Dog's cable? I'll use his guts for frapping!"

"Me!" snapped Flint. "I dunnit!"

"Your pardon, Sir," says Pew with a salute, turning pale. And that, mates, is the only time in my entire life I ever heard our Bosun apologise!

"Slipped his moorings, has 'e, Cap'n?" piped Ben Gunn peering from behind the Bosun's back.

"Nay, he dinna be dead," replied Flint. "But the next blasted Picaroon as defies an order o' mine will be, by thunder! Ben, ye and Gypsy take the swab for'ard until he comes alongside. Once we clears that infernal guard-ship and negotiates the narrows o' that blasted boom, he can roost aloft on look-out. A mast-heading might help blow some of the cobwebs out as be clogging his brain!"

As Black Dog was carried off like that much mutton, Flash Dan raised an eyebrow and asked a question: "Captain. A minor point, perhaps. But how, pray, do you propose stealing this vessel with two Forts, the Santa Anna and a Boom across . . ."

"I knows the signal for Safe Conduct," interrupted Flint. "Three lights on the boltsprit – two above one. And I've a party ashore now to cut the Boom cables, so's to give us ample . . ."

"Cables?" It was Flash Dan's turn to chop Flint short. "The Boom, Sir," began he very softly, "is secured to the sea-bed by chains attached to sheet anchors!"

Pew snarled a curse and Flint swore in language that made the Doctor blanch. I were too dumb-struck even to swear on hearing this piece o' Nautical News – you may lay to that!

"There be no hope to make nor mend now," growled Flint in the stony silence. "We're committed to this course. Nought for it but to cut-and-run with the wind and the ebb-tide up our coat tails. Our navigation better be on par with Magellan's, along o' the seamanship of Drake thrown in for good measure, if we're to clear the Boom mouth. There willna be a cat's whisker of lee-way if our Timoneers make any miscalculations. We should scrape past the Hundred Gunner with our signal – along of a rumpus ashore an' surprise."

"And Luck!" added the Doctor, arching his eyebrows. "*Fortuna favet fatuis*," murmured he, partaking a pinch of snuff.

"Aye, more'n our fair share," agreed Pew. "Every Man-Jack as be aboard best take to his Prayers!"

Darby M'Graw entered and reported – his beady, bright eyes darting about the cabin. "Coxun's compl'ments, Captin. Hands is all at station, fore an' aft, and the tide be near full turned."

"Thankee, Darby," said Flint pulling a gold watch from his pocket and studying the clock. "Bosun Pew, ensure all glims as be visible from outboard are doused, save the three needed for signal. Long John, ye and the Doctor hang-fire here. When ye receives two raps from the Poop, make signal to Bill's stink-pot party ashore, then join me at the wheel." He clicked his watch-case shut and glanced up, eyes flashing. "Quarters, Gentlemen, and may the Devil's Luck be with ye!"

I could feel the tension mounting throughout the ship. The very air we breathed seemed to be vibrating, like a taut hawse. Flash Dan helped me blow out all the lanthorns in the great cabin, barring one which I unhooked from its becket in the deck-head, afore taking station beside the stern-sheet windows.

"Thunder!" exclaimed I. "My nerve-ends ain't been this screwed up since I saw me first belly dancer on the Red Sea round."

"With Flint?" asked the Doctor.

"No, mate – England. I was Master Gunner under Ned England. Then I sided with Taylor, afore signing articles along o' Flint, not a month since when the Dagos declared war," I replied. "Have you an' the Cap'n struck some sort of bargain, along of your whispered chin-wag earlier?"

"I have a yearning for high adventure as well as unlimited wealth," sighed he. "Captain Flint has promised me an abundance of both if I sail with him and act as Ship's Surgeon."

"Just so long as a cannon ball don't replace your head!"

"Speaking of heads," grinned my debonair companion, his teeth sparkling in the gloomy glow of the glim set between us. "Tell me, John, has it been suggested to Captain Flint that he change his dentist?"

I was joining him in a hearty giggle when two raps overhead caught us both with a start.

Time for talking were past!

CHAPTER XV

ESCAPE FROM PORTO BELLO!

I lifted and lowered the glim to the window three times, then waited. In answer to my signal a tall tongue of flame licked over the warehouse wall some two cables length away, along the wharf. The tarred timbers, soused in turpentine by the speed of which the fire took hold, blazed like a beacon. Two more fires sprang up at different points from the first, followed by the flash and bang of a small-arm.

"Thunder!" cried I. "Gun-fire ain't on the cards. Quarter-deck, Flash Dan and lively!"

"At this rate our Mister Bones will have the whole of Porto Bello ablaze," remarked the Doctor, following me to the door.

I blew out the light, then we passed through onto the deck. Flint stood alongside the wheel with Job Anderson, Gypsy Fuller and a few more, all gazing over the starboard quarter rails past the jetty. Black Dog was sat on a 12-pounder's truck, sullen and silent, nursing a swollen jaw. A dark figure came hurrying along the deck, carrying a bulky object.

"Gun Crews is closed up, Cap'n," reported Hands. "But shiver my sides! Six o' the fourteen Long Twelves be blessed Quakers – see here!" said the Gunner, setting down a wooden stand attached to a dummy gun muzzle.

"Looks to be they intended converting her from Privateer to Merchantman," remarked Job Anderson.

It was common practice for Merchantmen and Traders to carry such deceptions, the idea being that reducing the weight of Cannon greatly increased the burthen for Cargo, yet the ship still would appear to be heavily armed. Sometimes 'Quakers' were used aboard RN vessels to make for greater cabin space or to disguise the loss o' guns smashed in action.

"Small matter," declared Flint. "We've enough iron to meet our needs for the moment." Turning to the Bosun's Mate, he bawled: "Avast, Black Dog! Dinna sit there in the Doldrums! Look alive and report for'ard! Tell Ben Gunn to hoist Signal as soon as we be under way! But if we comes under fire, he's to douse 'em – double damn quick!"

Shots and shouts from ashore were raising Cain in all quarters. I saw lanthorns bobbing about in the darkness like Will-o'-the-Wisps, interspaced by the flash and report of fire-arms, the harsh crack of musketry drowning the lesser bark o' pistols popping.

"Stab me!" swore Flint. "The shore party's run foul of soldiers b'the sound on it. I didna bank on a blasted pitched battle for a send off!"

The fighting came closer. Our party suddenly appeared at the jetty and clattered onto the boards – running hard. Some paused to fire at their pursuers, then raced on. One man went down, his death cry ringing clear. Another stumbled under the impact of a bullet. Two of his mates anchored an arm each about their necks and ran on, dragging him between them.

Flint stood feet astride, hands clasped behind his back, glancing at each man as he stumbled on deck from the gang-board set between the bulwarks. Nick Nutt, a Leading Hand newly appointed by Billy, came last.

"Sir!" gasped he. "We caught a Tartar by the Ears. Bumped one o' their patrols when we wus a-firing the . . ."

"Where's Mister Bones and Carijo?" demanded Flint, fierce as a Turk. "They ain't under hatches are they?"

"I don't rightly know, Sir. I ain't sure if they be above or below board, not now. The Boom be chained and . . ."

"I ken about the Boom!" snapped Flint. "If Bill ain't along of ye, where be he and Carijo at?"

"The Mate took Joe the Carib an' Mad Murdock in a Piragua to do mischief ag'in the Guard-Ship, Sir," continued Nutt. "Mister Bones 'as a flare-pot aboard and says for you to seek his signal at sea, Sir."

"STAND-BY NUMBER ONE!" hollered Israel Hands.

Flint gave forth a string of fruity language, but there was no time for reflection on what the Mate and a Crew of two could accomplish in a blessed dug-out canoe against a Hundred Gunner. The pursuing Spaniards had hove-to along the jetty. Busy re-loading, they was, afore making a final assault, when Hands yelled:

"FIRE!"

George Merry stopped swinging his match, blew the ash off the glowing end and dunked it in the vent field. He had to look sharp in taking his hand out of harm's way from the recoil of the cannon, for he lacked the safety of a lint-stock. This article were a staff about three foot long, bearing a point on one end and a crotch at t'other; the former was so you could stick it in the deck when helping to haul on the gun-tackle, while the latter held the match or fusee as some Gunners calls it.

The powder flashed down the channel to the touch-hole and the cannon recoiled onto its breeching ropes, spewing smoke, flame and a parcel o' case-shot. That there canvas bag of musket balls scythed into the Dons like a discharge from a Giant's Blunderbuss, which in fact was what it were – in a manner o' speaking. Those who escaped being killed or crippled fled in the face o' such carnage. Ran they did, slipping and sliding in the red muck that poured over the planking. Some of the lubbers jumped off the jetty – small blame to them, I say!

"STAND-BY TWO AND THREE!" bawled our Gunner yet again.

George closed up on Number Two, opposite Morgan, who stood alongside the third gun swinging his match.

"FIRE!" cried Israel stepping clear.

This time both pieces belched out bar-shot, aimed at the jetty itself. These brace o' balls, each one cut in half and joined by a foot long iron bar, tore the timbers to bits. Splinters flew and planks whirled away in all directions, along of the mangled remains of men. What with flames ashore and the drifting smoke of our discharge, Porto Bello looked to be suffering a major Fleet Action. But I had no time for sight-seeing as Flint yelled: "Cut clear for'ard! Cut free aft!" and the two hands stationed at each end of the mooring lines brought their boarding axes thunking down across the cables.

Free now in the force o' the ebb, our new ship shot forward like a live thing and the gang-board crashed clear of the bulwarks. Our stern started to swing. Job Anderson and Gypsy Fuller brought the ship back on line as the whole Crew gave a loud cheer. Full of pride, my heart pounding fit to pop, I took up a speaking trumpet and gave my first Sailing Orders aboard the *Walrus*.

"LOOSE SPRITS'LS AND DRIVER! HOIST THE JIBS!"

Barring them as was serving the guns, the Crew rushed forward and aft to obey my commands, urged on by the harsh, cruel voice o' the Bosun. By the powers, but Pew were a cold un! His rope's end sounded across the back o' more'n one and the fear he inspired gave wings to feet that were all but flying!

"Move, you blasted skulks! Look alive or I'll see you dead! Damn my eyes if I don't!" raged he.

We couldn't cram more canvas on our yards, seeing as we had to feel our way. The Boom and the Guard-Ship reduced the harbour mouth to a bottleneck with barely half a cable's length of sea room between. Close hauled as we were on the larboard tack, there was no space to allow for error. Two points of miscalculation either way would cause us to collide with either the Boom or the *Santa Anna*. Should we be rumbled, then a broadside from our enemy's 18 and 32 Pounders 'ud blow us all over Porto Bello. Bluff, Surprise and a goodly go o' Lady Luck were our only chance. But thanks to the brisk boldness of Mister William Bones, a Mad Mute and a Carib Savage, the massive Three-Decker was soon to have her own worries.

"With your permission, Captain, I shall begin to earn my bread and go below to attend the wounded," says Flash Dan.

Flint nodded: "As ye will, Doctor," replied he, watching the Gunners reload and a right royal foul-up they were making of it, to be sure! Dropping ball and bar-shot all over the deck, so they was!

"Avast!" cried Hands. "Swab it first, you fool, afore you puts a fresh charge in! Any sparks left in that bore and you'll dis'ppear through the blasted port – along o' the rammer!"

"Ensure the cartridge be inserted seam down'ards with the arse-end put in first!" added George Merry.

"I ain't no Gunner!" grumbled the offender.

"Ye will be ere I'm done with'e!" retorted Flint fiercely. "Providing ye dinna blow us all inta Hades afore we can clear the harbour!"

"Captain! Captain Flint!" came a sudden cry from the Fo'c'sle. "Look to the Guard-Ship! Her cable's afire – burning brighter than a heretic on a Papist pyre it be, Sir!"

"Shrivel my soul!" exclaimed Pew. "This here's a bold, brave blow from our mate, Bill!"

Framed by the back-drop of a million twinkly, bright stars we saw the Ship, her spars and rigging looming blackly on our starboard bow, and to be sure, both her for'ard anchor cables were fierce aflame. I never saw the like in all my days at sea! Fire was the main fear of any Crew, for flames would devour sun-dried timbers and tarred rigging quicker than a starving Piccaninny tossed a biscuit!

Now that there Ship were maybe 2,000 Tons burthen and fifty feet in the beam. To hold her against the current she needed three anchors: two Bowers up for'ard and a Sheet anchor astern. She was also rigged with a Spring-Rope, so as by means of the capstan she could winch herself around to present a broadside facing the bay or the open sea.

Her Crew was all in a clove-hitch, clustered on the cat-heads and along the bowsprit, yelling and a-bawling to each other. Buckets were being hauled aboard by ropes tied to the handles, but the dousing was delivered from too high up and too far away. Only a fine spray reached the flaming hawsers. Using the twin tongues of fire for a marker, I gave correction to our course.

"Two points to port!" I ordered the Helmsman. "An' hold steady!"

As Job Anderson and Fuller worked the wheel, our Cox'n with his glims glued on the compass-card in the binacle, both the burning cables parted with a loud: 'Thwack!' The severed lines snaked back like a pair of writhing serpents whose thick coils caught the starboard cat-head and swept several men into the sea. Their cries were all but drowned by the jubilant cheering from our Crew – Ben Gunn's being the most prominent. Always enjoyed the misfortunes of others, did Ben!

"That'll learn 'em to leave out too much cable, instead of riding apeek o' the anchor!" declared our Carpenter, hugging hisself with glee.

Swept along on the ebb, aided by our sprit and jib-sails, we bore down on the *Santa Anna* at a rapid rate. Caught in the current, the great Ship's bows swung round to port. Her stern cable went slack. Round she went and still more, until we could see only her stern-sheets as she was pulled up short on the sheet-anchor. For half a heart-beat she hung there on a single hawse. If all had been Bristol Fashion there was a good chance it would have held, but Billy's Gang had tampered with that too. Cut part way through, I reckon, by the speed with which it snapped. Quick as a Jew's self control over losing a half-penny! Away she went, turning stem to stern, spinning dizzily same as a child's top – completely at the mercy of the tide.

"By the Eyes of Argus!" cried Anderson. "Are they blind? Why don't the lubbers put the helm hard over and get some steerage-way on her?"

The great Ship continued her crazy course, then slammed sideways into the Boom. *Santa Anna*'s weight and the force of the current opened the bottle-neck entrance by at least another fifty yards afore the Boom's sheet-anchors held both Ship and logs in stays. Of the Three Decker, all that confronted us was her stern-sheet windows. The impact tore two of the sticks clean out of her, the fore and main-masts crashing by the board. Only her Mizzen remained, lopsided amid a mass o' splintered spars and tangled rigging. A visit from the Blessed Pope hisself couldn't have caused more chaos, you may lay to it!

"Boil my blood and fall on!" roared Flint triumphantly. "She's stricken! All's plain sailing from here on out!"

It were just at that moment the Forts opened fire. By the time we heard the guns go off, cannon balls were dropping in the sea around us sending up great gouts o' spray. But we minded the falling shot no more than a shower of rain. Several rounds ripped through our rigging causing only minor damage, seeing as our main canvas was still furled.

"Barbecue!" barks Flint to me. "Ye've the reputation o' being something of a Gunner! I wants for ye an' Hands an' Merry to put me a three gun salute through their stern-sheet windys as we bear down and fly by! Black Dog! Aloft with ye to the main-peek! Keep ye yore weather eye peeled for the fire-pot signal from Bill's boat!"

"GUN CAPTAINS – CLOSE UP!" cried Hands.

Me, Merry and the Master Gunner took station at our respective Pieces, the Crews all abustle with both Handspec and Crow as we bawled commands to elevate the Long Tom's muzzle to maximum. The *Walrus* would be the size of her namesake alongside a whale once we drew level with the *Santa Anna* and we'd need every inch o' height to put our shot through the ruptured ship's stern.

Small effort to imagine the wreckage and carnage aboard, caused by the great guns that would have torn loose, what with her deck listing at a sharp angle against the Boom. The Three Decker's Artillery wouldn't be lashed secure – 'Housed' in the sea phrase – not on a Guard-Ship ready for action. Many a Captain would have thought Mercy, shown Quarter and sailed past. But that were never Flint's way, not when dealing with the Dons. He had declared War on all the World with naught but revenge in his head and a bloodlust in his eye for anything Spanish.

"The Devil burn the bunch of 'em!" cried he, shaking both fists and baring those terrible teeth as hatred distorted his battered face. "But for the want of heated shot, I'd leave yon wreck a-blaze!"

I crouched behind the breech, peering along the upper sight, trying to gauge the height of our roll in relation to Long Tom's mouth. Morgan knelt on one knee beside the starboard train-truck, blowing gently on the glowing match in his hand. By the stance he took, without notice, I knew that here was another Gunner of RN calibre.

A final salvo and the Forts ceased fire. They couldn't bombard us for fear of hitting their own ship and the surrounding sea was full of swimming Spaniards. One of their last shots splintered our bulwark amidships and another bounced off the Taffarel, carrying away the larboard lantern from its crane.

Our target loomed larger than a house, her high stern-sheet windows ablaze with light from numerous glims that hung within. Israel Hands gave orders and his gun roared in response, hurling out a brace of balls. A moment later the dense smoke from his discharge was thickened by the blast from George Merry's piece.

Then it was our turn!

"STAND BY!" I yelled.

Squinting along the side-sights all I could see was a thick, white wall of swirling smoke, but the wind of our headway soon swept it aft in tattered streamers. I watched the line of Long Tom's muzzle elevate the big ship's shattered stern. Half her ward-room windows were blown in and her main gallery hung in ruins, the balustrades dangling like a row o' broken teeth. I waited until my gun muzzle reached the peek on the upward roll, then yelled: "FIRE!" and stepped clear a bit smart.

Tom Morgan's Match sent our Long Twelve bucking back onto its breechings, spewing smoke and flame, bar and ball. As we passed beneath the great stern and the smoke cleared, we saw the fruits of our efforts. Her port side quarter gallery was shot away and the casement hung on a single hinge. Our Crew, clustered along the starboard side and bunched in the lower shrouds of the fore and main mast rigging, sent up a loud "Huzza!" Next instant we swept through the wide gap in the Boom and were home free -surging out into the open sea.

"My Lads!" bawled Flint through a speaking trumpet. "I'll give a Golden Moidore to every Man-Jack who played a part in this night's work! And when the Mate be safe aboard, I'll order a double go of rum for all hands! Aloft wi' ye and keep sharp look-out for Bill's Boat!"

The hands swarmed up the ratlings, cheering like work-house charity children given extra gruel.

PEECE FOUR

ON THE ACCOUNT!

CHAPTER XVI

POP GOES THE WEASEL!

We picked Billy's Crew up not a quarter league from the harbour mouth. Half a dozen hands spotted the flare of his fire-pot the moment he used his Flasher. I gave orders to 'Come about' and we 'Hove-to' – our sails all a-back, shivering in the face of the wind.

Billy brought the Piragua alongside in a brace of shakes and a trim little craft she were, to be sure, complete with a lateen sail. Our crew hauled the three Heroes aboard, hollering 'emselves hoarse. The dug-out was cast adrift with the fire-pot still burning. She would be a good draw off if the Dons gave chase.

Once underway again, this time with fore-sails unfurled to boost our progress, Billy explained about the Guard-Ship. The other two Heroes of the hour, Joe the Carib and Mad Murdock the Mute, stood by grinning, cup in hand, while the crew drank their health from a keg of rum that were broached beside the wheel. The mystery of why the *Santa Anna* failed to steer was soon solved.

"Mad Murdock it were, mates! Jammed her rudder googings with a brace of wedges!" boomed Bones, clamping an arm around the grinning Mute's thin shoulders. "I couldn't fathom at first what he wanted with the quoins he snatched from under a beached Long-Boat, but it topped my trick o' soaking the cables in turpentine!"

"By thunder!" exclaimed Flint. "Ye may not have a tongue to wag, my mute friend, but yore headpiece matches Sir Isaac Newton's for brain power!"

The first pink flush of sunrise saw us safely back in our secret cove, berthed alongside the Barca-Longa in the lee of the high cliffs. Although she were a large ship, by Privateering standards, *Walrus* had a surprisingly shallow draft that gave access to creeks and inlets that would bar most other vessels of the same burthen.

Quarter-Master McGinty came up from below and greeted us with my old Parrot perched on his shoulder. He had bivouaced the main part of the Ship's

Company on a nice clean stretch o' white sand with bowers and lean-tos bordering the shady cool of the jungle. When we hove into sight the Duty Watch on board the *Weasel* fired the swivel and aroused the camp ashore. Cheer after cheer rolled out to greet us, their huzzas echoing against the cliffs, as we let go our hook.

Excepting those opposed to Piracy, a narrow handful, the rest of the crew plunged into the water, one and all, and came splashing towards us. Triumph near turned to Tragedy in the excitement when five clotpolls, in finding 'emselves out their depth, realised they couldn't swim. They were duely rescued by the Puritan Party on the beach and dragged ashore half drowned. By the powers, but we had some chuckle-headed lubbers among that lot o' would-be-Buccaneers!

Willing hands were soon working the capstan bars to off-load the Ship's Boats, of which the *Walrus* had three: a Chaloupe or Long-Boat; a six oared Yawl; and a very flat, broad bottomed boat towed astern called a Moses – used for hauling hogsheads, mainly. The *Weasel*'s Pinnace made a fourth.

All manner of delicacies were to be found in *Walrus*'s Hold, being formally bound for the Alcaidede of Trinidad. While we were off loading such luxuries as Westphalia bacon, pickled oysters, bottles of Madeira and butts of Claret for a Royal break-fast ashore, it was discovered we had us a little stowaway on board – shiver my sides! He was a young Negro, a nipper of around nine or ten I reckoned him to be.

Israel Hands, it were, as dragged him out by the scruff from behind some barrels and found hisself holding a tiger by the tail. A jaguar 'ud appear as a playful pup alongside that lad. He struggled and kicked, bit and punched too, so he did, when chance presented itself. The younker were pistol proof to such degree that the Gunner called on Black Dog to bear a hand in hauling him topside. The crew hollered 'emselves hoarse, vapouring in favour o' the Negro nipper.

"Go to it, Sambo, give 'im a drubbin!"

"Two ag'in one ain't a square deal!"

"Article rules, Black Dog, article rules!"

And when the Bosun's Mate cuffed the lad alongside the lug, there was some all set to give Black Dog a good drubbing. Eventually, both of 'em managed to dump their squirming cargo afore Flint.

The Cap'n scowled down at the lad, who gazed up into that broad, broken face with its piercing blue eyes without so much as a flicker o' fear.

Dressed all in his usual black, Flint looked like the Devil Incarnate a'standing on that there deck, "Ain't ye a-feared, Sonny?" growled the towering Buccaneer. "Ain't ye a-quaking in yore shoes?"

"No, Suh. I ain't got no shoons ta quake in. I is bin bare foot since bein' born!" replied the Innocence, frowning up at the shrunken head on Flint's chest. Our Cap'n's face softened, then he smiled – flashing them pointed teeth. The younker's eyes went wide as saucers in his pitch-black face and the whole of the crew ruptured into a great roar o' laughter.

That were how 'Pip' – late Cabin Boy to Capitan Pizzaro – joined our Company and a braver lad never set sail upon the sea. Why, I seen him cool as an iceberg amid shot and shell, beating us in to close-quarters on the Irish Drum O'Brien made for him without missing a blessed stroke! Flint's new Cabin Boy soon became a firm favourite along o' the crew, who added their own handle to his name – 'Tiger!' One and all we called him, 'Tiger Pip'!

The Spanish Prisoners were made to jump overboard and swim ashore. But once in the water, Flint, Pew, Billy Bones and a few others started pot-shotting at 'em with Small-Arms for target practice. Only three reached the beach alive where they were set to work under guard, chopping firewood. The Puritan Party, led by the Snooty Cove, bemoaned the wanton cruelty of it, but their deputation to Flint fell on deaf ears. They soon changed their toon and battened down their hatches when our Cap'n gave 'em the chance to change places.

On shore we fired up a Feast fit for a King, and then drank as if the world were about to run dry. Flint's Flyers spread themselves among their mates in the various groups around the cook-fires, for everybody wanted to know the long and the short of who done what and how. Empty 'necked' bottles soon lay strewn about the beach. It were quicker, you see, to knock the necks off than to waste time drawing the corks – thirsty men being short on patience.

Us Officers and Artists were clustered about Flint's fire-side – the Ward-Room of the gathering, so to speak. Our clique consisted of Billy Bones, Darby M'Graw, QM McGinty, Job Anderson, Pew, Black Dog, Hands, Merry, Morgan, Ben Gunn, Joe the Carib, Tiger Pip, who kept our tankards topped up, Flash Dan the Doctor and Me.

"'Tis fifty years agone when last I clapped me beadys on Porto Bello," stated One Arm McGinty looking wistful. "Aye, ship-mates, over half a century ago since Morgan ransacked it in '68 to the toon of two hundred and fifty thousand peeces of eight! There wus more forts a-guardin' of it in them days, mind! But Morgan was the man fer tactics. Made the Priests and Monks carry the scalin' ladders when we broach'd the walls. Them Fat Friars gave better protection from bullets than shutters. They didn't splinter when struck, heh, heh," cackled the Old Stander, "just screech'd and died all a-wriggly like fat worms chopp'd wi' a spade. Ah, they wus happy days under 'Arry Morgan!"

"Toast o' the Main were Morgan. Could be me an' him is related, both having the same handle and hailing from the same Home Town of Llanrhymney in Glamorganshire – look you," boasted the Gunner's Mate, puffing out his chest with pride. "Us Welshmen is born leaders, so we are. Runs in the blood, see!"

"Ha!" gibed Merry, his single earring of silver flashing in the sun. "You couldn't lead a pig to market, Tom! And all as runs in your blood is pilfered booze!"

A broadside o' mirth rocked our circle.

"Now look you 'ere, George Merry!" flushed Morgan, his Welsh blood running hot. "Ship-mates we may be, but I ain't a-standin' . . ."

A cry of anger and a clash of steel cut him short, then a great commotion came from among the men in an outlying group. Jumping to their feet, those around us gave voice to the fray taking place along the beach. Cap'n Flint fluttered nervously on my shoulder as our crowd aroused themselves to see what were amiss.

Two of the hands had fallen together by the ears. A-going like a pair of Tartars, they was, taking huge swipes at each other using both cutlass and dirk. One I recognised as being the Leading Hand, Nick Nutt, newly appointed by Billy. The other I knew not. Although bigger and meaner looking than the Leading Hand, he was being driven towards the sea along of every cut and thrust from the smaller man.

Flint slowly got to his feet, rolling the cud of coca leaves he were chewing on, his eyes glinting like crumbs of blue glass beneath the shady brim of his black sombrero. "What be the manner of this rupture?" snaps he, glancing around him for an answer.

"'Tis Leading Hand Nutt, Sir, having dry-blows with his old Bosun – him as wants no truck with Piracy," replied Pew.

"Grudge fight, Cap'n. They hate each other worse than a Whig do a Tory!" added Black Dog necking the cork off another bottle with a flat-o'-the-cutlass blow.

"I made a point of keeping the Puritan Party wi'out Arms," muttered QM McGinty, rasping his hand over unshaven, salt-white jowls. "Now where did he lay his mitts on a hanger and poignard, d'yer suppose?"

"Borrowed the blasted tools, where else!" growled Billy Bones. "You want I should lay 'em alongside, Sir?"

"The hands is out of discipline for the moment, Bill. Let 'em fight on. Besides, I ain't seen a first rate set-to since Tortuga!" said Flint and started striding towards the beach.

We all fell in and followed him, clucking along like a brood o' cygnets behind a swan. Our future Ship's Company dropped their vapouring and stepped aside for Flint and us lesser mortals, but the two antagonists on the shore line had eyes only for each other.

Nimble Nick was running rings around the Bosun. Prancing about like a French fencing master, he were, while the bigger man blundered his lunges with all the grace of a half blind bull, striking thin air mostly. Our crew gave a loud Huzza! as the Leading Hand's thrusting blade sliced a gash in Matey's thigh and the blood flowed. Nutt forced the big man into the sea which turned red in their wake. Back he went and still further, until the rolling swell was lapping their waists.

"What's Nutty Nick aiming t'do, sink the swab?" voiced Job Anderson from alongside of me.

Then the newly elected leader of the Puritan Party confronted Flint. "Sir!" says he, all haughty and puffed up with self importance. "I call upon you and your sense of fair play to end this diabolical display before murder is done!"

"Murther?" croaked Flint, cheeking his narcotic quid. "'Tis cutlash for cutlash! Dirk against Dirk! Blow for blow! Both be men full grown – so they are! Ye can give a Christian Burial to the loser, along of a Bible Reading, if ye be so minded. There now, what could be fairer and squarer than that, by thunder!"

A clash of steel and a thin scream marked the end. Their cutlasses were locked together against the guards and I saw Nutt with his dirk buried deep in the Bosun's side. Dropping his own dagger, the Bosun clutched hisself as Nutt withdrew the fluted blade that had done for him. The dying man stood swaying, his hanger arm extended, gazing in disbelief at us who watched in silence on the beach. His cutlass slipped from nerveless fingers. Then he fell forward to float face down, bobbing on the gentle swell amid tattered tendrils of pinky red. Sheathing his own hardware, the Leading Hand ducked under water and emerged with the weapons of the late departed. Wading ashore he squelched up the beach with his sea-boots streaming and presented both blades to a grinning Gypsy Fuller.

"I thanky, ship-mate," says Nick Nutt. "If ever a bilge rat needed his hash settled, it were that swab!"

The Puritan Party buried the Bosun under the leafy spread of a big Red Mangrove, while their pious leader read from the Scriptures. The Bible belonged to Flint, used in the Swearing of Oaths when signing Articles. After that solemn service, held amid the drunken revelry of our blasphemous crew, a plank was nailed to the trunk with these words branded on it by a musket ramrod heated red-hot.

RUEBEN PHIPPS
BOATSWAIN
DEPARTED THIS LIFE
SEPT 13th 1727

"Sir! I trust you will honour your word and allow my men to leave in the lugger?" enquired the Puritan Leader to ours as he returned Flint's Bible. "Also, I would deem it praiseworthy if you gave me custody of the prisoners."

"Whenever ye be so minded. I've a few articles to transfer; arms, and personal traps, but I'll see ye have ample rations enough to reach Jamacia," returned Flint. "Along o' yore Spanish charges."

Those of us who heared this statement couldn't give credit to our ears. The Captain was consenting to let Spaniards escape with their lives? I for one felt a deep chill within me – you may lay to that!

"I wish to weigh anchor as soon as possible, before any more of my men fall foul of yours," continued Snooty Head. "It is nearing noon and the tide will shortly be on the ebb. I await your convenience, Captain!"

With that the Puritan Leader gave a slight bow and returned to his own group. Flint called a party of us together and we rowed out to the *Weasel*. Our personal belongings were soon shipped aboard *Walrus*, along with the Serpent Headed Swivel Gun and all the Small-Arms. Oddly enough, most of the *Weasel*'s powder was left in her hold.

"*Walrus*'s magazines be full," said Flint, "and I ain't storing powder between decks where it might blow."

Flint and Billy sweated and grunted in hauling on a large, padlocked wicker basket which they transferred to *Walrus*. The basket was heavy and gave off a damp, musty smell – the same as you get from mouldy clothes.

"What might be in this weighty hamper, Sir?" enquired Job Anderson in helping to haul it below to the bread-room where it were stored.

"Ah," sighed Flint. "This be our insurance, Laddie, to guard against pilfering of any purchase we make on the Pirate round," explained he and winked at Billy, who grinned back.

When re-victualling the *Weasel* was concluded we returned to the beach, save for Flint and Billy Bones. They were both below decks a long time.

"Me'n the Captain will remain aboard to help row the Long-Boat back," said Billy to me. "The Pinnace alone won't ferry out all them Puritan lubbers in one go!"

"Aye, aye, Sir!" replied I and cast off. It was only when we were halfway to the beach, I thought it odd for the Cap'n and First Mate to designate 'emselves to Common Seamen's work.

Before departing, the snooty Puritan Leader stood up on the thwart of the

Pinnace and addressed our crowd who lay around their fires, drinking, yarning, singing or sleeping.

"As you know we are at War!" boomed he, turning his head to all quarters. "I appeal to every Loyal Englishman here to cast off from this Evil you are about to embark on, which can only lead to the Gallows and the Gibbet on Execution Dock! I beseech you, in the King's Name, to follow me and help preserve our Great and Glorious Country . . ."

"Bilge!" cried one of our crowd leaping to his feet. By the look on his face, I thought another killing was on offer! "Great and Glorious country, is it? You tell me that, you swab! Me as was transported to slave in the Indies for poachin' a b----y rabbit t'feed a starvin' wife and three little uns! And as fer yer precious King George! In pity o' his poor imprisoned wife, may he die crushed and gaspin' between the Elephant and Castle! Here now, take this in the Devil's Name an' be Damned!" roared the enraged Rover and sent a bottle hurling past the Patriot's head.

Those who were able staggered to their feet, snarling like dogs. Already half-seas-over on wine, and now with their drunken passions inflamed to fever pitch, our crowd sent a barrage o' broken bottles arching across the beach at the Puritan Party as they pushed off. Despite the entreaties of our four ship-mates, aboard to bring the Long-Boat back, the deluge of abuse and necked bottles continued until the QM piped up.

"Avast! Avast, Lads! Belay this bedlam! Flint's orders were for 'em to depart in peace – not pieces! Leave the lubbers be!"

"Aye, they'll be in pieces soon enough, eh, Q?" sniggered Darby M'Graw, giving McGinty a sly nudge. The words were only whispered, mind, but loud enough for me to hear. They sat down at the fire-side again, cackling like a brace of old crones.

Flint waited until the *Weasel* was clear of *Walrus* then returned to the beach, pulling a strong oar along o' the rest of the crew – him and Billy both. When the Long-Boat was beached they flopped down by the fire.

"Happy as pigs in a barn-yard they be," chuckled the Mate. "Off to do their dooty for King and Country – 'eroes one an' all!"

Flint gave an evil grin holding out his heavy silver goblet that Tiger Pip filled to the brim with neat rum. "We ain't heard the last o' those patriotic bucks. Stab me if I lie," said he and roared with laughter.

"Morgan were the man t'do his dooty," began McGinty after Flint's mirth died down, "but they didn't do theirs along o' him. Wanted to be buried at sea, did 'Arry. Instead the lubbers planted 'im in the Palisadoes at Port Royal."

"Seamen as gets laid under hatches ashore, ag'in their will, don't rest easy. Mark wot I say. Spirits tend to walk," piped Ben Gunn.

"Spirits ain't up for much," replied Israel Hands. "As m'father used to say: 'Tis the livin' you have to watch out for, lad. The dead don't count fer nuthin' 'cept compost!"

"Mayhap yea, mayhap nay, but hark ye t'this, my children," continued the QM squinting to watch the Lugger being borne on the ebb towards the gap in the cliffs. "Morgan went below near noon. A Saturday, it were, and four years later, almost t'the day and the same blessed moment on the clock, an earthquake pitched his grave into the sea along o' three quarters of Port Royal. Two thousand died in two minutes, shiver me fin! I know! I see it! I wus there, I wus! Damn near went below m'self, by thunder!"

"Aye, the Terror of '92, that were," declared Black Dog. "An old Uncle of mine made mention on it one time."

"Was it there you lost your larboard wing, Q?" asked Pew, his evil eyes flashing to the wrinkled stump of McGinty's left arm.

"Port Royal it were, Bosun, but not durin' the eruption. It was way back in '69. Aboard Morgan's old Flagship, the *Oxford*, I wus when she blow'd apart," replied the old Buccaneer, tamping down the tobacco in his carved, meerschaum bowl and leaning forward to spit into the fire. "'Arry claimed it wus the odious French as tried to do fer 'im. But I reckon some drunken Gunner went below wi' no cap to his pipe and we went up, mates – whoomph!"

Now during the time this small talk was going on, Flint, Billy, Darby and the Quarter-Master were sat peering at the Barca-Longa. She'd passed the narrows and was hoisting her lug-sails, just getting nicely underway.

"Powder and uncapped pipes don't mix too well," remarked Billy, studying his own short stemmed weed-burner.

"Aye, Bill. Accidents do 'appen when least expected," grinned M'Graw. "'Specially if slow matches gets mislaid between decks."

"Only lubbers 'ud sail on Friday the Thirteenth," voiced Merry, frowning from the Mate to M'Graw. George, like me, was finding it hard to follow the lay o' this conversation.

I was looking straight at the Lugger. Beating up for the open sea, she was, towing the Pinnace astern, her dark shape clear cut against the blue sky. Then she disappeared in a blinding, orange flash and there was only the Pinnace bobbing upside down beneath a big ball of dirty, grey smoke that drifted over the spot where *Weasel* had been. The sound of the explosion slammed against the cliffs, echoing and rolling on like thunder. Most of our crowd, flat on their backs and snoring lustily, never stirred. Others sat gazing seaward, mouths agape in a drunken stupor.

"Ah well," sighed Flint sipping his booze. "Pop goes the *Weasel*!"

CHAPTER XVII

MAKING PURCHASE!

Beneath the billowing white clouds of canvas the deck canted over and the sea came surging through our lee scuppers like it were boiling. Feet apart, his hands clasped behind him, Flint stood as solid as the binnacle I was braced against with the tails of his black, silk head-scarf streaming past his face. Behind us, Job Anderson and Tom Morgan wrestled with the ocean's high swell to hold the wheel steady.

Nigh on a month had passed since the *Weasel* had gone 'Pop!' We lay berthed in a creek for a week getting things ship-shape-and-Bristol-fashion, repairing our rigging and sorting out the Stores and Arms etcetera.

The 'Quakers' we used for fire-wood and we rearranged some of the guns, mounting the Serpent-Headed Swivel on the poop. Trying to bluff an enemy were all very well, until they picked up the gauntlet and made challenge. Dummy guns wouldn't be much good then, except to make a greater hazard from flizzings.

Our People were divided into Watches, Port and Starboard, and assigned to Messes along the same lines as the Royal Navy. When we came to Quarters, each of our sixteen 12-Pounders now had a full crew. Gun Drill and Ship Handling had been the order of every day for the past three weeks. Any grumble from the lower-deck, Flint nipped in the bud. He used Words and Wealth. The feel and the chink of gold in greedy fingers works wonders with them as has the fever for it – and who ain't? Just how much blessed blunt Flint had stashed below in his cabin I don't know, but it must've been a tidy sum. "A comfortable drop of dew from Heaven," as Sir Francis Drake used to say.

Most Pirate Crews operated on a 'No Prize – No Pay' basis. Not Flint! He organised competitions between the Gun Crews, giving a bonus to the fastest individual Team for loading, laying, firing and hitting the mark. Targets ranged from sand-spits on deserted islands to empty hogsheads, barrels strung together and set adrift. The same was done for those who sailed the ship, matching the teams of Top-Men against their mates on opposite masts – Fore, Main and Mizen. When Bosun Pew piped 'Secure' at Eight Bells each afternoon, it was a tired but content crew that sat down to good victuals and a well earned cup o' cheer. Evenings were spent drinking, smoking and yarning, same as ever, less those who were on Duty Watch. Then you weren't allowed nothing stronger than lime juice, coffee or maybe chocolate on Sundays, as in Article Bound. We had us some real Chinee tea on board too, along o' porcelain cups kept in the Great Cabin. Us Officers of Rank supped and tittered like Lords in Parlyment on the days that Flint got to feeling a bit dainty. Along of our Lording it, the crew demanded a double rum issue so's not to feel cheated!

"Thunder!" exclaimed Billy steadying hisself alongside Flint, the scar on his cheek now a dirty, livid white. "I reckon this Ship's Company 'ud out-sail or out-fight a Frigate!"

"I'd settle for out-sailing," returned Flint drily. "There dinna be na profit in trading Dry Blows with the blasted Royal Navy!"

Just as well we were on par with a War-Ship. It saved our bacon later, but there was a few of us as left one or two o' their rashers behind and some who lost a whole ham – shiver my sides!

We were putting *Walrus* through her final paces and during these Sea-Trials she shone far above any ship I ever sailed in – including Edward England's *Cassandra*. Flew over the water, *Walrus* did, her speed being a good eleven knots. Now that ain't bad for a ship of those days and we still had the Top-Sails and Gallents furled.

Flint took up one of the speaking trumpets that hung on either side o' the binnacle and handed it to me. "Cram on all canvas, Barbecue!" ordered he, glancing aloft. "Every last stitch, by thunder! We'll see how fast this War-Horse can run, given a free rein!"

I exchanged worried looks with Billy. A brisk breeze was blowing, coming on stronger all the time, and the sea was running high and heavy. With a full spread of canvas we could spring a mast, shred sails or even lose our tops altogether.

"Is that wise, Cap'n?" I asked. "We could crack our sticks or have 'em go by the board!"

"I'd rather lose 'em here, this moment, than wait 'til I have a brace of Navy Sloops snapping at my heels," replies he. "Broken masts now is better than being blown out the water later!"

"Aye, aye, Sir!" and right he was. Raising the trumpet to my mouth, I bawled: "LOOSE TOPS'LS AND GALLENTS!"

The Top-Men lept for the upper shrouds, keeping to the weather-side so they were blown into the rigging and not out of it. I watched them scampering aloft like monkeys, my 'eart a-going dot-and-carry-one, the same as when I first climbed a mast-head. As our added canvas captured the wind we surged forward at even greater speed, reaching around fourteen knots I reckon. Masts, block, sheet and shackles – all held as *Walrus* plowed through the sea with snorting scuppers, blowing spray from her bows. Flint slapped his thigh in delight; Billy puffed out his nostrils, snorting in harmony along o' the singing ship; and I gave a great sigh of relief. We had us a vessel that I rated second to none!

Now for all you young readers as knows nothing o' Tall Ships, I think I ought to make mention of them in general and the *Walrus* in particular. A multitude of craft sailed the seas in my day of all shapes and sizes. Some were designed for speed, like the single-masted Sloops favoured by the Free Traders for smuggling, and by the Royal Navy for patrolling in shallow water. Then you had double-masted Schooners and Snows of ninety to a hundred tons, a favourite with many who plied their Trade in the waters o' the Caribbean – Pirates or otherwise. Next came Brigantines or 'Brigs' as they were termed. At 150 tons these versatile vessels carried a combination of canvas; square sails to catch a quartering wind, while a fore-and-aft rig served best when sailing to windward.

The biggest Prizes from a Gentleman o' Fortune's point of view were the great 700-ton Indiamen, the same as I clapped aboard under England off the Malabar and Coromandel Coasts of India. Spanish Galleons still sailed from the Main of the Americas, but they were becoming few and far between nowadays. Why, in all the years we hunted the Caribbee in company with Flint, only around twelve Treasure Ships set out for Spain. The Golden Age of Piracy was past its peak, but the pickings were still good if you knew where to ply for purchase.

Greatest of all the Ships were the First Raters. Nothing short of floating Fortresses. Huge hulls, such as the *Santissima Trinidad*, were in excess of 2,000 tons burthen. Her red and white straked hull housed four decks and carried an arsenal of 136 Guns with a complement of 1,000 Seamen and Soldiers. A far cry from them as put to sea with seventy-five! Britannia had her giants too. The biggest and the best can still be seen in Portsmouth Dockyard to this same day – HMS *Victory*!

Ships in my time were faced with two main hazards. The first was fire and the second – rot, both wet and dry. In warm, tropical waters there were two more to contend with – Weed and the Teredo Worm.

The Weed, which we called 'Slawk', was thin, green and slimy. You could boil and eat it, if nought else were in the pot. It grew at a very rapid rate and if keels weren't careened every three or four months, you had a six foot forest flowing beneath your hull. Ships towing that amount of weed became slow and sluggish and hard to steer. A light pair of heels be essential to stay alive in our trade, especially when RN top-sails hoved into view on the horizon – you may lay to that!

Teredos were a far greater menace, to be sure. They were soft shelled molluscs, more than worms, and armed with batteries of fine, saw teeth. Hulls became honey-combed like a blessed bee-hive in a matter o' months and the first you knew of it was when the bottom fell out of the boat and there you were, sipping salt water instead of Arrack alongside Davy Jones! Regular Careening was the only answer at that time, but this was a hard and lengthy operation. All stores and guns had to be removed in some lone creek or cove. The Ship was then beached, hauled up on log rollers by a stout rope passed around a tree where it was wound in on the capstan, then her bottom was breamed by fire to loosen the filth. After that she was scraped and patched before being smeared with a mixture of tallow, sulphur and resin. Mucky labour it was too – and risky with the fear of being attacked when a strange sail was sighted on the horizon.

When careening became due, but with no time or suitable spot on hand, we resorted to what was termed in the navy as 'Boot-Topping'. Everything was shifted to larboard so the ship heeled over to within a limit of a safety margin, then the starboard hull was scraped and tallowed from boats to as far below the water-line as was possible. A repeat performance gave the port side a dose o' the same. Not until half a century past my time were hulls coated in copper sheathing which greatly reduced the damage done by shell-fish, worms and weed. The first Ship to undergo this trial was His Majesty's Frigate *Alarm* in 1761.

Now *Walrus* be a Ship fit to fly an Admiral's Ancient, and I ain't just a-saying of it because I'm her Master. Launched at Jamaica around the turn o' the century, her 124-foot hull was of cedar-wood that grows in abundance on the Bermudas. Worm resistant, it was, and double planked with a layer of tarred felt between for good measure. At 300-tons burthen she were heavy for a Ship of her size, but being built for Privateering, *Walrus* was made to withstand broadsides – her ribs and knees thicker and more closely set than those of an Indiaman. There again, surprisingly enough, her draft was quite shallow, drawing only ten feet of water when fully laden. Our war-horse could negotiate shoals and shallows, whereas an RN Sloop along o' the same burthen couldn't. I reckon it was because she were broader in the beam than most of her Class.

As I made a mention on a previous page, some Ships were designed for speed, manoeuvrability or fire-power. The *Walrus* had all three! Mounting seventeen ports aside to take 34 cannon, she was also pierced for 23 pairs of oars. Even when becalmed in the Doldrums and our 3,200 square yards o' canvas were useless, we could still move at three knots an hour with a pair of cursing Pirates pulling at each of the 46 sweeps. Heavy work, to be sure, but it was better than staying in irons whistling for a wind.

Our Figurehead was a sight to behold. A real *Walrus*, it were, stuffed and sun-dried with a hide as hard as our hull and bolted on just below the Bowsprit. Jutting down from either side of his upper jaw were two ivory tusks, each a foot long! Figureheads were often first rate sculptures hewn from a single block of oak. You had Greek Gods and Goddesses; Mermaids and Sea-Serpents; Dolphins and Eagles. Stems from the dark days of the Ancient Mariners, it do, like the Pagan Gods the Vikings carried aboard their Long-Ships.

There's few who be more superstitious than Sailormen, ancient or modern, you may lay to it! Christening a Ship with wine was a practice dating back to the Greeks and Phoenicians – an offering to Neptune. Whistling on deck was a sure way to bring on a high wind. When the sun was over the yard-arm, it was considered wise to pour a dram of rum over the side for the 'Old Man'. Placing a silver coin under the step of a Ship's mast was an assurance o' Good Luck. Yet spitting to windward would work in reverse! Some believe that to stick a knife in the mast of a becalmed Ship would bring on a wind from the way in which the knife-handle was pointing – but I never took matters that far!

That evening, after we'd shortened sail for the night and secured, our Captain officially christened *Walrus* with wine.

"Is you going to change the name and get a new Totem, Sir?" pipes Ben Gunn as we all stood solemn on the Fo'c'sle, where Flint had just emptied a full bottle of Claret over our tusked protector. "This old Sea-Slug ain't very ornamental is he."

"Sea-Slug?" croaks Flint tossing the necked bottle overboard, still with a bit in the bottom for Neptune. "Boil my blood, Benjamin Gunn, if ye ain't the King of all numbskulls! Why, this here Bull Walrus be one of the bravest creatures in Davy Jone's Domain. Even Orcas steers clear of these War-Horses. That's what *Walrus* means – 'War-Horse'! Now mark you this. Only Fools changes Ships' names. Bad luck don't blow no harder than on them who sail under a false figurehead, ye may be sure! England done it and died a beggar man on Madagascar! Blackbeard done it and lost his napper to decorate a boltsprit! I hope when we calls on ye, Ben, for first class carpentry, ye make better use of your head-piece other than just as a place to hang yore teeth!"

The whole crew roared with laughter as poor Ben, turning beetroot red and grinning like a loony, wriggled with embarrassment, twisting his hands like a washerwoman with a snapped clothes line.

"Up with Old Roger!" cried Flint. "Mister Morgan! Break ye out my own

Ancient, if ye please! My lads! Afore ye sight land again, I'll give ye enough gold to play Duck and Drake with!"

Amid wild "Huzzars!" George Merry sent the Skull and Cross Bones soaring up to flutter from the Mizen Peek, while Morgan, with a single jerk on a halliard, broke out Flint's personal Pennant – flown as a Flag of No Quarter in memory of his dead Wife. This twelve foot banner of red silk, forked at the end and bearing the name 'NESTER', emblazoned in pure gold thread, streamed from the main mast-head.

Under Jim Flint's brilliant direction we plundered in the Caribbee from New Spain to Surinam and as far North as the Cape Fear River way up in the Carolinas – Blackbeard's old haunt. Aye, mates, we 'Made Purchase' from all manner o' Tall Ships of all nations. Ransacked and razed five towns too! The Trail of Terror as was carved along in the wake of *Walrus*'s crimson career, were never equalled by another single Ship!

As I said earlier, the Golden Age of Piracy was gone. Buccaneering Bases, those used by the Old Guard such as Providence, Tortuga and Maricaibo, were all under New Management. The Freebooters were either given the 'Act of Grace', driven out or set to sun-drying. And you've heard QM McGinty tell of what befell Morgan's old stamping ground after he went below at Port Royal.

Civilisation was slowly creeping athwart the Caribbean – Snivelisation I calls it – what with navies of most Nations on constant patrol, as well I know, having been part and parcel to it myself! In them troubled times, Towns and whole Islands changed hands with such a rapid rate you didn't know where you was at from one minute to the next. The main tussle in the Caribbee was between the Spanish, English, French and Dutch. In the old days us Buccaneers roamed in thousands. The Freebooters had Fleets of their own, such as sailed under Morgan. The Portuguese dealt with their holdings in the Brazils, for the most part, and never gained no footing in the West Indies.

Despite all 'Appeals to the Little Stick', Pirates still had strong holds in and around the Spanish Lake. They operated from along the Eastern Seaboard, the Carolinas and such, clear across to the Antilles Islands and on down to Surinam. Most were Privateers sailing under Letters of Marque, which were just Licences issued to Ships o' one Nation by their Government, authorising 'em to attack and plunder shipping of another! Flint had a fistful, used to forge his own in case mishap and bluff were called for. Not that it mattered a Doit; a bona-fide Buccaneer turned black and looked just as ornamental swinging in chains as any low caste cow-killer without a Letter o' Mart. As Billy Bones often said: "Dead men don't bite, nor can they complain."

For most Land Lubbers, Pirate Plunder or 'Purchase' as we calls it, only comes in the form o' finger trickling Treasure: Doubloons, Moidores and Peeces of Eight. Well so it do, but there be other Booty besides hard cash or 'Specie' to give correction. Coined money in bulk was a rare thing barring Treasure Ships, you see, and those didn't happen by every day o' the week. They sailed in Flotillas, mostly, and were too strong for us to attack. No, Ship-mates, all that Gleams ain't Gold – as the saying goes. There were diamonds and ivory from the Guinea Coast, gold-dust too. The mines in Peru yielded silver that was smelted into Tortas. New Granada was rich in emeralds, while the oyster-beds around the Island of Margarita, off the coast of Venezuela, grew pearls by the bucket full.

Ships from the Old World brought all manner of merchandise to the New: Lyons silk and Valenciennes lace, Half-ankers of Schiedem, a Dutch liqueur, and Hollander Gin – Schnapps some calls it. The Spanish Nobility furnished their houses with the finest from Europe. Glass from Venice; satins from Florence; mirrors from Saint Gobain and furniture from London and Paris. We sometimes captured cargos of whale oil, bee's wax and great rolls of tobacco. There were bales of cochineal from New Spain and casks of indigo dye from India – all well worth clapping aboard for. Sacks of coffee and bags containing cocoa, tea and limes were always in high demand and fetched peak prices. Spanish Plate Ships leaving the Main were a goodly catch – Plate or Plata being pure bar-silver. We would shadow these rare Treasure convoys, providing they weren't chained together, in the hope of picking off a lame duck if it fell behind come the dark. I've a tale to tell about silver bricks later, I have, as 'ud make a Hindu holy man kick his sacred cow – shiver my sides!

Now all this wealth, sometimes amounting to more than a 'Great Gun', were about as much use as diamonds to a starving beggar in the desert until turned into real 'rhino' so's each man could collect his fair share, according to station. Our main hazard lay in finding a secure berth – somewhere we could relax and enjoy a fling ashore afore setting off to sea again to beat-up for more Prizes. Here, Flint proved himself to be priceless yet again. Him it was as knowed the best places to sell our Purchase for the best deal and fill our coffers to over-flowing. If ever a man put to sea better organised than James Flint, it must've been the Ark builder – blessed Noah hisself!

The chests containing our Blunt were kept in the Bread-Room, situated at the aft end of the hold. Now you Readers remember the large, padlocked wicker hamper that Flint and Billy transferred from the *Weasel* to *Walrus*, well, that was also housed there. Nobody knew what was in it except the Captain, the Mate, the Quarter-Master and Darby M'Graw. This matter was discussed among the Fo'c'sle Hands and finally a Deputation, led by Merry, confronted Flint.

"Your pardon, Sir," says George with a salute, "but according to fo'c'sle council, you stands in breach o' the rules."

"Why so?" asked Flint softly, his blue eyes glittering like glass.

"It states in your 'Articles', no secret to be kept from the Company. Yet you has a private possession in the Bread-Room! This crew wants in on it, Sir, as is our due!" demanded George amid nods and grunts of assent from the Deputation.

"Aah," sighed Flint, staring at each of their tight faces in turn. "Ye be in the right on it," replied he. "Follow me!"

One and all we trooped down onto the Orlop-Deck, where Flint paused above the hatch leading down into the hold. "As Captain of this Crew, I give ye leave, Mister Merry, to take whom ye please into the bread-room to see that which ye seek!" said he and stepped aside, giving Billy an evil grin.

Now I've a sixth sense that gets triggered off by deep matters of such moments and the hairs on my nape were setting my tarry queue all a-quiver. So instead of following the others, I sat me down on a biscuit barrel.

"Ain't you sallying forth below, Long John?" asked the Mate as Merry, Hands, Morgan and Anderson disappeared into the hold.

"Dinna ye be a wee bit curious, Barbecue?" added Flint with a sly gleam in his eye.

"Curiosity killed the cat, Cap'n!" replied I. "Reckon I'll lay-by a-while."

"Ah, John, John. Ain't ye the wise one," breathed the Big Buccaneer.

No sooner was the bobbing light from George Merry's glim lost in the dark depths of the hold, than Flint and Billy replaced the hatch-cover and sat upon it – the pair of 'em back to back and sniggering like simpletons. Flint pulled a heavy gold watch from his pocket and held it aloft to catch the lantern's light. "Any moment now, Bill," says he, still grinning.

The confused babble that broke out below conveyed one word – Panic! There came a clatter of trampling feet and a cry was followed by a splash as someone fell into the bilges. They came crashing up the steps in a mad rush and began hammering on the hatch-cover, yelling entreaties.

"Hark, Lads!" chucked Flint, cupping a hand to his ear in mockery of the mayhem below. "Do ye hear rats a-scuffling?"

Next instant, Flint and Billy, in company with the hatch-cover, were flung in the air and landed all a-heap as four wild-eyed bodies burst from the hold. They collapsed upon the deck, panting, trembling – their faces looking whiter than the Holy Ghost.

"By the powers, Cap'n, you as near done for the lot o' us along o' shock, look you," wheezed Morgan.

George Merry and Job Anderson just lay all flat-a-back gasping for air with their eyeballs rolling.

"A snake!" croaked Hands – him it was as were dripping wet. "Biggest serpent in all the world . . . curled in the bread-room . . . like . . . like a baby in a crib!"

"Aye, ye have just made the acquaintance of Samson," drawled Flint, picking hisself up off the deck. "There'll be nay pilfering o' purchase where he rules the roost!"

To be sure, no Seaman ventured below without Licence after those who saw it spread the word that Flint's Secret was an anaconda! Knowing that fifteen feet of coiled death lurked in the hold, ration parties seeking supplies insisted Samson was secured in the bread-room before going below. Even then, they demanded a double-rum issue as a caulker for carrying out what they insisted were Logged as: A Dangerous Duty Fit to Freeze the Mind and Cause a Severe Case of the Flux!"

Never the one to risk drifting onto a lee-shore, our Captain had three Havens. The first and main base was Nanny Town, built slap-bang in the very lap of those seeking to destroy us. Aye, mates, we were berthed in the British Colony o' Jamaica itself! You wouldn't look for to find a felon hiding in New-Gate disguised as a turn-key, now would'e? But I'll explain more about Nanny Town a little later.

Flint's second sanctuary was Paramaribo, located fifteen miles from the mouth of the Surinam River. Surinam, or Dutch Guiana as it came to be called, was first settled by the British, then fell to the Hollanders. Recaptured by the English, it was finally handed back to the Dutch in exchange for their Colony of 'New Amsterdam' on the Hudson River, which they renamed – 'New York'!

Paramaribo was populated by all manner o' People: English, Dutch, French, some Portugeeses, Negros, Sambos and Indians – even a few from Spanish descent. Everybody took to each other like a miser to money and one an' all prospered. Along the river-banks for sixty miles up-stream to Torarica were close on five hundred plantations with sugar works numbering around two score and ten. At Paramaribo we had a Fort to defend us from the marauding Spanish and English who plagued these waters – not to mention them blasted Buccaneers!

The Beauty of the Surinam River was manifold. First and foremost, you could sail straight up to Torarica. Flint's particular Crony, a Dutchman named De Groot – him as bought much of our Purchase – owned an Estate on the out-skirts of Paramaribo. The place were on par with a Palace, if somewhat topsy-turvy for my taste. He had marble statues in the garden and huge plants in the house. An' topping the stiffest yard-arm to nothing, him and Flint took tea in the blessed potting shed!

As to the country? Paradise it were – pure Paradise! The climate was soft as a babby's skin and healthy – why, you could spend a year running around like so many Sons of Adam and catch no more'n a sun-tan. Being below Latitude

10 Degrees North, we were spared the horror of hurricanes. Mind you, I been in storms at sea that lasted for days with pumps a-goin' non-stop, masts crashing by the board and a shrieking wind that sounded like a thousand banshees wailing over the end o' the world!

From the coast, for twenty miles inland, everywhere is low and flat, hardly rising above the high water mark. Beyond stretches of rich, heavy loam, brought down by the river's spate, ridges of sand sprinkled with shells showed where the coast-line was at in ancient times. Billy Bones collected half a dozen of these shells, curiously spotted they was, and he carried 'em around in his sea-chest for years! When I asked him why, he said: "The sea be in my blood, Barbecue, and when I be land-locked in some snug berth ashore, they gives me comfort o' nights. I sleeps with one alongside each lug and the sound of the sea lulls me to slumber."

The forests were filled with richly plumed birds and the lagoons had flocks of flamingos. I seen masses of orchids a-top of twelve foot stems; and in some lagoons there grew water-lilies with leaves six feet cross the beam. But amid all this splendour there was horror too, mates. Jaguars stalked the jungle at night – spotted death on four feet. Shoals of the vicious little Piranha fishes infested the river and basking on the mud-banks were black Cayman – huge creatures with teeth like tusks. Another horror was a weird type of eel found on the river bottom. Just to touch it could prove fatal, for some invisible strange force gave a jolt that rocked a body to its very bearings. The Indians were mortal a-feared of 'em and wouldn't go near even a dead un. Old De Groot, who had Books o' Knowledge by the ton, said it was due to 'Electrickery' or some such Mystic Power. Despite all the nasty things, I fell in love with the place at first sight and decided, then and there, that when I retired from the sea I'd end my days here.

But here I go again, blabbing on about this and that – tacking away from the main tale. I'll never make a blessed Story-Teller, me!

As to Refuge number three – more of a Work-House, it were, than a Rest-Home. It was here we did our repairs, careening and what-not. Dock-Yard duties, in a manner o' speaking. Skeleton Island lay ESE and by East, somewhere off the coast of Surinam and far from the main Trade Routes. Your pardon for not speaking more plain, but you'll know the long and the short of it at the stern of this story.

Shaped like a fat dragon standing up, Skeleton Island had a brace of land-locked harbours known as North and South Inlet. We used the southern berth, mostly, on account of strong currents that run northward along the west coast. Captain Kidd's Anchorage, Flint called it. Three Hills running south, all in line astern of each other, were named Fore, Main and Mizen in the manner of a ship's masts. On the centre and highest hill we always kept look-outs, to watch the surrounding seas for danger. Reason enough that all hands referred to it as the 'Spy-Glass'.

A previous crew who sailed with Flint, now 'retired' and living in the lap of luxury, according to Billy, had built a block-house near the southern anchorage, encircled by a stockade of sharpened stakes. Here it were, we dragged the guns ashore and mounted 'em around the block-house, facing all points of the compass in case of attack. Stocked up with rations and arms we was on par with the Tower of London for defence!

We used other natural harbours besides Skeleton Island, bearing in mind we needed to bream and careen the *Walrus*'s hull every three months to keep a light pair of heels. One such favourite place was Coxun's Hole at the east end of Cuba. Another was Old Providence, used by the Brethren of the Coast in Morgan's Day, lying a hundred and fifty miles from the Mosquito Shore of Nicaragua. If caught short in the Gulf o' Mexico, we'd hole-up in the Dry Tortugas or at Ten Thousand Islands off the west coast of Palm Key. Safe, snug berths they were, where we didn't have the worry of being laid aboard while our ship was in irons. The worst that could befall our crew was in taking a tumble when drunk and breaking a bone – if not our necks. Then there was always the risk o' getting your cake carved through a rupture among Mates when Out of Discipline, especially when rum tankards were topped full and tempers overflowed!

Now it was Flint's habit to bury accumulated Treasure. His reason was that should *Walrus* founder in a storm or maybe run aground and abandoned if hard pressed by the Royal Navy, then the Blunt wouldn't be lost. I had to agree with this sound insurance against losing all. Flint, Billy, Darby and Old McGinty already had a King's Ransom stashed away – buried on Skeleton Island. Darby M'Graw told me when drunk, but denied it when sober. Flash Dan warned me to keep a weather-eye on the Captain and his close cronies. He wouldn't say for why. The only answer he'd give me was: "Deep dealings, Long John my lad – deep dealings."

Buccaneering weren't all booze and tap-room brawls. By the powers, but I seen some black days at sea, I have. Battle, murder and a close-run from all quarters. That was the way of it when we clapped aboard the *Santa Rosario* fresh out from Caracas, bound for Port-au-Prince in Hispaniola and points west. A real close-run with 'The Reaper', that were, barring one other – shiver my sides!

CHAPTER XVIII

CLAPPING ABOARD!

We were cruising off the coast of Caracas, when, on the morning of the third day, there came a cry from the Crow's Nest: "DECK AHOY!" bawled our Main-Top Captain, Gypsy Fuller.

"HOLLOA!" shouted Billy Bones through cupped hands, confirming that we down below had heard him.

"SAIL-HO, BEFORE THE STARBOARD BEAM!" replied Fuller. "BEATING UP TO THE NOR' WEST!"

Flint and the Mate mounted the poop, each clamping a spy-glass to his eye, but as yet they could see nothing. Our intended prize was still below the horizon, you see, hid from us as were on deck. The wind was two points abaft the beam, northerly, and our course was ESE.

"Steer sou'east, Barbecue," ordered Flint. "And loose all sails."

"Aye, aye, Sir!" returned I. "Man the braces! Hands aloft! Lively there!"

We crammed on the canvas and our yards creaked as the crew hauled them round to cup the wind from the quarter. All was drawing alow and aloft and we stood on under a heavy press of sail – increasing speed at a rapid rate. Within minutes the stranger's top-sails hove into sight.

"Keep our canvas full-and-by, Job," says I to Anderson who was alongside the wheel opposite Mad Murdock.

We were lying windward of the stranger and had the weather-gage on her, while she was 'close-hauled', tacking or sailing zig-zag into the northern Trade Winds. Caution was our key word, until it were known what manner o' ship she be. Running a-tiptoe across the water we was, so to speak, ready to strike or flee.

Bearing down on her starboard bow, we soon identified her by the great scarlet and gold Maltese Cross emblazoned upon her fore-sail. Although she was frigate built, deep-waisted and what not, her structure fore an' aft had been altered to resemble a Galleon. She was launched as an Indiaman, right enough, but now the red and yellow striped Flag o' Spain fluttered from the mizen peek halliards.

"Hoist Spanish colours!" cried Flint, making a careful study of her, noting the number of guns. "We'll gammon 'em for the moment. Meantime – Bosun! Clear for Action!"

Pew's pipe trilled the order and our People became all a-bustle. In the same manner as a ship o' the Royal Navy, all items not necessary to fire the guns were stowed in the hold. Our Long Twelves were cast loose from their housing but not run-out, for to do so would give our game away. Half a League separated us when the Spaniard suddenly tacked and made to go-about. We none of us fathomed the Dons had got wind of our intentions by sighting our Tusked Totem. In all Spanish circles, unbeknown to us at the time, the Old Walrus berthed below the bowsprit was now as famous a figurehead for privateering on the High Seas as Dick Turpin's pock-marked features were for robbery on the High Toby.

Our presence promoted more'n a little panic among her crew. In going-about the manoeuvre was as clumsy as drunken gentry poling a punt on the blessed Thames. At one point she canted so far to leeward, the wind having broached her to, I reckoned she'd capsize on the next swell – 'Doing a Duck' to coin a Buccaneering phrase.

"Boil my blood!" roared Flint slapping his thigh. "Did ye ever see such a collection o' muddle-headed lubbers between wind and water!"

"Aye, her Capitano will be tearing at his wig and using some nice pickled language no doubt," sneered Pew.

"Now why should they about-ship and head back to port, I wonder? And us a-flying of a friendly flag too, so we are!" mused Flint.

"Solados be aboard, by thunder!" exclaimed Billy who still had the ship under close study.

I took a go of my glass and sure enough, I saw a score o' Musqueteers clambering up the ratlings to man all three Fighting Tops. Focusing on the high, curved taffarel I spyed the name '*Santa Rosario*', as was wrote below the ornamental scrolls. The gold lettering suddenly disappeared when twin balls o' smoke belched from her stern-chasers.

"So-ho!" says Flint. "They be ripe for mischief and intend to take a bite of us. I'll wager a Groat to a Golden Guinea there's riches in the offering ere we strike!"

"Aye Sir," agreed Billy. "She sits heavy enough for a Plate Ship, but we'll have a hard haul in broaching her and clapping aboard. The swabs have the sharpest edge on us in men and metal two-fold." The Mate glanced at Flint, his face tense. "Reckon we should veer off, Jim?"

"Hang-fire, Bill, hang-fire," replied the Captain. "Time enough to cut-and-run if the need arises. Until then, let's haul to the wind and see what Fate or Fortune blows our way."

What did blow our way gave me many a bad dream afterwards.

The Spaniard's random shots fetched nowhere near us and none saw any spume or spray to mark their fall. We stood on towards her weather-quarter with all our sails billowing like the wings of some great white bird. She caught the wind and crowded on every inch of canvas, but before an hour was out we were positioning to give battle.

"Run up Old Roger! Let go my Pennant o' no Quarter!" cried Flint, popping a wad of coca leaves into his hatch. "No point acting the play now. Master Gunner, report aft!"

"Israel Hands, lay aft!" squawked Old Phineas McGinty, looking like the resurrected aftermath of the Armada, dressed in the dented breast-plate and buckled morion of a Spanish Grandee who lived in Drake's Day. His cry was repeated for'ard.

Flint descended the steps o' the poop ladder, snapping his spy-glass shut. Beside the rail stanchions stood our little Negro nipper, Tiger Pip, clutching the Irish drum that O'Brien had made for him. His black face beaming with sweat and excitement, he grinned up at the Buccaneer.

"Is I to 'Beat t' Quarters' now, Capt'in?" asked he, flicking his pink tongue over his broad, dry lips.

"Aye, my son! Let her rip – loud and lively!"

Amid the 'Thumpety . . . thump! . . . Thumpety . . . thump! of Tiger Pip's drumming, our crew came alive. The Bosun's Party, under Black Dog, slid down the standing rigging after securing top-chains to the yards – happen that the support rope be shot away. Port lids were raised and the guns run-out, ready primed with their crews raring to have a go.

Our people wore all manner of clothes to give protection and aid at close-quarters. A firm favourite was sailcloth troons smeared thickly with pitch, together with sleeveless, ox-hide jerkins – some bearing studs of brass. They were tough enough to turn aside a cutlass cut or thrusting dirk. Flint cmerged from his cabin with Darby in tow, clad in a Brigandine. This article was a kind of quilted jacket as had iron plates sewn onto it. Welsh Bowmen wore 'em in Olden Days, according to Morgan, when they drubbed the Froggies at Crecy and Agincourt. Good for repelling musketry and cold steel, but against ball and bar-shot it would serve no better than a cook's pudding cloth!

Weapons we had a-plenty: Halberds; Pikes; Pole-Axes; Muskets and a few of the new, cut-down conversions called Musketoons – designed for use in the Cavalry. Fixed to the ship's bulwarks by a pintle were bell-barrelled

Blunderbusses that could reduce men to so much gruel at close range. All hands carried either a Dirk or Poignard and of course – Cutlasses. Most had at least a brace of Pistols slung about 'em. Some favoured French Swords; others used Spanish Sabres or Rapiers. These latter tools of ill office were apt to snap in a lay-man's hands as never learnt the noble art o' fencing. Few Buccaneers of my acquaintance were able to mince about using fancy footwork like a French Dancing Master to perform their butchery, but one who could and did was as deadly as a Fer-de-Lance when he cried: "Touché!" – Flash Dan the Doctor.

Flint's great, curved, clam-shell hilted Cutlass hung by a baldric looped over his right shoulder. From the left a bandolier of holsters supported two brace of heavy, large bored Pistols. Stuck in his belt in a sheath of patterned brass was a long dagger from the Malays called a Kriss. Wavy bladed, it was, with an ebony grip all intricately carved.

Some of our numbers were divided into 'Stink-Pot' parties. Their aim was to make smoke and cause confusion among the enemy. Others took on the role of grenadiers to throw 'Grenadoes'. These home-made bombs were rum bottles filled with powder that had a fast fusee attached in the neck. You had to look lively and get rid of it once the fuse was lit because it exploded within four or five seconds. To cut a longer fuse would only serve the swabs time enough to lob the blasted things back!

Flint was priming the pans on his pops, assisted by Darby M'Graw who held the powder flask, when Hands reported breathless and streaming with sweat: "Cap'n?" gasps he, knuckling his forehead in salute.

"See ye here, Israel," began the Buccaneer. "This enticing woman we be about to seize by the ears has sharp claws, I'm thinking. She has an entourage of Solados alow and aloft, eighteen pounders at her waist and mayhap a Grenadier or two tucked behind her Comb. When we close on her, clear those platforms ere they pepper us with all manner o' mischief. A few parcels of Langrage through her sails won't go amiss, but bring ye her sticks by the board if ye can reap such bounty," concluded Flint.

"Aye, Sir, and for our Bonus I've positioned a pair of Swivels on the Main-Top along o' Tom Morgan in charge. Lays a good gun, does Tom. Three goes of case-shot from them brace o' beauties be worth a score of Musqueteers in deck clearing," grinned the Gunner.

Flint made a brief inspection of the Gun-Deck, partnered by Billy, then turned his attention back to our Prize. "All's in order, Long John," he reported. "Bring us to close-quarters whenever ye be so minded."

Being, 'Master', it was my chore to position the *Walrus* so's our Guns could give the Dons a good drubbing alow and aloft, with as little damage and danger to ourselves as possible. The ideal situation for us was to cut in close across the ship's stern, then rake the whole length of her deck with a broadside – point blank. I veered *Walrus* to larboard, seeking plenty of sea room afore sweeping round onto the starboard tack. Our Seamen were all a pully-hauly at the braces as we bore down on the *Santa Rosario*'s larboard beam. From stem to stern she suddenly erupted smoke, spitting a red tongued broadside at us.

At two and a half cables length distance, moving fairly fast across our bows, she missed mostly, but scored some small success up for'ard. Like the French, Spanish Gunners tended to shoot high, firing on the upward roll. Holes appeared in the fore and main courses. Several Seamen cluing up the canvas, to put us under fighting sails, were swept from their horses by a mixture o' ball, bar and chain-shot. One unlucky lubber, minus both legs amidships, got hisself caught in the clue-garnets with an arm locked tight around a stirrup rope. There he dangled, mates, like a blessed Dancing Doll upon a wire, screaming and swaying while spattering all below him in a gory, red rain. There was some real fruity language coming down to us from the Gunners up for'ard, to be sure!

Our Sprit-Sail Yard was shot through, leaving a great gouge in the Jib-Boom. The sail itself sagged, flapping over our Tusked Protector, with its severed cordage trailing in the cut-water beneath the plunging prow. Bits that were blown off the Beak-Head showered flizzings over the Fo'c'sle. A Double-Headed-Angel skimmed the fore-mast, bounced off a cannon's breech and went whirling through two Gunners, reducing 'em to bundles o' raw, quivering meat. The mess were frightful, mates. Made me feel glad I had no part in swabbing parties. Put me clean off dinner, it did!

"Shrivel my Soul!" raged Pew. "Five good men gone below and the deck were only holy-stoned yesterday – blast their blood!"

The *Santa Rosario* held on course and so did we. Close to a cable's length away, Israel let fly with the larboard Bow-Chaser. Starboard of him, George Merry touched off its twin. Now there be 'gunners' and GUNNERS, but Israel Hands had what us artists call 'The Touch'. In all the years I sailed afore the mast, his match was never met with!

Splinters whirled away from the *Santa Rosario*'s main-mast. Along of the same moment, George Merry's parcel of Langrel scoured her mizen fighting-top. Sweeping through sails, rigging and men, it rendered to shreds all that lay before that deadly mixture of bars, nails, bolts, gravel and glass. The huge trunk o' the main sail jumped, tottered and split under the impact of Israel's well placed ball. Pushed by the pressure of wind and assisted by the weight of her canvass the whole mass fell for'ard, crashing across the larboard half of the fore yard-arm. Among the jumbled wreckage were the puppet figures of the Musqueteers and Top-Men. Some of 'em were flyers and gave a goodly display o' the acrobatics afore falling to their doom. Arms and legs all a-whirly, they was. Our lot cheered in the manner of Demented Demons, one rousing "Huzza!" following t'other.

Fists clenched, teeth bared in a terrible grin, Flint was enraptured. The destruction of anything Spanish was meat and drink to him. "Dance, ye Devil's Spawn!" shrieked he. "Dance and Die!"

I'd timed our turn to a point near perfection. Calculated to mere fathoms, it was, as we cut across the dead-water swirling in the cripple's wake. From fifty yards we engaged our larboard battery.

"FIRE AS YER GUNS BEAR!" cried Israel, his sharp eye scanning the Crews to see if all was closed-up and positioned proper.

Number One roared in response, double-shotted with ball. Numbers Two and Three discharged the same to shatter the Spaniard's stern. The remaining fourteen Long Toms were loaded along of various calling cards of ill office: Case, Grape and Star-Shot with a goodly go of Langrel for booster.

To make myself more plain, so's you Readers will know what I'm jawing about: 'Case-Shot' be musket balls parcelled in sailcloth. RN Gunners refer to it as 'Canister', because the bullets are contained in a cylindrical tin-box. 'Grape-Shot' consists of small balls, around half a pound in weight, packed and corded up in a thick canvas bag the same size as a cannon's bore. 'Star-Shot' is a combination of three balls, each attached to a separate bar and fastened on a link, much in the manner of keys on a ring. When fired the balls extend every which way, spinning same as the Spanish Bolas do. As to 'Langrel' or 'Langrage', if you be Gentry, this were a mixture of our own making. Being always short o' foundry ammunition we used all sorts of scrap, ranging from bits of chopped bar-iron and lead clippings to broken bottles.

This motley collection was now carving through the *Santa Rosario*'s ruptured stern-sheets, sweeping the length of her deck and clouting the crew for six, as they say in Cricket. Smoke and flame spat bravely back at us as both Stern-Chasers made a defiant reply. They barked but once, then fell to ruin amid a blast o' Grape and Langrel from Numbers Four and Five. Their shots passed either side of our main-mast, cutting a few cords of running rigging, but causing no great harm. The *Santa Rosario*'s aft section resembled inside an Irish pot-house after Saint Patrick's night. From Transom to Taffarel her whole stern was a-gape; windows, gallery, cove and counter – the lot were blowed to ruination.

With most of her sails in shreds and the wreckage that lay over her larboard bow acting as a sheet anchor, the *Santa Rosario* slowed to the point where she was more or less drifting. The wind, in bearing down upon our starboard side, pushed us beam on to her shattered stern.

"Helm hard-a-weather!" I hollered on seeing the Don's splintered taffarel looming above the smoke amidships.

Anderson and Mad Murdock spun the spokes of the great, double wheel and our bows swung to larboard, bringing the *Walrus*'s head nearer and nearer the *Santa Rosario*'s side. We struck her starboard gallery abaft our midships, right where I was stationed on the Quarter-Deck. Our head slewed round and crashed into the *Rosario*, level with her main-chains. The Grappling Parties, cheering their heads off, slung their hooks over the high bulwarks to ensnare our Prize and hold her close. Musketry from her Fore-Mast Fighting-Top began to splinter our deck. Two hands were hard hit and carried below to the surgeon. Then Tom Morgan's Swivels, situated on our own Main-Top, got the measure o' the Spanish Musqueteers with a double go of Case-Shot and sent 'em to say 'Hail' to 'Holy Mary'!

"Secure grapnels!" bawled Billy Bones.

Brandishing a pair of pistols, Flint leapt onto our bulwarks via the poop steps, nimble as a cat: "Grenadiers to the fore!" cried he above the din. "Stand-by, Boarders!"

To the accompaniment of Tiger Pip's drumming and a brace of musicians blowing conch-shell trumpets, along of Phineas McGinty the Old Quarter-Master, bashing a copper gong, our gang vapoured with a roar. Deserting all guns, the crews split into their respective parties. While our main force chanted war-cries and waved their weapons in defiance, clashing cutlasses, those armed with Stink-Pots and Grenadoes hurled them up and over onto the Don's deck, the spluttering fusees leaving streamers of smoke in their wake. Bang after bang added to the clamour and dense clouds of oily, black smoke poured from our Prize as if she were a-fire.

"Boarder's away!" bellowed Flint as soon as the bombs exploded.

The first party followed Flint and entered the *Rosario*'s gaping stern galleries. Billy Bones led the second assault. The *Santa Rosario*'s bulwarks being seven or eight feet above ours, Bill's bunch clapped aboard by sinking hatchets and pole-axes into the ship's side and using them as steps. Along of the crash in becoming locked together the *Walrus* was now on *Rosario*'s lee-side. This placed us in calmer water which made boarding her a bit more easy, not having a heavy swell to contend with. All hands swarmed up and through the gun-ports, while others clambered onto the chains. Here it were, mates, that the tide turned against us – so to speak. Near swamped and sank the lot o' us, so it did!

Unbeknownst to our people the Dons had retreated into 'Close-Quarters'. This strong barrier of thick timbers, loop-holed for Musketry, was thrown up across the fo'c'sle. In Drake's Day it was called the Fore or Forward Castle. That be where the word, 'Fo'c'sle' comes from. And that's what confronted Flint's Crew – a castle, bristling with fire-arms!

Because of the thick smoke swirling from the sulphur-soaked rags of our own shattered stink-pots, Bill's Gang couldn't see the fortifications. Our Broadside had caused ruination on a grand scale, right enough. The decks were strewn with dead and dying and several of the Big Guns were dismounted. Wreckage lay everywhere. Concealed amongst it were several small Caissons with fast fusees leading to the Barricade. These powder-filled chests were loaded with musket balls, nails and splinters.

Flint joined Bill's bunch. Both parties, puzzled by the absence of defenders, were still seeking someone to fight when the Dons fired their bombs. For a Booster they let go a withering blast of Musketry. In two ticks on the clock the *Walrus* lost a third of her Complement. Still reeling under this onslaught, our crew was, when some fifty Spaniards swarmed up from below decks and attacked from astern. At the same time, those in close-quarters charged from up for'ard. Caught like paper in a press, Flint's survivors were reduced to the fight o' their lives.

Pew was forward with his Mates, attending to the wreckage on the bowsprit. I were checking the compasses in the binnacle for damage when the caissons exploded. You can imagine our surprise, being as we thought the battle was more or less won.

"What in Blue Hades be happening, Job?" yelled I to Anderson in alarm as the volley of musketry drowned my voice.

Next came a great roar and clash of arms. The Bosun's Party paused on the fo'c'sle, mouths a-gape, as my two Timoneers sprang up off their knees after lashing the helm amidships to a deck ring.

"WE BE BOARDED!" screamed Anderson as a score of Spaniards, led by a tall, villainous looking Lieutenant, came leaping down from the bulwark onto our deck abaft the beam.

Armed with both sword and pistol the Officer locked his glims on me. "Strike your Devil's Flag, o buccaneering dog!" demanded he in perfect English. "Down on your knees and beg for Quarter!"

Just then Flint and the remnants of the crew fought their way back aboard in a tight bunch, jumping onto the fo'c'sle, our bow being level with the *Santa Rosario*'s mid-section. At that point Mad Murdock launched hisself at the Lieutenant, swinging his sabre. Distracted by the clamour up for'ard, the Don didn't have time to parry the blow with his tuck. Murdock's heavy blade lopped off his head in a single swipe. It rolled across the deck and came to rest against the aft hatch coaming. I swear to this same blessed day that his starboard glim winked at me!

My own mode of self preservation I placed on a brace of double-barrelled pistols made by Pettijean of London. Drawing both barkers from the deep pockets of my fine, red coat I swept back the cocks with the heel o' my hands – right and left. Firing right, left, left and right again, I triggered all four barrels into the bunched Spaniard's stunned, horrified faces. All my bullets drummed up more trade for Saint Peter.

"Cut and run, mates!" I cried and sprinted for the sanctuary of the Fo'c'sle to join Flint's Gang with Anderson hard on my heels.

I expected Murdock to follow us, but he weren't dubbed 'Mad' for nothing. He flung hisself into the Dons, swinging his big sabre in a frenzy of hate. Him and Flint were on par for Spaniard splitting – you may lay to that! With a cry of rage they closed around Mad Murdock like an angry swarm of hornets, stabbing, hacking and firing point-blank. Him as was made Mute by Papist Cruelty must have been dead on his feet, but he done in three more o' the swabs before he went down. Even after he fell they continued to belabour his twitching, blood-soaked body as if a-feared he might rise up again. By the time they had finished their butchery, me'n Job had joined Flint.

"By thunder, Barbecue!" exclaimed he to me. "Here be a narrow corner! Out-foxed us with close-quarters and a brace o' blasted caissons!"

Flint were hatless and bloody, the tails of his head-scarf caked in gore. His Brigandine had saved him from serious hurt. Three of the thin, iron plates were lead-smeared and buckled by bullets. He was peppered by bits and pieces in the arms and legs, mostly, with a chunk torn off the top of his left ear. Billy took a minor flesh-wound from a ball in his thigh; but Nick Nutt, the Leading Hand, collected splinters in his left elbow that locked the limb rigid for the rest of his life.

"Shiver me fin!" voiced One Arm McGinty, flapping his stump. "Did thee ever see such brisk boldness from the likes o' Mad Murdock!" The old QM's ancient armour looked to be more battered than before and was speckled with dark splashes of blood.

"Aye, Phineas. Many a good man has gone below board this day and we're next in line, I reckon," replied Billy Bones.

"Damnation take these Dago dogs!" grated Flint through his fearsome teeth.

Our crowd cut the for'ard grapnel lines and guarded the gap between *Walrus*'s Bows and the *Rosario*'s bulwarks with a row of Pikemen. Grouped about and below the fo'c'sle, we faced the Dons. Many of them still lined the Man-o'-War's sides. Those aboard us were packed in the waist like salted herrings in a barrel.

"Stand-by, lads, and steady!" roared Flint. "It'll be sink or swim for us all in two shakes of a shark's tail!"

"Engleeshmen! I would speak with your Capitano! Does he survive?"

Casting our eyes up to the *Santa Rosario*'s high side we saw this hunch-backed, bottle green coated figure, begrimed in powder smoke, with his hands cupped to his mouth. At first, I thought he was wearing a black cap, but then realised it was his hair smarmed down on his skull with pomade or some such sweet smelling bilge.

"Is it Quarter ye'd be wanting?" mocked Flint. "If so, strike ye yore Ancient and lively!"

Those among the Dons who were 'Linguisters' erupted into a great roar of laughter. I could now see the Spanish Captain's face clearly. Squat and swarthy, it was, with small piggy eyes and a brace of front teeth like those on our Tusked Totem. Leering at us, he was, and with large, pointed ears, looking like some over-sized mad rabbit!

"Ah, you Engleesh! Defeated, yet you remain undaunted! Bravo! But hear me now! Surrender and I will give you good quarter! Resist, and all who escape the sword shall hang from my yard-arms!"

"Play 'em for a time, Jim – keep 'em jawing!" hissed Billy Bones, thrusting his scarred face between me'n Flint. "Cast you a sly peek at the Poop an' cock a glim to the Main-Top."

Deliverance comes in many strange guises and until I rolled me weather-eye to the forementioned Stations, our plight appeared blacker than a Piccaninny playing in a tar-pot, so it did. Apart from me, my two Helmsmen and the Bosun's Party, who had remained aboard to care for the ship, there was Morgan's Gunners along o' Joe the Carib still aloft, while down below we had Flash Dan and his Loblolly Men, to attend the wounded, in company of Darby M'Graw and Ben Gunn's Carpenters. This hidden force had now sneaked top-side by way of the stern-sheet windows.

With half an eyeball on the Spanish Capitano, I watched the activity taking place upon the Poop. Between the stanchions. I could see the red waistcoat on the Doctor, the skinny, scarecrow figure of Ben Gunn and Tiger Pip's black, woolly head bobbing about. There were four Swivel Guns pintled to the quarter-rails, one either side and two facing for'ard with bodies hunched down behind them all.

"Your ship's figurehead is well known to us, Capitano Flynn," continued the hunch-backed Spaniard. "I, Don Claudio de Beaumont, shall be rewarded by the King himself! Long has your name been mentioned in the Court of His most Catholic Majesty!"

"Along of some right Royal Oaths, I'll wager," muttered Flint to the Mate.

"Look sharp, lads!" shouted Anderson as six Grenadoes trailing smoke arched from the Poop and fell amidships among the Spaniards crowding the waist. Before we could duck they exploded with a flash and a roar.

The blasts were puddened by the packed bodies that served as bolsters between us and the shell-shards, so we suffered no hurt. But it cleared the Dons off our deck like a giant cutlass swipe – the glass splinters from the rum-bottles scything through 'em right, left and centre. Some of those right next to the explosions were flung into the air, looking like rag-puppets savaged by hounds.

Flash Dan, still clad in the blood-stained apron that announced his trade, was on his feet in an instant yelling: "FIRE!"

As his Rapier descended, giving the signal, Six Swivels raked the Dons from alow and aloft with a mixture of Case-Shot and Langrel. Tom Morgan's Gunners then lobbed Grenadoes down onto the *Santa Rosario*'s deck. Pure Bedlam, it were! What with shots, shouts, bangs, screams and yells, I couldn't hear myself choke on the acrid powder fumes that wafted for'ard on the breeze.

"At 'em all hands – all hands!" cried Flint surging forward. He bounded onto the Poop at the head of our crowd, then together with Flash Dan and Billy beside him, he boarded the *Santa Rosario* and leapt into a tight little group of Officers – his cutlass swinging.

Of all the sea-fights I ever took part in, none surpassed this one for sheer butchery, by thunder! Our crowd, what was left of 'em, went crazy wild. More men were chopped down like that much pork, than ever I see since being bundled aboard a King's Ship. Cry Murder if you've a mind, but too much killing creams into a blood-lust. It don't matter a Doit, mates, whether you be a Prince blasting Widgeon on the Wing with a Fowling Piece or a Pauper chasing Rabbits in a hay-field with a Brick-Bat; when hot blood seeps into your eye 'tis only the killing that counts – you may lay to it! That was the way of it with us Pirates, hell-bent on releasing Papist Souls from their mortal coil.

Flint, Bones, Flash Dan, Hands and Me were all cut and thrust along of both cutlass and dagger. Old QM McGinty swung a Broad-Sword, regardless of who was in the way. Joe the Carib dealt out death from the Main-Top, using his bow to fire five-foot arrows. When he ran out of shafts he turned to his Blow-Gun along of deadly, red plumed Darts. Each sliver of bamboo was dipped in Curare – a poison as causes palsy. I saw Morgan and his Gunners slide down the standing rigging, cutlasses clamped in their teeth, nigh on breaking their necks to share in the slaughter. Foxy-faced Darby M'Graw favoured several brace of pistols that he fired from the *Rosario*'s Poop-Deck, while Tiger Pip done the loading of 'em. Alongside was Batty Ben Gunn, brandishing a Musketoon. But our 'Chippy' fired more abuse from abaft the fighting than musket balls into it! Black Dog killed any way he could, preferably from behind. And then there was Pew, shiver my sides! Still clutching the Pole-axe he'd been clearing away wreckage with, he were swinging it for all he was worth – like a butcher's boy chopping scrag!

Flint was terrifying to behold. Pointed teeth bared, framed by blue tinged lips, eyeballs bulging and with that hideous shrunken head swinging on his heaving chest like a pendulum, he cut and carved his way through men – reducing them to mince-meat with his great, curved cutlass.

As for Flash Dan! Dancing about skewering Dons left, right and centre on his Long Rapier. His Sword-Play was pure poetry to watch, not that I had time to make much of an audience. Bawling out: "NEXT!" he was, in-between thrusts, and laughing his head off – and him a man of medicine who partook of the Hippocratic Oath too!

Our casualty rate continued as well, mind! The Spaniards fought back as ferocious as any Madagascar Savage I ever met with. Some of us received only minor cuts and contusions. I saw a Cooper's Mate get his nose knocked askew by a musket butt. Took a slight hurt myself in the foot, along of a sabre jab. And to top it all, Black Dog lost two talons!

The way of it were this: Black Dog stood facing three Dons. Ankle deep in purple gore and hard pressed, he was hemmed in under the Poop-steps. Me'n Hands, it was, who rescued and delivered him from certain destruction. Just as we struck to level the odds, the centre assailant aimed a blow which the Bosun's Mate parried with his poignard. We saw the long dagger fall to the deck. The sabre swipe had severed its lower quillon, together with the third and fourth fingers on Black Dog's left hand. With a snarl that matched his name the Bosun's Mate avenged hisself, thrusting his cutlass point through the throat of the Man who had maimed him.

"*Madre de Dios*! Quarter, Señors! Quarter!"

"Begorrah, they've struck, ship-mates!" bawled O'Brien.

"The day's our! We've won, we have!" cackled Ben Gunn dancing about on the Poop, clapping his hands in glee as the Spanish Flag came fluttering down.

"Shrivel my soul," panted Pew, resting on the long handle of his dripping Pole-axe. "If any swab ever tells me that Buccaneers don't earn their bread, I'll split 'em from Peek to Kelson!"

CHAPTER XIX

SERPENTS, SHARKS AND SILVER BARS!

Barring the three Officers and two fat Friars, the captured Crew were battened down below in their for'ard hold. Only a pitiful few survived our onslaught, maybe two score from close on three hundred. Our own state weren't much better, mind. Reduced to forty-eight hands, we was, along of half as many sore wounded. And us what sailed with a hundred and fifty-five! I was bemoaning the loss o' Mad Murdock, a Trump of a Timoneer, when the Quarter-Master dispersed my blues by winking and saying: "Bear up, John. Dead men compensate the living for the loss of their company. Look on it this way, my son. The less as survives an engagement, then the more Blunt there is to share!"

Now I calls that logical thinking, to be sure, and felt much brighter.

While Old McGinty supervised the ransacking of the *Santa Rosario*, the Spanish Captain was conducted aboard by Billy. Apart from a twisted spine, we now saw that the poor swab had a shrivelled leg. He limped at the head of his Officers wearing a built up boot. Flanked by the Priests, he held his country's Colours over his left arm and carried a cup-hilted Rapier resting on his right, sheathed, it were, with the pommel extended towards Flint and the case a-laying across the crook of his elbow.

"You may have my Ship, my Flag and my Sword, Capitano Flynn. Small good will they serve you!" leered he, bowing and offering the articles.

As he spoke, his face reminded me of a cornered stoat ready to strike. I weren't far off from the mark, neither! Flint's mood was as black as Judge Jeffreys' favourite cap. He spat on the Flag and dashed it to the deck, stamping upon it. Snatching the sword he slammed it against my chest. His impatient gesture for me to take it near knocked me over. Little did we know that the Don's Tuck was to be the saving of us all.

"There!" cried Flint, grinding the Flag under the heel of his sea-boot, standing on Ceremony so to speak. "That's what I think o' ye and yore blasted, accursed ancient! Cost me a good crew, so ye have, and afore this day is done I'll . . ."

Dumbfounded, we watched as the Spaniard turned his deformed back on the raging Buccaneer and faced his Officers. Was it Cool Courage or Demented Foolery? I thought Flint would strike him down then and there. Instead, he stood with bulging eyeballs, while his face became a horrible mottled mauve colour – bloating fit to burst. Opening and closing his mouth, he was, like a stranded guppy.

"Señors," began the Spanish Captain, speaking calmly in his native tongue, addressing his Officers grouped beside the aft-hatchway, "I thank you for your Services. Give me this, your last Loyalty, and trust in the Blessed Virgin to care for our Souls." Rounding on Flint he snapped: "As for you and your dogs – long may they howl at the Devil in Hell!"

The Friars solemnly crossed 'emselves.

We were still recoiling from this Curse when the Deformed Don stamped on Flint's foot with his clubbed boot and drawing what we took to be a small pistol from his pocket, he nipped over the hatch coaming. For a cripple he matched the speed of a striking barracouta, by thunder! Afore we could say: 'Jack Sprat!' he'd disappeared below decks, slamming the sliding cover shut. The Dons immediately stationed 'emselves over the lid and adopted the stance of prize-fighters ready for a bout o' fisticuffs. The two Friars dropped to their knees and began to blabber Prayers in Latin as Flint, hobbling in short circles and near potty with pain, vented his rage on our gaping crew.

"Dinna stand there like a bunch o' dead-eyed zombies!" he roared, shaking both fists. "After the swab and bring him to book!"

"Beware, mates! Armed, he is, with a pocket-pistol!" warned Black Dog, nursing the blood-stained scarf that was wrapped around his ruined left hand.

"Nay, matey. 'Twere a tinder-lighter. Only a tinder-lighter. I see it plain as print, I did," said Ben Gunn. "Small cause for alarm."

The Carpenter's words left us cold as pack-ice to a man. Realisation flooded Flint's face, turning it from mauve to a ghastly shade of grey. "Small cause for alarm?" shrieked he. "Boil my blood! If the mannikin snaps a flasher in the magazine . . ." His voice trailed off.

We all turned to the colour of chalk now that the Hunch-Back's intentions became horribly clear. His aim was to blow up the Ship! In a solid body we hurled ourselves upon the hatch defenders and laid 'em alongside in a brace of shakes. During the scuffle both Friars were knocked flying. Pew cursed as he tore a finger-nail in wrenching the hatch open.

"Down! Down!" urged the First Mate, pushing me against Black Dog, who in turn tumbled upon the Bosun and caused more pickled language.

"Broach the swap to!" bawled Flint from the rear. "Cut the cur down afore he blows us into Tooth-Picks and Purgatory!"

Bunched together we clattered below, passing through the lower-deck and on down into the very bowls of *Walrus*. Pew were leading. I followed Black Dog. Behind me I could hear Billy snorting through his nose, blowing for breath. In rear of him came Morgan, Hands and Merry. Dark and gloomy, it was, below decks. Since clearing for action, only such glims as were essential to see where you were at remained alight. No more than a faint glimmer for guidance really. All else was in deep shadow, black as pitch. We crowded onto the Orlop-Deck, sweating, gasping and stooped near double in five foot o' head room. A score or more wounded men lay sprawled on the bare, overlapping planks awaiting the attentions of Flash Dan who was still top-side.

"Avast, ship-mates," called a feeble voice. "Be you seeking a crippled, midge of a man in a gold-laced coat?" enquired he.

Ignoring various pleas for water, we peered into the weak light cast from one of two lanterns and saw this fellow propped against the corner of a knee. He had a blood-soaked bandage around his head and by the waxy sheen on his face, I reckoned him to be 'Writing his Will'.

"Which way is he gone?" demanded Pew, seizing the man by his baldric belt and shaking him cruel. "Did he go below?"

"Aye, Bosun . . . aye. Peg-Leg Lawson took a'ter 'im . . . along . . . along o' my dirk," gasped the dying gunner.

"Ship's Cook?" exclaimed Morgan. "Why, Pete ain't capable o' killing a pig in a manger!"

"Aye, nobody minds him!" added Merry.

"One cripple to clap aboard another – bah!" snapped Billy Bones. "Follow me and lively!" He paused on the first step leading into the hold, peering into the darkness below. "Hand me a glim, Barbecue," ordered he.

I unhooked a lantern from its becket and passed it to Pew, who gave it to the First Mate. We descended the hold with our hearts in our mouths, as the saying goes, half expecting each foot-fall to be our last. Foul air filled our lungs and the only sound was the gentle slap of bilge-water. Fear held us in his clammy grip for another reason, for this was Samson's domain. Now although Flint's anaconda was safely secured in the bread-room, guarding the Blunt and other valuables, just the mere thought of being in close-quarters along o' those sinister, silky coils made my skin crawl. Israel Hands voiced my very thoughts from the middle of our mob.

"If Samson shows up, I'm shifting top-side," declared the Gunner.

"If we don't look sharp and bring the Hunch-Back t' heel, we'll all be going top-side – double damn quick!" snarled Pew.

Billy suddenly halted. The rest of us crowded close around him. In the faint glow given off by the tin-lined light-room adjoining the Magazine, we saw

Pete Lawson the Cook sprawled on his back with a dirk protruding from his chest. His peg-leg was broken, smashed by a kick from the Don's clubbed-boot, I shouldn't wonder. We advanced a few feet and froze. Beyond the Magazine's open door-way, framed against the light that shone through the thick pane of glass partitioning the glim from the powder, stood the Spanish Captain. Tinder-lighter in one hand and a bag of mealed priming powder in the other, he glanced up, his face livid with hate and determination. No longer did his appearance smack of a mad rabbit. More akin to 'Old Nick' as he stood there preparing to send us down to the pit!

"One spark, mates!" hissed Billy from between clenched teeth. "One spark and we'll be making our excuses to Saint Peter!"

I've witnessed some heart stopping situations in my time, I have, but few came closer to causing apoplexy than this un. I was still carrying the Cripple's Rapier. Almost without thinking on it I unsheathed the tuck and holding it close against the cup, flung it same as savages do a dart. The heavy, triangular blade flashed across the intervening ten feet like a streak o' quick-silver and struck the swab in the right fore-arm. The point hit bone and bounced out, but the shock of it caused the Spaniard to drop both bag and lighter. Topping my cry of triumph came one of pain. The Hunch-Back scurried out of the Magazine streaming blood like a stuck pig and swerving hard-a-port, he disappeared into the darkness aft.

Heavy foot-falls, clumping down the steps behind us, announced our Captain's arrival in company of Darby M'Graw, Ben Gunn and the Doctor. "That crippled Dago cur has done for the Cook!" snapped Flint as he eyed the empty Magazine with relief flooding his face. He sat down on a spare tier of cable that lay faked alongside the shot-locker. Grimacing from the pain in his foot, he asked: "Where's the Deformed Dog at?"

"Long John wounded him in the wing with his own sword, Sir," replied Pew, tipping his forelock in salute. "Hiding somewhere astern, he is."

"Throwed it like a blessed Black Man spearing beef, by thunder!" grinned Black Dog, showing his stained and broken teeth.

"Saved the lot of us so he did, see! Crew, ship, prize an' all. Mark you that, Cap'n Flint!" said Morgan.

"He's as good as a Talisman aboard this 'ere ship, is Barbecue," added Hands, looking all solemn like a Chaplain delivering of a Sermon.

"*In toto*," murmured Flash Dan and gave me a glance that bordered on brotherly love. The Doctor was indeed a deep-minded man, to be sure.

"Ah," sighed Flint, well pleased. "I knew that, soon as I clapped eyes on him. I'll call a Fo'c'sle Council later and propose Long John be given a cut over and above his Dividend for this day's work." He winced again, holding his injured foot that rested on his left knee. "Damme, Doctor. My toes feels to be broke. Oblige me and take a look to . . ."

For a second time the Spanish Captain interrupted Flint; only now it was a scream that caused him to clue-up his words, not insolence. This long, continuous shriek o' mortal terror rolled and echoed throughout the hold.

Flint leapt to his feet, his injured toes forgotten. The eleven of us stood transfixed, as if by Enchantment, while the colour drained from our faces. Abruptly, the shriek dropped off as though the victim were suddenly gagged.

"Dear Heart! But will someone tell me wot that were?" croaked Ben Gunn through ashen lips, grovelling all over Darby M'Graw.

"Sounds like oor hump-backed friend has met with something that he dinna be too keen on," said Flint smiling around at us.

"Samson, by thunder!" cried Merry.

"That spikes it for me! 'Bout-ship, mates – I'm off!" said Israel Hands and started for the steps.

"Avast ye, Master Gunner! Dinna ye go a-deserting of yore post!" bawled Flint. "Samson ain't free. I only lets him out to hunt the hold. Yonder Dago ventured where he should'na. Give me the glim, Bill."

Flint took the lantern and limped aft. We all followed, filing along the floor timbers set athwart the keel, treading on each other's heels for fear of being abandoned in the dark. Water slopped on either side as we passed casks, cases, boxes and bales. Rats scurried from our tramping feet, plopping into the bilges.

The bread-room, now transformed into our 'Treasure House' – known as 'The Coffers Cave' – lay astern between the Sail and Fish-Rooms. We saw that the bolt had been drawn back and a foetid smell hung heavy in the air already reeking of bilge, hemp and tar. Flint raised the glim to the grill, but it was too dark to see inside. Without hesitation he opened the door and entered. Us faint hearts crowded the doorway and peered in. Those in front drew back against thems as pushed from behind. Me'n Hands were the two coves doing the main pushing!

The Serpent's stench became overpowering. Near stupefied us, it did. Stank worse than Black Dog's stockings do on a hot day! At first all we saw were two blood-red rubies, glowing like hot coals in a grate. Then, after Flint lifted the lantern higher, the rubies became a pair o' eyes – glittering and unwinking. From among the Money Chests, piled Plata and the tall, curved Elephant's Tusks stacked and roped to the bulkhead, the snake crooked its huge, triangular shaped head and hissed murderously. Its large, forked tongue flickered in and out – tasting our smell according to what Flint told us.

We all of us stared, mesmerised. Caught in those crushing coils, there was little to be seen of the Spaniard. Patches of green and gold marked his coat with occasional white streaks where his breeks were. His crippled foot jutted grotesquely from one end of this mottled mass o' deadly meat, while only a tuft of pomaded black hair was visible at the other. Between the thick, centre coils a hand stuck out – topped by a ruffled, lace cuff. The fingers were curved like claws, bloated and turning black.

"See how its tail anchors t'that Elephant's Tooth, look you," said Tom Morgan in an awed whisper.

"Sammy has to do that to get a good squeeze on his dinner, don't he, Capt'in?" said the Steward.

"Aye, Darby. That there tusk of ivory is his lever," explained Flint. "All constrictors need to anchor their tail to get sufficient purchase in order to crush their prey, afore they swallows it."

"You mean t'say Samson'll devour the Don?" asked Ben Gunn aghast.

"That he will, Chippy. Coat, breeks, clubbed boot an' all. When Sam has digested his rations, in a fortnight or so, he'll regurgitate the clothes, boots and bones. That wakes him up, ye ken, and tells him 'tis time to restock his larder. H'ain't Nature wonderful!" sighed Flint, viewing his creature with the look o' love that a Mother has for her Babe.

"He'll find rats poor fare after this feast, I'm thinking," says I, feeling ready to break bulk along o' my ballast. "I just hope he don't develop a taste for Human Truffles, Cap'n!"

"Oh calamity! Oh cruelty!" wailed Ben Gunn. He put both hands to his head, mumbled: "Oh dear," and fainted clean away.

Darby M'Graw caught him before he hit the deck. Our chuckles were short-lived when we had to carry the Carpenter top-side, so's fresh air could revive him. Cursed something wicked, we did! I thought our little party in the hold would conclude the Horrors and Tragedies for one day, but I was sadly mistaken, mates, by a long sea mile!

"*Salve!*" greeted Flash Dan on reaching the Orlop-Deck, where the wounded awaited his attention. *"Ars longa, vita brevis!"* grinned he. Setting his sword aside, he picked up a long bladed, surgeon's knife and addressed the four, blood-stained Loblolly Boys: "Right, my fine fellows, bring on the first Lucky Lad for doctor's block!" ordered the Master Surgeon, indicating to the canvas covered chests that served for the operating table, then cheerfully began to whet the knife-blade on the sole of his boot.

Thunder! Was I glad to clear that hell-hole before he started to carve-up, but you could hear the screams throughout the entire ship!

Our dead lay in neat rows, ready for decent burial as befitted Brave Brethren. Normally it was Mad Murdock's duty as Sail-Maker to sew 'em into their hammocks, weighted with a ball, but since he'd gone below hisself the task fell to Ben Gunn's Carpenters and the Riggers under Shamus O'Brien – as prime a pair of Idiots as ever set sail! They flung the Spanish bodies overboard without ceremony. Soon, scores o' corpses were bobbing about in the swell around both ships.

"Tiburons!" came the cry. "Hundreds of 'em!"

One glance showed the surrounding sea swarming with Sharks. Packs of 'em, drawn by the scent of blood, came from all points. There were all manner o' species: Makos, Tigers, Hammer-Heads and a huge White Devil of a sort I had never seen before. Pew referred to it by a Spanish name: '*El Blanco Muerte*' – 'The White Death!' Israel called it a 'Hayen' and knew it well from his whaling days.

"That there fish," says the Gunner to me, "be so ferocious it's been seen to attack small boats – cutters, canoes and the like."

The dead bodies were pulled below or ripped asunder on the surface, the same as 'Flogger Finch' was – you mind Flogger? I make mention of it because there among the Pack, larger and more savage than when last I see him, was Clipped Fin. No mistaking the chunk missing from his pennon.

Flint's face glowed – glowed it did, mates, for we were afloat in a boiling sea of Spanish Blood. 'The Plank! Bring aft the Black Plank! Grab those swabs!" shrieked he, pointing at the cowering prisoners who had tried to thwart our pursuit of their Mad Captain.

The three Officers were quickly seized, being already bound.

"What of these Papist Monks, Sir?" asked Pew.

"Them G-d D----d Friars above any!" returned Flint with a blasphemous oath. "Those dogs inflict more cruelty in the name o' the Church, God and Goodness than Barbarians do in Honest Mischief!"

Many a West Indian was flayed, garrotted or burnt alive at the stake to save his Soul. If that be Religion and God's Mercy, well then, give me Pew's Philosophy any day: "Rhino, Rum and Baccy with a Good Run-Ashore, a Buxom Strumpet to sit on your knee by way o' variation and Amen to it!"

The Officers went by the board for starters. Prodded with Pikes along the plank that was lashed in the gangway gap of the bulwarks, they cried and pleaded afore being bounced off into the turbulent briny where snapping jaws awaited them. Frantic with fear, first one Friar, then t'other was bundled out onto the board. The second swab sat astride the end and faced us with tears streaming down his fat cheeks. He clamped his legs around the plank and refused all efforts to push him off.

Joe the Carib loaded a dart into his blow-gun and put the red plumed barb dead centre o' the Friar's plump thigh. In a few seconds, after the poison had caused palsy, so that his face went slack and he was panting for breath, a boarding pike tumbled him into the sea. The Sharks pounced upon him, quicker than a Jew flinging hisself at a penny on a cobble-stone. And then, shiver my sides, those Fiendish Fishes turned and tore at each other in a Frenzy o' Feeding!

For the Record, along of those o' you who are interested in plain facts, I ought to clear the decks regarding the truth about us Pirates forcing prisoners to 'Walk the Plank'. Now out of all the Buccaneers o' my day and even those I never met with, Blackbeard, Kidd and Long Ben Avery, only one 'sweated' prisoners by means of the Board. Flint, shipmates – James Flint Esquire were that Genteel!

The *Santa Rosario* was sunk along of her human cargo – wounded and captive alike. Even Flint his own self was sick of the slaughter. A slow match leading into the Magazine done the trick a treat and we watched her blow up. We couldn't care for 'em and mercy for Spaniards weren't part nor parcel of Flint's code o' conduct. Besides, we had ourselves to watch out for and Dead Men don't Tell Tales!

"There, but for Barbecue, goes us, mates," says Billy all solemn.

"I reckon we showed Mercy," said Flint gruffly, looking old and tired. "Better being blown to bits, than torn apart by gnashing teeth!"

Our dead had yet to be disposed of. Men who slip their moorings in the Tropics tend to ripen rather quickly, you see. After promising a bonus to Ben Gunn's burial party to keep sewing, assisted by O'Brien and his Riggers, us Officers trooped aft for respite and rum in Flint's cabin, while the Crew, what remained of 'em, went for'ard for a dose o' the same. My first drink went down the hatch without touching the sides!

Flint was well pleased with the Inventory handed him by QM McGinty. Piled upon our deck was: Fifty great Rolls of Tobacco steeped in Rum; Boxes of Loaf Sugar; Ten Cerons of Wax; Six Hundred Bottles of Cognac; and Four Hundred Ingots o' rough Silver. In addition there were the Officers' Chests containing such knick-knacks as Gold Watches, Jewelled Brooches, Silks and Money. The clothes were placed in the QM's Common Chest.

A very handsome pair of Juan Pigrav Pistols, bearing gold escutcheons, with silver butts and trigger guards went to Gypsy Fuller. Him it was who first sighted the sail of our Prize and in accordance along of our Rules, the finest brace of Barkers found aboard her were his. The silly lubber went and sold 'em to Billy Bones for Twenty Pound. Twenty Pound, mind – I'd have payed Forty!

Flint considered the departed Capitano's 'Despatch Box' to be the greatest Prize by far. Pew found this lead-lined article among the wreckage in the Great Cabin. Within it was a canvas envelope containing a Document. All sealed in wax and pink ribbon, it were. Now this here Paper gave details concerning all manner o' Monies, amounting to the toon of Three Hundred and Fifty Thousand

Pounds! All this Blunt had been salvaged from a brace of wrecks off Sarasota and was due to be shipped from that Port at Palm Key by the *Santa Rosario*, three months hence. The ship we had sunk was to have called first at Vera Cruz, there to refit, afore picking up the Rhino. Needless to mention, mates, who planned to collect it now!

A knock came on the cabin door and Ben Gunn tottered to our table with an eyeball in each Watch, as the saying goes, one above and one below and both Bloodshot! "All hands is tucked up snug, Sir, ready to abandon ship," stated our Carpenter and began giggling, suspiciously the worst for drink.

"Benjamin Gunn!" said Flint fiercely. "Tell me true now. Have ye been a boozing on dooty? And ye who be in charge along o' the Dead!"

"Only a dram, Captain. Toasting the newly departed, we was. Shamus the Rigger nicked a few bottle o' brandy to wet our pipes with. Thirsty work sewing on deck, says me, and us wi' no awning, asking your pardon, Sir," replied the Chippy, wriggling like an eel and looking coy.

"What's this?" snapped Billy. "O'Brien breaking bulk, by thunder!"

Flint flapped his hand, waving aside the Mate's anger. "We all needed a caulker after this day's doings, especially those a-serving of mess-mates who have Crossed over the Bar into the tranquil waters of Eternity. Small harm done, Bill."

Small harm done indeed! The whole blessed Burial Party was half-seas-over on pilfered Cognac. Empty bottles were strewn everywhere and the result proved to be on par with the Black Death for pure disaster!

We gathered all solemn on deck, standing two by two alongside the Dear Departed, while Flint quoted from the 'Book of Books': "Man that is Born of Woman liveth but for a short time and is cut down like a Flower . . ." I remember looking around me and thinking: 'We got a right bunch o' Nose-Gays here.' Mind you, we all smelt rather high, along of the perfume from the Dead. Flint concluded with a mixture of his own verse: "Ashes to Earth and Earth to Dust, if the Good Lord will-na have ye – then the Devil must!"

After he was done, Israel Hands passed along the starboard battery and touched off a Thirteen Gun Salute in final farewell. Unlucky for some, you might say! To the trilling o' Bosun Pew's silver call, we lifted our charges and gave 'em 'Jonah's Toss'. Time and again we lifted the canvas-wrapped corpses, stacked like cord-wood upon the deck, and heaved seventy-eight of our former crew over the side. Sank like stones, they did, being weighted as they was – and how! In lifting the feet of the last man me'n Morgan were handling, I felt the weights to be square-shaped.

"What ballast did you burden 'em with, Ben?" I asked. "Did you use bar-iron instead o' ball?"

"Nay, Mister Silver," replied he, well pleased. "Seeing as we're short on shot, and seeing we has an abundance of spare bricks, I used them. I'm a saving soul, I am."

My blood ran cold; Billy's eyeballs bulged from his head; while Black Dog and Pew both near turned the colour o' white-wash.

"Spare bricks! Spare bricks!" repeated the Bosun, sounding the same as my Old Parrot. "Spare bricks o' what?" he demanded and began furiously puffing on his pipe, drawing the smoke deep into his lungs by way of comfort to sooth taut nerves.

"Why, the spare lead bricks just newly shipped aboard," beamed Ben.

A weird, gargling noise came from Pew as he bit through his pipe-stem. The smoke inside him blocked his breathing and he fell to his knees, coughing and choking with Black Dog pounding his back.

The rest of us never so much as moved a muscle. We just stood gaping at Ben Gunn with our jaw-bone on our boots. Then, as if propelled by some silent, inner signal, we all rushed to where the plunder was piled. Smashed wooden boxes and a few scattered Ingots were all that remained of the Silver Wealth we had paid such a high price for.

"You chuckle-headed numbskull! Who in Hades told you the blasted Tortas be lead bricks?" roared Billy on the verge of having apoplexy.

"Him there! O'Brien it were, Mister Bones!" squawked the Carpenter and turned the colour of tallow.

The drink drained from the Rigger's face. "Oi t'ought it were lead, I did, bein' weighty an' all," concluded the rank Irelander, scratching his balding pate and looking about as intelligent as a Pauper running Parliament.

"I'M GOING TO KILL 'EM! I'M GOING TO CUT 'EM UP, AN INCH AT A TIME, AND FEED 'EM TO THE FISHES!"

This demented shriek came from Pew who drew his dagger and started towards the quaking Carpenter. Teeth bared, his yellowish greeny-grey eyes bulging and burning in his head, his lank, red hair framed the face of a fiend that twitched with uncontrollable rage and hate. It took the combined efforts of Black Dog, Morgan, Merry, Hands and Big Job Anderson to restrain him, while all the time he pleaded with them. "Just one little stab, mates! Just one little cut!" begged our Bosun as they dragged him below to where the Doctor gave him a soothing potion of rum and laudanum.

Meantime, Ben Gunn had shot up the rigging, fast as a rocket-flare fired from a mortar, to perch like a monkey on the main-mast cross-trees. Took over an hour to coax him back down.

"Sink me for a lime sucking lubber," sighed Billy and sat down weakly upon a bale for fear he might keel over. "If brains was Plata, O'Brien and Ben couldn't muster enough to forge a blasted pinhead."

There came a deep, rich chuckle from behind us and we turned to see Flint standing there with his Bible still clutched under his arm. "Boil my blood and fall on!" exclaimed he, grinning around at us. "If this here situation dinna give the lie to the fact that a Mon canna take his Money with him, I'll take up pig-farming by way of a living – ye ken that!"

Throwing back his head the Big Buccaneer roared with laughter. Killing Spaniards was all that mattered to him. The Wealth we amassed was just a carrot he used to dangle in the face of us donkeys, so we would follow him and do his bidding.

That's how those who died in stealing the Blunt came to collect the lion's share and carry it to the grave. Israel Hands and Shamus O'Brien braced themselves several times for dry blows, until Flint swore to slit the ears and nose on him who struck first. Our mood remained as sullen as winter, bound for Nanny Town. There were some of the Crew all for pitching the whole burial party over the side, along of the departed, but we were short-handed enough.

Old Phineas McGinty's logic summed it square: "Wot's sunk be sunk, shipmates. None can make nor mend and we'd only place ourselves in harm's way, falling together by the ears. Think towards Sarasota, lads. In a few weeks from now, we'll all be rolling in Rhino. Aye, mates – three hundred and fifty thousand pounds worth!"

But an awful lot was to happen to both Ship and Crew ere we laid our grubby hands on that Blunt. Some of us were destined to be changed men for all that remained of our time. Several of our present number would never live to see it. Two of our Staunch Company in particular wouldn't see the Blunt. One, because he got buried and the other because he ended up blind!

All hands were needed to sail the ship; even Flint took a turn at the helm. With a fair quartering wind, along of a full spread of canvas, we covered the seven hundred and fifty miles back to our base in Jamaica in just over a week. The dimness of a false dawn found us anchored off the mouth of the Rio Grande. We made our signal to those on look-out ashore, hoisting two lanterns aloft on the cross-jack yard, and when the answering wink of light assured us all was well, we lowered boats and warped the *Walrus* up-stream into a snug berth among towering trunks of red mangroves.

CHAPTER XX

NANNY TOWN!

Nanny town originated from slaves set free by the Spanish in the 1650s, boosted by runaways from English Plantations after they mutinied in 1690. Their Leader was Joe the Carib's father, Cudjoe, a big Coromantee slave from the Guinea Coast. Carijo had spent most of his life living with his Mother's people, since his Father, after raising Cain in Clarendon and escaping to the Spanish Main, returned to take charge and lead the runaways in Revolt.

Flint bore a great compassion for slaves, having been one hisself. There were a few English among 'em too, both men and women. These were known as 'Poor Whites', people who had slipped their cable after being sold into bondage because of debt back in England – transported for being poor! Ahh, Rule Britannia! The White Community called them 'Red Shanks'. Despised by the rich, the same as the poor are any place, some sought sanctuary in Nanny Town when eventually released by their owners. The Red Shanks played a brave part in our private world. They spied for Cudjoe and acted as go-betweens in Barter with the surrounding towns and settlements. Gypsy Fuller had married one – a big, buxom oyster wench from Billingsgate. She set up as landlady of a pot-house that became the Headquarters of our Crew when we were berthed in the Blue Mountains.

Set apart from all others, Cudjoe's Community came to be called 'Maroons'. To be 'Marooned', mates, was a Fate worse than Death itself. It was an old pirate practice from way back. We used it to punish any of the Brotherhood who deserved to be laid aside. Left alone on a deserted island with maybe a bottle of water, one small-arm plus a little powder and shot, most who were handed such a sentence died raving mad – if they didn't put a ball through their own brains first!

Situated on a thousand foot bluff in the Blue Mountains, twenty-five miles NSE of Kingston, surrounded by thick forest and swamps, Nanny Town was indeed 'marooned', but safe from attack as the Bank of England – or so we supposed at the time! When the *Walrus* was safely hidden in one of the many Tributaries of the Rio Grande, the Maroons arrived with mules. By mid-morning the wounded, along of our Purchase, were all transported nine hundred feet up the Blue Mountains into Nanny Town. And a rough, hard climb we had of it to be sure, but better aching legs than an aching neck – stretched beneath a gibbet-cum-yard-arm!

No Conquering Legion returning in triumph to Rome received a warmer welcome. Laughing girls, all bright and gay in coloured dresses, bombarded us with flowers, while cheering children ran alongside our mule-train clapping their hands in delight. Cudjoe greeted each of us with open arms. His show of affection for his son, Joe the Carib, together with Flint, would have shamed a Papist slobbering over the Pope! Except for a sprinkle of salt and pepper in his curly thatch, this strong, squat, ex-Coromantee slave showed no sign that he was past sixty. Ageless he was, like our Ancient Quarter-Master. While he and Flint conferred over the unloading and stowage of the plunder, we were served cool tankards of chowder beer by a smiling mixture of Sambo and Negro women. Draped garlands of flowers around our necks, they did, and gave a bonus to some o' us whose luck was at the Peak.

Here it was that Charlotte Eleanor first entered my sinful life. After giving me my nosegay and beer, Cap'n Flint being perched as usual upon my shoulder, received a juicy chunk of pine-apple. And then, by thunder, this Buxom Beauty kissed my grubby cheek and ran away laughing. My heart went dot-and-carry-one, hammering from between my ears. My mind's eye can still capture that first sight of her as she skipped off. Her dark eyes and pearly teeth were all a-sparkle, her black face radiant. Aye, radiant and shining same as a sunbeam with her woolly head done up in a blue, speckled bandanna. Built like a Man-o'-War, she were, broad on the beam with all points rounded in the right quarters! I felt as if I was standing barefoot in feathers – shiver my sides.

Being hot, tired and dirty, feeling somewhat out of salts, we all took a well needed soothing bath in a cool, mountain stream – a rarity for us Buccaneers. Why, even Black Dog made a splash. And if ever a Mortal Seaman needed dousing down that day, it were me – and you may lay to it! After changing into a clean shift of rigging we shone like new pins, one an' all. Looked smart as paint, we did, ready for the evening's festivities.

Surrounded by jungle-covered mountains on three sides with the nine hundred foot fall off on t'other, the town was well protected against tempest or attack. The buildings, a mixture of adobe bricks and timber, roofed with palmetto, were set in the Spanish style around a main Plaza. Neat and clean they were too – a far cry from the likes of Providence, Port Royal, Tortuga and other buccaneering bases of old. This Maroon community was self-sufficient in all things. There was a tannery and a tailor. A sugar mill for the making of rum. Market stalls sold meat, fruit, fish and vegetables. And for colourful contrast they had a blacksmith who was white, alongside a baker dark as pitch! There were three taverns, our favourite being Joan Fuller's. That was where us Officers boarded; Flint's wardroom, it were, in a manner of speaking.

That this here Town were 'Lawless', I'll allow, with few Rules and Regulations to govern it. But this wild, freebooter system worked a treat. Here, there were no profiteering politicians playing the people for their own ends. Why, I'll sign my affy-davy there's more corruption and dark doings in places as be run by proper Parliament. Look ye to London Town. Thicker with foot-pads and felons than fleas on a cur-dog in high summer, so it is!

At dusk we gathered in the Plaza, seated at long tables piled high with fare fit for Royalty. The mainstay of the Maroons was barbecued pork, yams and plantains; but in our honour they had laid on fathoms of mouth watering fancies. Seeing that when our Purchase was sold most of the money would flow back to them, they could afford to be generous. Having palates honed to the taste of salt beef and ship's biscuit for so long, you can imagine with what relish we attacked the following:

Boiled chicken. Roast suckling pig covered in a sauce made from their brains along with nutmeg, sage and salt, all cooked in Claret wine. We had stewed eels; pork collops; young goats with puddings of blood and thyme packed in their bellies. There was veal and cauliflower; green peas and larded ducks, well seasoned with oranges, lemons and lymes. Huge pies contained minced tongue and tripe. There were pewter platters of lobster, sole and sturgeon. Bowls brimming with anchovies and olives, almond cheese-cakes and custards. And roasting on spits set over a long fire in the centre of the Plaza – four oxen. Enough food to feed the five thousands, thinks you, but all this wasn't just for us. There were close on three hundred people partaking in the Feast.

Our wounded wanted for nothing. Berthed snug and secure in gaudy, Indian hammocks they had pretty Negresses to fetch and carry anything their heart desired and to fan them cool. A female hand on a fevered brow can work wonders – as well I know. But for the skill and careful nursing of our Doctor, Flash Dan, many who now lay enjoying being pampered would have been under hatches. We had wine by the butt; beer by the barrel; rum and brandy by the bottle. Nanny Town was the nearest us Buccaneers would ever come to reaching Heaven, I reckon!

The Spanish Lake, in my day, was a melting-pot for all People: Mulattos were created by a Negro and European union; Quadroons came from Mulattos and White parents; Sambos were the offspring of Negros and Caribs, while Negros and Spanish Indians produced the Cholos. A rum blend of humanity, to be sure! For gaiety and colour this mixture, collectively called the Maroons, made a livelier picture than the combined brushes o' Rembrandt or Hogarth could ever have done. The flowered waist-coats, ruffled shirts and finely laced, bright plumed hats of the men-folk matched the billowing, multi-coloured petty-coats on the women as they bobbed, weaved and whirled together in a wild dance to hollow log drumming. This man-made race showed no shame in being tainted by either whitewash or tar-brush. Proud, they were, proud and beautiful in belonging to Nature's children. And I was proud and privileged to be part and parcel of 'em, seeing as I took one to wife. But there I goes again, over-stepping the Story!

The Maroons created a unique form of entertainment, found nowhere else in all the World. They calls it: 'The Limbo'! Now it ain't so much a dance – more of a contest. Two notched stakes, driven in the sand about two yards apart, support a pole that be wrapped in rags soaked in turpentine and set a-fire. The idea is for each dancer to pass beneath the Flaming Bar with only the sole or sides of the foot allowed contact along o' the deck. After each pass, the marker is lowered a notch. If anybody dislodges the Bar or loses their balance, then apart from getting slightly singed, they be out of the game.

There are few who can match the rhythm and grace of a Darkie when it comes to dancing – you may lay to that! 'Tis the throb of drums stirred into their blood over the centuries that gives 'em such flavour, I reckon. The men wore only their open-kneed breeches, while the women, shiver my liver, stripped to a loin cloth or long strings o' skirted beads belted about their waist. By the powers, but we saw some Bold, Beautiful Sights as would blast the eyeballs off a Bishop!

Flames from the cook-fires reflected a mixture of black, brown and dusty skins as the dancers shimmied and shook, twisting their shoulders and limbs in perfect time to the drumming. They moved forward, crab-like in column, bending their knees and opening their legs wide on approaching the Flaming Bar. Leaned over backwards, they did, to such a degree you'd think Newton's Law would have 'em fall flat on their backs. Many did, until the last one left, who passed under the lowest mark, was declared the winner and rewarded. A young Mulatto girl wriggled her way through a space of eighteen inches to win.

Our crowd sat bewitched and boggle-eyed. Silent as sleeping mice, they were, in staring at the raw-skinned spectacle o' the dancing wenches. Jim Flint and Billy Bones leaned so far forward, I expected 'em to fall off the blessed bench at any moment – and our First Mate snorting through his nose like a grampus. Pew's leering countenance wore the look of a first-rate lecher. Black Dog sat with his left arm in a sling, along of his finger stumps now neatly parcelled and tarred, and bit clean through the stem of his clay-pipe. There was Ben Gunn absentmindedly licking his lips, savouring some of the beer that Israel Hands was spilling over his head. The Master Gunner stood behind him – mesmerised. Even our little Tiger Pip, who served at table filling tankards, poured a whole jug of ale into one pot as he stood with his mouth a-gape and eyes like saucers – and him not yet spliced into his teens, sink me for a Sinner!

Bright eyed and laughing, my Charlotte swished her beaded skirt every time she passed, moving her hips like poetry in rolling her beam-ends at me. She came to grief early, being a point or two on the large side. Near choked on my custard tart while watching her! When she came and sat on my lap I gave her a gold chain for consolation, seeing she had suffered a slight burn to starboard. I took away the sting with a soothing smear o' butter. Tit for tat, she made me a present of two small gold earrings. I wear 'em to this same day. Pierced my lugs then and there, along of her own hands and a red-hot needle. Not that I felt any pain, mind! Smelt like a flower garden, she did, and her skin were as cool and as soft and as smooth as silk and . . . and . . .

I'd best hang fire here, mates, afore I crosses me nib and puts a blob o' blots all over this here page of me copy-book. My old quill be quivering too much from the memory of it, you see!

Rough and uncouth as we were, the Ladies of Colour cottoned to our Crew like barnacles to a hull. Female company was a rare luxury for us and we tended to mind our manners in currying their favours. Billy Bones was looking mellow enough to melt, sitting there with his arm draped over the smooth, bare shoulders of a dusty skinned Quadroon. His thick veined, sinewy fore-arm bore several old tattoos: 'Here's Luck', 'A Fair Wind', and 'Billy Bones His Fancy', were all wrote in neat print. Darby M'Graw was just putting the finishing touches to a fourth on his bicep. It showed a picture of a man dangling from a gibbet. Darby branded Bill's flesh by means of a bamboo splinter dipped in a blue dye. Pew was an interested spectator, in between fawning over a fat Negress. And even Flint appeared near normal with a pretty poppet perched on each knee. We treated those women like Queens and they in turn rendered many a service to us: washing clothes, mending 'em, cooking and doing this, that and the other, but mainly Cooking and The Other! Even Black Dog found a doe-eyed wanton to darn his socks! Now that, mates, be – 'True Love'!

Our Purchase was sold by Public Auction. After Cudjoe's runners spread the word, wealthy merchants and plantation owners travelled miles to make a dishonest dollar. Their blood had caused no stain in the stealing of it and they ran no risk of swinging – so much for 'Respectability'!

Flint and Phineas McGinty handled the share-out, seated in Joan Fuller's tap-room. Pew and Billy stood behind them, policing the proceedings, so to speak, acting the role of 'Master-At-Arms'. Each crew member, in answer to his name being called by the QM, would approach the table with a cheery, "Aye, Sir!" and salute. McGinty, squinting through a pair of square rimmed spectacles, read off the man's score from a ledger, while Flint counted out the amount due from the Guineas, Doubloons and Peeces of Eight that gleamed in neat piles before him.

Some received more – some less. As in Article Bound, us Officers were paid a percentage in accordance to our station. The Captain, First Mate, Quarter-Master and the Doctor each collected Two Shares of a prize. The Sailing Master (Me) along with the Boatswain, Gunner and Carpenter got One and One Half Shares. All other Officers got One Share and a Quarter.

The Cooper's Mate, nick-named 'Port Tack', since his nose was smashed askew in the fight, and a tall long boned, yellow-haired lubber called Allardyce tried to cause a grumble among mates. They wanted those who were responsible for burying the bar silver with the dead, to forfeit their shares. The Fo'c'sle hands, however, voted 'em down. Our Carpenter was a favourite butt among the Company and O'Brien, according to Israel, was only: 'A poor Irish bog-hopper, born without benefit o' brains!' Ben Gunn screwed hisself into a blue funk in case he was tipped 'The Black Spot'. That be a Summons, ship-mates, and can mean anything from Banishment to Marooning – or even Death!

"I smell trouble brewing in that Nasee quarter," stated Flint. None of us then knew just how firm his words were to be spliced.

The wounded also collected over and above their Common Cut. Their Lawful Compensation for the loss of a limb or to be crippled by some other rupture was 800 Dollars. A Joint was worth: 400. But an Eye was priced at: 1,000! Money from public stock paid for lesser hurts proportionally. The loss of Black Dog's two talons netted him a hundred dollars, while Billy Bones received five and twenty for the ball that Flash Dan dug out of his thigh. My gashed foot fetched four stitches, but Rhino wise it weren't worth a Groat. I did, however, get a reward of a Hundred Pound from the Public Purse for skewering the Hunch-Back Captain and saving the ship – along with all our lives.

Red was the rose in our Nanny Town Garden, as the saying is; but along o' roses you get thorns. News of an Ill Wind which was blowing a mass of briars our way first fetched us on the boozy breath of two Merchants who had lingered for the last pickings of our plunder. Noon, it was, and I was sat in the shady cool of Cudjoe's summer house, partaking of tea and a pipe in company o' Flint, QM McGinty, Billy Bones, our host and the two Merchants.

It weren't a proper tea-party, not like the Gentry has it. Not with Cudjoe spiking the pot with rum, Flint dunking coca leaves in his cup, McGinty blowing down the tea-pot's spout to clear a blockage, and Billy slurping his brew from the blessed saucer. But we was Posh for the standard o' them parts, mind! Drinking out of real Chinee Porcelain we was, shipped all the way from K'ang Hai along o' matching milk-jug and saucers. Billy busted his!

Pleasanter surroundings you wouldn't look for to find in all the wide Caribbee. Why, the Coromantee's garden might have been landscaped by Capability Brown hisself, what with its rockeries, fish-ponds, water-falls and bright bunches of sweet, smelly flowers. The town lay quiet under a hot sun. Most of our Crew were still a-slumber sleeping off a wild night's revelry that had continued into the early hours.

"'Tis no jest, Gentlemen," says the first Merchant, a podgy cove called Duckett, well dressed and streaming sweat. "Two Regiments of Foot, mostly Regulars, newly transported from Gibraltar. I hear the Authorities have also brought in trackers from as far afield as the Mosquito Coast."

"None better for man-hunting on all the Main," stated the second Merchant, Wade by name, nodding his gaunt napper.

Cudjoe's big, white teeth gleamed like tombstones. "Ah, Man," grinned he. "I bin fightin' Red-Coats since b'fore the turn of the cen'ury. Aye, close on forty year a-gone. We Maroons is stuck in the British craw an' they can't spit us out, nohow. Moskito bloodhounds or no!"

"A certain Captain Stoddart has other ideas," continued Duckett, mopping his fat face with a large bandanna. "He commands a newly formed force known as 'Rangers', assisted by a Company of armed, trustworthy slaves."

"Indeed, yes. The Confidential Black Shot, is what they are called. And to whet their appetites they have the promise of a ten pound bounty, payable on each Maroon's head they bring in," added Wade with an aloof, all-knowing air that I for one found irksome.

"I dinna much care for the tune of this," remarked Flint, thoughtfully rolling his quid of coca leaves. "Blunt be a mighty powerful booster to a head-hunter's ambition."

"Top of the morning, Cap'n!" called out Ben Gunn, peering over the wall. "I thought seeing on how Mister Silver has taken such a shine to Miss Charlotte, her as serves your table, he might like to know she's hard-pressed at this same moment, along of the evil attentions o' Port Tack!"

"Where at?" cried I, jumping up in such haste I overturned my chair and caused Billy to drop his saucer.

"Gypsy's Patch – where else? You going to trim his lamp, Long John?" asked the Carpenter eagerly.

"Trim it?" I roared. "I'll bring his blasted shutter down so 'ard, it'll snuff the swab's light – permanent!"

Clearing the wall as if it wasn't there, I raced up the alley, tore across the

Plaza and burst into the bar like a Furicano. Gypsy was still a-bed upstairs and Joan was at market. The Cooper's Mate was grappled alongside Charlotte, watched by Allardyce who sat lolling and leering drunkenly in his chair.

I saw at a glance that my Negress needed no assistance from me. Port Tack was on his knees with his arms locked about my Beloved's waist. He was so drunk that, but for holding onto her, he'd have fallen flat on his nasee mug. Charlotte had drubbed one of his glims closed, skinned her sweet knuckles against his teeth, and was now giving him a thick-ear. Screwing it, she were, as if winding a clock, like my big sister done on me when I were a cheeky younker – and it don't half make your head hum!

But the fact that he had clapped his foul hands aboard my Beauty, her being as good as a man's own wife already, made blind rage my master for the moment. I drew my hanger and would have split him from pate to wind-pipe had Flint not come a-running in at the head o' the others.

"Avast, Barbecue! Stay ye yore hand! No cold killing!" cried he. "The dog ain't even armed!"

Now to kill a fellow Buccaneer in a fair fight, except as laid down under the Articles for Duelling, was bad enough. But to strike him down undefended along of a foul stroke – Death was the only sentence any crew could give. Considering the future course Port Tack was to steer, for others besides himself, it would have been in the common interest to have laid him low then and there. Instead, I contented myself with a flat-o'-cutlass-blow that sprawled him senseless at Charlotte's trim feet.

"You, Allardyce! Haul this lubber back to his berth!" ordered Billy Bones. "Ben, you bear a hand!"

"And tell the dog, when he comes to, if he ever so much as touches the foot-prints o' this dear, sweet girl again, I'll see 'im stood ankle deep in his own purple innards! Tell 'im to steer well clear of my Intended! You tell the swab that, by thunder!" I shouted after them.

There now, I'd gone and said it. Let the cat clean out the bag, I had. Charlotte looked at me in amazement. They all did. Then her pretty, black face broke into a smile fit to dazzle the sun itself.

"Why, John," says she, all coy. "I never knowed we was betrothed. I thank you, kind Suh," and she gave me a curtsy on par with a Duchess stubbing a toe to German George.

I felt like Royalty at that moment, mind!

"Long John Silver, ye be the most close-hauled, tight-lipped Rover I ever sailed alongside of!" boomed Flint. "Stab me if ye ain't! Look to him, lads! Turned redder than my Pennant o' No Quarter!"

"What be a-miss, mates?" yawned Gypsy Fuller from a-top the stairs, still dressed in his night-shirt and tassled cap.

"Charlotte's a Miss, but not for long, man," grinned Cudjoe. "She'n Barbecue is a-goin' to git spliced!"

"Shiver me fin, mess-mates," moaned Old McGinty with a sad shake of his head. "White Doves don't nest with Blackbirds, 'taint in nature, and you can't cook fish alongside meat, my son!" says he to me.

But we were well used to the Old Stander and his grumbling, so nobody minded him. Flint bellied us up to the Bar and sat my Intended a-top on it. Gypsy poured measures all round, 'On the house,' and Flint proposed a Toast to the future Mister and Missus John Samuel Silver.

Our Wedding was set for Sunday and Flint were to officiate – him having the same powers as Chaplain, being a Sea Captain an' all. Meantime, we had us a roistering two days in which the hands performed all manner o' roguery along of high jinx. Spent pounds as if they was pennies, while boozing fit to bust. Fortunes were won and lost in gaming at cards or dice. Cock-fights were popular too. Some lubbers simply throwed their Rhino away, Shamus O'Brien paid a gay young wanton three hundred Dollars to see her dance naked upon a barrel. By the powers, I'd have danced in the raw upon a barrel for that kind of Blunt – you may lay to it! And Ben Gunn, shiver my sides, played Chuck Farthin with blessed Doubloons – Doubloons, mind! Ah, much was the Booty, stained with blood, won in an hour of clapping aboard, then once ashore, lost in a moment of high passion for either a doxy or a pair o' dice!

Drunken fights were common place. A spilt drink, a wrong card or arguments over the favours of someone's Flash Packet – thems were the main causes. None suffered serious mischief, although the Doctor's needle never stopped in stitching split chins and chops. They boozed and brawled, gambled and danced, an' a right Royal Time was had by one and all!

As for myself: I never wasted good money o' mine. Weren't much the one for gambling, brawling nor dancing neither. I only attended around two Country Hops in my entire young days, but I enjoy watching others make merry, mind. Charlotte Eleanor loved to dance, being a Darkie, while I was content to just sit back alongside a full tankard and admire cargos. For many, this merry gathering of the ungodly was to be their last fling above board come Sunrise!

I'd slung my hammock alongside Charlotte's on Gypsy Fuller's balcony, it being cooler than the stuffy room listening to Billy Bones snoring his head off next door. Just on cock-crow I was surfacing from a deep sleep, my mouth dry from too much Brandy and with an urgent need to visit 'The Temple of Cloacina', when a dull explosion echoed in my brain. At first I paid it no mind. Up at 'Gun-Fire' was always my habit while in Port, until I remembered we were anchored in no road awaiting on a harbour to open. No morning gun was fired in Nanny Town! The next blast blew me clean out of bed as half the Balcony disappeared in swirling dust, smoke and flying palm fronds. Landed smack a-top o' my Beloved, I did!

"John Silver," murmured she, slipping her arms around my neck, her silky voice still drugged by drink and sleep. "You be a dandy man and right cuddly, but we ain't wed yet. You is jumping the gun, Suh."

"Guns is poppin', to be sure! But mine ain't even cocked, Missy!" I replied, jumping into my boots as conch-shell trumpets began their mournful bellow of alarm.

Three big bangs followed in succession, a broadside you might say, and a great mushroom of smoke and flour geysered up amid fluttering Palmetto thatch from the bakery opposite. Then I saw red fingers o' fire licking at the remains of our roof. Charlotte came wide awake, her big eyes rolling like a brace of tennis balls.

"Oh, John!" she cried. "Is the earth quaking?"

"Attack! Attack! Stand t' yer Arms – all hands!" squawked Old McGinty from the square below. Rushing about, he was, clad in a striped night-shirt, breast-plate and morion – brandishing his broad-sword.

"Out, lads! Show a leg there and lively!" bawled Billy Bones from within the Tavern whose fronded roof was now fiercely ablaze.

"Budge, you snivelling skulks!" came Pew's nasal snarl for a booster to get some of the Crew members moving who were berthed in a front bedroom.

"Me britches, mates! Where's me britches?" wailed Ben Gunn.

Doors slammed open to the tune of shouts and tramping feet. With no time even to collect my coat from the press, I grabbed my Parrot, Cutlass and Pistols; then seizing my Popsy's trembling hand, I bounded down the stairs dragging her astern. Joan and Gypsy Fuller were in the bar-parlour stuffing money and clothes into a parfleche. Flint sat athwart an iron-bound strong-box, pulling on a sea-boot, calmly listening to Joe the Carib's excited jabber as he relayed his father's instructions.

"Fadder, him take peoples to Cock-Pit Country. Red-Coat an' Black Shots come! Plenty many! Fadder tell me, tell you sail t' Black Ribber. He say, him send word along o' brudders at Accompong!" blurted the Maroon Leader's son, standing there holding a musket and his blow-gun with a quiver full of five-foot arrows and his beloved bow slung across his broad back.

"Can ye no muster me an extra dozen men, Joe, for to help warp out the *Walrus*?" asked Flint, slipping a baldric belt over his shoulder.

"Most Men's along o' wife and picc'ninny. No leave 'em. Many dead. Many little bit dead," returned Joe grimly.

Flint swore a low oath, then, on spying me, he said: "Barbecue, when we reaches the ship, along of all hands, muster me a Pulling Party for to man the sweeps!"

Billy burst through the door with Darby M'Graw and the Q M in tow – the latter still wearing his night-shirt and armour. "Time for us t' cut and run, Jim! There be Infantry and Irreg'lars pouring down the North slope!" reported the First Mate.

"How in Hades they got Artillery a-top that there mountain, beats me plain it do, Capt'in. Growed blessed wings, I reckon!" gasped M'Graw.

"Doctor Hunter be wanting stretcher parties for the wounded, Sir!" piped the QM. He stood with his Broad-Sword resting upon his shoulder, looking like Cervantes's *Don Quixote*.

"No time! Any as canna move under his own wind will have ta remain becalmed and take a chance along of the Red-Coats and Jack Ketch!" came Flint's curt reply. "If we lose the ship, we lose all – including oor Lives!"

I turned back to Charlotte and found her missing. None saw where she went. At that point a shell caught us amidships and the deck-head caved in. A beam crashed across the bar, nearly braining Darby. Another partly blocked the doorway. The room filled with plaster-dust and the acrid stench of powder smoke. Blinded and coughing we all stumbled outside in Flint's wake, him and Billy clearing the way along of hauling the strong-box between them.

"'Urry up 'Usband! Don't be draggin' yer stern at a time like this!" urged Joan Fuller, a former Billingsgate oyster wench, deported and indentured for stealing a cod with which to feed an ailing Mother.

"Sharp's the word, Wife," grinned Gypsy cheerfully, stumbling under the bulging Parfleche. "My oh my, but ain't it warm t' day!"

I was frantic to find Charlotte. Glancing to all points, I were, when Tiger Pip rushed around the corner and near knocked me flat a-back. "You seen my missus, younker?" cried I, seizing him by the scruff.

"No, suh, Mister Silver, I ain't!" replied he, clutching his treasured Irish Drum in one hand and a Brass Trumpet in t'other. Turning to Flint, he asked: "Is you a-wantin' me to blow Retreat, Capt'in?"

"Save ye yore breath, my son," growled the Buccaneer. "The only cove as be blowing a horn around here is Gabriel!"

The Tavern's palmetto roof was now a roaring inferno, along with most of Nanny Town. I was on the verge o' turning myself inside-out when, to the amazement of us all, Charlotte appeared in the pot-house doorway. Clutched in her hand was the buckskin money-bag I'd placed under my pillow for safe keeping.

"By thunder, Girl!" cried I. "Risking life and limb to save Long John's Fist! You're a bold, Black Beauty o' a Blade, to be sure!"

"We shall need money to marry, John. What with new clothes to buy and a ring to pay for. Then I shall have to purchase . . ."

The tavern roof collapsed with a crash amid a shower of sparks, cutting off her clotpoll chatter. Only a woman could talk of such things at such a time – you may lay to it!

"Com'on, Duckie!" says Joan Fuller, seizing her hand, and we all raced after the crew, streaming towards the defile that marked the dizzy pathway down to the mangroves where *Walrus* lay berthed.

We passed some pitiful sights in crossing the Plaza. Men, women, aye and little children too, lay huddled in heaps or were sprawled among the scattered baggage they had tried to salvage. From the Heights that came to be called 'Stoddart's Mountain', in memory of him who was bombarding us, those blasted nine-pounders kept banging away, showering the town in case-shot and shell. Spurts of dust, caused by striking musket-balls, were popping all over the Square. Everywhere was shrouded in smoke, covering us from sight of the Enemy. A great pall of it hung above Nanny Town, billowing blackly against the blue sky.

Charlotte Eleanor broke free of Joan to snatch a squalling waif from its dead Mother's arms. None of our crew were killed, but two more joined the walking wounded who were being helped along by staunch mess-mates. Random shots were what got 'em, I reckon. Mixed up among our crowd were several Maroons and the two Merchants – Messrs Duckett and Wade.

We trod a nightmare journey down that narrow path with a sheer fall-off to starboard. And a right raggle-taggle crew we looked in descending it. Flint and Billy were still hauling the strong-box between 'em. Ben Gunn was clad in just his shirt and drawers. Some were bare foot, a few only partly clothed, but all were armed. Capping the scene was the sight of Charlotte bringing up astern with a bawling mite in her arms – an infant not yet weaned.

I mind the rout for this main reason, for I was made aware of just how all a-back are those who have suffered and survived amputation. There was this poor cove on a crutch, his right foot gone, trying his best to keep an even keel on that treacherous slope, when his timber leg suddenly slid to starboard. Over balanced on the brink, he did, and fell screaming into the mangroves five hundred feet below. 'Better off dead,' thought I, 'than to be a cripple begging for bread!' But I was to change my tune, mates, because after panting up *Walrus*'s gang-board, along o' Charlotte, the next time I trod on terra firma again, I myself would be minus five toes!

"What's this? Petty-coats and babbys!" cried Old McGinty as we stepped on deck. "You can't allow it, Cap'n Flint! 'Tain't in Articles and any lubber knows that women aboard Tall Ships only brings bad luck!"

"Stow yer yap, yer old goat! Less yer care t' try and give me Jonah's Toss!" retorted Joan Fuller and seizing the brim of the QM's morion, she jammed it down over his eyes.

"Belay ye yore greetin, Quarter-Master. I'd ship a hundred petty-coats to help pull the sweeps. Aye, and a parcel of Piccaninnies too, sink my Soul!" replied Flint. "Stab me, but ain't this a Frosty Friday!"

"Friday?" queried McGinty, pushing his Helmet back up so he could see. He quickly calculated on his fingers and his wrinkled, brown old face turned grey. "Oh, shiver me fin!" wailed he. "You can't sail this day, Cap'n – not t'day! 'Tis Friday the Black Thirteen!"

Flint hisself went pale at this, we all did, but he quickly bore up: "If we dinna set sail now we'll no sail at all, 'cepting locked below in oor own irons, along o' the Red-Coats clapping us aboard! Man the sweeps – all hands! Every man-jack as can crawl! Aye, an' ye ladies o' leisure too, by thunder!" roared he.

"Well-I-say," sobbed the Old Stander, slumping against a gun-carriage. "What wi' Long John toting white handled knives; wounded mates laid aside and petty-coats aboard. Now here's us a-setting sail along o' the Blackest Day as ever was for ships and seafarin' men. Oh, Doom! Oh, Disaster! We be bound for Davy Jones's Locker – one an' all! I feels it in me fin!"

BOOK 2

PEECE FIVE

DISASTER AND DELIVERANCE!

CHAPTER XXI

THE FLYING DUTCHMAN!

McGinty's wailings of woe were broached to by a slice o' luck none of us looked to find: the tide was on the turn. Along of slipping our cable, we steered to mid-stream and drifted seawards on the ebb. The sweeps were manned with a will, for speed was now a sound insurance for safety.

Charlotte placed the waif in Flint's hammock, the Cap'n having graciously assigned his quarters to the Ladies. Then the pair of 'em rolled up their shirt sleeves and took their place alongside the men, pulling at one of the great oars that was run out athwart-ships. Our chronic shortage of hands restricted us to using only thirteen pairs o' sweeps from the twenty-three, the Able Bodies being boosted by the wounded. The Maroons among us pulled a good oar. But the two Merchants, Ducket and Wade, re-christened, 'Bucket and Spade' by the Crew, the former being short and fat, while t'other was tall and thin, saw fit not to blister their hands – at first! That was afore Pew politely introduced his pleasant self, along of a rope's end. Worked like a pair o' Red Shanks, they did, each of 'em turning purple in the face with the effort of pulling! Even Flint and the First Mate, Billy Bones, sweated and swore alongside the fo'c'sle hands, while me'n Job Anderson held the helm steady and Tiger Pip thumped out the time to every stroke of the oars on his Irish drum.

We cleared the creek of the Rio Grande without sight nor sniff of a Red Coat. Once out in the open sea we shipped oars and hoisted sail. It was at that moment, mates, that our luck evaporated quicker than the blobs of sweat that dripped from straining bodies onto the hot deck. From this time forth, Old McGinty's Dirge of Doom sailed right alongside, until it finally clapped us aboard!

As you Readers will remember, we was to head for the Black River, situated around eight miles WSW of Kingston as the crow flies. But both wind and current was against us and it blowed so hard there were no hope o' beating-up into it. Then a blasted RN Fourth Rate of 60 Guns loomed on the horizon, so we sailed with the wind up our coat-tails. In fleeing from the Royal Navy, yet another fact was sheeted home – our old War-Horse was badly in need of careening. Had the wallowing, heavy hulled 60 Gunner been a Nimble Frigate, she might well have fetched us. As it turned out we didn't lose her until we got shrouded in a safe blanket o' darkness.

For nigh on a week it continued blowing big guns that pushed us far off our intended course. We passed between Cuba and Hispaniola, scudding out into the North Atlantic under Goose-Wings. Rations ran low since we had not re-victualled at Nanny Town, being too busy enjoying ourselves, and with no chance to water ship our situation weren't too tickety-boo!

Since we were so direly under-manned, every able-bodied hand was needed to sail the ship. At one point we had to claw-off from the dreaded *Abreojos* – 'The Eye Opener' – as it be known in Spanish Circles. This complex of surface level reefs, Cayes we calls 'em, bore many names on various maps: Plate Wrack; Phip's Wrack; North Riff and Silver Bank. It was here that William Phips salvaged gold and silver from the wreck of the *Nuestra Señora de la Concepcion* to the value of Three Hundred and Twenty Thousand Pounds. He done it by using a diving bell back in 1687. But to one and all who sailed those waters they called it 'The Graveyard of Ships'. Many a Tall Ship had mysteriously disappeared in this remote region and some of 'em were no place near the Cayes. These weird, dangerous waters stretched from the tip o' Palm Key in the West, across to Barbados in the East, then extending on up – the apex of the area being Bermuda to the North. On some more recent maps this triangular section of Ocean was marked as 'The Devil's Sea'!

To crown our near disaster, the Babby gave up its ghost. There was no milk aboard and it were too young to take gruel. Flash Dan had devised a teat from a silk glove, which he filled with sugar water, but it were no go. The poor mite vomited any nourishment that Charlotte was able to give him. Strangely enough the weather dropped off on the day our little Piccaninny died a nameless death. Almost becalmed, we was, as if both wind and waves were hushed in sympathy. 'Twere a solemn crowd as stood gathered on the Quarter-Deck. The Women were wet-eyed; Ben Gunn had the snivels; and Flint kept choking on the words in reading from The Book of Books. Shamus O'Brien crooned a mournful Irish Dirge while the tiny soul, wrapped in its swaddling with a half-pound swivel ball at its feet, were gently lowered overboard on a halliard and committed into the Arms of the Almighty.

"A bad sign this, ship-mates," stated the Old Quarter-Master, blinking back his tears.

"I rather think the Good Lord chose to remove such Gentle Innocence from such wicked company as we," replied Flash Dan with a sad smile, then he murmured: "*Sinite parvulos ad me venire.*"

"Come now, Doctor," returned Flint "This crew is too solemn by a long sea mile. God rest the wee waif, I say, but stand-by to come about. Darby! Lay aft and break out the Rum! A double go for all hands, by way of a bracer, while I holds Council!"

As M'Graw disappeared below to fetch the keg, Flint mounted the poop steps and bade us gather round. "My Lads – and Lassies," began he, giving the girls a ghastly smile with his pointed teeth, "we be doon to a pint of water per day and the barrels o' junk as are left be as salt as Lot's Wife! Our War-Horse needs new tack and his backside, if it ain't breamed soon, the blasted barnacles on it will be sewed!

"Now, it be my intention to steer a course for Georgia," continued he. "I ken of a new Settlement on the Savannah River that offers us Safety and a warm welcome. The Governor's Father and me wore the Queen's Coat, when we were younkers, and drubbed the Froggies together at Blenheim under the Immortal Churchill. There we shall re-fit and re-organise; then along of a fresh Crew, we'll beat-up for the Jolly Dollars that be a-waiting for us at Sarasota!"

Darby appeared from between decks, wide-eyed, pale and empty handed. "Capt'in," croaked he. "Samson is a-woke up. Heard 'im coughin', I did, and when I peered in the Coffers Cave . . . Well, Sir, yew'd best come and clap yewer deadlights on wot I saw there – shiver my Soul!"

We all tramped below and descended to the hold. Flint opened the door of the bread-room where his Serpent resided and the sight within sent a ripple o' fear slicing through the Company. Both Joan Fuller and Charlotte screamed, then my Beloved swooned away into the Doctor's arms.

In the gloom of the glims we saw Samson slithering up the port planking, seeking a way out, but it was the grinning skull set a-top a clubbed boot and surrounded by crossed bones that shook us to our very bearings. It were the remains of Don Claudio de Beaumont – you mind the hunch-backed Spanish Capitano? He couldn't have popped up at a worse moment, Morale being as it were at that time. His big teeth seemed to be mocking us in triumph. A coldness swept into the hold – like being in a Crypt!

"It's an Omen as ever was," whispered Tom Morgan fearfully. "Look you how he leers, mates. No good'll come o' this – mark my word,"

"I'll lay another along o' that," stated Merry, his single earring of silver reflecting the light as he turned his head for sole attention. "Did any present body so much as hear a scuffle or plop from a rat in the bilges when we entered the hold?"

"Right you are George. I ain't seen hide nor hair of one during the time I inspected for leaks between decks – not since we set sail," declared Ben Gunn.

As the significance of this sank in, our Chippy stood wringing his hands with a worried look on his face. You could grow a full beard in the time it took for things to register in Ben's poor brain!

"Aye," returned Port Tack. "And any lubber knows 'tis only a doomed ship that gets deserted by its rats!"

"Then why might you still be aboard?" I snapped, glaring daggers at the Cooper's Mate – him who had manhandled my Charlotte.

"Belay all this Tom Fool, bitter talk!" retorted Flint, his face twitching in anger along o' the need for drugs and rum. "Ye have been confined in the company of women for so long, ye be starting to squabble like 'em! The rodents are lying low for fear of my Snake. And in regards to yon pile o' bones; why, that be oor Emblem – a sign of success!"

We all backed hastily away as Samson crooked his ugly head around the door jamb. Israel Hands was all but climbing into Black Dog's pocket. As for our two reluctant Buccaneers, Messrs Bucket and Spade, they had fled top-side long since. With flickering tongue and glowing eyes, the Serpent glided between Flint's sea-boots and slipped silently into the bilges.

"Off ye go my Bonney Beauty," crooned Flint. "Just wedge that there quoin against the door, Bosun. He'll be back in his berth once he's had his fill o' rodents."

"If he can find any aboard this Cursed Ship!" spat Port Tack.

Flint's eyes flashed fire in the dim light. "If he canna, I'll feed him ye! One more sour word and the Cooper will be needing a new Mate! Now collect ye up yon bones in a gunny sack and sling 'em overboard," concluded the Captain softly. "Dinna cross me na more this day."

It was a right dejected looking Crew that returned top-side, to be sure. Aye, mates, cast down but cautious, we were, for Flint was in a killing mood. 'Up Spirits' soon raised ours somewhat. But hardly had we supped the first sip, when the Look-Out hailed us from the mast-head.

"DECK HOAY!"

"HOLLOA!" returned I through cupped hands.

"SHIP T' STARBOARD! THREE POINTS B'FORE THE BEAM!" yelled he.

Flint, the First Mate and Me snapped our glasses open and scanned the expanse of Ocean that lay North-West by North.

"Thunder!" exclaimed Flint. "She's cast-away and derelict b'the look of her. And unless my Bring 'em Closer be a deceiving of me, we be bordering a break-off from the Sargasso Sea. Stab me and fall on!"

Focusing my own glass I saw what had once been a great vessel of three masts, but she was now little more than a hulk festooned with streamers of weed, shreds of tattered canvas and the remains of rotten rigging. Her Mizen was gone, the Main had snapped off at the Fighting-Top and only her Main-Yard-Arm and two spars on the Fore-Mast were still slung – held up by chains. She was drifting in a meadow of Gulf-weed and giant kelps that had been massed together by wind and ocean currents. The Sargasso Sea, from whence it came, is as large as a continent. This tangled carpet of weed was so thick you could near walk upon it. Columbus took two weeks to clear this floating forest, when first he sailed to the New World. It be a strange fact o' nature, ship-mates, but every blessed eel on Earth begins its life there before swimming off all around the Globe!

"There be something odd here," remarked the Mate. Turning to Flint, he pointed with his spy-glass. "Look to her Quarter, Jim. A high, narrow stern like that un with a broad buttock below ain't in character along o' ships now days. An' those poop lanthorns be Dutch or I'm a Turk!"

"Stab me," breathed Flint softly, "Ye be in the right on it, Bill. Why, Fly-Boats of her cut stopped hoisting sail a hundred years ago."

"What means it, mates? A Dead Ship adrift in a Dead Sea. Let's leave her be, that's my vote," said George Merry.

"Begging your pardon, Ship-Mate, but I intends to board that there Old Flight and see for myself the manner of her rupture," replied Flint firmly. "Stand-by to go about!" bawled he.

The Crew rushed to their stations. We altered course and swung round. Approaching with the hulk to leeward, we had a clear view of her stern. Between streamers of weed hanging over her Escutcheon could still be seen the faded, gilded letters of her name:

CHARON

Once alongside, grappling irons were thrown over her Bulwarks and we secured to the cleats. The *Walrus* felt strange beneath our feet. Being buoyed-up on that carpet of kelp and bladder-wrack, there was no roll or the rising and falling of a swell. Nothing moved and we had the sensation of being suspended in space.

"Weird, I calls it," voiced Morgan, scratching his whiskers in bewilderment. "Hanging in stays upon the sea like this ain't in nature."

"Aye, Tom," agreed Merry. "An, what kind of a name is that for a Ship now, I ask you?"

"Greek Mythology, my man. Charon is the Ferryman of Death, so Legend has it, who carries the souls of the damned across the River Styx to Hades," explained Flash Dan with a seriousness that was a rarity for him.

Both George Merry and the Welshman swallowed hard, glancing nervously at each other, while their mahogany faces turned several shades lighter. Our Crew huddled closer. Charlotte held onto my arm and I saw fear mirrored in her dark eyes. We scanned the reeking, weed encrusted timbers that loomed over us and the stillness an' silence o' that old Ship smacked straight from the Grave, mates.

A shadow flashed across the deck, followed by a scream, high and thin. All heads snapped back and we gazed aloft in time to see the look-out plummeting down. He bounced off the Main-Yard and landed in the Cutter, smashing a thwart with his impact. At the same instant we beheld a huge white albatross sweep upwards to perch upon the weed strewn, jagged stump of the derelict's mizen-mast.

"Hell's Teeth!" snarled Pew. "That blasted bird must've knocked Bibby clean from the Cross-Trees!"

"Then here goes!" growled Allardyce and drawing a long-barrelled French pistol from his sash, he took a pace forward, aimed and fired.

Flint's cry of: "Avast!" was drowned in the sound of the shot. The big bird rocked back on its perch, flapping mighty wings to maintain balance, while its snowy breast exploded in a puff of blood and feathers. This splendid creature glided sideways off the Mizen and disappeared past the Poop onto the deck below.

"Boil my Blood!" roared Flint in the stunned silence. Bounding forward he snatched away the Barker with one hand and seizing a fistful of lank, yellow hair with t'other, dragged Allardyce down to his knees. "Dinna ye ken what ye've done? Ye've sent the Soul o' some long dead Seaman down to Purgatory! Put a Curse on my Ship, ye have, an' Damned all as be aboard here! What Evil befalls this Crew be on yore own head!"

"Don't do me no 'arm, Cap'n!" pleaded Allardyce. "I ain't right sharp on the lore o' Seafarin' Men! I thought dolphins wus Seamen's Spirits – I swear!"

"Only them as die drowning in Davy Jones's Domain become pilots, ye chuckle-headed numbskull!"

"Captain!"

The urgency in Flash Dan's voice checked Flint. He flung Allardyce from him and sent the pistol spinning barrel over butt into the sea as he strode to where the Doctor, Billy Bones and Pew stood gazing into the Cutter like they were star-struck. Only then did we all crowd close to view the mortal remains of Samuel Bibby. Death had failed to hide the stark terror that was stamped on his skull-like features. The horror-filled face with its bared teeth and wild, bulging eyes sent Joan Fuller's hand flying to her mouth to stifle a scream, while Charlotte's grip near broke my arm.

"He died of apoplexy," said Flash Dan to Flint, pointing at the corpse. "Killed by sheer fright."

"Thunder! He wears the look of a mon who's stood eye-ball to eye-ball along of the Evil One hisself," gasped our Captain.

"Yew ever see a Seaman so stricken, mates?" asked Darby in awe. "'Taint in keeping with anything Mortal."

"You'd be stricken, Steward, if a blasted bird with wings as wide as a fore-s'l knocked you out the trees!" retorted Black Dog.

"He weren't knocked from the nest!" stated Billy, his countenance like granite. "The bird was way astern and Bibby was facing for'ard. I see that much along o' his dive."

"I don't follow the course o' this conversation. It's neither heads nor tails an' that's a fact!" bemoaned Merry.

"Shiver my sides!" exclaimed I, "So it weren't the bird as put a pawl on poor old Sam's 'art – he never even saw it!"

The Mate nodded, his eyes flicking onto Flint. "My reckoning is he spied something top-side on this old hulk, Jim," said he softly.

A coldness crept over me and I felt Charlotte shiver.

"By the coral encrusted Bones of Drake, I'll fathom what's what aboard this tramp if I have to pull it apart plank by plank!" vowed Flint, popping a parcel of coca leaves into his mouth and gazing up at the hulk, his glims hard and glittering.

Tiger Pip rushed over and clung to the Captain's coat, his eyes starting from his head: "Don' you board dat dead boat, Capt'in!" begged he. "Dem Duppies'll git you, sure!"

"Hush, my son," soothed Flint, patting the Child's woolly thatch. "If there's any haunting to be done between decks – I'll do it."

Charlotte gave comfort to the lad as Flint, followed by the Doctor, Billy, Pew and Me hauled ourselves up a grappling line and boarded the derelict, amidships. Not another man-jack of our Crew dared venture onto her. Small blame on them, I say. After moving up for'ard and our mates were lost to view, I could have gone a bit o' comfort m'self, mind!

The Ship stank of the sea. Every lungful of air was rank with the heavy, pungent smell of wet weed. Her timbers were grey and cracked, like an elephant's skin, and the gaping decks creaked under each foot fall.

"Look sharp, lads! Spread out a bit lively," urged Flint. "We dinna want to be falling through the bottom on this old bucket."

Missing planks left great gaps in the deck, along of wide cracks where the caulking had come adrift. Her Fo'c'sle was in ruins, the wood warped and split. Now while all had remained silent and still aboard *Walrus*, we became conscious of sound and movement on this dead Ship. The remains of her masts, long since sprung, groaned in sympathy with the creaking old timbers as she rolled on the ocean's swell. Wreckage were everywhere. Abaft the Midships lay a barrier of fallen spars, toppled sticks and dangling blocks, entangled in a mass o' rotten rigging and decaying canvas that hung from the stump of the Main-Mast. Hiding the stern from sight, encompassing this curtain of cordage and splintered timbers, were giant kelps measuring a hundred feet or more and branches of Gulf-weed with clusters o' air blisters clinging between the leaves like bunches of grapes.

"No guns or carriages aboard," observed Billy, peering down the for'ard hatchway.

"Anchors are gone too, Sir," remarked Pew with a glance at the Cat-Heads.

"Aye, jettisoned long ago for fear of foundering in some great tempest," said Flint. His face began to twitch and his hand crept onto the butt of a Pistol. For the first time ever, I was seeing our Captain – a-feared.

Mind you, mess-mates, the rest of us weren't exactly the picture of boldness, to be sure!

"I'll wager my wig and scholarship this old tub has since braved scores of storms, especially in these waters."

"Aye, Doctor. Wild waters would have thrown the weed upon her, pile on pile," confirmed the Mate. He tapped a ring-bolt with his toe. The iron was red rusty and came away in flakes.

"What with unmanned pumps, her boards and caulking sprung, why, the bilges must be brim full by now," said Pew gingerly testing the first step leading down to the lower-deck. Brittle as dried bones, the wood snapped under his weight.

"Nay, Bosun," warned Flint. "It dinna be safe to venture below."

"Reminds me of an old ship-mate I once watched a-riding in a cart as rotten as this," reminisced Pew. "The blasted boards gave way beneath his feet an' he might have busted both legs, but for one saving factor."

"What were that, Pew?" I asked, falling for it hook, line and sinker.

"The rope around his neck!" smirked our Bosun, tongue in cheek.

"Forsooth! Will one of you nautical gentlemen kindly explain to a poor land lubber how it is this hulk continues cruising instead of having sunk a century ago?" asked Flash Dan, pursing his lips and cocking an inquiring eyebrow at each of us in turn.

"'Tis her cushion of kelp and the air in the bladder-wrack as be buoying her up, I reckon," replied Flint thoughtfully.

"By the powers," said I. "Her hull must be as foul as a Turk's armpit, along o' worms and weed."

Flint rasped a hand over his stubbly chin. "Stab me," murmured he, looking puzzled. "The Sargasso Sea lies to the East, yet the Gulf Stream Current runs from the West. How come she drifted against it?"

"And this 'ere weed, Cap'n, it's WET!" Pew picked up a piece and licked the long, leathery stem. "Salt too. Yet the Ship's timbers be as dry as the Barbary Coast. Shrivel my Soul, Sir, but nothing makes mortal sense aboard this old bucket!"

Flint gave us all a tight-mouthed look, his face still twitching, then turned and retreated aft. We followed, treading the boards as if walking on eggs, and picked our way with care. Pew was first to clear the curtain of weed that was draped amidships. He suddenly hove-to with a start and a strangled cry of: "Shrivel my Soul!" Stumbling back he clawed a pistol from his belt and came on aim.

The sight that met my gaze in brushing aside the leathery streamers of kelp made my blood run cold. Lashed behind the great, brass-bound wheel on the Quarter-Deck stood a Man, or rather the remains of one, and crouched upon his shoulder, one wing trailing with its head tucked under the other, sat the dying Albatross.

"Stab me and fall on!" exclaimed Flint, his clam-shell hilted Hanger half drawn. "What Evil Sign is this?"

"He ain't much of a gay sight to look upon, I'll allow, but he's near as comed to dust as makes no difference. Dead men don't bite, Cap'n!" said Billy putting on a bold front and striding forward. But I heard his innards rumble from where I was at – for all his bravado.

"*Dei gratia, de mortuis nil nisi bonum*," said the Doctor crossing himself.

Cautiously we approached the Spectral Seaman. A 'gay sight' wasn't the word for it. There he stood, mates, secured to the wheel by a broad leather belt, one hoary hand firmly grasping a spoke, while the other was balled into a fist and raised in silent defiance towards the sky. His clothes proclaimed him a Captain or some such man of office. Once of best quality velvet, the old fashioned doublet and pantaloons were now tattered and faded, mere rags of their former glory, stained by sun and salt along o' the juices from his own demise and decomposition.

But it was his face which arrested our gaze. A skull covered in skin, it were, with a ragged, pointed beard, bared teeth and empty eye-sockets staring in vacant rage into infinity. Topping the stiffest yard to nothing was the fact that his long hair, lank and mousey looking, still blew in the breeze. Well, parts of it did, for tufts had fallen away here and there, exposing patches o' greyish bone.

"Odds bodikins! I shouldn't care to hazard a guess on how many years his life has been departed from this mortal coil," stated the Doctor, peering at the Corpse with professional interest. "Mummified he is!"

"What's his Blessed Mother got to do along of it?" asked Pew screwing up his evil eyes in a frown.

"The man is salted and sun-dried – preserved by the elements," explained Flash Dan. "Embalmed by Nature, so to speak, the same as the Ancient Egyptians were with aromatic oils, herbs and spices."

"Aye," nodded Pew with understanding. "Them Gypsy Kings as was planted in the Pirrymids!"

"This Cove 'ud make poor fare for jerked-beef," remarked I tightly, feeling far from my usual jovial self. "Starved to death by the look of him."

The Albatross suddenly lifted its head and fixed us with bright button eyes, unwinking and dark as lamp-black. In the same instant the Spectre lowered his fist to point an accusing, bony finger at Flint. Pure shock anchored us to the deck. In irons, we was, hardly able to breathe.

"BEWARE YE, CAPTAIN FLINT! I WHO AM CURSED BY GOD AND DOOMED TO SAIL THE SEVEN SEAS FOR ALL ETERNITY IN DEFIANCE OF HIM, GIVE YE WARNING! FOR WHEN NEXT YE SPY ME AND MY SHIP, ON THAT DAY YE AND YOUR CREW SHALL COME TO GRIEVOUS RUIN!" boomed the hollow voice of this Terrible Spectre.

"Thunder!" exclaimed Billy Bones. "The Flying Dutchman!"

"BEGONE!" echoed the Ghost.

Since clapping aboard we had lain becalmed with nary a cat's paw to ruffle the glassy surface of the sea. Now the Ship gave a violent lurch, dipping her bows, and a great, ice cold wind came upon us. Unbalanced in both mind and body, we fled. With Flint and the Doctor hot-footing it in the van, we launched ourselves from that accursed Ship, jumping eight feet onto *Walrus*'s deck. Pew landed smack a'top O'Brien and laid him out cold.

"She's foundering, mates!" warned Merry, clinging to the for'ard line.

"Cast off! Cast off!" cried Flint, turning blue in the face.

"Helm hard-a-lee," croaked I to Anderson. "Close up the crew, Job, for I ain't got breath left with which to holler."

"Man the braces!" bawled my Chief Timoneer spinning his spokes.

"Don't hang a leg there! Look lively you swabs!" screeched Pew, venting his rage and fear upon those who were trying to revive the Irelander.

The confusion and terror in those first few moments was on par with a Press-Gang let loose in a Nunnery. Our Crew ran hither and thither, spreading panic faster than the plague, while battling against this strange wind. The oddity of it was that the sea remained calm as a mill-pond!

"Starboard braces heave away!" cried Black Dog.

Along of all grappling lines released and with the helm hard over our head swung away from the wreck as the sails bellied before the wind. I was braced against the binnacle beside Billy. Flint was clinging to the stanchions o' the poop steps, while the rest of our people steadied themselves as best they could, grabbing cleats, cannons or the bulwarks. We all watched awe-struck as the *Charon* slipped silently and smoothly into the carpet of kelp with not so much as a ripple or bubble breaking the surface. No sooner had she sunk from sight than the wind ceased.

"What manner o' mischief is this, Cap'n?" cried Israel Hands, his face ashen. "In all my years afore the mast, man and boy, I ain't never seen a wind like that with the briny staying calm as a corpse!"

"Him as could tie a Gunner's Knot to that would have a headpiece on 'im fit for Parliment!" voiced Merry and the rest of the Crew clamoured in support of what were said.

"Belay, my lads!" interrupted Flint, raising his hands for silence. "The sea be a strange mistress and here's us slap-bang in the middle of what be known as the Devil's Domain! So, the sooner we slip these bewitched waters – the better! Break out the rum, Darby!" ordered he and everybody cheered. Vapoured fit to split, they did!

That was the way of it, ship-mates. Only Old QM McGinty and Flint's little steward Darby M'Graw knew what took place aboard the *Charon*. Our Captain thought it best to keep mum and not frighten the Company; but being in such close confines the news circulated the Fo'c'sle faster than a secret among women! "*In vino veritas*!" as the Doctor said. And within hours all hands knew the long and the short of it. There was much grumbling between decks, augmented by Messrs Port Tack and Allardyce, more so after the rum gave out.

Five days dry! Five days without rum and every one were living on nerve ends, along of biscuit crumbs and a tea-spoon of tepid, stinking water per person. A right starving time we had of it, to be sure. Flint fared the worst. Rum was meat and drink to him – barring drugs. Sometimes he ranted and raved, violent to the point where it took four of us to hold him down, while Flash Dan calmed him by taking his lancet and opening a vein. The bleeding done us all good, I reckon. Other times Flint cringed and grovelled in the Mate's cabin, plagued by countless faces of the men he had murdered. Between bouts, coca leaves and warmed wine served to steady him and he was much of his old self.

Billy Bones devoured plugs o' twist like they was candy bars and Ben Gunn were Mast-Headed for pinching cheese. Port Tack got paraded before Flint, charged with smoking below decks without a cap to his pipe. In any other Company the Cooper's Mate would have received 'Moses's Law' written across his shoulders – forty stripes, lacking one. But since Flint was a 'Shell-Back' hisself and still suffered dreams o' the lash cracking over his own hide, he never inflicted a flogging on others. The most a Man could expect by way of corporal punishment would be to 'Run the Gauntlet' and endure a drubbing from all hands. Port Tack's sentence was to holy-stone both decks from stem to stern and polish all brass-work with the fine, red brick-dust that caused him to sneeze non-stop.

With lime juice all out and no fresh rations, scurvy began to take a firm grip on some of the Crew. Those who were low on salts, the wounded and sick, suffered first. Hair fell away in handfuls and teeth became loose in their sockets. By the time Palm Key's swampy coast-line hove into sight on the horizon, we were a sad pack of dogs to look upon and no mistake – you may lay to it!

Nearing the end o' the Morning Watch, it were, as we cruised along the East Coast, seeking a likely spot to drop anchor and water ship. Under sails that had been shortened for the night, our speed was down to a snail's pace. To starboard the rising sun appeared like a blood-red ball perched upon the rim of a glassy sea. On our larboard side a thick, white wall of mist rolled out across the water from the Everglades.

Those on duty were about to be relieved by the Fore-Noon Watch, mustering below, when without warning we became enveloped in a greenish vapour that descended upon us from out of nowhere. Tom Morgan, who was time-keeping up for'ard, clanged the Ship's Bell in alarm. Black Dog, stationed at the wheel, blew on his whistle – piping 'All Hands!' The *Walrus* suddenly lurched and lifted. I felt the deck rise beneath my feet as I grabbed the binnacle for balance. The compass had gone crazy wild, its needle spinning round all points on the blessed card. Bodies erupted from both hatches, fore and aft, Pew and Hands being among the first on deck.

"We be run-aground!" cried Black Dog as Flint and Billy stumbled from the Mate's cabin. Behind them, I saw the frightened faces of the women peering from the passage.

"Bilge!" bawled the Bosun in reply to Black Dog's remark. "I can feel we still has head-way!"

"But there ain't no roll, Pew," retorted the Gunner. "Why, 'tis as if we be sailing through thin air!"

"Israel's right!" voiced Gypsy Fuller.

"Blast yore eyes, Barbecue! Ye should ha' summoned all hands afore ye sailed into this soup!" roared Flint, purple with rage.

"There were no time, Sir! It clapped aboard on us not sixty seconds gone – like a blasted bolt straight out of the blue!" I replied, meeting his mad stare with steady measure.

"Ship t' starboard! Cutting athwart our bow!" screamed a frantic seaman from up for'ard.

"Hard-a-port!" I yelled.

My intention was to turn *Walrus* into the wind, bringing our few sails all a-back, whereas we'd heave-to. But as Joe the Carib and Billy Bones clawed at the spokes to assist Black Dog, the wheel spun free. Slack as a main-sail in the Doldrums, it were!

"Thunder!" cried Billy, "*Walrus* don't answer the rudder!"

"The Ship! 'Tis the Flying Dutchman!" Pew's voice was more of a shriek than a shout.

"An here's us sailing above her deck! Oh how can this be? We're dead men all, mates!" wailed Old McGinty clapping both hands to his head.

Then that weird, ice cold wind came cutting into us, flesh cringing, same as a stroke from the cat, but none took notice of the discomfort. All eyes were glued on the Ghost Ship. Israel Hands was right. The *Walrus* was floating on thin air, suspended above the sea amid swirling green vapour that stank of things Long Dead.

Transformed to her former Majesty, gleaming in an eerie white light that shimmered like burnished silver as seen in a deep pool, the *Charon* bore down upon our starboard bow with all sails set. The Dutchman were there behind the wheel, his hair streaming past his face, and perched upon his shoulder sat the Albatross. The pair of them were also restored to their former state, except the Great Bird was now blood-red with its mighty wings flapping wide.

Both Man and Bird glittered along o' the same ghostly light that illuminated the Ship. Most of Flint's Flying Forty fell to the deck grovelling. Some raised their hands in supplication, calling upon the Saviour they had rejected for salvation and deliverance from Doom. Drugged up to the gills on coca leaves, the Captain became a raging, demented demon.

"Rot ye for a parcel of hen-hearted numbskulls!" roared he, eyeballs rolling at the cowering crew. "Damnation seize my soul if I'll let that Dutchman cock his hat athwart my hawse twice! Dam'me, no!"

Flint turned and, bounding onto the poop, he jerked the calf-skin jacket off the serpent-headed swivel. In a brace o' shakes he flashed flame from his tinder-lighter onto a match. As the Ghost-Ship swept past our bows, pitching and rolling as if tossed by some invisible tempest, Flint trained the gun dead-centre of the Dutchman and fired.

"Take that ye Damned Duppie!" he shrieked as the case-shot raked the Quarter-Deck.

But that spray of musket balls merely became green flashes, each blessed bullet turning to flickering blobs of Saint Elmo's Fire where they struck. Hollow laughter mocked us and the Spectre shook his fist before veering. The swirling vapour began to vanish, sucked in by the *Charon*'s stern-sheet windows, or so it seemed. We smacked the sea a mighty 'Wallop!' and found ourselves floating upon tranquil waters once more, along of light airs and a blue sky. The Ghost-Ship turned transparent, shimmering, and finally fusing with the fog bank – she disappeared.

The crew slowly got to their feet, gazing about them mystified. Flint slumped against the swivel and brushed a hand wearily over his forehead in a daze. His face looked ghastly, all mottled blue and grey.

"Rum! Bring me rum!" he ordered.

"Kill-devil's all out, Capt'in," replied M'Graw with a nervous glance at Billy Bones.

"It'll have to be rack, Jim," soothed the First Mate.

"Wine then," returned Flint, "and plenty of it. I'll drink it below." He tottered down from the poop, his eyes glazed and unseeing.

Tiger Pip put a guiding arm around his waist and led him into the passage way. Joan Fuller and Charlotte Eleanor took charge then and helped him into the great cabin.

"Wot now, ship-mates?" grated Port Tack, hands on hips, looking a sight braver than he did several minutes ago. "Here we be, bows on t'our Day o' Judgement, and us along of a Cap'n full seas over on drugs and damnation! So wot do we do? Hang in stays and whistle for a wind? I calls . . ."

"Here's what you do, matey!" snapped Billy, confronting the glowering Cooper's Mate. "You'll put your helm amidships, talk soft and lay-to! That tongue o' yours has too much lee-way!" The next instant, Port Tack was taken all a-back when a crashing blow from Billy's right fist smacked him between the eyes and laid him senseless upon the deck.

"Anchor Parties – close up!" cried the Mate. "Long John, we'll heave-to in yonder creek!"

CHAPTER XXII

THE BATTLE OF LOWETHER'S FOLLY – DRY BLOWS!

Most of the Company were employed under the Bosun, rowing the Ship's boats into the Everglades until striking fresh water, then filling relays of kegs and transporting them back to *Walrus*. Being in ever-gladed country, those ashore had the edge in comfort over us who remained on board transferring the water from the small barrels into the huge casks housed amidships in the hold. Below decks was stifling, while those of us working the winding tackle top-side broiled in our own sweat – baked by a blazing sun. Anchored where we were, the inshore breeze missed us.

Flint, Darby and Joe the Carib went a-hunting, taking one of the Ship's pintle guns ashore with 'em. Joe had his Blow-Pipe; Flint and his little steward carried the big, brass-barrelled Blunderbuss between them. Billy was against the idea of such a minor gang going off alone. The swamps swarmed with alligators and poisonous snakes. One serpent was known as a cotton mouthed creature because with its jaws a-gape, the thick, white saliva in its throat resembled a cotton ball. These Glades were also home to the dreaded Seminole Indians, who since having tasted Spanish cruelty, weren't too polite in their treatment of White Men.

Despite the First Mate's entreaties regarding risk, the jaunt proved a bonanza for all hands. With one blast, Flint bagged more'n two dozen ducks alongside a marsh, so close were they confined, while Joe killed three small swamp deer along of his Blow-Gun. Delicate, beautiful little animals they were and some of us, especially the women-folk, thought the slaughter shameful. But for growling bellies it made a much needed change from worm ridden cheese and weevil filled biscuit – both hard as iron. In addition to our diet, Joe the Carib found some water melons, cabbage palm and above all – limes!

Camp was made on a sand-spit and once the fires were lit, Joan Fuller and Charlotte prepared a feast fit for Kings. Since I remained aboard supervising the working party, loading the last of the water kegs, our rations were rowed out to us. Flash Dan was in the Chaloupe. He had come to collect some medicines for the wounded hands ashore and the worst of our scurvy cases who had running sores.

"Top o' the morning, Doctor," I greeted as he scrambled up the gangway cleats, agile as a monkey.

"That man Lowether," began he, "is a scatter-brained, numbskulled nincompoop. I have tried explaining to him, until blue in the face, that being buried up to his fool neck in dry sand is no cure for scurvy. What he needs is fresh greens and lime juiced water. But will the clotpoll heed me – look there!"

I trained my glass on where the Doctor pointed and sure enough I saw Ebenezer Lowether, our Sail-Maker, buried up to his gills at the end of the sand-spit. Grinning like a loony, he was, displaying his gappy teeth. Nearby, Job Anderson and George Merry were calling out to the crew, holding up little white balls they had collected in their hats.

"Seems some good has come from Lowether's Folly after all," I said. "The Coxun's found a cache o' turtle's eggs by the look of it. A rarity for these here parts, to be sure."

"Splended! I shall take mine hard-boiled with just a dash of salt and vinegar for dressing," replied Flash Dan rubbing his hands together in anticipation of such a treat.

After the noon-day meal, being main-hot, Ben Gunn got the Mate's permission to lead a swimming party over the Ship's side. The girls swam out from the beach and joined them. Joan Fuller was dressed in a brightly patterned piece of chintzes, same as a sari, but Charlotte wore only her gold chain and turquoise earrings – shiver my sides! Two thirds of those ashore plunged in alongside her, clothes an' all! Israel Hands, Billy, Black Dog and Me were the only four who remained aboard. In ogling the shimmering, naked form of my Intended, Hands over reached hisself hanging out the gangway. Lost balance and fell in, he did, along of a little help from the toe o' my boot!

"John!" cried she. "Come on, the water's wonderous cool!"

Now I wants it known I does wash, but too much bathing is apt to weaken a body. Besides, it ain't healthy swimming on a full stomach – belly cramp can put you in dire straits! Anyhow, I stripped down to my buckskin breeches, kicked off my sea-boots and took the plunge. No sooner had I surfaced, than a horrible thought flashed through my mind and I voiced my fears aloud. "Thunder! It'll go hard on us if them alligators has a hankering after some sea-food and leaves the swamp!"

"Rest easy, Mister Silver. The Mate told me that gators don't venture this far down river," assured Ben Gunn between splutters. "Ain't that so, Mister Bones?" sang out he. "Gators won't clapp aboard on us swimming in this creek, says you!"

"Aye, Ben!" returned Billy, leaning on the bulwarks watching us. He removed the pipe from his mouth and spat casually into the water. "They be too a-feared o' the sharks!"

A stream of bubbles was Ben's only reply. The rest of us left him floundering as we struck out for the ship and sanctuary. Windmills weren't the word for it the way our arms were a-going!

"Ladies first! Ladies t' the fore, lads!" cried I, clawing my way up the cleats in the lead. But only to give the girls a quicker hand up, mind! Not that mine were needed. There were more mitts boosting them inboard than suckers on a Squid!

Billy Bones puffed smoke through his nose with pleasure, feeling mildly amused over the chaos he had caused. Black Dog stood alongside him, cackling like some demented crone. Jest or no, their smiles soon faded for scarcely was the last man inboard, Ben Gunn of course, when there came a cry of: "SHARK HO!" and a lone killer cruised into our creek. Whether it was the scent of duck guts and deer lights, dumped and carried out on the ebb, that brought him or the fish had premonitions of the rich pickings to come, I cannot say. All I knew for a fact was that this Sea Rover were my old acquaintance from the deep – Clipped Fin. Alone he was now, his stripped body bigger and more voracious.

'Trouble Comes In Threes,' so the saying goes. First it was the reappearance of that Accursed Dutchman; then along with the Shark from the Sea, there came a distant, BOOM! BOOM! BOOM! of raw-hide drums from the Everglades. Heads began bobbing up through hatches and peering out of gun ports, listening. I also had an ear cocked as I slowly finished dressing and for the last time in my life – pulled on a PAIR of sea-boots.

Old McGinty, who had ushered the girls below to rig them out in clothes from the common chest before the crew suffered too much eye-strain, poked his head above the coaming. "Hark at that, Long John," says he. "Them Sem'noles has wind of us, I reckon. The shore party'll need to look lively. Budging into the boats, is they?"

"Budging ain't the word for it, 'Q'! I never seen a band o' cripples move faster'n the able-bodies helping 'em!" replied I.

One bunch was tumbling into the Chaloupe under Flint, while the Doctor directed the launching of the Yawl. Although beached by the retreating tide, that boat slid down the sand like it were on greased skids. All hands pulled a strong oar and were soon alongside with Clipped Fin for close company, skulking in their wake. Flint and Flash Dan shinned aboard amid the Crew who clustered around the gangway to assist the sick and wounded. The Chaloupe and Yawl were secured by their painters to the Moses Boat, made fast to the

Main-Chains.

"By thunder, Cap'n!" cried Job Anderson peering towards the shore. "We done clean forgot Sails Lowether! Left 'im high and dry, buried up to his ears, so we have!"

Only then did we become conscious of a thin, plaintive cry wailing out across the water above the throbbing drums. I snapped open my spy-glass and got a close-up of the Sail-Maker's head, him who had replaced Mad Murdock. Eyeballs bulging, face bloated with effort, his mouth was a wide 'O' and his loose, gappy teeth wobbled from the force of bellowing lungs.

"Serves the silly dullard right!" returned the Doctor looking sour. "*Reducto ad absurdum*!"

"Reduced to the absurd," translated Flint. "Aye, he be all o' that. But we canna leave the swab to stew and starve in sand or mayhap for Savages to make sport with. Bosun! Take ye the Yawl, along of six, and . . ."

Something 'whooshed!' over our stern, severed a mizen back-stay, chopped through a bit more standing rigging on the starboard fore-shrouds, then sent a great geyser of water soaring skywards between us and the beach. We all rushed to larboard with the dull rumble of the round-shot's discharge echoing in our ears. Sweeping across the narrow neck of the creek was a Frigate with tattered streamers of smoke eddying in her wake. In spying us she only had time for the one shot afore veering off.

"Boil my blood!" grated Flint, grinding those terrible teeth together in a snarl of Rage. "Here's us caught short by a blasted Cruiser, while catering for a Fool!"

I clamped my glass to her as she made to come about and below the billowing White Ensign that proclaimed her Squadron, the bold letters on her Taffarel leapt out at me – letters I had often cleaned with my own two hands:

AGAMEMNON.

"It's *Rolling Aggie*! My old *Agony*!" I cried, sounding rather jubilant.

"Well ain't that ducky for you and lucky for us!" retorted Pew from behind me. "When they learn that their old ship-mate, Barbecue, be aboard on us, they'll no doubt heave-to and signal us alongside to partake o' tea with the Captain, like good companions every one, instead of blowing us to bits!"

The significance of the Bosun's sarcasm hit me like a go o' grape-shot. Over a decade had passed since I'd been given 'Jonah's Toss' from her quarterdeck. She would have returned to home waters and Paid Off half a dozen times during those years, so it wouldn't be the same Captain and Crew that I'd sailed with. Small odds it! What mattered was she were Royal Navy – her guns manned by seamen second to none! I could hear the roll of her Marine Drummers, 'Beating to Arms', as she rounded the point and was lost to view.

"How big is her bite, Long John – what teeth does she carry?" asked Flint from behind me. Calm and composed once more, he lowered his glass.

"She's a thirty-two gunner, twelves and sixes, Sir. Or were when I was aboard her," I replied. "She can't come in close, not in these waters. Her draft be too deep for this creek."

"Packing that power o' punch she don't need to! Along of blockading the mouth, she can stand off and pound us to pieces at leisure. Anchored as we are, like a rat tied to a rope with our arse in the air, one goodly Broadside through our stern'll finish us," returned Billy grimly.

"Aye, there's nought for it but to meet her head-on and exchange Dry Blows – ball for ball," said Flint. Cupping huge hands to his mouth, he cried: "Quarter Gunners! Check ye yore Artillery! Port Watch! Clear for Action! Starboard Watch! As direction by the Master! Carpenter!" continued he. "Fetch for'ard yore axe and stand-by to cut loose the anchor, when Long John gives the word! 'Tis Cut-and-Run for us, my Lads, or the Devil along with Damnation!"

The Captain's bull-like roar galvanised the Crew into instant response. The trilling of Black Dog's silver call, as he piped, "Up Hammocks', added to the clamour caused by the Mate, the Bosun, the Gunner and Me – all bellowing our various orders at once. Men rushed everywhere, some of them colliding in their haste to obey. Speed was of the essence and every one aboard *Walrus* knew their very lives depended on doing the task allotted to 'em and doing it well!

The Quarter Gunners, each with four Long Twelves to his charge, unhoused their Cannons and checked that every piece had sufficient instruments for them to function proper – Rammers, Sponges, Worms, Priming-Irons, Lintstocks, Crows and Handspecs. Billy Bones supervised the hoisting of nets, strung above the deck, to catch any falling debris that might be shot-away. Sound insurance against being brained by a block. Hammocks were stowed in the Quarter-Nettings to act as a bolster between those of us exposed on the open deck and the Enemy's small-arms fire.

Under Pew, the Bosun's Party lashed thick wreaths of cordage, called Pudening, around our Main and Fore-Yards in place of Chains, securing them to the Masts in case the supporting ropes got severed. The Ship's Boats being already in the water, saved a deal of time in lowering 'em. They were always towed astern during an engagement to cut down the risk of injury from 'Flizzings' – flying splinters.

Israel Hands, assisted by 'Bucket and Spade', along of Tiger Pip, Joan Fuller and Charlotte, were hard at it, bringing up cartridges that the Gunner handed out to them from the magazine. A finer pair of powder-monkeys you wouldn't look to find! As Israel passed out the loads from behind a wet blanket, draped over the doorway for added safety, each flannel bag containing a four-pound charge was taken top-side on the double and carefully placed inside thick, rope tiers behind the gun's train-tackle.

My Charlotte Eleanor looked a picture in her speckled shirt, worn open to the waist, and the baggy, bell-bottomed canvass ducks that ended just below her knees. I mind her yet, racing about barefoot, a brace o' salt-boxes bouncing around on her broad hips, her black face shiney with sweat and her teeth flashing as she gave me a breezy grin. I can still see the sparkling gleam of excitement in her dark eyes, enhanced by turquoise earrings swinging from her lobes and my gold chain glinting above her heaving bosom. Black Magic, she were, but I had no time to dwell on it!

While others prepared to receive or give punishment, along of our RN adversary, my main priority was to get the Ship under way with all haste. I sent half the starboard watch aloft to help the Top-Men under Gypsy Fuller. Others I employed to position the great oars, ready to boost us along on the failing ebb when we reached slack-water. Having just over fifty able-bodied Hands we could either sail the Ship satisfactory or by reducing the Gun's Crews from nine to six Men, operate both batteries – but we couldn't sail and fight full strength at the same time!

"CARPENTER CLOSED-UP, SIR!" came the report from for'ard and I pictured the spindly figure of Ben Gunn down on the Cable-Deck, stood with his pole-axe poised, a-waiting my order. He'd need to look lively after slicing through the hawse, for a taut cable suddenly cut can be as dangerous as a kicking horse.

I raised the speaker to my mouth: "CUT LOOSE! HOIST JIB-S'L AND DRIVER! HELM HARD-A-LEE!" Tilting the trumpet higher, its polished copper flashed like fire. "TOP-MEN AHOAY!" I yelled.

"HOLLOA?" Came Fuller's reply.

"LOOSE MAIN AND FORE-TOP S'LS! STAND-BY LEE BRACES!" I bawled.

Snowy canvas flapped in the breeze as *Walrus* came free from the anchor with a jerk and her head swung round. Anderson expertly spun his spokes and brought our war-horse under control. The Top-Men leapt like monkeys down to the lower yards.

"LEE BRACES, HEAVE AWAY!" I cried and with that order we were committed.

Our Seamen hauled to the wind and we slowly crept towards the open sea and a date with destiny I would long remember. Manning the great sweeps increased our speed by a couple of knots, but we were still only crawling when we struck the slack water at the mouth o' the creek.

Agamemnon came sweeping round on a starboard tack, her main courses hauled up in the brails. Her guns were run out, protruding from the ports like a row o' black teeth ready to take a bite at us. On her Tops I saw clusters of Red-Coated Marines. She had as many men to her Small-Arms as we had crew! From about a bow-shot away, 240 yards or thereabouts, as her Cannons came into line along of our Head, she engaged us. Tongues of flame amid white mushrooms of smoke licked out from the maw of her larboard guns – hungry for the taste of Buccaneer blood. They bled us too, with the very first ball!

Our Crew were rowing steady, keeping in rhythm to the beat of Tiger Pip's drum as he tapped out the time, when the shot struck two of the Starboard sweeps. Splinters flizzed every-which-way and such was the shock on the shaft of the oars, one Man lost most of his teeth, along of a busted jaw, while a second rower, his head still bandaged from the *Santa Rosario* Fight, received a blow that broke both arms.

"Heave ye Lads an' Lassies!" roared Flint who strained at a sweep beside the Mate. "Pull for the very lives o' ye!"

Charlotte Eleanor and Joan Fuller manned the oar opposite. In front of them, Flash Dan the Doctor partnered Black Dog. The Bosun's Mate was swearing Blue Fire at the next pair of rowers. Sweating and straining over the long shaft were the two merchants, Ducket and Wade, who kept losing the stroke.

More shots slammed into our Prow, Bowsprit and Fo'c'sle, gouging out great splinters which gashed our canvas and severed clew-lines. Some bad damage was done to the gammoning ropes that bound the inner quarter of the Bowsprit close to the Stem. *Rolling Aggie* swept by wreathed in smoke and prepared to come about again for yet another go at us, this time using her starboard battery. But she was now close-hauled, sailing into the wind, and needed sea-room in which to tack, so we had at least fifteen minutes respite. Faintly, from across the water, we heard the "Huzzas!" of her cheering crew.

"Shrivel my Soul! Listen to the swabs!" snarled Pew, bounding down from the Poop where he had just finished bending a bracer onto a severed mizen Back-Stay. "I'd give a Thousand in Gold never to clap eyes on a King's Ship again! Rot the Royal Navy!" raged he and shook his fist at the manouvering Frigate, little realising that his wish was soon to be granted within the hour!

At this point the wind fetched us more fully, turning up the larboard side of the Captain's broad-brimmed sombrero. "Avast!" he bellowed. "Enough of this galley-work! Time to show 'em we also have teeth!"

We shipped oars and veering with the Everglades to port, began clawing-off from the coast. Being so close in-shore we had little lee-way and the danger of running aground was dire indeed. Darby M'Graw came on deck carrying the

Captain's Brigandine. Flint donned the iron-plated jerkin, but didn't fasten it. QM McGinty appeared behind Billy, dressed in his battered breast-plate and morion.

"Long John!" snapped Flint, checking the priming in his Pistols. "*Walrus* will have to run free for the moment. Ye must claw-off as best ye can. Try ye to fetch us onto yon Frigate's weather-bow, so's we engage her to leeward and keep the wind."

"I ain't got sea-room enough t' spit in, Cap'n! *Aggie* has the edge on us. If I steer one more point nearer the wind we'll broach-to!"

Even as I answered, the *Agamemnon* completed her turn and started to beat-up towards us. She looked a proud sight with her Ensign fluttering, streaming out over the starboard quarter, her sails bellied and bow dipping, carving a broad V of frothing white water. Magnificent, she was, in her defiance – aye, and deadly!

"Hold on course then! It'll have to be Catch-as-Catch-Can!" came Flint's tight lipped reply. "Younker!" cried he, turning to Tiger Pip. "Beat to Quarters, Laddie! Bosun! Hoist 'Old Roger' and break out mine pennant!"

The 'thumpety-thump' of the Negro Nipper's drum drove our Top-Men down the standing rigging – sliding with a speed that made my innards roll. At the same instant, Pew jerked on a halliard line and Flint's twelve foot, forked banner of red silk, bearing the golden emblazed name of NESTER, his long dead wife, broke away from the main-mast head and streamed to leeward. I glanced astern and saw Nick Nutt, the Leading Hand, haul up our Ancient to flutter from the Mizen Peak. That great billowing, Black Flag, along with its Skull and Crossed Bones, never ceased to drive a thrill through my veins.

Billy picked up my trumpet and began bawling commands: "MAN THE STARBOARD BATTERY – ALL HANDS! GUN CAPTAINS, REPORT WHEN READY!"

Black Dog arrived breathless from below. "Carpenter reports two shot 'oles in the cable locker, Sir!" gasped he, knuckling his for'ed to Flint in salute. "He plugged 'em, but needs to parcel several seams as be a bit leaky. Permission to retain two mates, Sir?"

"Nay, nay! inform Doctor Hunter to assist the Carpenter, along of Mrs Fuller and Miss Charlotte. Everybody else I wants top-side to work the artillery. Tell Ben Gunn to keep close watch on the starboard timbers. 'Tis there we shall shortly receive shot inboard," returned Flint.

"Aye, aye, Sir!" replied the Bosun's Mate, giving another salute. "You ladies foller me!"

Charlotte paused, one foot on the hatch coaming: "Take care, John," said she amid the squeak of carriage-trucks as the guns were run-out between decks.

"Black clothes don't sit so well on a black skin!"

Then she was gone, following Joan and Black Dog below. In her place appeared the dented morion of Phineas McGinty. Beneath it his wrinkled, leathery old face twitched with agitation as his head swivelled from side to side, just above the coaming, peering at the planks.

"Neglect o' Dooty! That's what it is – neglect o' Dooty!" raved he, clanking onto the Upper-deck. "Bosun! Why ain't the decks bin doused and sanded? How can the Damned Guns be op'rated proper, if the Damned Crews be skiddin' about on gore!"

Pew's snarled commands set 'Bucket and Spade' pumping water up from the Well-Deck, which they swabbed over the boards. Tiger Pip followed them, scattering sand from a brace of buckets slung on a yoke around his neck. The water was to dampen the risk of any spilt powder being ignited by friction; and the sand to assist firm footing on decks that would soon be slippery with blood.

Ducket and Wade came down the deck, trailing their swabs. A more dejected duo were never seen afloat. Both wore the same worried look o' despair, like a pair of paupers with empty begging bowls. Their once fine clothes were filthy, torn and stained with salt and tar. They pulled up short and nervously confronted Flint, shuffling their feet.

'Fatty' Ducket, now not so fat, stood with rivulets of sweat trickling down his drawn, lean face – his suit hanging on his wasted frame like a sack. "Captain, we appeal to you," began he with a nervous twitch tugging at one of his puffy, red-rimmed gooseberry eyes. "I think we have given good service as sailors, if somewhat reluctant at times, but you cannot ask us to double in the role of gunners. From one Gentleman to another, I implore you to release us from the administrations of that terrible man, Pew, and allow us access to the safety of the Orlop-deck. My colleague and I are even willing to assist the Carpenter below."

"How kind and considerate," murmured Flint in a mellow voice, bouncing lightly up and down on the balls of his feet, but with an icy glint in his narrowed eyes.

"I – I am a G-God fearing Baptist, Sir . . . not a B-Buccaneer," stammered Wade. "I must get back to Jamaica – my wife, my children, my business . . ."

"My bleedin' heart!" growled Billy Bones.

"Stop, I beseech ye!" cried Flint raising a hand. "Ere ye reduce me to tears. Ye both be free to return to the bosom o' yore families."

Relief flooded the Merchants' faces, but only for an instant as Flint turned and stretched out his arm, indicating towards the open sea. "I hope the pair o' ye are bonny swimmers!" he snapped. "Failing that, ye'll have ta stand and fight alongside the rest of us! Refuse, and I'll inform Bosun Pew he has a brace o' mutineers in his party!" Flint suddenly seized them by their filthy, sweat-stained cravats and practically lifted both men off their feet. "Care ye to be a dead God fearing Baptist?" roared he, thrusting his face close to Wade's.

I thought 'Spade' was about to burst into tears, while 'Bucket' looked sicker than a Saracen forced to celebrate High Mass. The Captain glared from one to the other for a moment, then hurled them from him. They collided and sprawled onto the deck. I watched 'em crawl away on all fours like kicked curs, despising the very sight of such creatures who would sell their own Mothers into slavery to make a fast Guinea. Blood-money was fine by their standards – providing their blood wasn't spilt in the getting of it!

"All Guns double-shotted, primed and ready, Sir!" reported Hands.

"Here be two teeth still frapped," said Flint, nodding towards the Quarter-Deck's starboard twelves. "I reckon us Officers can make as much noise as any bona fide Gunner. Bill, holler below for Pew and Black Dog to report aft. Tell 'em to bring cartridges along o' Joe the Carib and that big Buck Maroon. The QM and Stiff Nick can maintain discipline on the Lower-deck. They've a brace of good arms between 'em, heh, heh."

Cackling over his own wit in referring to McGinty and the Leading Hand, whose larboard wing was locked solid after the Rosario Fight, Flint and the rest of us unhoused the two Long Twelves. We released the muzzle lashings, laid out the side and train-tackles, then put the thick breeching rope in order. Working one gun at a time we hauled them back on the train-tackle, ready for loading. And weighty they were too, each piece weighing in at around 1¼ tons. When the cartridges arrived, Israel sent Tiger Pip scampering down to the Gun-Room for a pair of huge powder horns.

"Full ones mind you, Younker!" bawled the Gunner after him.

Along of the Bosun's Party reporting, we divided into two Crews. Israel captained one. I had charge of the other. Under the guidance of the Master Gunner were Pew, Black Dog, Fatty Ducket and a huge Maroon called Big Robin. In my Crew I had Flint for Loader, dealing with both cartridge and ball. Billy's task was to sponge and ram-home. Wade the Merchant had the job of supplying Flint with charges and shot from the thick, rope garlands faked behind the gun. Affixing the slow burning fusee to the crotch on his lintstock was Joe the Carib.

"Stab me and fall on!" grinned my newly demoted Loader, streaming sweat, with that hideous head-piece swinging against his near naked chest. "Few Gunners get the chance to set the Captain and First Mate hopping it hot-foot, you may lay to that, Long John, my Lad!"

Flint rid himself of his heavy Brigandine. Hats, coats and cutlasses were laid aside under the Poop steps, so we weren't encumbered and then we ran-out our guns with a wild cheer.

All the Gun Crews were busy, most of them stripped to the waist. They tied bandannas tightly around their for'eds, pulling the sides over their ears. The purpose was two-fold: firstly, to act as a sweat-band and keep our glims clear; secondly, to protect our lugs from the concussion of the cannon's discharge. Some gunners preferred to operate in bare feet with their trousers rolled up to the knee.

I finished bruising the priming powder in the pan, grinding the coarse grains to the fineness of pepper, using the wooden knob on the end of my great Gunner's horn. Then I closed the vent, sliding the thick lead apron into place over the pan. The firing of my piece would be the signal for a full broadside from both decks.

Rolling Aggie plowed down upon us on a larboard tack, her bows digging deep for the wind had freshened. From just over a cable's length away she opened fire with her For'ard Guns as they came to bear. At the other end of our deck, crowding about the brace of Long Toms below the Fo'c'sle, I saw Morgan's crew duck as a round-shot punched a hole in the Jib-Sail. Port after port spat smoke and flame at us. I felt the initial shock of a ball striking our outer skin, but after that the solid hits became general and *Walrus* shuddered in a maelstrom of hot metal.

Ball, bar and grape-shot slammed inboard, tearing and splintering our timbers, ripping through sails and rigging, wounding, maiming, killing, and in some cases reducing grown men to so much bloody gruel. Judging by the screams from below on the main Gun-Deck, several of the distressed were having a hard time dying. Well, even Admirals have to take pot luck in a sea fight. Look to his Lordship, Horace Nelson, him as got his backbone smashed by a bullet off Cape Trafalgar – and from a common French Musqueteer to by thunder!

As I squinted along the side-sights, checking the lay, above the din o' this man-made Hell came the brave, defiant 'Thumpety-Thump! Thumpety-Thump!' of Tiger Pip's Irish drum. There he sat, mates, perched bold as brass upon the poop steps beating the pig's skin for all he was worth, grinning wider than a Cheshire Cat.

"Give it a go, my Son!" cried Flint. "I'm partial to a bit of music, along of my powder-smoke!"

"I is a-thumpin', Capt'in! I is a thumpin', Suh!" returned the Nipper, proud as a Grenadier.

Beyond the notches that marked the Gun's upper sight, I watched *Aggie's* plunging Bowsprit slide into view. When her entire Fo'c'sle was framed in the port, I waited 'til our gun-muzzle began dropping, along of *Walrus's* downward roll, then flicked open the apron and stepping smartly aside, yelled: "FIRE!"

Crouching beside the starboard train-truck, Joe the Carib blew ash from the fusee and, reaching up with his linstock, dunked the glowing end into the priming pan. Stationed alongside in a like manner, but further up for'ard, Pew done the same to Israel's piece. The priming powder popped in the pan with a puff o' smoke, then both cannons belched with a roar, spewing out a white wall of smoke lanced with flame and a brace o' balls as they slammed back into the breechings. There was a slight pause, then a thunderous volley crashed out from the Battery below, along of Morgan's two twelves up for'ard. I steadied myself against the cant of the deck as *Walrus* rolled to leeward under the recoil of the deafening discharge. Smoke swirled from both hatch-ways and a dense, white cloud billowed up beyond the Bulwarks – extending from stem to stern like a fog-bank. The wind blew it back in our faces and its acrid fumes set us to coughing along o' wiping our eyes.

"STOP YER VENTS!" bawled Old McGinty from below.

I quickly slid my own lead apron into place to smother any sparks as remained in the chamber. Meantime, Billy was all in a clove-hitch with the length of thick rope, stiffened by spun yarn, which had a sheep-skin sponge on one end and a wooden, cup-shaped rammer at the other. In dunking the sponge into the water-bucket, the rammer fouled itself in the gun-tackle. Snorting, sweating and swearing blue fire worse than a felon in New-Gate, Billy fumbled to free it.

"Come now, Mister Bones," taunted I in jest. "Bear up, if you please, and act a little livelier!"

Flint roared with laughter over my gentle gibe, looking like Hell's own Imp, but the Mate's face became more mottled than Samson's skin. Wade's polite snigger was cut short by the sponge socking him alongside the lug. In between cursing the cup and denouncing me, in-as-much that my parents never stood before Parson, Billy freed the rammer and commenced to clean the gun – swabbing out the bore prior to reloading. Livid, he was, and snorting with rage.

"Ah, temper, Bill, temper," soothed Flint, grinning with those terrible teeth. "Ye know what they say: B-----ds have the Best Luck!"

At this point in the Battle, the *Agamemnon*, in reaching the end of her pass, raked us with canister from the swivels manned by the Marines on her fighting-tops. Duckett was collecting a cartridge for Israel's gun when this deadly hail descended and swept the deck. He flung up his arms, spun and fell – shot through the head, shoulder and chest. I mind him yet, sprawled on his back, the red blood running from him in rivulets, his gooseberry eyes unblinking, staring at the sky.

"Deary, deary me. Our bucket's got a hole in it!" mocked Pew.

Up for'ard, two of Morgan's men were down. One was flopping about the deck like a stranded fish, while his mate crawled towards the Fo'c'sle dragging a shattered leg. Another casualty was the Quadroon partnering Anderson at the wheel. He lay slumped over the barrel between the spokes with a bullet in his back.

"I needs a help here!" called out the Coxun, dragging the dead man clear.

"Bosun!" snapped Flint. "Bear a hand at the helm! Joe! Take station between the guns, ye'll have to fire both!"

As the *Agony* veered to starboard and began to tack, her stern-chasers signalled a brief interlude to the engagement, along of putting the Seal of Fate on our chances of escape. One ball splintered the Taffarel and carried away the centre Poop Lanthorn, renting a great gash in the Driver Sail. The next shot brought our Mizen by the board, crashing across the Starboard Quarter.

Gypsy Fuller poked his head above the hatch coaming. "Quarter-Master's compliments, Sir! Five killed and eight wounded," reported he. "How would you have us engage the next bout o' Dry Blows – Broadside ag'in?"

"Independent fire, Fuller! Independent fire!" replied the captain. "A-fore ye returns to station, Mister! Just act sharp, like, and haul our Ancient inboard. Then nip aloft and bend it below my Pennant. It goes against my grain to fight the King's Men, and I'll nay risk fouling Navy etiquette by them thinking maybe I've struck!" Flint turned to the cringing merchant. "You there, Spade! Look alive and assist the Top-man, here, to salvage Old Roger!"

Gypsy bawled down the hatch, repeating Flint's order, and doubled onto the poop. Wade trotted after him, gingerly stepping around the dead body of his former companion. They clambered over the wreckage of splintered spars, ripped sails and tangled rigging and began to haul on the halliard to which our 'Jolly Roger' was attached. The Flag hung out-board, half trailing in the water from the Mizen Peak. In reaching out to retrieve it, the block supporting Wade's weight suddenly came free and with a cry of sheer terror, he plunged head-first into the sea.

"Man Overboard!" yelled Fuller.

We crowded the Bulwarks, gazing astern. There was poor old Spade being dragged along in the Ship's wake, clinging for dear life to a mass of severed cordage. I nipped onto the poop, to bear a hand and help Gypsy haul him inboard. Hardly had I grabbed the rope, when I saw *Agamemnon* come-about and start her drive towards us. Had we a full press o' sail, along of a light pair o'heels, we could have easily out-sailed her. But between the dead-water swirling astern and the terrified, upturned face of Wade, I saw the long streamers of slawk weed trailing from our hull like a blasted mobile meadow.

"Hell's Teeth!" exclaimed Fuller and froze in hauling on the rope.

Hell's Teeth indeed, for veering around the Port Quarter came the black battle-scared pennant of Clipped Fin. He passed slightly astern of Wade, taking off a leg, I reckon, by the sound of his scream. He continued to shriek and began clawing hand over hand along the rope, leaving a wide trail of blood-stained water in his wake. In his panic, Spade became hopelessly fouled in the tangle of rigging that trailed from the Mizen's Peak. The distance needed to haul him clear of the water was only eight feet, but it might as well have been eighty! Gypsy and I strained at the ropes, pulling as if for First Prize in some Tug-o'-War at a country fête. With mounting horror we watched the Shark sweep in for a second attack, surging through water streaked with tendrils of red. That deadly, black snout struck the merchant a terrific blow in the back; the cords went slack in our hands; a sudden swirl of water and both were gone.

"Can you match such a death to anything more horrible, Long John?" asked Gypsy in a hoarse whisper as we finished hauling in our Banner.

"No, but one just as final if *Rolling Aggie* catches us perched up here like a pair o' blessed crows!" I replied.

We reported to Flint, both of us bad shook to be sure.

"Spade's life for our Ancient. Fair exchange, I calls it," remarked he. "The worst tragedies happen at sea; and here's another bearing down upon us this same moment. Quarters, Lads! Stand-by more dry blows!"

Fuller scrambled up the ratlings of the Main-Mast with the big flag draped over his shoulder. *Agamemnon* closed to within three hundred yards, her main and fore courses billowing, and fired both bow guns in commencement of what was to be her fourth and final bite at us.

"FIRE AS YER GUNS BEAR!" came the QM's cry from below.

As *Agamemnon*'s bowsprit drew level with our stern her seamen brailed up the main courses so as not to by-pass their target. I ordered Flint and Billy to raise our breech, which they did using both handspec and crow. I booted the quoin further in on its bed to lower the gun's muzzle in line with *Agamemnon*'s ports. A quick check on the lay and the order to 'FIRE!' was rewarded by seeing splinters fly from one of her openings. Closing upon our starboard quarter, her bulk took away what little wind we had and our sails went slack so we stayed. Gun by gun we opposed her advances, but *Rolling Aggie* held her peace until she drew level. Beam to beam, we were, point-blank at fifty yards when her whole larboard battery roared in reply.

Our Gun-Port disintegrated. Splinters flizzed in all directions. I saw Israel's piece slew round under the impact of a ball, which in striking the breech, shattered into shards o' razor sharp iron. Big Robin the Maroon shrieked and crumpled to the deck clutching his side, where two ribs had been smashed in by a fragment of shot. At the same instance, I felt something slam into my left knee and I grabbed the pomiglion of our Cannon for support. Through a haze of smoke and pain, a distant voice was screaming: "My Leg! My Leg!"

That voice were MINE!

CHAPTER XXIII

WOODEN SHIPS – IRON MEN!

After my ears stopped singing and my vision cleared, the first thing I saw was the ship's wheel – or what was left of it! The side served by Anderson was still intact, although the Coxun lay sprawled in the lee o' the Poop. At a glance I reckoned him to have 'slipped his moorings' and gone to his own place. But all that remained of Pew's part of the wheel was half a lower rim with jagged, broken spokes protruding from the upper edge on the barrel around which the tiller ropes were wrapped. The Bosun was groping about on hands and knees, shaking his head same as a prize-fighter do in trying to recover from a hefty punch. Whether he was just dazed or dying from a mortal hurt, I couldn't tell. The scarf was gone from around his for'ed and his lank, red hair hung before his face like a curtain.

Billy Bones stood swaying, his countenance the colour of wax except for the scar – a dirty, livid white. He stuffed a neck-cloth beneath his shirt and buckled his broad belt over it to staunch the blood welling from his side. Joe the Carib bore several minor splinter wounds on his naked, tattooed back. And Israel Hands dripped gore from a gashed chin. Only Black Dog and Flint seemed unscathed.

"Barbecue! Ye be bleeding worse than a stuck-pig! Look t'yore leg, Man!" cried the Captain and with a pang o' pity I watched the Big Buccaneer gently lower the limp form of Tiger Pip onto the rope, shot-garlands faked behind the gun.

Our Nipper had been supplying both pieces with powder and ball, in place of 'Bucket and Spade'. There weren't a mark on him, mind, but his soft brown eyes were glazed by Death's hard hand. Concussion, caused by the wind of a passing round-shot, had snuffed out his young life quick as a candle in a gale. The saddest sight I ever saw, in all my years at sea, were that lad as lay dead with his beloved drum slung across his chest. I never sailed alongside a better boy than 'im – shiver my sides!

I wasn't slow to heed Flint's advice! Pain knifed through my left leg. Gritting my teeth I saw the red blood spurting from a rent in the knee o' my buck-skins, soaking my sea-boot along of each heart-beat. Using a piece of frapping, I bound the cord tightly around my thigh, by way of a tourniquet, pulling 'til the bleeding stopped, then tucked the end under itself and secured it so's not to slip.

While the wheel was unmanned and with a head-sea running, both wind and current had forced our rudder to Port, swinging *Walrus*'s bow towards the shore. Flint took charge o' the helm hisself. Using all his great strength he started to bring the Ship back on course, crowding *Agamemnon* even closer. Holding that shattered wheel in a grip of iron, our Captain achieved what normally took the combined power o' two, strong seamen.

"Joe! Tell the Quarter-Master to report top-side, along of two t'act for Timoneers!" cried he, the blue veins in his neck bulging with effort.

The Carib stuck his linstock in the deck and disappeared below. The battle raged on with *Agamemnon* holding level, blasting us point-blank from fifty feet. Our fore-top-mast hung upside down, suspended by its various blocks and braces, all in a tangle with the Fore-top-gallant-sails and rigging. The Fore-courses were mere crumpled masses o' shot torn canvas; and our Main-sail, also full of holes, served better as a sieve! Some of the RN gunners on *Aggie*'s upper deck were doing their best to render *Walrus* unsailable.

From where I was slumped clinging alongside my cannon's breech, I saw the starboard cat-head go whirling away and moments later, a ball carried *Walrus*'s bell overboard.

Rolling Aggie didn't rule it all her own way, to be sure! A steady bombardment from our battery below had reduced her Fore-mast, bringing it down by the board, which in turn rendered the Bowsprit into a tangled, splintered ruin. For added rupture there were gaping shot-holes along the length of her larboard side. Morgan's Gunners were still in the game, trading dry-blows from up Forard. More cannister, chain and multiple bar-shot tore through our rigging. Flizzing flew off the Main-mast and something bounced onto the nettings stretched above me. A dangling arm swung before my eyes, streaming blood, and I looked up into the wide-eyed dead face o' Gypsy Fuller.

Under the gimlet eye of our Master-Gunner, Black Dog and Billy Bones heaved their gun back in line of *Agamemnon*. There were now only enough hands to operate one piece. After straining over handspec and crow-bar, they reloaded. "Home!" cried Israel Hands on feeling the priming wire jump in the vent as Billy thrust the cartridge down to the chamber and withdrew the rammer. Israel held the iron needle poised above the touch-hole, ready to pierce the powder-bag with a brace o' hard jabs, when the harsh, guttural voice of Pew arrested one an' all.

"Avast, there! Someone bear me a hand! I wants a wipe to clear the blood from my blasted dead-lights! Lively now, one o' you skulking lubbers!" snarled he.

The Bosun stood half crouched, groping about with powder-blackened, blood-stained hands. The red hair that lay plastered against his for'ed and hung in matted tangles alongside his face was caked in gore, but it was his glims that rooted us to the spot. 'Blasted Dead-Lights' was the word for it! Flizzings from the shattered wheel had struck athwart the bridge of his great hooked nose, reducing both eyes to a sticky, translucent mess that trickled down his cheeks amid tears o' watery blood. In short, mates, Pew were Blind as a Bat!

Black Dog fetched him and led the way to where I was at. "Here's Long John, suffering a slight hurt hisself. He'll attend you, Pew. I'm needed on the gun." And with that the Bosun's Mate flashed me a withering 'You douse-the-fire-Jack-I-done-my-toast!' look and hopped it hot foot back to his station.

Grimy hands groped my person. "Whereabouts are you hit, Barbecue? Much pain, matey?" he asked, cocking his head to one side and gazing at my face with those unseeing, mangled orbs.

"In the knee – left leg. 'Tain't too bad a hurt, I reckon, but I don't feel too tickety-boo," replied I, instinctively trying to draw away from the eyeless horror. But his fingers closed on my shirt with the vice-like grip of talons.

"My glims is stinging, burning like b-damned, and I can't find my neck-cloth no-how. Give me the lend of a wipe!" demanded he.

Telling a Tincture o' Truth would serve no purpose, so swallowing the bile in my throat, I plowed straight in and pitched it to him red-hot: "'Tain't no use me 'Beating about the Bush', Pew!" croaked I, placing my mouth nearer his ear to carry my voice above the 'Crash!' of Israel's gun. "All the wipes in the world won't rekindle your glims. Your dead-lights is shuttered permanent, along of punctured eyeballs. You has to bear-up, Bosun and accept for all your days, you'll be as blind now as when but a babby-unborn in your mother's belly!"

Better men would have broke, but not our Bosun. Pew's mouth twitched and his hand tightened into a balled claw on my shirt. "My mother died the day I was hatched!" returned he in his familiar, guttural snarl. "But I survived that an' I'll survive this, by thunder! Ere I goes below, I'll live to roll in a coach with flunkeys to answer my every beck and call! Eyes? Black Dog will serve me for dead-lights! Now lead me alongside a piece of artillery. I can load a ball and haul tackle – blindfold!"

I bound up his eyes with my own scarf and Israel took him into his own Team. Cruelty were his passion, mates, and heartlessness his trade-mark, yet I never met his match for fearlessness. No Pirate, past nor present, were more pistol proof than Blind Pew – and you may lay to that!

McGinty and Joe the Carib, along of two t' act for Timoneers, appeared on deck in the nick of time to help save us from a first rate disaster. As Flint completed his exertions at the wheel and brought our head clear of the shore, the manoeuvre fetched us to within spitting distance of *Agamemnon*. So close were we that the main-yards grated, overlapped, then interlocked. Now for ships that sail too near alongside each other the sea acts in a peculiar push'n pull manner. While the bow-waves thrust the heads apart, the void left by the dead-water swirling astern draws the after-ends together. Our quarters kissed with a mighty 'Crash!' and sprang apart almost immediately, under tension o' the locked yard-arms, but not before a mixture of Seamen and Red-Coated Marines had leapt onto our Poop-Deck.

"We be boarded! Starboard Quarter!" cried QM McGinty. Drawing his big broad-sword he met a burly cutlass-bearing seaman half way up the poop steps amid a clash o' steel – not six feet from me.

Flint wasn't slow off the mark, neither! Flinging the coats aside from under those same steps where our weapons were at, he stuck his wavy bladed dagger between his pointed teeth, then snatched up a pistol and the clam-shell hilted cutlass. Nimble as a cat he vaulted the rails to lay alongside McGinty in a brace of shakes. Billy Bones, Black Dog, Israel Hands and Joe the Carib crowded me close, trampling the clothes underfoot including my fine, blue coat, in grasping for the first hanger that came to hand. But by then several Matelots and Marines had clambered across the wreckage littering the Poop. They swarmed down the larboard steps and fanned out over the Quarter-Deck, bellowing for blood.

"REPEL BOARDERS, ALL HANDS – ALL HANDS!" roared the Mate.

Far from being dead, as I'd first feared, our Coxun launched hisself into the attack, along o' the two Timoneers who were forced to abandon the wheel and fight for their lives. Although Job Anderson sported a lump the size of a duck's egg on his left temple and the eye was half closed, it didn't cloud his judgement in skewering a Seaman amidships with his first thrust. In a matter of moments the Quarter-Deck became a mass o' struggling figures, wreathed in smoke, hacking and hollering at each other – pure Bedlam!

I salvaged my coat from where it lay trampled upon the blood-stained boards and a right Royal mess it looked, to be sure. Inside its capacious pockets were my double-barrelled Pettijeans. A brace of pistols mustering four shots, each barrel double-loaded to bear a trump hand in the survival stakes, be a close comfort in time of Strife – you may lay to it! I pressed myself back against the Cannon's Breech and checked my priming. Pew positioned hisself on t'other side of me and together we a-waited what might come at us from out the fray.

Unattended, *Walrus* again swung towards the lee-shore, only this time we drew *Agamemnon* along with us. Trailing wreckage and the respective Ship's boats, both vessels sailed as if under the restraint o' drag anchors. Combining this along of variable light airs, the wind having dropped off again, we were within a point or two of drifting as made small difference. Any breeze that tried to belly the sails aboard either Ship, simply passed clean through the shot-torn canvas.

The smoke drifted with us, clinging about both Ships like a ragged, dirty grey shroud. Mere yards away I saw the flashing tongues o' flame from *Agamemnon*'s discharges, sinking into a dull red glow like the opening and closing of furnace fires in the foundry of this man made hell. Several grappling irons were thrown across, but Morgan's Gunners cut the lines clear – backed by more hands from below.

QM McGinty staggered down off the Poop, his broken broad-sword clattering onto the steps. "I've sprung a leak amidships on me larboard beam, Long John," gasped he. "Jim . . . the Cap'n . . . be . . . be hard pressed . . ." faltered the Old Stander and collapsed at my feet.

"Bear a hand, Pew!" cried I, guiding the groping Bosun.

Together we dragged our Quarter-Master into safety between the guns. I saw at a glance that Phineas was hard hit. His breast-plate showed a small hole on the lower left side, below the heart, from which a bright rill of blood trickled over the armour.

"Stay close, Pew, and keep low! The Cap'n needs aid!" I hollered above the din and lurched towards the Poop step stanchions.

My own part in the hurly-burly that raged about me was brief but bloody. A hatless Marine suddenly appeared out of the mêlée and barred my way. Wild eyed with the heat of battle, his bayoneted musket extended before him, his teeth flashed in his smoke-blackened face and he crouched ready to lunge at me. With no time for proper aim, I fired from the hip. The brace of balls from my right hand barrel lifted him off the deck even as his bayonet came up. One bullet struck his crossed straps; the other ruptured his throat. He fell away from me gargling in his own gore, which gushed from his mouth in a crimson flood.

Numb and lifeless, like so much deadwood, my leg supported my weight well enough without pain. I lurched up the steps, past the sprawled corpse of the Seaman McGinty and slain, and onto the poop. Flint was hard pressed to be sure. He held three tars at bay along of kriss and cutlass, keeping them penned behind the Mizen's wreckage, but a Sergeant of Marines was clambering over the tangle to broach him to from starboard. A Seaman and a Jolly already lay dead among the rigging. Flint's heavy pistol was close by them, resting against a block, its butt smeared with blood.

"Beware t' starboard, Cap'n, an' hold hard!"

Flint heeded my warning none too soon, pivoting just in time to parry the downward swing of the Sergeant's half-pike, catching it with the flat of his cutlass. I pistoled a Seaman, triggering off the remaining barrel on my right hand piece, and blew his brains apart. In the same breath, a single swipe from Flint's broad blade cleaved the Sergeant's skull asunder. The two surviving tars drew back, their eyes wide in horror as I levelled my left handed barker. But before I could dispatch them, along of my last two loads, *Agamemnon*'s keel sliced into the sand and she stuck. Her 700 tons burthen and 12 foot draft needed deeper water than *Walrus*, whose 300 tons drew only 8 feet. We were all flung off balance as the impact wrenched *Walrus* clear of the Frigate. Weakened by shot-torn rigging, our rival's Main-Top-Mast couldn't withstand the jolt of the sudden stop and came crashing down onto the deck. Two Marines were swept off the Fighting-Top and fell screaming to their deaths along with it.

"She's sewed, by thunder!" cried Flint, clinging to wreckage, pointing towards *Rolling Aggie* with his dripping cutlass.

I myself was momentarily all-aback, sprawled against the splintered quarter-rails. The two tars, seeing safety sliding away from them as the distance increased between us and *Agamemnon*, did a quick about-turn and jumped overboard. Their thin screams of distress told me that Clipped Fin was still cruising around like a blessed Arab bum-boat after baksheesh. So always look afore you leap, mates!

Several more shots came at us, the glow o' the cannon's discharge flaring briefly in the thick bank of eddying smoke that swirled between Ships, before all firing ceased. On the Quarter-Deck the final curtain was about to fall over the fight, but there were two main acts yet to be played.

The first featured a bearded Petty Officer, who was grappling with our Bosun. Blind Pew was on his knees, held by the hair with his head wrenched back. The PO's cutlass was poised to chop, but he stayed his hand on seeing his victim was without eyes.

"Lost yer lights 'ave yer – yer Judas haired swab!" roared the Petty O. "Shame on yerz for cheatin' honest sea-birds out of tasty tit-bits when yer swinging in chains on Execution Do . . ."

Guided by the voice, our Bosun sprang off the boards and seized the PO's throat in a grip of steel. He went over backwards, his legs kicked from beneath him, and dropped his cutlass in trying to ease that choking claw. Blind Pew was astride him in a flash, pinning one arm against the deck with his knee. Black Dog ran to the rescue, but ere he reached the struggle, Pew took the PO's head between his strong, scarred hands and with a single, savage jerk, snapped the man's thick neck like a dry stick. Me'n Flint heard it 'Crack!' from where we was at.

Will Shakespeare hisself couldn't have set a better scene for the Grand Finale that was played out on the Quarter-Deck. All the boarders were dead, barring three, but of those only two were capable o' putting up a fight. One was a Captain of Marines; the other were a thick set, yellow fanged Private who crouched astern of him. Alongside this bull-shouldered brute, nursing a dripping left arm, was a thin, scar-faced Corporal glaring about him with hot, mad eyes. Our Gang had all three hemmed in by the poop recess. The Marine Captain stood hatless, his fine coat torn, and with a broken tuck in his hand. Calm and erect, he a-waited the final rush that would cut him down.

"Avast!" bawled Flint. "Stay the hands, Bill! Belay there, Captain! Ask ye for Quarter and I'll grant mercy for ye and yore men! Ye have fought the good fight and it goes against my grain to trade blows with any as wears the King's Coat! What say ye?"

The Captain of Marines had turned at Flint's first call. He was on the verge of giving an answer, when the burly Private thrust upwards with his bayoneted musket and skewered him athwart the body – full way right in up to the socket!

"Go to it, Carver my Buck!" cried the scar-faced Corporal with savage glee.

We stood aghast at this foul act of Treachery – and from him who was one of His Majesty's Jollies, too! Mind you, mates, there was nothing Jolly about this sour looking swab. His mouth twisted into a yellow-toothed leer as he jerked the bayonet free and stepped back. The Marine Captain gaped at him, his face showing surprise and disbelief more'n pain. He remained on his feet for a few moments, swaying, doubled over clutching his side. Then his lights lost their lustre and rolled into his head. Only the whites were showing when he slumped to the deck – stone-dead!

"Blast your eyes, you butchering bullock!" cried Billy Bones starting forward, but hove-to when the Marine levelled his musket. With his lips drawn back over those yellow fangs, he looked more dangerous than one o' them diamond-backed rattling snakes found on the American Main!

"Hang-fire, Mister and stand-fast!" snarled he, bunching his thick shoulders. He faced midway between the Mate and Flint, his dark slitted eyes darting up and down from one to the other. "I suffered a Point of Honour, not a week since, along o' this lubber! Two dozen at the gratings for tarnished brass, on that swine's say so! An' me buttons wus as bright as any! Well, I've sunk him now, I have! There's no gain in killing me'n Pikey! Give us a berth aboard here and you'll find us hardy an' handy enough! Pikey can shoot the 'ead off a crow at a hundred paces and I can carve the 'art out of a man afore it stops beatin'!"

"Point taken," replied Flint. "Put up yore piece."

The Marine reversed his musket and 'thunked!' its bayonet into the deck, where the weapon's blood-stained butt bowed back and forth above the boards. Folding his arms, he gazed about him at his new found mess-mates. Port Tack, who had served on Morgan's Team, stepped forward and offered his meaty hand.

"Welcome aboard *Walrus*, matey," said he as they shook. "By wot handle are yer known?"

"Lowe! Ned Lowe!" returned the Marine, bearing his yellow fangs. "But among my late company, I were called 'Carver!' And this is Corporal Pike," added he, slapping Scar-Face on the shoulder. "Known to one and all as: 'The Mad Marine'!"

'Birds of a feather if ever there was,' thought I. 'A Buzzard and a Vulture!' For fair or foul, I didn't much care for the cut of Marine Carver Lowe and his cronie. Neither of 'em were cowards. Future actions proved that. But a bigger pair of curs you wouldn't find ashore or afloat on all the Seven Seas – you may lay to it!

"Thunder!" exclaimed Flint, glancing towards the shore. "Man the Helm! Lively there, afore we run aground! Clew-up all canvas, except the Jib! Black Dog! Detail a leadsman for the main-chains!"

The Bosun's Mate piped: 'All Hands,' but it was a pitiful few who answered the call from below – dirty, sweaty, smoke-blackened and bloody. To sail the ship into a safe berth was top priority now. The coast-line were broken up into small islands here-abouts and navigation was made tricky due to shallows. As we drifted in on the reflux of the tide, we lost sight of *Agamemnon*. She disappeared, swallowed by the smoke haze along of the gathering dusk.

After Flint helped me down off the poop, I declined to go below and remained at my station alongside the shattered wheel. The Surgeon had far more pressing casualties to attend – or so I thought! We were well into the Everglades when we let go our remaining anchor. The Leadsman's last call was recorded as: "By the Mark, Two Minus One!" which informed us we were afloat in eleven feet of water. At first glance we looked to be land-locked, riding at anchor in the centre of a small lake. The water was smooth as glass and crystal clear with several narrow channels leading into it. At low-tide our anchorage became a lagoon, the water level falling only a few feet, which left us slightly sewed ourselves, but we were safe enough.

Old Phineas McGinty wanted to remain on deck, propped up between the Guns. But Flint insisted he was taken down for the Surgeon's attention. The Quarter-Master cursed Flint roundly and those who bore him below. One first rate oath followed another, but the Old Stander's voice was weak – the air bubbling and wheezing about in his punctured lung.

A butt of wine was broached on the Fo'c'sle for all hands. In addition, those of us who were wounded received a small tot o' brandy from out the petty tally, by way of a bracer. Flint toured the lower Gun-Deck, along with Billy Bones, and returned top-side looking mortal white about the gills, excepting for his lips and nose. Tinged with blue, they was, in the light of the sinking sun – near matching the colour of the tattoos on his chest and forearms.

"Stab me and fall on," breathed he. "I havena seen such carnage since we broke the French Line at Blenheim. Five Ports shot out; three pieces up-ended and oor decks a-muck with the red blood of oor finest men."

"Aye," growled Billy, nodding his head in agreement. "Our scuppers is a-wash with purple gore, splintered bone and brains. Cast your glims for a look-see out-board, Barbecue. The blessed *Walrus* herself seems t'be bleeding from her very bowels."

And so it were, mates. For a hundred yards all around us the ship was riding the anchor in a crimson pool. Blood flowed from the scuppers and the gaping gashes in our starboard side, for all the world like *Walrus* were some Wounded Whale just escaped from the Harpoons o' the Hunters.

We watched a grim-faced Job Anderson help lower the limp, Lifeless form of Gypsy Fuller down from the nettings. "Him and me were young together an' many a rough sea did we sail. I'd best give a word o' comfort to his widder," remarked the Coxun and followed those who bore the body below.

Just on sunset, Flash Dan appeared through the aft hatchway – although now not quite so 'Flash'. His yellow, leather apron was smeared with the red muck of his calling, as were his hands, and there was dark splashes on the white, floppy sleeves of his fancy shirt rolled up to the elbows.

"A word, James," said the Doctor to Flint. "I deem it wise if the great cabin was prepared for the wounded. The Orlop Deck is no place for ailing men to rest and recuperate in. Upon my Soul, the stench from blood and vomit is enough to turn the stomach of a grave-yard ghoul."

The Surgeon gave a start on seeing the splinter-marked, bloody features of Pew, who stood between me and the Mate. Flash Dan's eyebrows arched as he looked from the Bosun to Billy's blood-stained side, and then down to the gore-smeared leg of my buckskins. "You three Brave Beauties should have reported below, long before this," rebuked he mildly. "It ain't good policy to leave wounds unattended for too long in this climate."

"We're all still standing," growled Billy. "Do Joan Fuller know she's a widder-woman yet?"

"Indeed, and she took the news with a staunch heart. She said: 'Many a bold man has met his Maker this day, so he's in good company.' Both she and Miss

Charlotte took Tiger Pip's passing a bit hard. But even now those brisk pair of poppets are serving the wounded," replied the Doctor. "Hold still, Bosun, and let me view your damage first," he ordered and gently untied the bandanna that I had used to bind up those shattered orbs. "My God, Man! How come you are still on your feet?" The Doctor blanched, staring into the ruined sockets.

"Beauty were never my strong point," came Pew's guttural reply, showing his small, curved, stoat-like teeth in a savage leer. "But I can still give orders, splice a rope or serve a gun!"

"I have seen the Dead, the Dying and now – the Damned." Flash Dan replaced the bandanna and patted Pew's shoulder. "I shall clean you up, my man, down below and make you as presentable to the public gaze as is humanly possible," said he and turned to the Mate.

"How fares Old Phineas?" asked Flint.

Flash Dan shook his head, pulling Billy's shirt aside. "I can do nothing for him, I fear. The ball has ruptured his internals and lies embedded too near the heart. We can only make his last hours as comfortable as conditions allow. But I do not think he will survive the night."

Flint cursed and Billy cried out under the Doctor's probing fingers.

"Rest easy, Mister Bones. A bad gash, to be sure, but nothing a few stitches won't rectify," soothed the physician straightening up. "Would some kind soul give me a pipe? Being a slave to tobacco is somewhat of a bind, working below decks, and I am dying for want of a puff. And now, John, let's attend to that leg of yours."

He seated me on the poop steps. Several loungers gathered round. Along of Flint and Billy, Israel Hands, Tom Morgan, George Merry and Job Anderson, Ben Gunn was also there, having just arrived from below with a report on the damage.

"All is secured, Sir," said our Carpenter to Flint. "But we be riding low in the water and with five foot in the bilges, we'll have to man the pumps afore we can budge from here."

"Well done to you and the ladies, Ben," congratulated Flint. "But before we can patch up and pump the ship, needs are that we patch up the crew, what's left of 'em, afore we budge anywhere!"

All eyes were on the Doctor. Taking my own ivory handled dirk from out of my blood-stained sea-boot, the same knife that Pew had used to save my life all those years ago, he slit open the leg of my buckskins from boot-top to tourniquet. The leather, normally soft and supple, had turned hard – stiff with congealed gore.

"Will someone pass forward a glim and give me a little light on this matter?" asked the Doctor, for he was now working in semi-darkness – the sun having all but set.

Job Anderson's long arm held the binnacle lantern that Flint fired-up with his 'Flasher'. Inquisitive heads peered forward in a tight, half circle as the surgeon pulled the stiffened leather apart. There came gasps and low mutterings of surprise. My knee-cap was a mass of jagged, splintered bone; and the exposed flesh of my leg had turned a mottled, dirty grey. I had no feeling in the limb whatsoever. The Doctor studied the damage in silence for a few moments, thoughtfully puffing his pipe. Finally, his clear blue eyes flicked upwards and locked on mine. I saw compassion mirrored in them, along of a sorry sadness.

"John Silver," said he very softly. "You are a man by reputation, so I'll not mince my words. The limb is lifeless and the flesh has already started to mortify. The tourniquet was left on too long, but in any case, your knee is shattered beyond my humble skill to repair it. In order to save your life – I must amputate your leg!"

CHAPTER XXIV

MINUS FIVE TOES!

"D'you hear that, mates?" piped Ben Gunn. "Long John's for the chop!"

Following those words a cold, creeping dread flooded through my system. I felt as if the blood in my veins were being replaced by someone tipping a bucket of ice-water through a hole in the top of my head. My heart sounded like a drum, booming and banging away between my ears. Seeing my stricken look, the surgeon reached for me.

"Hands off!" I cried and hopped a-top the poop steps, quick as a young lad, goaded by fear and panic. From there I pitched into the Doctor with a broadside of defiance. "You may lay to this, Flash Dan! I was born in one bit an' by the powers – I ain't dying in pieces! So hear this, one and all! I'll part the brains of him as first raises a finger ag'in me!"

To back up my threat I drew the one barker from my belt, that remained charged, and covered the crowd of up-turned faces below me. I saw Ben Gunn slip away and slink off down the hatchway. The evening grew chill with a mist that started to come off the water. Only a thin ribbon of red in the western sky marked the sunset. No one spoke or stirred; even *Walrus* stopped creaking and groaning. The silence was so heavy you could have cut the air with a jack-knife! Then I spied other lights and many of them, flickering like Will-o'-the-Wisps as they reflected on the vapoury waters of the lake. The lights were torches – torches stuck in the bows of approaching boats!

"Ye'd best stand-by for butchery else-where, ship-mates!" And pointed with my pistol, along of my yell o' triumph, so elated was I at drawing their attention off me.

All hands crowded the side. Flint and Billy snapped spy-glasses open.

"'Tis *Agamemnon*'s crew comed to clapp-aboard on us in revenge! Blasted long-boats, look you!" announced Morgan in his peculiar sing-song accent – the way of all Welshmen.

"The Devil burn the bunch of 'em mess o' swabs!" spat Anderson.

"Maybe we can call a parley and claim the King's pardon?" voiced some stout-hearted soul.

"No hope but to Strike and cry Quarter!" wailed a third.

"Perchance their surgeon is in need of a good assistant," said Flash Dan, sounding hopeful.

"Batten yore hatches and belay all this bilge talk, ye hen-hearted fools!" snarled Flint. "When since do RN landing parties advertise their presence along of a torch lit procession? This dinna be a Spithead Review and they ain't long-boats!"

"No, by thunder!" exclaimed Billy. "Them be dug-outs under a Flag o' Truce; I can see white bunting a-fluttering beneath the brands!"

At that point a voice hailed us from across the water: "SHIP AHOAY! HANG-FIRE, CAP'N FLINT! 'TIS ME, SIR, THE SAIL-MAKER, AND I'VE BROUGHT AID!"

"By the powers!" roared George Merry. "It's 'Sails Lowether', him as we left stranded high and dry – buried up to his bulwarks in sand!"

"And here's 'im in company of Seminole Savages, large as life!" concluded Black Dog.

Wild cheering from our crew echoed and rolled across to the Indians. They replied with a weird chant, whose tune kept them in time to the rise and fall of their paddles. So intent was I in watching the approaching boats, I didn't see the dark shadow that rushed up the Poop steps. Next moment I were locked in the tight embrace of my beloved Charlotte Eleanor.

"John, oh John," sobbed she, clinging close with her smooth, soft arms about my neck. "Ben Gunn tol' me of your terrible plight. What's to become of us? And here come the savages – will they devour us?"

"No, no, lovey! How 'Sails' done it, I dunno, but they have come to deliver us. Now don't you fret none over, Long John. I ain't sunk yet, not by a deep-sea-mile," soothed I, stroking her woolly head by way to give her comfort.

Secure for the moment in each other's warm embrace, we watched the boats glide alongside. A full moon peeped above the trees, bathing the bay in silvery beams which lit up the scene clear as day. And what a spectacle it were, mates. I never saw such colours since being brained in a brawl in Maracaibo one time!

Gay shirts of checked linen were slashed with silver ornaments, belts of turquoise and necklaces of pearl-shell, along of bright baubles. On many the moon-light glinted against yellow metal, be it brass or gold. Most wore head-dresses made from the rich plumage of unknown birds. All were armed with an assortment o' weapons: Knives – big as cleavers in alligator sheaths; Tomahawks and Hatchets; Long Spanish Pistols and a sprinkling of Arquebuses. These latter, 'Thunder-Sticks', as the Seminoles called 'em, were deemed antique in

Morgan's time. Cumbersome and heavy, they was, needing the support of a forked pole to fire them. The faces on these people were copper-coloured, smooth and beardless – their hair straight, long and black. Their features weren't marred with tattooing, but painted in such designs and colours they appeared like Demons fresh from the Pit.

"Avast you, Ebenezer Lowether! Tell them heathen friends o' yours t' douse their glims, afore they sets us a-fire!" bawled the Mate as the first of the dug-outs bumped the boards of *Walrus*'s outer-skin.

"Right you are, Sir!" acknowledged the Sail-Maker and sent his own brand hissing into the water. "But this 'ere gatherin' ain't heathens, Mister Bones! Most of 'em speaks perfect English, like wot me'n you does, Sir!"

"Me no heathen!" boomed a deep voice. "Me wears um the Holy Cross of God! Our Fadder, Him chant in Heaven, Harold be thy name! Hallelujah and Hail Mary! Give me the Glory and a Penny for the Story – Amen!"

More torches followed the first, spluttering into extinction amid vapours of steam. Bedecked in their beads and feathers, the Seminoles swarmed aboard of us. They didn't come empty handed either. Baskets of fruit and fresh cooked meat were soon being hoisted inboard, along of large stone flagons. When the stoppers were uncorked their contents gave off the rich aroma o' rum! From among the revelry and merry-making on the deck below, Ben Gunn brought me a pannikin.

"How do, Mister Silver. 'Barbecue could use a bracer,' thinks I. 'And right welcome,' says you," cackled the Carpenter handing me the noggin.

"Thankee, Ben," I replied and drank it out in one.

No sooner had I lowered the cup, when that wily old wood-worker turned and bawled below: "Long John's drained his caulker, Doctor! Swallowed every last drop – sweet as nature!"

"Wha . . . meansh thish, Ben?" mumbled I along o' slurred words. "Rum-sh taint'd." My ears were singing and my mouth held a bitter taste in it.

"Just a tincture of opium, Long John – Doctor's orders," replied he, grinning up at me.

Stricken by poppy juice – the Flower of Forgetfulness – my head started to spin and the world swam before my eyes. Charlotte held me close and as I clung all the tighter to her, I felt the pistol gently plucked from my nerveless grasp. Sinking down into the depths o' darkness, I was, when strong arms supported me from behind.

"Leave him, Lassie. I has him secure." Flint spoke right alongside my ear, but his voice sounded remote, coming from far, far away.

I awoke in a haze. My head felt as heavy as if I'd spent the last ten hours full-seas-over, while the taste in my mouth was on par with the bottom of my bird's cage! Sweat stung my eyes. The lighting was dim, the air rank with the acrid tang o' burnt powder, blood and vomit. I was in the Doctor's domain – the dreaded Orlop Deck. A face swam into view, black and shiny, blurring for a moment as a cool cloth was wiped over my burning brow. The buzzing in my brain became distinct words.

"He be coming alongside, Sir," came a voice that I thought belonged to George Merry. The light grew brighter as the glim was moved closer.

"You is safe, John, and in good hands," soothed Charlotte, wiping that cool cloth over my face again.

I lay a-top several sea-chests aligned together, resting upon a canvas covered, blood-stained pallet of straw – what we called a donkey's breakfast. My head was cradled by the softness of Charlotte's lap. In the gloom I saw a row of wounded men. Some sat propped against the ship's knees. The more badly injured lay upon the bare, overlapping boards with their heads cushioned on bunched clothing. I saw Flint standing bowed beside Billy, in company of Joe the Carib and some Seminoles. Then Flash Dan's face blocked my view as he stooped over me.

"John," said he, squinting, the wrinkles around his eyes crinkling into crow's feet. "I have never operated on a man against his Will. Are you in full command of your faculties? You understand my words?"

"Aye, Doctor. You be plain enough," murmured I.

"Then I shall be plainer," returned he. "As I told you when we were top-side, your knee is smashed beyond mortal repair. The limb is dead and once the flesh starts to mortify and the poison penetrates your system, my skill will become void. Take amputation and life is still within your grasp. Refuse, then all you can look to is a lingering, painful death and the coldness of a watery grave. The only consolation I can give, along with that choice, is possible clemency from your Maker."

"You promised we was to be wed, John. Would you have me destitute, to wander unwanted and uncared for in this cruel, sinful, wicked world? Or perhaps to be seized and bound into slavery – or worse!" chided my Beloved gently and her tears fell soft upon my face, sweet and warm.

That decided me, that did! A cripple? Then so be it! I gripped her hand and crushed it to my lips, catching Flash Dan's clear eye in my own misty gaze. "Do as you must, Doctor," said I in a firm voice, yet coarse and dry, grating like gravel. "You just carve away as if 'twere Christmas, for you'll hear no murmur from me."

Even the groans of the wounded seemed to diminish as Flash Dan straightened himself and snapped his fingers – brisk and business like. In the silence the noise sounded on par to a brace o' pistol shots. A beaker was passed to Charlotte, who fed me another go of the same mixture that laid me low before – opium and rum.

Now Daniel Hunter was a physician far in advance of his time. I knew from his past performances at the chopping block that he always warmed his instruments, prior to a carve-up, to lessen the initial shock o' cold steel on warm flesh. He also kept his patient drugged as much as possible. After I drained the draft, a musket-ball was placed between my teeth. This was to stop me biting my tongue. And to keep from swallowing the bullet, a knotted string was attached to a hole bored through it. Flash Dan's own invention, that was. Some saw-bones used a gag of rope or a leather strap, but this method stemmed a man's breathing. The Doctor and a Loblolly Boy were just exchanging my own crude tourniquet for a belted screw-clamp, when a cry o' fear, spliced with pure terror, resounded through the deck.

"The Serpent!" screamed several voices.

"Samson's surfaced, Capt'in!" informed Darby M'Graw, matter-of-factly.

"Save us in the Name o' Mercy!" wailed one of the sorely wounded.

I have a hazy recollection of seeing Samson's ugly, flat head weaving to and fro above the hatch-coaming on the hold. Flint reached his pet in a brace of shakes. He looped a coil about his broad shoulders, tucked the head under his arm and trudged off top-side dragging several yards of mottled death behind him. The Seminoles stood boggle-eyed and spellbound. But I was too dozy to give it much thought. Strong hands held my arms, while Charlotte cradled my head and hugged me close – her big, soft bosoms pressed against my cheek. I remember thinking that if I died under the Doctor's knife this night, my present position would be the nearest I'd ever get to Paradise!"

Blackness enveloped me like a blanket as I slipped the cable of consciousness and drifted down into oblivion. But I wasn't at peace for long. Raw pain, white-hot and nerve-shredding, brought me to as sickening waves of agony tore at the very core of my being. My eyes snapped open and I bit on the musket-ball as if trying to crack a nut. Charlotte's heaving bosoms partly blocked my view. All I could see was the glint of her gold chain as it swung before my face. I struggled to move, but those holding me tightened their grip – clamping me firmly against that make-shift butcher's block.

"Hold on, Lovey. Doctor's nearly done," came Charlotte's reassuring voice. "You is going to be jus' fine, John."

"Make haste with that pitch, my man!" said Flash Dan, cool and composed.

"Just fine!" "Just Fine!" Her words kept repeating themselves, echoing and rebounding about in my brain as I fought to keep sane amid the horror of this Hell on earth. I screwed my eyes tight shut, arching my back, and bit on that bullet with all my might as the steady 'swish . . . swish . . . swish' of the surgeon's saw increased my agony to the omega of all pain. Could a mortal man take much more? Suddenly my upper molar cracked against the pressure of the ball and a powder keg seemed to explode within my skull. I distinctly saw an orange flash – then sweet blackness.

Old Man Death kept me suspended on the point of his scythe for three days. Apart from the shock of amputation and having lost a great deal of blood, both before and during the 'carve-up', I also fell victim to a raging fever. I clung to life, hovering between semi and sub-consciousness. But in this detached world the pain was ever present. The Doctor fed me bitter drinks of Peruvian bark to fight the fever, along of laudanum to pacify the pain. The former drug was some help, but the latter did little for my relief.

Sometimes in a state of semi-wakefulness I saw images crystal clear and heard distinct voices; then again, just objects and meaningless murmurings. I comprehended enough to know I was lying in a hammock, slung in the great cabin. Once, I saw Flint sitting at his desk in his big, carved chair – writing. All around him were wounded men sprawled on comfy pallets. I remember Charlotte bending over me, in company of Flash Dan. She were bathing my face and speaking soft, soothing words.

Attacks of delirium was what I suffered from the most – that and the pain. I can't rightly recall all those abominable fancies, but the few I clearly remember make me go clammy to this very day. Drained me of energy, they did, same as them vampire bats do in sucking the blood of man and beast in the Brazils.

On one such occasion I imagined Flint were knelt alongside the hammock, gnawing my leg off – his terrible pointed teeth all agape and dripping with gore. Then his face changed into the severed shrunken head of the Grandee. It kept popping up over the hammock like a Jack-in-the-box, snapping at my thigh. I kicked out with both feet and tried to flee, but couldn't move, for I found myself held fast in Samson's mottled coils. The Grandee's shrunken napper became the snake's, which had swallowed my leg up to the hip. You see, shipmates, in all my delirious dreams I still possessed ten toes!

The final straw that broke the camel's back, as the saying is, or in this case, my fever, was when I was being towed through the sea by Old Clipped Fin with 'Flogger' Finch astride him. You remember 'Flogger'? Then Ben Gunn and Joe the Carib, watched by two Seminole Indians, started to remove my leg by use of the Carpenter's big bow-saw. I awoke screaming, my stump hurting like blue-blazes. Soaked in sweat, I was, cold and trembling. But above all, clear-headed and – ALIVE!

CHAPTER XXV

SANCTUARY IN SAVANNAH!

Charlotte Eleanor and Joan Fuller shared a Pallet beneath my Hammock, not just to meet my needs, mind, but to be close at hand to attend all the other wounded berthed in the great cabin. The girls appeared one on either side of me, Charlotte radiant, her black face beaming. Joan looked drawn and tired, having seen her husband laid to his Eternal Rest only two short days ago. Gypsy was buried at sea with thirty-three others, along of our Negro Nipper, Tiger Pip. The Seminoles ferried them out to deep water, the bodies laying athwart the canoes, stacked like cord-wood. Charlotte told me that Flint carried Tiger Pip, parcelled up in the remains of our Mizen-Sail, and slipped him over the side last with his own hands – Sweet Innocence resting alongside Savage Sinners!

"How do you feel, John?" asked my Black Beauty stroking my cheek, now dark and rough with stubble.

"I ain't the full man I used t'be, Missey, and that's fer sure," replied I in a croaking whisper. "I could go a drink o' nice, cool water."

You Readers can well imagine the state I were in – me asking for water!

Joan Fuller produced a bottle gourd containing beverage. It tasted like nectar, sliding down my parched pipe. Pleasant and wholesome, it was, a mixture of spring water, sugar and just a tincture o' lime juice. The vessel was forcibly dragged from my lips and left me gasping.

"Easy, Long John. Drink more slowly or you'll suffer the cramps," warned Joan giving me an affectionate pat.

"By thunder, but that's some better. No booze ever tasted sweeter," I panted and greedily seized the bottle for another go, being as dry as the Gobi Desert.

The candles in the lanterns that hung about the great cabin had burnt low, leaving the glass smoky and brown as amber. This dimness was just being boosted by the light from a false dawn, when a feeble voice called from the hammock slung alongside mine.

"Is that yoreself, young Silver? Are yer moorings all made fast and secure now, matey?" inquired QM McGinty.

"Why, Quarter-Master!" exclaimed I. "Ain't you a sight for sore eyes. And here were me thinking you was under hatches."

The 'Old Stander' was indeed a sight. Contrary to the Doctor's words, he had outlasted four nights instead of one. But his face had fallen in and his wrinkled skin was ashen, translucent like oiled paper, his lips tinged black. Only his eyes seemed alive. Deep sunk in hollow sockets, they burned with the same inner fire that had carried him through over half a century of sea-fights.

"Ah, Barbecue. I ain't long for this world," sighed he. "While the light o' this noo day gets brighter, mine grows dim. Ere the sun sits above the yard-arm, I shall be below saluting Sir 'Arry, for I feels Death a-pulling on me fin and filling me 'ead with shadows."

His voice, although faint, had aroused our two Guardian Angels from their slumber. Charlotte was alongside me, while Joan knelt beside the Old Man holding his hand. "Hush now, Phineas," soothed the widow. "You must rest and not waste your strength."

"No, no," wheezed the QM. "I'm outward bound for the last time and I knows it. Will one o' you kind, dear Ladies inform Jim Flint that the Quarter-Master 'ud appreciate a word along o' his Captain." The Old Man closed his eyes and lay breathing hard, his mouth a black O in his sunken, shrivelled face.

"I shall go. You stay with your man, dearie," said Joan.

"Ought you to summon, Doctor Hunter, also?" suggested Charlotte.

"Aye, I'll bring 'em both." Joan smiled at me and was gone.

Several of the wounded were arousing and Charlotte went about her work, dishing out drinks of beverage with words of comfort. Flint came hurrying, clad in just his shirt and breeches. Bare foot, he was, and I saw the puckered rings of purple flesh above both ankles where the gyves had rubbed the skin for the three years he were a prisoner of the Grandee. Flash Dan followed along of Joan Fuller and behind her was Darby M'Graw, now sporting a blog o' black leather over his left eye. Just visible below the patch lay the tell-tale tip of a serrated scar. Pew, it seemed, wasn't the only one to have lost his glims.

"Well, Long John my lad, ye look to be brighter than a polished button," said Flint bearing those cannibal teeth in a ghastly grin of pleasure. "The Doctor here will have ye 'Ship-Shape-and-Bristol-Fashion' 'ere we dock at Savannah, for we sail on the next full tide." His manner became grave as he bent over McGinty and whispered. "Phineas, what be all this tom-fool talk about ye slipping yore cable?"

Flash Dan winked at me as he held McGinty's shrivelled paw to feel his pulse and laid a hand against his brow. He and Flint exchanged glances and the former shook his head. “No hope, I fear,” said the Doctor sadly. “He sinks by the second.”

The Old Man’s eyes fluttered open. “Captain, I has comed to the end of me course,” murmured he. “I’ve seen a sight o’ times, I have, since shipping aboard a Brig out of Town-Side. Me, a nine year old cabin boy. For all the shot and shell I see fly, I never reckoned an ounce o’ lead ’ud lay me low. Took a British ball to carry me ’ome, mind! No Don ever put me down for long, not even when I took three bullets aboard the old *Naiad*. You mind our Old Ship, Cap’n? Pity . . . pity we had to blow . . .”

“Hush, hush now, Phineas, old friend!”

Flint’s tone was fierce and forceful in silencing the dying man. The Old Stander’s eyes closed and he lay wheezing and gasping for breath. I saw that Flint was very agitated. He knelt gripping McGinty’s hand, his face twitching along with his thick, blunt fingers as if he wanted to throttle the QM. What caught my eye was the withering glance that the Doctor flashed at the Captain – like a judge about to pass sentence. If I’d blinked I’d have missed it, but that stern-faced flicker told me he knew something about Flint that I didn’t. We were to sail a good few thousand more leagues before I found out what it was!

I thought Phineas was about to croak when his glims snapped open. He rallied and resumed talking. His words were weak, but clear; and by the strain on Flint’s face, I expected it to crack at any moment!

“Long, long ago in some far distant place, I lost me ’art and soul to a golden haired maiden with Spanish eyes. But too many lies and deceits fouled our Union. What started pure, became tainted and poisoned. Ours weren’t two ships as passed in the night. Mine foundered. She sent me to the bottom and I sank without trace – Doomed from the first.”

The QM coughed and a spew of blood came from his mouth. Flash Dan wiped his lips, while Flint, now less on edge, told him gently to ‘Hush’ again. But the Old Stander just swallowed and carried on speaking.

“Like that affair of forbidden love, my romance along o’ the sea be laced with Hardship and Pain; Heart-Ache and Disappointment; of Tears, Treachery and Mistrust, bound by Black Rages, spliced with Dark Despair. I see her face afore mine eyes to this same moment. Memories fade, yet her features remain – sharp and clear as three degrees upon a compass card. Ahh,” sighed he. “When will I see you again?”

The Old Man fell silent, except for his belaboured breathing. He lay with his eyes closed for a moment. When he opened them again he turned his head towards the stern-sheet windows. By the faraway look on his face, he was seeing things that were lost to us.

“You must rest, Phineas,” soothed Flint, his own glims misty.

"La Mer has been both Mother and Father to me since then," continued the Quarter-Master, unheeding the Captain. "Aye, along of Wife and Lover, Best Friend and Worst Enemy. Dead seamen don't sleep easy ashore. I want t'spend my Eternal Rest lying snug and deep on her bed, dressed in me armour and 'elmet with me hammock for a winding sheet and a ball between my sea-boots. For last, I nominates Long John Silver, to succeed in my stead, along o' Quarter-Master. That's my vote when it comes to Fo'c'sle Council." The Old Stander coughed blood again. "Wants t' see La Mer," he gasped and struggled to sit up.

Flint and the Doctor supported him, the latter wiping his mouth. For a long moment he gazed through the open windows at the blue waters of the lagoon, bathed in dawn's dim light, and the vast expanse of Ocean that lay beyond – framed by a brace of islands. Who knows what pictures from the past he saw there. Broadsides of flame and Tall Ships foundering. Faces of men who are no more. Maybe even the Girl with the Golden Hair. Suddenly, in a voice clear and steady, he chanted: "You wus a Flyer Morgan; You wus the lad to crowd; When you wus in your Flag-Ship; But now you's in your shroud!"

And with that utterance, along of a rattle from deep within his throat, Phineas McGinty fell back into the arms of Flint and Flash Dan – Dead!

"*Me illumina, Domine*," said the Doctor crossing himself.

I won't harp too hard on the voyage to Savannah; but several small points need to be logged, so you Readers'll know the long and the short of what's past and how it ties in with the present and future.

Most of our repairs were completed when I was still in Limbo, fighting off those fearsome fantasies along of my fever. *Walrus*, you will remember, lost both Mizen and Fore-Top-Mast. Spliced with that, the rigging was so slashed and the sticks so splintered and unsound, the whole lot had to be unstepped and jury masts mounted in their stead. For further convenience we left most of our cannons ashore in safe keeping of the Seminoles, to whom Flint intended to return. The reason was two-fold. Firstly to lighten the Ship, along of our damage sustained on the water-line, and secondly to reduce *Walrus* from looking too much like a Privateer. The way to Savannah led through dangerous seas – patrolled regularly by the RN.

Under a single square of canvas with two Jib-Sails up For'ard, *Walrus* sailed out into the scene of what all on board referred to as 'The Battle of Lowether's Folly'. Seminole scouts reported *Agamemnon* long gone. She came clear of the sand on the first full tide, and were last seen beating-up to the South-West, probably back to her base in Jamaica – leastways, that's where the 'White Squadron' was stationed in my day.

Flint and the Seminole Leader hit it off right from the first. The Chief was a tall, strong, good looking Indian named Coosa. But on account of his bright blouse, one and all we called him 'Red Shirt'. Him it was who had saved Ebenezer Lowether and dug the silly Sail-Maker from the sand. They had followed the course of the fight, hugging the shore in their dug-outs. Red Shirt and the Captain signed 'Articles'.

Shortly before we set sail, our Captain 'cleared lower decks'. All hands mustered aft where Flint addressed them. He had already told us wounded of his intentions.

"My lads!" began he, speaking from a-top the Poop. "Trading dry-blows with the Royal Navy has set us all-aback and the Treasure amassed at Saratoga will have ta hang in stays for awhile! But after we have refitted at Savannah and topped up oor crew along o' fresh hands, I vote to give it a go! If the Blunt is still there, then come Hell or High Water, I intend to seize it, Lock, Stock and Barrel – what say ye, Lads?"

Their wild cheering carried clear across the Lagoon and sent a flock of flamingos flapping lazily into the air, their plumage forming a pink cloud against the blue.

Red Shirt and twelve warriors shipped with us to see the Wonders of the White Man's World. Under guidance from our gang, they turned out to be pretty good seamen too! When the lack o' food forced Samson up from the hold and Flint had carted him off like a babe in arms, our Captain's standing shot past the peak in the eyes of the Indians. Never had they seen such a Serpent and to show their esteem, they brought a live pig aboard. Boggle-eyed in amazement they watched Samson crush and swallow the unfortunate creature. After his fill of pork, the anaconda curled hisself under the poop-steps and slept – as was his habit.

We were on our way to Savannah, sailing North when *Walrus* hove-to at sunset and the whole crew convened for the Quarter-Master's burial. True to his last wishes he was buckled into his armour and morion, then along o' the broken broad-sword clasped to his chest, Sails Lowether sewed him into his hammock with a twelve pound ball at his feet.

I was still weak as a kitten, but determined to attend. Charlotte shaved and bathed me and combed my hair. Dressed in a clean, striped night-shirt, property of the late Gypsy Fuller, I was wrapped in a blanket and carried out onto the Quarter-Deck by Morgan and Merry. They placed me upon a chair, along o' my stump all parcelled and tarred. I was sat with my back to the Fo'c'sle,, when I first heard a sound that was to become as common to the Crew as the 'clunk' of my Crutch – the sinister tap . . . tap . . . tapping of Blind Pew's stick. The Bosun arrived in company of Black Dog. An old sea-cloak covered his shoulders, for the evening was chilly, and a green shade curved above the upper part o' his great hooked nose, hiding those horrible empty eye-sockets now plugged with oakum and pitch.

"Hard days, Long John. Hard days an' damned dark!" says he in reply to my greeting. "You've danced your last samba, so I hear. The blasted pair of us will end up sharing the same beggin' bowl, I reckon!"

Flint officiated. Conducted the matter of moment with all the decorum of a Country Squire, he did. It weren't so much a Service for Old Phineas – more of a Tribute! The mortal remains of the 'Old Stander' lay a-top of our Black Plank, balanced between the bulwark and a barrel, covered by the Skull and Crossed Bones o' the Black Flag under which he had lived, fought and sailed for so long.

"I willna dwell on what be wrote in the 'Book of Books'," began Flint, tapping the Bible beneath his arm. "Phineas didna believe in the Power of an Almighty, ye ken. Like most forged in the same mould, he lived by Articles as far removed from Heaven as is Hell. But he was apt to show more mercy to his captives than Heaven ever bestowed upon its victims of Religion – ye needs only to read on Ancient Rome for that! Well, he'll know the truth on it now!"

A catspaw of wind ruffled the smooth, blue water and sighed a sad lament through what little rigging we had. I felt a lump in the back of my throat and swallowed hard several times to clear it. Charlotte and Joan Fuller were weeping quietly. Ben Gunn and Darby M'Graw also had a touch of the snivels and were sharing the same handkerchief to wipe their eyes, until Ben blew his nose in it!

"The burial of this 'Old Stander' dinna be just the death of another brother," continued the Captain. "We Gentlemen of Fortune, gathered here this day, bear witness to the end of an era. Phineas McGinty were the last of the 'Old Guard', an original 'Cow Killer', one who had sailed under the command of the immortal Morgan. His demise marks a mile-stone in the History of the Sea. No Pirate along o' his ilk will sail these waters more." Flint gave Israel the nod. "Nineteen Guns, if ye please, Master-Gunner and Amen to it!"

While Hands went from piece to piece, touching off, Morgan and Merry, assisted by several others, reloaded and run-out. True to our role in the guise of an Honest Merchantman, we only carried eight cannon – four a-side. As the highest salute in Naval tradition boomed and rolled out into the red glow of sunset, the plank was slowly lifted from the barrel end by Flint and Billy Bones. The Mate, greatly weakened by his wound, had lain confined to his berth since the fight. Along of the Final Salute from our guns, us Officers discharged small-arms over the Black Flag as Phineas McGinty slipped into the peace and silent solitude of the sea. The last o' the 'Old Guard' had gone Home!

Flint made no idle boast when he stated we'd be well received in Savannah. While we were still warping the *Walrus* up-river, an Armada of small boats turned out to bear a hand. James Oglethorpe, him who was selected Governor, came aboard in person and made much of our arrival. He called our Captain 'Uncle Jim'!

"This smart, young man were Christened in honour of me," explained Flint proudly. "My Godson, so to speak."

Georgia, so named for his nibs, German George the Second, was the last of Thirteen Colonies settled by the British. Unlucky for some, you might say, since a Revolution in later years cost the Crown the Americas. When Jamey Oglethorpe first sailed upstream back in 1733, he had only one hundred and sixteen immigrants, poor people mainly, debtors and those who were destitute. Originally, he founded the settlement, which he named after the Savannah River, as a colony for England's paupers – a place where they could begin a new life. In briefly fifteen months the population was boosted by tradesmen and merchants, along of some persecuted Protestants from Europe. Shortly before we warped in, a bunch of Lutheran refugees arrived from Germany. 'Slazburgers' they were called, but of course our crowd ruptured it to: 'Salty Burglars!'

Unlike most other English holdings in the New World, slavery wasn't allowed in Savannah, leastways, not until after 1749. But by that late date, most of Flint's Buccaneers were long gone and piracy as we knew it, was fast fading into the past.

We struck lucky from the first. Oglethorpe had only shortly returned from London, where he had presented the great Creek Chief, Tomochichi, to the Lord Trustees of the Coloney. Our Indians got on great guns with both the white settlers and Tomochichi's people. The former were just curios, but the latter were related, the Seminoles being an off-shoot of the Creek Nation. Joe the Carib became something of a celebrity among all three factions. Our Seminoles became known as 'The Twelve Apostles', for they were always spouting bits from the Bible, although most of it was well mixed and jumbled.

Flint established us ashore by buying a tavern, the same as he'd done in Nanny Town. Charlotte and Joan Fuller were given licence by the Governor to manage it. They did a roaring trade in The Rover's Rest, for we were a novelty in those parts. People came out o' curiosity and to hear how we had drubbed the 'Spaniards' to a stalemate in a running fight. Many a drink was brought me by a spellbound audience, listening along of my narration regarding the loss o' my leg.

"There were me, shipmates, a-serving of my gun, when this 'ere cannon ball cut me off at the hip! But I minded it no more'n a flea-bite! Stood firm, I did, on my one remaining leg! Ankle deep in me own gore, I was!"

By the powers, but there were some pasty faces present by the time I'd finished 'swinging the lamp' and 'shooting my line ashore' – you may lay to that, mates! But Pew was the one. He drew a bigger crowd than a troupe of half naked houri belly dancers would have done, did our Bosun! The town's folk went in awe of him and got a thrill out of being frightened. Mind you, some of the children suffered nightmares after clapping their eyes on Blind Pew. I reckon he'll give the Devil a bad turn when his time comes to go below!

All hands were given three days 'Out of Discipline', but with strict orders not to molest the public. During this rest, afore refitting *Walrus*, if such it could be called along of all the merry-making, Compensation for the Wounded was paid out as in Article Bound.

Blind Pew's statement of: "I'd give a thousand in Gold never to clap eyes on a King's ship again!" made during the fight, earned him Double that amount. I never plucked up bottle enough to ask him if he were happy with his wish! Darby M'Graw received one thousand dollars; and for the loss of my left leg, I were awarded, eight hundred. When the last Claim for Compensation had been squared, Flint rapped the table with a pistol butt and called for "Order!"

"Fo'c'sle Council, my lads!" cried he. "Time for ye to vote in new officers, to replace those who have gone below! But first, Benjamin Gunn has a Presentation to make! Ye have the floor, Ben!"

The Carpenter was pushed forward amid much mirth from our gang. He stood wriggling like an eel with embarrassment, a soppy grin on his face, which flushed beetroot red. Nervously, his thin hands fidgeted with a crutch of polished cedar. The tip was brass-bound, to save the end from splitting, and the arm-pit support was well padded in red velvet.

"Seeing as how you're all a-back and becalmed, along o' losing your larboard truck, Barbecue, I thought maybe this old timber 'ud serve to support your hull in hobbling to the Tap-Room for a refill of wot you fancies. I built it to the Doctor's own specifications, I did, so it'll fit snug as a sea-boot," concluded the Carpenter, handing it to me.

"Thankee, Ben," said I. "And right handsome it is, to be sure!"

Our Chippy returned to his place, accompanied by cheers and shouts of encouragement for me to: "Give it a go, Barbecue!"

Willing hands assisted me to rise from my seat. It felt strange in gathering my balance perched on one pin, for although my leg was gone, I could still feel my foot. Tingled, it did, with what we called Pins-and-Needles. With the crutch firmly under my arm-pit I gradually let go my weight upon it. Then along o' baited breath, I hobbled the first few steps since losing my limb. The whole Crew came to their feet as one man and gave vent to a thunderous, "Huzza!" that near lifted the roof.

"Long John Silver sails again, look you!" bawled Morgan.

PEECE SIX

OF SAVAGE SEAS AND MEN!

CHAPTER XXVI

FLINT'S NEW QUARTER-MASTER!

"As in Articles so stated," began Flint after the clamour died down and I were once more seated, "the choosing of a First Mate and Bosun remains my right alone. Other Officers of Rank are voted in by Fo'c'sle Council, except in time of engagement. Mister William Bones will hold his present appointment. Pew, is it the intention and desire of ye to remain along of this Company and serve in the same capacity?"

"Aye, aye, Sir!" replied the Bosun, half rising from his chair and cocking an ear towards the Captain.

"Then so be it!"

During the course of the evening, George Merry was promoted to Leading Hand, being as his predecessor, 'Stiff-Armed' Nick Nutt, had had his head replaced by a cannon-ball. George took charge of the Larboard Battery, while Tom Morgan held the same office on the Starboard side. Black Dog became Third Mate under Blind Pew, and Job Anderson doubled in my old role of Sailing-Master. He still retained his title of Coxswain, but it meant a greater proportion o' prize money. Finally, it came to the question of a new Quarter-Master – the most important affair of moment.

Next to the Captain and First Mate, the Quarter-Master was the most powerful personage aboard a Privateer. His responsibilities ranged from Good Order and Discipline among the Company, to arresting private feuds and arguments and awarding punishments; or if it came to dry blows, refereeing duels between the aggrieved parties. By far, his most important role was the fair distribution of all public property, which covered everything from clothes and rations to weapons and prize money. The QM was a man respected among mates, but above all – 'TRUSTED!'

"There be three names forwarded to me, nominating each for Quarter-Master," resumed Flint. "George Merry, Port Tack and John Silver. I shall now make it known that the predecessor along of that post, Phineas McGinty, voted from his death-bed for John Silver as the man most able to succeed him. Since us Officers has no vote in this affair, any as canna make the mark of his choice upon the paper, Mister Bones will so oblige ye. When all slips are secure in my sombrero, I'll make Tally and give Verdict!"

"Hang-fire, Cap'n!" cried Port Tack springing up, his face livid. "I has a right, according to Council Rules, to voice my say afore votes is cast! The same as any whose name be there for election!"

"Aye," drawled Flint, his eyes icy. "Ye ever was the one with more wind than most. Speak ye yore piece and be done!"

Port Tack glowered about him as a ripple of sniggers accompanied the Captain's words. The crew fell silent in the face of such menace and the Cooper's Mate turned to where I was sat alongside Flint with Charlotte standing behind me, her hands square on my shoulders.

"Wot kind o' Company be this?" demanded he. "You has a Bosun who's blind and now there's some about to elect a cripple for Quarter-Master! Lay along o' this, mess-mates – heed me now! When we clapps aboard a Prize, how do a one legged QM lead us t' take charge, as in dooty bound? Is he t'be hoisted in a Bosun's Chair and dumped on deck same as a bag o' blasted cocoa? I'll work and sweat to earn my bread at sea, along o' the next man, but I don't cotton to haul no cripple around like so much spoilt cargo!"

"Avast!" cried I and made to rise, but Charlotte's grip anchored me firm.

Mumblings, for and against, greeted Port Tack's outburst as he sat down scowling. Heated discussions broke out. His following was small in the Company. I noted a few of 'em, but they didn't meet my gaze. Small wonder, for I was in a rare rage with a face redder than fresh beef on a butcher's block – you may lay to that! George Merry came to his feet in a flash, raising his hands for 'Order'. Flint remained impassive, stoney-faced, but wary. Billy Bones sucked noisily at a hollow tooth. Blind Pew sat like a statue. Rock still, he were, with his head cocked to one side listening, while Black Dog whispered in his lug – no doubt describing the tense scene.

"Easy all, ship-mates! No call for us to fall together by the ears!" remarked Merry and the argufying dropped off. "My rival ain't too choice along o' his words, I'll allow, but I don't reckon he meant to give the offence he did. There's none here'll deny Long John be Pistol Proof – a brisk hand as ever was. And honest? Why, he'd be the last man in this 'ere crew to Dutch Trade a mate – straight as a rammer is, John!"

"And generous!" voiced Israel Hands. "I can vouch fer that!"

Merry took advantage of the murmurings o' assent to wet his whistle with a gulp of ale before continuing. "Now, Brother Port Tack, has a point when he says the role o' Quarter-Master should fall on the able-bodied shoulders of an active man. I'd be first to stand-down and give Barbecue my vote if I thought it weren't an unfair burthen to place on a body supported by only one leg. QM McGinty his own self said how tiring he found it to keep an even keel in rough seas – him with one arm. To be fair and square, mates, we be dooty-bound to think o' poor John's plight and not just ourselves!" concluded Merry and sat down to hearty applause from all around.

'Diplomatic George as ever was,' thought I and pulled myself up along of my timber leg. "Thank'e, Mister Merry," I said hobbling dot-and-dash to the centre of the floor. "Well now, since everybody's had his say, I'll make so bold as to have mine! I've given much thought to my future, I have. Soon I shall be duty-bound to this sweet girl here in Holy Wedlock. My days o' roving afore the mast be belayed! I'm five years away from fifty, mark you, and I intends to concentrate my energies on becoming a good tempered landlord. Vote for whom you please, but don't elect me – I'm done with the High Seas!"

Flint's jaw dropped; Billy's eyes bulged and Pew gave such a start, it took Black Dog to steady him from falling off his stool. You would have heard a finger stir in the silence that followed my statement. I turned, intending to hobble back to my place, when Carver Lowe ruptured the quiet.

"Apprentice pot-man be about the level o' yer mark!" sneered he, lolling drunkenly in his seat, a clay pipe clenched between his yellow teeth. "So much yer can manage t' serve more ale than yer spill. If trade drops off yer won't be able to sell yer Black-Bird in these parts, slavery bein' banned! Still, the Protestants hereabouts are pitying souls. Along o' yer crutch an' beggin' bowl, yer shouldn't starve in the street when they clap eyes on only half a man!"

Flint came to his feet with a thunderous oath and a snarl on his face that would frighten a mad dog. Billy's big, meaty hands balled into huge fists. But I stayed them with a raised palm in the Peace Sign.

"My argument, Gentlemen!" I cried and hobbling slowly forward, stopped in centre of Port Tack and Carver Lowe, who sat alongside Allardyce. "Having been in this Company less time than it takes to walk a turn around the deck, you with the ink on your Articles scarcely dry, I'll be gracious." In addressing, Carver, I casually placed my right hand on the beam above me and shifted my weight for better balance. "I'm easy going as a rule with good nature to all. But had you bothered to check the force o' my current afore setting sail along of your insolence, ye'd fathom that no man cocks his hat athwart me or mine and sees a good day afterwards!" I took a firm hold on the beam above me. "And seeing as we be out o' Discipline . . ." I brought up the crutch and jabbed Carver clean between the eyes with the tip.

The former 'Bullock' went over backwards, as if pole-axed, with blood streaming down his face from a half-moon gash on his for'ed. Before Port

Tack recovered from his surprise, I swung my timber leg and delivered him a blow alongside the lug that sent him sprawling. The Mad Marine came to his feet in a flash, eyes blazing, but he was pulled up short when Israel's dagger pricked him beneath the chin.

"One move, Pikey, an'?" grinned the Gunner, speaking soft, giving another gentle jab.

Carver was out cold, but the Cooper's Mate were only dazed. He fumbled for the pistol in his sash and dragged it out. The double click sounded clear as with his left hand he cocked the dog's-head clamping the flint. I knocked the barker from his grasp, which exploded, and the bullet plowed a great gouge in the floor-boards leaving a long splinter standing. My timber 'cracked!' him athwart the pate and he slumped senseless beside his smoking gun.

"There'll be a hard frost in Hades afore either o' you pair of beauties crosses this old cripple again, along of his crutch!" cried I, standing waist deep in wafting powder smoke and with that, I hobbled through the haze back to my berth.

"Long John's the man fer me!" yelled Morgan, raising his tankard.

"If he don't join this crew and sail as Quarter-Master, I'll resign, I will, by thunder!" vowed Israel Hands, putting his dagger away.

"Barbecue for QM!" roared Merry and the Company vapoured in support of me to a man. Ain't it nice to know you're wanted!

You Readers didn't really think Old John would resign, did you? Not with three hundred thousand pounds a-waiting to be plucked from Spanish coffers at Sarasota. If it were still there, mind! Now I don't know all the mysteries of navigation, to be sure, but I do know how to navigate men along of my way o'thinking – you may lay to that, mates! Human Nature being what it is, you needs only to tell 'em they can't have something and they'll be screeching for it in a brace o' shakes – especially when cut in the mould of Flint's flock.

Barring Port Tack's crowd, they were mine to a man!

"Well, as to this kind offer, I ain't too sure," said I, rolling my eyeballs to all quarters, while rasping a hand thoughtfully over my stubbly chin. My hesitation fell heavy in the hushed silence. "Y'see, mates, the more my mind dwells on the comforts of a safe berth ashore, the more reluctant I feel to face hardships afloat and maybe another encounter with a blasted round-shot."

The whole crew came to their feet, clamouring for me to act as QM, even those who had picked up Carver, along of Port Tack, and set them to rights. 'One more word,' thinks I, 'and they'll be a-begging of me on bended knee.' I cast a glance at Flint and shiver my timber if he wasn't in a blue funk over the outcome. His tongue flicked dry lips. All the booze had gone to his nose and it glowed blue. He were in a high sweat, being that if I hopped out, most of his best men might vote to Split the Bearskin and break up the Company. Gold meant nought to him. Killing Spaniards was all he craved for in Revenge of Her who died so tragic.

"John Silver," says he, scarce able to breathe, "if ye sign my Articles alongside the slot reserved for QM, I'll gi' ye ma written affy-davy, here and now this same moment, making Charlotte Eleanor owner o' this here Public House in partnership of ye and Mrs Fuller! A handsomer offer ye'll nay find – not if ye spends the next hundred years afloat! Stab me or sink me for a sinner!"

"You'd do that to splice my services, Cap'n?" I asked, truly astounded.

"Down to every last bottle, barrel and keg, by thunder!" confirmed he. "Ye be worth yore weight in gold-dust to me, Barbecue!"

"My Girl," said I turning to Charlotte, "you now be part owner of this 'ere grog-shop!" To her amazed cry of delight I picked up the pen and dipping it in the ink-pot, held the quill aloft. "Ship-Mates! You now has a new Quarter-Master!" I cried and signed my name with a flourish.

The cheering near brought the walls down! One and all drained his tankard and began beating the table-tops with an insistent chant for 'RUM!' I hopped along o' my timber and took station behind the bar. Wedged well secure on my crutch, I worked the taps, filling tankards as fast as Joan and Charlotte could fetch 'em. Flint came to his feet, bellowing the opening line of:

"Fifteen men on a dead man's chest!"

And the whole house shook as we all bore chorus:

"Yo-ho-ho and a bottle of rum!"

Three weeks later I was aboard *Walrus* finding my sea-legs. Those twenty-one days were so hectic, to such a degree, I near met myself coming back. Turning in 'Round Robins' weren't the word for it! My duties included directing the stowing of stores and ballast, rations, water, and supervising the renewal of all the steerage ropes. Then we had a week of sea trials, putting *Walrus* through her paces, and exercising the fresh hands at Gunnery. By way of interest, the heading on the local news-sheets read: 'RICHARD TURPIN HANGED AT YORK!' That was back in April, mind. Topping all this, me'n Charlotte got spliced. Married in Church, we was!

Seeing our crowd in that Holy Place was on par with a bunch o' Quakers holding high jinx in a pot-house – the like were never seen! Chaplain didn't feel too tickety-boo towards our lot. Billy Bones got his yeoman drunk on rum; and some chuckle-heads, under the guidance of Ben Gunn, left the font full o' babby alligators. The Christening parties that replaced us had its female members fainting every-which-way. To cap a grand day, the Vicar locked hisself in the Vestry and drained the Communial Wine. Stayed there all night, he did, singing Bawdy Ballads. Savannah ain't been the same since!

It was a tearful farewell that Charlotte took along of me when I hobbled aboard *Walrus* on that bright July morning, my parrot upon my shoulder. Joan Fuller gave her comfort. Governor Oglethorpe saw 'Uncle Jim' off and a sad little group of women and children waved husbands and fathers on their way as we drifted downstream on the ebb.

Walrus cut a brave sight, mirrored in the clear water from peak to transom. Breamed and careened, her sides freshly paid with tar, oil and red oker – the masts gleaming under several coats of pine varnish – she shone like a new pin. From the brass-bound wheel of polished oak aft, to the bright bell for'ard, there wasn't a sign of the damage the decks had suffered at 'The Battle of Lowether's Folly' – decks that were now holy-stoned to a dazzling whiteness.

Our new crew were the most motley collection o' Humanity as ever put to sea. There were around twenty Germans, several French, five Negros, two Mulattos, and Wun Hung Lo, a Chinee Cook. Where Flint dredged him up from, I don't rightly remember. In contrast to our catch, there was a towering, blond headed Danish seaman called the 'Great Dane' and a swarthy, black bearded Gunner sporting huge gold earrings known as 'Black Bart', his name being Bartholomew the Portuguese. Then there was 'Pop-Eye', a Creek Indian with optics like organ stops. He had earned his bread serving as a harpooner in the whaling fishery. Many was the yarn he swopped with Hands, Israel having fought Leviathan hisself. In place of a spear, Pop-Eye carried a great killing lance, its point heart-shaped and broad as a man's palm. He could cast this missile from the Poop and hit a mark chalked on an empty keg placed upon the Fo'c'sle! We also had aboard a Mannikin from the African Main. Short and broad, he was, black as pitch with the strength of three. His name was 'Jacko', but to one and all he was the 'Poisoned Dwarf'.

Our stop-over in the bay that marked 'The Battle of Lowether's Folly' was brief. We spent the night ashore in a Seminole Chiki, loaded our Cannons in the morning and with eighty warriors to boost our attack on Sarasota, set sail on the evening tide. For as far as Cape Florida we sailed under British Colours. But on beating-up into the Gulf Stream, tacking along the West Coast o' Palm Key, we hoisted the French Flag.

I were suffering a bad patch around this time. Although my stump had healed clean, there was this blasted ligature that refused to come adrift. Caused me no end o' pain and discomfort, it did, but I stuck it like a man, refusing the Doctor's drugs. There was a precious sight more reason than one as to why I preferred to remain clear headed.

Since I'd clapped 'em aboard, Carver Lowe and Port Tack had kept their own council, along of the Mad Marine and a few other Cronies, avoiding me when possible. Carver now sported a great, crescent-shaped scar on his for'ed – courtesy o' yours truly. Except for a sour look or two, they minded me as if I weren't there. For my part I kept my wits sharp, my hanger loose and my Pettijean Pistols handy within my coat pockets. I didn't fear treachery, but I didn't trust 'em neither!

Pew were pure Magic the way he handled his handicap. Attended by Black Dog, he went aloft, spliced ropes, hauled sails and tackles, and ruled the Fo'c'sle with a rod of iron. One more accomplishment, worthy of note, was his prowess at throwing a knife or firing a pistol. Guided by the slightest sound, uttered by someone hid behind the target, our Bosun could sink blade or ball, chest high, into a foot wide board at twelve paces. Few were the Fo'c'sle hands who weren't a-feared of Blind Pew!

As for my own self being in stays, along of my timber support, I found my sea-legs early. Mainly, it was a question o' balance, getting what we call the 'Feel of the Ship'. To be sure, it depended on what kind of sea were running. Beating-up in the Gulf Stream against a head-sea caused *Walrus* to roll and pitch as she plowed through the swell. To assist my movements on deck, various lines were rigged. 'Long John's Earrings' the Crew called them. When hauling myself along, hand over hand, I trailed my crutch by a lanyard looped around my neck.

I recall one narrow corner. The night being dark with strong wind and rain, the seas were running high. Each rolling crest was white capped like the Cape Horn greybeards found in the Storm King's domain. I were working my way up from the Fo'c'sle, trailing my timber, when the hand-line I was hauling on snapped and the billowing sea that broached our beam pitched me into the scuppers. Near swept me overboard, it did. Tom Morgan raised the alarm from his station alongside the wheel. Merry and M'Graw dragged me clear. Black Dog, who was up for'ard on Watch, examined the haliard's end and said afterwards that the rope had been part-way severed with a knife cut!

Now who might have done that, I wonder?

CHAPTER XXVII

THE SACKING OF SARASOTA!

For the umpteenth time I studied my watch-face in the dim light from the Binnacle. A faint smudge of pink silhouetted the shore-line, whose palm tops showed clear half a league distant. Our crew were at 'Rest', the Gunners huddled between their pieces, while the Seamen sat in little groups about the deck. All hands had 'Cleared for Action' and 'Closed-up' an hour since before sunrise.

We were hove-to off Sarasota. Flint and a third of our Company had gone ashore the previous afternoon, reinforced by the Seminoles now almost a hundred strong. The plan was simple. Come the dawn, *Walrus* was to sweep into Sarasota Bay and engage the shore batteries. With all the attention focused on us, Flint's force of a hundred and fifty would attack from out the swamps, taking the entire town by surprise from the rear. No one would expect a foe to come from that quarter. *Walrus*'s final role was to close in alongside the jetty, where all hands would launch off in a frontal assault.

Despite the cool of the morning, I was sweating. My hands had gone clammy and there was a dryness in my throat, along of a tightness in my guts. Such symptoms be standard in a body screwing itself up to brace against an Engagement. To be sure, any man who claims he ain't a-feared afore facing a broadside, is either a liar or a fool!

My thoughts flickered to Charlotte and I fingered an earring in fond memory o' her. Our three days of honeymooning, spent in the privacy of the Governor's summer house situated on the coast, were the most wonderous I ever knowed. Much Mooning did we do and sweet was the honey of our togetherness. There lay I, swinging lazily in a hammock with Charlotte feeding me juicy tit-bits, Almonds, Cynamon and Nuts from the Brazils, while keeping me cool along of a feathered fan brought from New Spain or 'Mexico' as our Colonials were now calling it. I even found time to read *A General History of the Robberies and Murders of the most notorious Pyrates*, by Captain Charles Johnson. But of course there was no mention of Me or Flint's crowd, save for Israel Hands, him as having sailed along o' Blackbeard.

The tap-tap-tapping of Blind Pew's stick fetched me back aboard.

"High time for us to bear-away, Pew," I informed him.

"Aye, Barbecue. This waiting is what gives a man the jitters. That, an standing off an' on same as a blasted bum-boat, rolling about like a bottle. The sooner I smell battle smoke – the better!" concluded the Bosun in his usual guttural snarl and placing his Silver Call between his thin, cruel lips, he piped: "Hands to Sailing Stations."

"UP HELM!" cried, Job Anderson, now conning the ship in my old role of Sailing-Master. "MAN THE BRACES THERE! HOIST JIB-SAILS! LEE-BRACES, HEAVE AWAY!"

The two Timoneers, Pop-Eye the Creek Indian and Joe the Carib, spun their spokes putting the helm hard over. Men hauled on the braces and the Fore-Main-Yard creaked round. There came a 'Crack!' as the shivering canvas cupped the wind. *Walrus*'s bow swung to starboard, the deck canting as the sails bellied out and we began to make headway. Top-Men clambered aloft, ready to un-clew our 'Fighting Sails', while *Walrus* dipped and plowed towards the red gap in the horizon that marked the opening to Sarasota Bay. Twenty minutes later with billowing canvas and the cutwater boiling beneath our bows, we ran out both batteries and swept into the Attack.

"UP WITH 'OLD ROGER'! BREAK OUT THE CAPTAIN'S PENNANT!" I yelled, being as it were me in overall command since Flint and the First Mate were ashore.

Our Crew gave three hearty 'Cheers!' as the Skull and Cross Bones were hoisted to the Mizen Peek and Flint's Red Banner of 'No Quarter' broke from the Main-Mast-Head – streaming to leeward. Now I ain't no Patriot, not I, but to give the Sons of Spain an added smack in the eye, I had the Union Flag fluttering on the jack-staff.

Sarasota was a sad sight in matching it alongside other Spanish settlements. Originally, the French had tried to colonise a town here, until Spain booted them out and took over. Sarasota was one of the few remaining claw marks left by Spain on the American Eastern Main. '*El Animoso*' was fast loosing his Royal Grip on the New World. Spanish influence was wide spread, mind, but although the Dons could still muster a force to be reckoned with, their hey-day as a major Power was past in the Caribbee.

The years had taken a heavy toll on the small fort over-looking the rickety jetty that curved out into the bay. Although long since fallen into disrepair, I saw through my spy-glass that the ruin still retained some big teeth. I counted eight menacing black muzzles belonging to 18- or 24-pounders. Set apart from the miserable collection of dilapidated, wooden houses, the one solid structure was the Jesuit Mission. Built of adobe bricks, it were, and surrounded by a high wall. From a flag-pole afixed to the belfry fluttered the Blue Standard of Barcelona, bearing a black clad Monk holding a Rosary.

Set between the Town and the Mission, but bordering the shore, was a Redoubt. Constructed from palm logs and sand-filled wicker baskets, this fortification housed another four cannon. Riding at anchor within the Bay was a Schooner and a brace of single-masted vessels. To me, they looked much like 'Menchews' that were used on the Malabar Coast to carry cargo.

"I cannot, for the very life of me, see a King's Ransom being hoarded here," remarked Flash Dan at my elbow. "Personally, I'd say this place doesn't look capable of mustering a single Silver Rider."

"If the *Santa Rosario*'s 'Red Tape' be correct, it's accumulated riches from various countries – including salvaged Rhino from two wrecks. Aye, and all to the tune o' three hundred thousand pounds, shiver my timber!" I replied, feeling my eyeballs burn at the mere thought of so much money. "I just hope the blessed Blunt is still here!"

"Three points to starboard!" cried Anderson, conning the ship so's our cannon would align with the shore batteries.

I wedged my rump against the binnacle and shifted my crutch as *Walrus* changed direction and heeled to the wind.

"FIRE AS YER GUNS BEAR!" bawled Merry from below.

The four Long Toms on the upper-deck's larboard side were manned by a mixture of Germans and Negros. Israel Hands commanded the Quarter-Deck's two Twelves; Black Dog supervised their sisters up for'ard. Pew, having cast aside his sea-cloak, was acting as Israel's loader.

"Stand clear!" cried Black Dog.

His order to "FIRE!" was lost in the shattering roar of the lower batteries' for'ard guns. I felt the timbers quiver and shake beneath me as the deafening discharges came closer and closer. Smoke rolled up from the hatch-ways and billowed above the bulwarks, where the wind blew it to leeward in tattered streamers.

Israel's two pieces belched flame, recoiling onto their breeching-ropes. The acrid bite o' the powder-smoke in my throat took me back in an instant to the horror of our last action. Blind Pew was uncanny to watch. His every movement was sharp and sure. Not once did he falter or fumble. None as never knowed him would guess that the green shade concealed empty eye-sockets plugged with pitch and oakum.

The Mission's bell began tolling out its mournful message of alarm as through my spy-glass, I watched our shot rupture the Fort's sea-ward wall. One of the small twin turrets had already collapsed and a great pall of mortar dust and smoke hung over the ruin. I saw the bronzed breech of a big gun sticking up like a cock-eyed bollard from the jumbled masonry piled in the shallows. But despite all this ruination, red tongues of flame spat defiantly back at us along the parapet in returned fire, while the Colours were run-up to flutter from the flag-pole's peek.

"STAND-BY TO COME ABOUT!" bellowed Anderson through a speaking trumpet and Seamen rushed in response to man the braces.

As we swept past the Schooner our starboard battery, under Morgan, delivered a Broadside. Me'n the Doctor swung our telescopes in time to see the Main and Mizen Masts brought down by the board. Two men jumped off her shattered stern and struck out for the jetty. Made the water fly, they did! Not a port-lid was raised nor a gun run out against us. I reckoned the Crew were all ashore – I reckoned wrong! With part of her bow stove in below the water-line, the Schooner started to settle by her head.

"Strange?" remarked Flash Dan, lowering his spy-glass. "Did you observe her flag, John? I caught a glimpse of it through the rigging, just as the Mizen fell, but noticed no red strakes."

"Yellow be more sharp to the eye at this distance, Doctor," replied I and thought no more of it.

Anxiously, I scanned the town for any sign of Flint's attacking force. Instead, my glass captured smoke mushrooming from the Redoubt. Shots were falling all around us now, sending up spouts o' spray. Some fell short. Several passed to leeward. Only three fetched us. One splintered the Poop's planking, passing through to cause chaos in the Mate's cabin. Another punched a hole in a head-sail. The third shot, grape I reckon, carried away half the fore-tops'l-yard, taking a Top-Man with it. I never saw the going of him, but Black Dog's Gunners were peppered in blood-spots and loud did they curse.

"STAND-BY, YOU'RE GOING ABOUT!" yelled Anderson. "HELM HARD-A-LEE!"

While the order was relayed along the Lower-Deck, a warning for Gunners to brace themselves and chock their guns, Joe and Pop-Eye spun their spokes. *Walrus* turned into the wind with her head-sails shivering as the Seamen loosened their sheets, bowlines and braces. When our old War-Horse had fallen off five or six points, the Coxun cried: "Let go and haul!"

Straining, our sailors hauled to the wind, wheeling the Main-Fore-Yard about the mast. The canvas filled with a 'Crack!' – this time bellied out from a starboard tack. To save *Walrus* falling off still further, the two Timoneers put the helm hard over. With all sails trimmed we began making head-way again and none too soon, for in slowing down when coming about, we were a sitting duck. Those of us nearest the wheel cowered, turning our backs towards the quarter-rail stanchions as a ball reduced 'em to flying splinters.

In rushing across the deck to man the pieces now opposite the shore batteries, two of Israel's Gunners were hit. A German suffered only a minor gash on his arm, which Flash Dan bound up in a green handkerchief. The big Negro was less fortunate. Struck full centre in the chest by a jagged flizzing, he fell like a pole-axed bovine not a yard away. Bright was his blood, trickling into crimson designs upon the sanded deck, shaped by the ship's roll. Pretty patterns, to be sure, but treacherous footing for the likes o' me along of my timber leg!

"Forsooth!" said Flash Dan as splinters 'Flizzed!' across the deck and several pieces of severed rigging writhed above us like tortured snakes. "Captain Flint's assault should have started long before now. If those Seminoles of his have failed to negotiate the swamps, *Walrus* will need to draw off. This work is becoming too warm."

"We'll make one more pass, Doctor. If nought develops ashore, I'll order about-ship and bear away."

Under the circumstances there wasn't much else I could do. If we hove-to and berthed alongside the jetty, as planned, the shore guns would reduce *Walrus* to a wreck. Kindling wouldn't be the word for it after being chewed by those big teeth! One possible danger was laid aside at any rate, for as we plowed back past the Schooner we saw she had settled on the bottom. Only her Fore-Top-Mast was visible above water, surrounded by a flotsam of splintered spars and tangled ropes. I noticed half a dozen bodies, floating face down, bobbing among the wreckage. Odd it was, to be sure, that none opposed us earlier.

In beating-up back towards the town, Morgan's battery delivered a broadside at the Redoubt and reduced it to rubble. A goodly aim from all guns, that were! The four cannons remained silent thereafter. We came about yet again and Merry's Gunners sent another withering blast of iron smacking into the old Fort. As *Walrus* tacked for the third and final time the Fort still showed fight with three pieces firing steady, and whenever one of the heavy balls fetched us, it tore through our timbers like they was tarred paper. Apart from damage to the ship, casualties among the crew were creeping higher.

"Pass the word to Mister Morgan below! A broadside into the town, for luck, then we'll stand-off to see if Cap'n Flint comes through!"

No sooner had Allardyce nipped beneath the hatch coaming with my directive, when Pew paused at his work alongside Israel's piece, his hand cupped to his ear. "Hark, mates! Musket fire! I can hear Musketry!" cried he.

We all strained our lugs but heard nothing, save for a muffled report as the port hurled another double discharge at us. One ball tore a gap in our bulwark; the second splintered a port-lid, smashing through timbers a foot thick to cause more execution among our Crew. Smoke rolled over the bay like a fog-bank, hiding half the town. Focusing my glass upon the Fort, I saw the yellow and red straked Flag o' Spain being hauled down in jerky accompaniment to the popping of small-arms.

"There be shooting sure enough, Bosun!" said Israel to a leering Pew.

"The swabs 'ave struck!" I yelled, but seconds later the 'Jolly Roger' was fluttering above the eddying smoke in place of Spanish Colours. "No, by thunder – it's Flint!"

"Odds bodkins! Strike up the band!" bawled Flash Dan.

Our jubilant clamour was suddenly lost in the shattering roar of Morgan's broadside. Double shotted for good measure, the starboard pieces poured a mixture of ball, bar and grape-shot into Sarasota. Some of the load must have ruptured a brace o' breakfast fires, I reckon, for the town was soon fiercely ablaze, burning in two places. Fanned by a stiff, inshore breeze the flames spread faster than a flight in an Irish pot-house.

"LARBOARD YOUR HELM, THREE POINTS! CLUE TOPS'LS! STAND-BY TO BACK HEAD-SAILS!" yelled Anderson through his trumpet and brought *Walrus* veering in towards the jetty, graceful as a gull.

"Landing Parties, close-up!" cried Pew and piped: 'All Hands to Quarters.'

There came a mad rush from below, both hatches streaming men whose hot eyes and eager faces showed that their minds were already mulling on the prospect of Plunder. All of them were bristling with weapons. Pistols slung by bright ribbon, tied to the trigger-guard, dangled from brawny shoulders. Cutlasses there were a-plenty, along of Poignards, Pikes and Pole-Axes, Halberds and Hatchets, Muskets and Musketoons. Two men out of ten carried a brace of 'salt-boxes', each containing two, square-shaped rum bottles filled with powder and fitted with three inch fusees. These were our grenadiers. Gathered on the Fo'c'sle, our Musicians caused a great clamour what with drums a-thumping, bugles a-blaring and all accompanied by the dull, mournful moan of conch-shell trumpets. Yet above all this din, I seemed to hear the Ghostly 'Thumpety . . . thump! . . . Thumpety . . . thump!' of Tiger Pip's Irish drum, beating us in as ever he done.

"LAY ALL FLAT-A-BACK!" bawled Anderson.

Walrus bumped the jetty and slithered along it, then with head-sails backed we hove-to. The cable-men jumped down onto the groaning, creaking timbers and made secure – fore and aft.

"Look to your priming, all hands!" cried our Master Gunner.

"Remain along o' your respective parties! Gun Captains t'keep each his own Crew in order – follow me!" I roared and looping the crutch lanyard around my neck, lowered myself hand over hand down *Walrus*'s side by way of a grappling rope.

Once assembled on the jetty I led off thumping my way along the boards, dot-and-dash, my chest heaving like a Smithy's bellows. The Crew were divided into three Companies, each with a Gun Captain acting the role of Corporal, much in the same manner as if we'd worn the King's Coat and served in a Regiment o' Foot – God 'elp the Crown!

While sheathed in smoke we were well shielded and safe. But then the blasted wind veered, which blowed away our cover and brought us under small-arms fire from a block-house sunk in the sand behind the ruined Redoubt. The air about us was soon popping to the tune of hot lead that whistled past our lug-holes.

"Break for the Fort, mates!" I yelled, waving the Company to by-pass me as more musket balls hummed overhead.

My bold Buccaneers needed no second bidding. Broke and ran, they did, stampeding past me like a herd o' frightened Friesians. But Flash Dan, who should have remained aboard with his Loblolly Boys attending to the wounded, in company with Anderson and the Carpenter's Crowd, strode along beside me. For sheer, cool nerve you'd be hard pressed to find his double. He stationed hisself to starboard, positioned between me and the intense musket fire.

"A lovely day for cricket," remarked the Doctor as a ball splintered the boards before us and whined off into space. To look at him you'd think he was taking the air in blessed St James's, shiver my timber!

Black Dog drew abreast of us, leading Blind Pew by the hand. "Here's Long John and the Doctor, ambling along like they was taking a turn around the deck before supper," informed the Bosun's Mate for the benefit of his sightless charge. "Best budge, shipmates!" added he.

"If I had the Wings of Pegasus on this one remaining ankle o' mine, you'd see nought of me but coat-tails!" grated I, gasping and sweating fit to simmer in my own heat.

"Belay all this hurry-hurry, Humphrey!" croaked Pew, his lank, red hair blowing past his face in the breeze. "Bide your time. I'm too long in the tooth for rushing about like a ship's younker. This here's good company, so we'll keep consort to Flash Dan and Barbecue. The rest o' them swabs ain't got the pluck of a weevil in a broken biscuit – shrivel my soul!"

Black Dog was not a happy looking, 'Humphrey', but he slowed his pace to comply with Pew – the Bosun now being the one outboard and nearest the oncoming bullets. For the moment, owing to the curve of the jetty, I took a small degree o' comfort in the fact, that, before any lead could hit me, it first had to pass through Pew, Black Dog and then Flash Dan! But it didn't last. Soon, all four of us were exposed to the firing.

Can you picture it, mates, the four of us plowing our way up the rubble of the Fort's east wall, the two able-bodies assisting a cripple with one leg and a blind man? Looked like rejects from Greenwich, we did. The poor Doctor were hard put to it in keeping me on an even keel; even so I fell over three times. Some good came from my contusions, however, for along o' the second tumble, I felt a sharp pain in my stump and found myself free of the troublesome ligature, which dropped out the wide, loose leg of my canvas trousers. Reaching to just below my knee, I wore the bell-bottom ducks for comfort and convenience, bearing in mind that dressing with only one leg was apt to be a bit tricky. On my right foot, instead of a heavy sea-boot, I now had a soft, silver-buckled shoe with a blue and white striped stocking. My stump gave no more trouble, except when the weather turned. Served me better than a barometer!

Me'n Flash Dan were floundering about, stumbling over the loose stones and stirring up the dust, when Flint his own self appeared to bear a hand. And what a sight for sore eyes he was – caked in dried, thick black mud from sea-boots to baldric belt.

"Welcome, Barbecue, and here be the good Doctor, looking like he's just stepped out of 'Cockfords'!" greeted the Big Buccaneer. "Hop aboard my back, Long John my lad, and I'll haul ye alongside a brandy keg in a brace of shakes!"

I were big and heavy, but Flint was bigger and stronger. Piggy-backed me into the Fort where my crowd, in company of his Crew, were ransacking the wine cellars – tossing bottles from hand to hand. Several Indians appeared half-seas-over already. Flint paused to bellow some orders, to ease up on the wine, then lumbered on past five or six dead Spaniards, sprawled about the rubble strewn courtyard, and dumped me in the shady cool of the ruined keep. Billy was there with Darby M'Graw and Red-Shirt the Seminole. All of 'em were muddy, bloody and stinking.

One-Eyed Darby poured brandy from a half-anker that stood wedged on the table between two bricks, passing the earthenware bowls to Israel Hands, Black Dog, Pew and Me. Flash Dan busied hisself administering to some wounded Seamen and Seminoles who sat slumped against the wall. Not two feet from the up-turned bucket on which I sat, lay a Spanish Officer with his throat cut from ear to ear and – scalped. Pleasant company all round, to be sure!

"A close-run, Cap'n," I remarked, filling a pipe. "We was about to bear-away. Pew here was the first to hear your gun-fire."

"Stab me and fall on," sighed Flint mopping his face. "Those swamps be crawling with serpent beasties. Three brisk hands and a brace of bucks those cotton-mouthed creatures cost my Crew. Then to cap disaster, a bunch of Friars working the fields spied us. We took ten for prisoner, but two other swabs escaped and spread the alarm. Now the whole blasted town's taken refuge in the Mission. That's where the Blunt's at. Port Tack and Carver Lowe sweated a swab for information. They havena got artillery, but plenty of Musqueteers manning the walls."

"A frontal assault 'ud cost us dear, Jim," said Billy snorting through his fleshy, broken veined nose. But he seemed more concerned with the black muck that caked him.

"Aye, an' there's the block-house set dead-centre with sharp-shooters covering every-which way," added M'Graw, puffing out smoke while picking at a dried scab on his cheek.

Flint gulped brandy, his broad, beat-up old face furrowed in thought. "We'll attack from three sides," says he at length. "Darby, send O'Brien to repair on board and bring off the Carpenter's chippies. Ben can supervise the making of scaling ladders. Yore Grenadiers, Long John, will have ta blow oot the block-house afore we budge."

"Can't the ship's guns be brought to bear?" asked the Bosun, hunched over sitting on a beam of timber like a buzzard, his drink in one hand with a pipe in the other.

"Nay, Pew. The block-house be too deeply sunk in sand; and if we reduce the Mission to rubble, it would serve small purpose ta maybe bury the Blunt under tons o' masonry," replied Flint as Darby went out calling for the rank Irelander. "I'll nay risk it."

"Do you reckon the Friar was bluffing about the two men-o'-war due in here any day from Vera Cruz?" inquired Billy, scraping the caked mud off his clothes using a gully with a crooked handle.

Flint shrugged. "Mayhap there be a tincture o' truth in it. We'll keep a weather-eye to windward."

"He didn't blab 'til Carver cut off his lug," reminded the Mate.

"Which one?" cried Pew brightening over this piece of gay news.

"Why, I don't rightly recall, Bosun. What odds it?" asked Billy looking puzzled. "Starboard, I think."

Pew slapped his thigh in delight, spilling part of his booze. "I'd have had both of 'em off! Aye, and his eye-balls to boot! Bleeding 'ud do them Papist Pigs a service! They've split blood a-plenty!"

"Right you are, now 'tis oor turn. Let's set-to with a will and organise killing parties. Pipe 'All Hands,' Bill!" ordered Flint and tossed down the remains of his drink.

Most of the ramshackle town was still intact. The changing wind had turned the fires back on themselves, which were now all but burnt out. Under guidance from Ben Gun's carpenters, all hands turned-to and soon knocked together a score of scaling ladders. Rough'n ready they were, to be sure, made from beams, shutters, house-timbers and such like, but they would serve to get us over the wall.

Divided into three groups, our assault parties moved through the deserted streets onto the edge of town. We saw no sign of life, save for a few pitiful, skulking dogs. Mangy creatures, they were, half starved, ill-kept and vicious. Taking cover behind the low walls, Flint commanded one team; Billy the second; and me the third with the Doctor acting as my mobile assistant.

While the Musqueteers of all three parties peppered the block-house, firing volley after volley, five of my Grenadiers rushed across the open stretch o' sand, keeping close to the shore. Each held a brace of glass grenadoes, their fusees trailing smoke. Before they reached the ruined Redoubt, two were bowled over by sharp-shooters and a third, sore wounded, ditched his bombs and began crawling back towards us. The silly swab should have smothered the slow-matches first, for when they exploded the shards of flying glass carved him into a quivering, bloody carcase.

Of the other two, pistol proof Buccaneers, one was killed in trying to push his grenadoes through the fire-slits in the low wall, while the other, after a mad-cap dash back to safety, reported dismal failure.

"It ain't no go, Long John," gasped he. "Them blasted musket slits is too narrow fer the bombs t'pass through!"

"Forsooth!" exclaimed Flash Dan. "Bowled at first bat!"

Flint swore like Satan. "Boil my blood! Here be a fine finale to oor bugle blowing! Stab me! Sunk afore we've even set sail – by thunder!"

We all of us felt flatter'n a hooked skate, mates. Then Red-Shirt came to the fore. "I, Coosa, shall deliver those Spanish Dogs and drive them from their lair!" boasted the Seminole, striking his chest. "Fear not, Friend Flinty. See to it your Musqueteers stand ready with good aim!"

Red Shirt rounded up the 'Twelve Apostles' and after a brief chin-wag they loped off, six of 'em carrying large, leather sacks.

"Now where might they be going?" voiced Billy Bones as we watched the Indians skirt the town and head for the trees. "The blasted block-house ain't that-away!"

"You wait – you see," replied Red-Shirt smiling. "Get plenty aid," added he with a nod and a wink. We tried to draw him out, but he just chuckled and grinned, refusing to say any more.

While the Seminoles were away, I got to thinking about the coming assault. Sight of a wooden effigy of the Virgin, standing in an alcove, first caught my attention. But when I saw our prisoner Priests being herded into a pig-pen, my mind went back to a camp-fire on a distant beach and the Memoirs of my old Quarter-Master, who I'd listened to all them years ago. Birth of my plan sent me clumping hot-foot, literally, to break the word t' Flint. It were a Plan Re-Born, in a manner o' speaking.

"Jim!" says I, sliding m'self down alongside him behind the wall. "D'you mind when we were waiting for the *Weasel* to blow, and what Old McGinty said on how Morgan attacked Porto Bello?" Blank stares was all I got from him and Darby. "Morgan used the Friars for a buffer to protect his Buccaneers! Made 'em carry the shutters!"

Recollection flooded Flint's face. "By thunder, Barbecue! Och, but there be only one fault along of that statement!" exclaimed he, slamming a fist into his meaty palm.

"What can be wrong wi' it, Capt'in?" asked Darby.

"I should ha' thought on it first!" returned he and roared with laughter.

When the Indians showed, close on an hour later, their leather bags were bulging. With the wind once more blowing in our favour, we fired the buildings bordering the town. Under cover of the smoke that billowed towards the Mission, the six Seminoles bearing the bags dashed for the Redoubt. For added protection against bullets, they crowded behind a brace of thick shutters. A few shots came at them, but they made hazy targets in the eddying smoke. Soon all six were on the block-house roof, safely sheltered by their shutters from any Mission sharp-shooters who might be able to make 'em out.

Their next move was to empty the bag's contents into the square smoke-hole set in the roof. Shouts and shots came from within, along of a hideous scream. The block-house door flew open and seven Spaniards rushed out, weaponless and near raving to judge from their antics. An eighth man remained clinging to the frame, beating at something on his leg.

With that, Flint blew a modulated blast on his silver-call and we all surged forward. Bunched together in our van were the ten Friars, each one linked to his fellow by a rope around the neck. To add a bit o' polish to the plan, I made the leading Priest carry the carved statue of the Virgin – him who had lost a lug to Carver Lowe. And what a Grand Procession it were, mates. Made me feel quite 'Holy', it did!

In the smoke and confusion the fleeing block-house defenders were mistaken for Buccaneers. Four got shot by their own men from the Mission wall, while a Seminole brought down and tomahawked another, along of a mighty leap off the block-house roof. But the remaining two suddenly fell to the ground in a fit. Writhing and kicking, they was, and frothing at the mouth.

"At 'em, all hands!" roared Flint with his hanger raised high.

"Follow me, my crew!" cried Billy brandishing his own cutlass.

"*Aut Vincere aut Mori*!" yelled the Doctor storming forward at the head of my gang, his thin rapier flashing like quick-silver.

"Charge Mates – charge!" bawled I, waving my crutch in excitement, and promptly fell over. Pop-Eye picked me up. Leading from astern has its advantages, to be sure. I like to keep a buffer between me and musket balls – you lives longer! Besides, it ain't my fault if I can't run as fast as them who has Ten Toes, now is it?

Since my party were the frontal assault group, the Friars remained with us as our force split into three. Sight of those black-robed figures in our van had already caused chaos upon the Mission wall. My Gang pulled away from me. I was alone in coming abreast of the block-house and there met a sight that froze the blood in my veins. Sprawled in the doorway was a dead Spaniard. His face was bloated and black, his lips foam flecked, his eyes sightless – staring at the sky. But horror of horrors, crawling over his body, their forked tongues flickering, were a score of cotton-mouthed serpents. Aye, and some of them rattling snakes too – shiver my liver.

My old crutch near caught fire from the friction with which I started to shift. Then – Disaster! True it is, mates, 'More Haste – Less Speed!' In my hurry to get clear, I stumbled over wreckage from the ruined Redoubt and sprawled full length. Before I could recover myself, three of the Hellish creatures reached me – two cotton-mouths and a rattler. I clubbed one snake with my crutch, and was jabbing at a second when the rattler coiled, shaking his tail like dry seeds in a gourd, and crooked his head ready to strike. One more second would have seen me impaled upon his fangs. Next moment the snake lay writhing in two segments, his thick, diamond patterned back severed by Pop-Eye's quivering lance. The Creek Indian leapt over my prone body and dispatched the remaining cotton-mouth with a swipe of his cutlass.

"By thunder, Pop-Eye! You couldn't have done me more service had you been my blessed Mother!" I said to the grinning Savage.

"Flash Danny, him see you close hauled, Long Johnny," replied he, picking me up, along o' my cocked hat and crutch, and setting both to rights. "Send, Pop-Eye, much plenty quick to settle serpent's hash."

"We'd best budge, matey, afore the rest of 'em settle ours!"

The other reptiles were fast slithering out over the sand, so we lost little time in making ourselves scarce. Shots and yells now came from all quarters and the din was dreadful. My Gang had carried their wall that housed the big, double gates and fierce fighting was taking place on top of it. By the sound of the hurly-burly taking place on the flanks, Billy and Flint were in-board also.

I saw Bartholomew the Portuguese wielding a sabre and there was the 'Great Dane', like his fore-fathers, the Norsemen of Old, doing execution with a pole-axe. Perched on a ladder behind Black Dog was the hunched figure of Blind

Pew. The Bosun was bawling the odds, waving his stick and urging his men to commit greater carnage. I stood spellbound, watching the crimson coated doctor, jabbing and stabbing along of poignard and rapier. A strange man was Daniel Hunter. I never knew which he enjoyed more – slicing flesh or sewing it back up!

Me'n Pop-Eye passed the Friars. All were sprawled where they had fallen, after being cut loose from their fellows, and I noticed the splintered statue o' the Virgin laying across the chest of the one-eared Priest. 'Peace be unto ye, Brothers,' thought I in hopping past – and you can't get no more peaceful than what they was!

The Creek Indian scaled a ladder first, then hauled me inboard on the end of a rope. Once I were top-side, safely settled on my crutch, he gave a blood-curdling war-cry and rushed off to join in the mêlée taking place in the court-yard below. But the fight was won. Already I could hear Spanish voices crying for 'Quarter!' Backed against the Chapel, the survivors burst through the doors under pressure from the crowding pirates. Triumphant yells mingled with the screams of terrified women and children who had sought Sanctuary there.

Now some things I can't make mention of for very shame! This much I will say: there ain't no depths o' knavery nor debauchery a Buccaneer won't sink to if the prize be either money or a molly – you may lay to that!

While others sought to reap sordid fruits for their efforts, I went in search o' richer rewards. I wanted to see that Treasure, I did, and feel it trickling through me fingers. Dead and dying were everywhere: Spaniards, Buccaneers and Seminoles lay slumped over the wall, sprawled down the steps and strewn about the yard, but I minded them not at all. In this game a Rover's luck was either good, fair or bad. At the moment mine was 'Full and By' – and that's all as mattered to Long John Silver!

Carefully, I hopped down some twisty steps and found myself under the wall, standing in a narrow, arched corridor with doors set on either side. Gloomy, it was, and cool. I clumped along, opening several doors, in search of the cellars, but these tiny cells were the late Monks' habitat. The furnishings were Spartan in the extreme. Rounding an alcove, a big bored pistol was suddenly thrust under my nose.

"Friend or Foe? Speak or Die!"

The owner's face was in deep shadow, but the voice I knew like my own. "Pew!" I gasped as my heart bounced back up from my belly.

"Barbecue!" breathed he with the same relief. "I've lost me bearings a bit, along o' Black Dog."

We moved on, Pew clutching my coat-tail, while I took the precaution of having one of my twin-barrelled Pettijeans in my right hand with both dogs at full-cock. At the end of the corridor was a double-door, comprised of slats, and from behind this barrier came a low murmur. Cautiously, I pushed one door open and saw a long room with pallets arranged on either side. Upon these 'Donkey's Breakfasts' lay scores of delirious, moaning men. The stench was frightful.

"Shiver my timber!" I exclaimed, coming close to gagging.

"What is it, Long John? What be that 'orrid smell?" asked the Bosun taking a tighter hold of my coat-tail.

"'Tis a sort o' Hospital, Pew – the Mission sick-bay."

Along of my reply the man nearest the door raised hisself weakly upon an elbow. His eyes were yellow, the same colour as the dry, translucent skin stretched tight over his face. "Water, Señors," begged he in Spanish.

"What sickness ails ye?" I demanded in the same lingo, already guessing what the answer would be.

"*Vomito . . . Vomito Prieto*," gasped the Don and slumped back on his bed.

"Out, Pew!" cried I and, pushing the Blind Bosun before me, slammed the door. "The whole blasted Company within is laid low along o' Yellow Jack!"

CHAPTER XXVIII

TREASURE – YELLOW JACK – AND A TEMPEST!

Me'n Pew clumped and tapped our way in search of Flint. Everywhere we saw bands of Seminoles collecting weapons. They cared nought for gold or silver. Red Shirt's agreement with Flint was that their reward would be to have all the captured arms and powder. En route across the corpse-strewn courtyard, we encountered a screaming wench with Carver Lowe clawing at her skirts.

"Avast! Belay that!" I cried, hobbling forward with Pew holding onto my coat-tail tapping his stick.

Stained by blood and powder smoke, limping from a minor leg wound, the burly ex Marine let go the girl and swung about. "What score is this, Quarter-Master?" snarled he, rounding upon us in fury as the Filly ran off. "Is it fer yerself yer wants my 'Flash Packet' or the Blind Bosun there? I reckon the pair o' you are finding slim pickings, eh – what with only three legs and two eye-balls between the brace o' you!" Then he threw back his head and roared with laughter.

Guided by the sound of the Marine's mirth, Pew rushed past me. Before Carver recovered from his surprise, the Bosun had him held fast in an arm-lock with a hoary hand crushed tight against the back of his bull-neck.

"Make mockery of your betters, would you!" hissed Pew and put pressure on Lowe's locked limb.

"M'arm!" shrieked he with his head forced down, causing the half-moon scar I'd given him to pulsate redly on his for'ed. "Yer busting m'arm!"

"One more word and I'll bust your b---dy neck! Take us to the Captain – march!" ordered the Bosun and grinned in savage glee as exerting more pressure, he drew another agonised scream from his victim.

His face distorted by agony, Carver Lowe led us into what I suppose was the vestry-room of the Church. All the major Buccaneers were gathered there, grouped around a half naked Prior who was tied to a chair. The Monk had suffered a severe sweating. He sat slumped in his seat, his body scored by cuts and streaming blood. When we clumped in, Black Dog was on the verge of fixing smouldering fusees between his toes, watched by Flint, Billy Bones, Morgan, Merry and a good few more. The Doctor was standing beside Israel Hands, thoughtfully puffing on his pipe.

"What means this?" demanded Flint, his face working with vexation as Pew sent his prisoner to sprawl headlong at the Buccaneer's feet.

"Insubordination, Sir! Both to myself and the QM here!" replied the Bosun, resting on his stick, which he'd tucked under his arm, and cocking an ear towards Flint.

"They resented me clapping aboard a doxy – as is m'right! Him there!" cried Carver, pointing an accusing finger at me.

"All hands is 'Out of Discipline' for the moment, Quarter-Master. They can do as they please," reminded Billy, eyeing me as if I were a Raw OD who hadn't yet got his feet wet.

"Then get 'em back in Discipline – and lively!" snapped I to the Mate. "The whole blasted town be rife along o' Yellow Jack!"

I couldn't have caused more of a stir had I backed up my words with a Grenadoe. Bedlam broke out to such a degree that Flint fired a barker into the ceiling to bring the Company to order: "Avast!" roared he. "Belay all this bellowing! Is it Buccaneers or bleating Sheep that I command here?"

"So it was a Yellow Flag I observed before the schooner sank," remarked Flash Dan, drawing calm and cool on his pipe.

"That were my verdict, Doctor – so it was!" cried Morgan. "But no lubber heeded me – mark you!"

On stating what Pew and I had found in the sick-quarters, Billy ordered our Trumpeter to sound: 'Muster All Hands' and recall them from their looting and raping parties.

Flint removed his sombrero, leaving his bald head covered by the black scarf with its long ends trailing over his left shoulder: "Och, if it's nay one thing 'tis another," sighed he. "We must abandon here and ship-aboard *Walrus* with all haste. But our problem lies along o' this obstinate beastie!" snarled our leader, viciously slapping his hat across the face of the sweated Prior. "The Blunt be in the cellar, secured behind a sturdy locked door of oak and iron. This Papist swab has hid the blasted key and will'na tell where it's at!"

"Why not blow in the door, Sir, and be done with it? One keg should make us all rich," said I seating myself at the table to ease my aching leg and rasping a hand over unshaven jowls.

"Aye, and risk bringing doon the cellar roof, plus all as be above it!" retorted Flint with a look as sullen as winter. "Come now, Barbecue, ye has a head-piece upon yore shoulders, not a blasted dead-eye – think on it!"

"Lead me to him! I'll give him a go with Ahmed's woolding cord! He'll either blab or feel his eyeballs pop from their sockets!" hissed Pew.

"Send for Ahmed the Moor!" bawled George Merry and the call was repeated.

Now, 'woolding', mates, be the most Devilish form o' torture ever devised by man. H'invented by the Moors, it were, them as rules the Barbary coasts. Early French Privateers much favoured it and this method of extracting information was the special fancy of Jean François Nau – better known in Buccaneering circles as L'Olonnois, so named after the town in which he was born. This instrument of pain consisted of a cord as had two knots tied in it that fitted a-top the eye lids. When the cord was placed around the victim's head and tightened by means of twisting it with a stick or some other article, pressure from the knots forced the eyes from their sockets 'til they popped clean out of the skull. I don't hold with torture, not I! I'm a kind soul at heart and ain't given over to cruelty. Live and Let Live, that be my Motto. Mind you, there's some as would take the liberty to call me a liar – the swabs!

When the evil-looking, scar-faced Turk arrived, Black Dog took the cord off him and obliged our Blind Bosun – leading him over to the cringing Prior. The sight of Pew bearing down to do a mischief upon a body would be enough to reduce the Devil hisself into crying, 'Quarter!' Pew's claw-like hands made their groping approach and explored the shirking Monk's features. The cord was deftly slipped into position and the Bosun started to tighten it using his stick. Four turns was all it took, mates, afore the Prior shrieked the information we were all a-waiting to hear.

"The Madonna! The Madonna, Señors! The key lies within her hollow!"

Pew released his sobbing victim with a disappointed snarl. Flint reached for the Statue, set in a niche in the wall behind the chair, but Billy beat him to it. Quick as a flash the Mate snatched it and smashed it to smithereens upon the table. There, amid the clay fragments, lay the big key. Flint picked it up, balancing it in the palm of his meaty hand, eyeing all our eager, greedy faces. Then he tossed it to me.

"Do ye yore duty, Quarter-Master! The Blunt be yore part o' ship. A full inventory, mind! Black Dog will show ye the way!" said Flint, grinning like a shark along o' his pointed gnashers.

Key in one hand, crutch in t'other, I followed the Bosun's Mate in a flurry and fever of excitement with the rest of the Crew crowding close behind me. Out the room we went and turned down a narrow, twisty stairway that led to a corridor, like what I was in before, only this one were lit by burning pine brands soaked in pitch and set in iron beckets upon the wall. As Black Dog stopped alongside an iron-bound door and reached for one of the torches, there came a ghastly, blood-curdling scream from behind us in the Vestry.

"Flint's sunk the Friar, hark you," whispered Morgan. But we paid the death-cry no mind. With trembling fingers I fed the key into the lock and turned it to the tune of sharp intakes of breath all around me.

"In! In!" cried Blind Pew on hearing the click. Stood behind me, he was, his crab-like tallons clawing and plucking at my coat.

Black Dog entered first and held the light aloft. I were near knocked off my timber perch by the mad rush as the swabs surged in behind me. We all of us pulled up short and stood bewitched. Aches and pains were swept aside in seconds as we stood there soaking in the sight that greeted us. The pure magic of that moment, mates, gives me comfort to this very day – 'Aladdin's Cave', it were!

Stacked in the centre of the room were quadrilaterals built from bars of gold. To starboard were more of the same four sided constructions made of silver. When Black Dog fired the torches set in each wall we saw huge chests, brass-bound and with their hump-backed lids wide open. From every coffer came the dull gleam of minted money. The Crew went crazy wild. Laughing, shouting, they seized fistfuls of the Blunt. Trickling it through their fingers, they poured it over themselves and each other and flung handfuls into the air. No sooner did they lose one pile, they grabbed another. I saw Blind Pew on his knees, kissing the coins in his cupped hands. Ben Gunn was sat alongside him, laughing and crying all in the same breath, while showering hisself in specie.

Billy Bones, Flash Dan, Israel Hands, Merry, Morgan and Me all drooled over the same chest. The Doctor picked out a single coin, turning it in his skilled, slender fingers. He held a 500 Mohur piece from India. Pure gold, it were, and measured around five inches in diameter. "Must be the biggest bit o' Blunt in all the world," whispered Israel, his eyes bulging in awe. The rest of us just looked at the Rhino; but when Merry reached for a feel of it, Billy slapped his hand.

"Hang-fire, George," croaked the Mate, blowing through his fleshy nose. "Let me drink it in for a moment longer, matey."

When we finally did bring ourselves to touch it, trickling through our fingers were monies from all the countries in the World: Silver Daalders from Holland and Golden Ducats from Denmark. Spanish Doubloons and Ducatoons; French Louis D'ors; and of course countless Peeces of Eight – both Cobs and Reals. There were Oriental round bits, square bits and bits with a hole bored through the centre so's you could string 'em together. I never saw so much specie in all my born days – shiver my timber!

"I'll have to mount a Guard over this little lot, mess-mates," I said in a voice that somehow didn't sound like mine.

"Ah, but – *quis custodiet ipsos custodes*?" sighed Flash Dan smiling, flipping the huge Indian coin and deftly catching it between forefinger and thumb. "You will need a noggin of laudanum for the headache you'll have after logging this hoard, John!"

"Look you 'ere, Doctor. I don't fathom all the Greek talk you be always spouting!" complained Morgan. "Why not speak English, plain an' proper, like wot we all does – see!"

Well, the long and the short of it, ship-mates, was this. Twelve hours it took us to ship the Blunt aboard *Walrus* working in non-stop relays out to the jetty and back for more. My task was such that I clewed up with quill-driver's cramp, for every single coin had to be counted and its value logged. When we finally sailed away from Sarasota, into the sinking sun, the Mission was mere rubble and what remained of the Town we left ablaze – a fiery beacon to mark our success!

What of the Dead, the Dying and the Damned, thinks you? Well we done 'em a favour, I reckon, along o' their suffering from Yellow Jack. Not that any of it were my doing, mind! I never had no hand in senseless slaughter. Flint, he done it! Cut the living heart out o' that poor Papist Prior, so he did! It lay on the Vestry table, still steaming when we returned top-side. Duty is duty as well I know and none better, but I've never killed except in defence of my own Self – and me a poor, helpless cripple with only five toes and a timber leg to take me through the trials and tribulations of Life!

Excitement of so much Treasure ruled out the fear of Yellow Jack. Few heeded the Doctor's advice: "Should any of you feel faint or dizzy and give rise to vomiting, report to my Dispensary without delay." Only one fever afflicted Flint's Crew at that time – GOLD!

Several Seminoles were the first to fall sick. The very same day we landed them back into the laps of their loved ones, Flash Dan confirmed five cases of the dreaded *Vomito Prieto*. There was precious little he could do, except pump 'em full of Peruvian bark. I never knew the fate of Red-Shirt's people, but like most Savages afflicted by white-man's diseases, I expect it decimated their village something cruel afore it disappeared. Why, mumps, measles and even sneezy colds killed thousands of Indians in the Americas. What was common to us was catastrophic to them. Smallpox alone near annihilated the whole Cherokee nation at one time, reducing a numerous proud race to a mere pitiful few.

Two days after departing from the Seminoles, our Ship's Company took a nose-dive. Started dropping upon the deck like stranded flying-fish, they did. Flash Dan and his Loblolly Boys worked around the clock attending the sick. But by then, us able-bodied hands were bracing ourselves to do battle with a much greater adversary than Yellow Jack – the mighty sea itself!

I mind that morning like it was yesterday. We were well into the Hurricane season now, nearing August, and the previous day had been most uncomfortable – hot and rainy. Sunrise found us becalmed. Motionless, we was, floating in a sea the colour of lead with nary a cat's paw to ruffle the surface. The damning of that dawn was heralded by huge beams o' light that cut through the great masses of black and mauve clouds bunched on the Eastern horizon, pouring down from the Heavens like pillars of gold-dust.

"I dinna care ta look on this," growled Flint, tapping at the barometer that hung on the bulkhead in his cabin, where us Officers had gathered. "If the mercury falls any lower, it'll abandon the blasted glass altogether!"

"Aye, Jim," I agreed. "My stump tells me such weather has fanfared the downfall o' many a fine ship."

We clued-up our main and fore courses and furled all top-sails. The Ship's boats were double lashed; port lid mantelets were closed and caulked; gun housings were checked; all stern-sheet windows were removed and replaced by deadlights. The Bosun's Mates lashed preventers to all braces, stays and shrouds. Everything movable was firmly secured. The last act in this grim game, before Hunraken hit us, would be to batten down the hatches when Flint or the Mate gave the word.

We waited.

Around Four Bells of the Fore-Noon watch, purple squalls appeared in the distance and the sky changed from blue to bronze with the sun dim and remote, shining like a silver coin as seen in a deep pool. The sea began to breathe along of a slow, strong swell. Short waves fetched us, marring the surface with whitish, grey streaks. The breeze became a wind, but before noon it was blowing big guns. Daylight disappeared under a canopy of cloud, blacker than Flint's hatred for Spain. Echoes from Thor's Hammer rumbled and rolled low overhead; then lightning tore the sky asunder. Rain slashed down and a hurricane of wind set the seas to running mountains high. Our masts and rigging became enveloped in a flickering, green light known as Saint Elmo's Fire – Greek Fire some call it – and a Fore-Sail that tore loose from its furlings was reduced to fluttering rags in seconds. All we could do was to scud before the wind under goose-wings – that and pray our luck would hold!

Now I've weathered a few storms afloat in my time, I have, but none never came close to comparing with this fury – and you may lay to that! Most hurricanes sweep in across the Gulf, from East to West, and blow themselves out in a day or two against the Coast of the American Main. Not so this raging beast. We were battered and blown every-which-way for night on a week without sense of direction, since our compasses spun in crazy circles.

The Moses Boat that was towed astern swamped and sank, snapping the painter. Our six-oared yawl broke free and was smashed, but it was salvaged and repaired later. Scudding before the wind it took all of four Timoneers to keep *Walrus* stern on to the storm, each man lashed to the wheel. One Seaman from the relief watch suffered a Pooping before he could secure hisself and was swept away. Another was flung against the Binnacle by the same giant wave. Although he was saved and carried below, the Doctor declared his back to be broke. He died shortly afterwards.

At a crucial stage of our struggle, *Walrus* came that close to doing a duck that my tarred queue still quivers at the memory of it. One of the great water casks, housed amidships in the hold, broke loose and smashed against the samson post – nought to do with Flint's Snake! Now these barrels were positioned to help balance the Ship. Huge, they was, each one weighing over a ton. To save ourselves from total disaster, we had to stove-in the remainder and pump the bilges for Dear Life!

There be a saying among us Seamen who lived under sail: 'One hand for the Ship and one for Yourself!' In that terrible tempest both hands were needed to keep *Walrus* from foundering – even mine! I took my turn lashed alongside the wheel and helped maintain the pumps, sat upon my rump. Manned day and night, they were, for Ben Gunn and his Carpenters had only half completed the repairs to the damage sustained during the attack on Sarasota and with smashed hatch covers to boot, we shipped tons of water that poured down the companion-ways below decks.

Walrus gained brief respite from the battering when we found ourselves floating in fairly tranquil waters. We had to 'about-ship', you see, mates, and head into the storm to save our stern from being stove-in under the constant pounding from savage seas. This comparatively calm patch was known as the 'Hurricane's Eye' – its centre. But no sooner had the Chinee cook, Wun Hung Lo, served up our first hot meal in days, than we were once again battling for survival against the fury of God's elements.

When the wind finally abated and the mighty seas subsided into a heavy swell, we anchored and staggered to our berths. Bruised, battered and some of them sick, many of the Crew simply slumped down upon the deck where they stood at station. Slept as if dead, they did! For ten hours solid I matched Billy Bones, snore for snore, stretched out alongside the Mate in a soaking hammock.

I surfaced from that deep sleep slowly. Stiff, sore and sluggish, and with my pipe parched, it took me a while to realise *Walrus* was still afloat and I were still alive. Rum was the main-stay, mates! It boosted our weak and weary bodies in the same way as the first sight of a handsome wench do after spending months at sea.

"A goodly go of kill-devil be the key in a crisis – there ain't no bigger bracer!" declared Billy and right he was.

After the Mate got up and left the cabin to report to Flint, I spied the corner of a note-book sticking out from beneath the folded coat he'd used for a pillow. I browsed through it with idle interest and realised I was reading his Account-Book. The first pages contained only doodles, such as a man makes from idleness. There was a sketch, the same as Darby done on his arm at Nanny Town, a gallows with a Pirate dangling. Other writings were the same words tattooed on his forearms: 'Here's Luck', 'A Fair Wind', and 'Billy Bones His Fancy'. In addition there was: 'Mister W. Bones – Mate', 'No more Rum', and 'Off Palm Key he got it'. What was he referring to, I wonder? Pew having his deadlights snuffed? Me, along of losing my leg? Or the iron that sliced his own side? On the next five or six pages there was a column of dates down the left margin, then a varying number of crosses along the line with various amounts of money entered in the right hand margin. I saw that according to his last tally, our Mister William Bones was worth a staggering: £71,351 15*s* 4*d*! He could live like a Lord for the rest of his life with a bank-roll like that! So why was he still risking life and limb – a-roving with Flint?

Hearing heavy foot-falls, I quickly replaced the book.

All hands set-to in clearing the decks of wreckage, opening port-lids and making *Walrus* Ship-Shape-and-Bristol-Fashion. I took an inventory o' the damage done to our stores in the hold. Ruination was everywhere, the bilges being a-wash with staves from busted barrels, tangled bits of junk and lumps of salt meat. It was as well the storm abated when it did, since a four-pound slab of pork was found to be blocking the mawmar of the bilge pump. The rising water had seeped into the magazine and ruined scores of cartridges stacked on the deck. Gun-powder, when wet, dries hard as mortar, you see, mates.

While the crew busied themselves over their 'Sailor's Pleasure', sorting and airing contents of sea-chests and putting soaked clothes and bedding out to dry in the sun, Flint held a Ward-Room Council with us Officers. He'd housed his Serpent there for safety during the storm and the creature was now coiled in a corner o' the great cabin, eyeing us with an unwinking, glittery stare. Israel Hands near climbed up the bulkhead! I reckon the only two aboard who were unaffected by the tempest were Samson and my Cap'n Flint. That old Parrot o' mine slept through it, mostly, but when she wasn't dozing on her perch, she spent the time swearing blue fire and cursing all who came near her – in between screeching: "Stop rocking the boat, you swabs!"

"According to my sightings and calculations, we be off the Louisiana coast between the Cenis and Madalena Rivers," stated Flint, tapping the chart on the table with a pair of silver dividers. "Now I for one have nay sailed these waters. Do any among ye ken the lie o' the coast that confronts us?"

"French territory and vast. That's all I know, Jim," replied Bones blowing through his fleshy, broken veined nose – a sure sign of the heavy drinker.

"Ain't Morgan got a Froggie in his Battery?" I asked, glancing from the Mate to M'Graw. "Maybe he can bear a hand along o' this 'ere pow-wow."

"That he has, Barbecue. A Gunner named Jean-Baptiste La Beck," replied One Eyed Darby. "Want for me t' fetch 'im, Capt'in?"

"Do!" said Flint and went on to discuss the plight of our seventeen sick, along with the critical shortage of water.

Only five had died from Yellow Jack and Flash Dan reckoned he now had the disease in stays. Billy Bones suffered a minor dose, but Rum and Jesuit powder kept him going. Flint missed it and so did I. What worried the Doctor was the mental and physical condition of our Captain. Drink and drugs were beginning to tell on his battered, broad old broken face. It was becoming more gaunt with black, puffy pouches beneath the eyes. His countenance was marred by tiny, purple veins and entirely tinged with blue now. That were due to excessive rum drinking – according to Flash Dan.

"*Messieurs*?" enquired the Frenchman on reporting with M'Graw.

"Look ye to this chart, Frenchy. What can ye tell me of the coast? Do ye ken it at all?" asked Flint, pouring the man a drink and handing it to him, personal like, in his best drawing-room manner.

"*Mon Dieu*!" exclaimed La Beck. "Know it? No! But I know of it by reputation! A bad country, Monsieur le Capitaine, inhabited by the Karankawas. Giant Indians, fiends in human form who feast upon the flesh of man. It is called the Cannibal Coast on French maps. *Sacré Bleu*, but must you put us into such a place?"

"Nay, providing ye and the Ship's Company can survive on salt water!" returned Flint. "Bosun, capstan party to close-up. Weigh anchor and make sail. We should sight terra firma within three hours if the wind holds."

The cry of: 'LAND-HO!' came from the cross-trees by late afternoon. We hove-to and dropped our hook five hundred yards from the beach, allowing for the fall of the tide. Being nearly dark, we didn't venture ashore until early the next day. During the evening, Ben Gunn and his chippies knocked a raft together from spare timber and barrels, on which to carry water-kegs, since we had lost our Moses Boat.

When our Ship's Company learned of the land they were at, and what it contained, they weren't too sharp in volunteering to water ship. Flint would stay aboard *Walrus*. He was too fly to trust the Company as would remain not to seize the chance to up-anchor and sail away with over three hundred thousand pounds. Us Senior Officers drew lots to see who was to lead the Landing Party – the same form of selection being carried out in the Fo'c'sle. There were four short straws amid a bunch of long ones. Hands drew the first, muttering: "I never 'ave no luck, me!" Job Anderson pulled the Second; Billy Bones the Third; and the Fourth fell to yours truly! After a final drink with Flint, the order for what remained of the evening was to check, clean and carefully load our small-arms. As I looked to the priming of my twin-barrelled Pettijean pistols, I got a queasy feeling in the pit of my stomach that I didn't much care for!

CHAPTER XXIX

CANNIBALS!

Next morning we launched the long boat along of its make-shift consort, by means of the capstan, and pulled for the shore. Me'n the Mate sat in the stern-sheets – Billy steering. Straining at the eight sweeps were: Darby M'Graw, Joe the Carib, Tom Morgan, George Merry, Carver Lowe, Pike the Mad Marine, Pop-Eye and the Froggie, Jean-Baptiste La Beck. Being towed astern on the raft was a force fifteen strong, which included: Job Anderson, Israel Hands, Ben Gunn, Bartholomew the Portuguese, Black Dog and Blind Pew. Now the Bosun didn't have to come, but he volunteered to control the beach party – and who better! No one would dare shirk in his presence, even if he was blind!

It took the long-boat's Crew close on half an hour of hard pulling to reach the beach, towing the raft against the ebb o' the tide. To ferry the full barrels of water back on board, we had a hawse leading from the raft to the capstan. Once one load were winched out to *Walrus*, there was a hand-line with which to haul the raft back to shore. I reckoned three round trips would fulfil our needs regarding fresh water.

Blind Pew, Black Dog and four seamen remained with the raft and boat. Me'n Israel took command of the water detail, while Billy Bones and Job Anderson organised our escort. All of us were heavily armed. In addition of my trusty cutlass and the double-barrelled Pettijeans in my coat pockets, I carried a brace of large bored barkers hooked on my belt and a short dagger. Looped over my right shoulder was a powder flask and bullet bag. On the left, slung across my back was a musketoon crammed with buck-shot. Perched a-top the upturned butt was Cap'n Flint. I thought she might admire to have a flutter ashore and maybe peck at a fresh berry or two.

Previous to our landing, Flint had taken a bearing from the mast-head to a fringe of woods visible across a cane-break. Where there were trees, there was water. Clutching my compass I plowed my way up the soft, white sand on the beach and entered a forest of tall canes, the fluffy cotton coloured tops of which towered twelve feet above the deck. Joe the Carib and Pop-Eye took the lead, hacking a path through the giant stems on the line I indicated. When they grew tired, two fresh hands took over.

Cut off from the in-shore breeze, the air became hot and humid and our clothes were soon sweat-soaked. The going was good, the ground flat and firm, but by the time we gained the woods after a quarter of a mile, my lungs were on their last gasp.

"Stand-Easy for ten minutes, lads!" I ordered and seating myself against the trunk of a great live oak, I fired my pipe which gave cause for more wheezing.

Homo sapiens, as the Doctor calls his fellows, are the only creatures to so abuse their bodies along of Baccy and Booze. Smoking and drinking be the folly o' Fools! Mind you, mates, I was led astray on both these bad habits by older men who should have known better. Still, I'm too addicted and set now to change my ways. 'Tis only the tar that be holding my lungs together, I reckon!

"Out pipes and let's be on with it!" growled Billy. "Pop-Eye's found a pond just beyond them pines!"

Pop-Eye's pond turned out to be a small lake, cool and secluded. We saw no sign of the Karankawas, so when the water kegs were filled and the detail started for the beach with Billy, I stayed on in company of Ben Gunn, Hands and M'Graw. While Ben went searching for suitable timber, to assist in ship-repairs, I flashed up a fire on which to cook the midday meal of fried junk. The trees dispersed the smoke, mostly, and I was careful to use only dry, dead wood.

Hands and One Eye Darby were stocking fire-wood for the Ship's galley and I was slicing pork, when Ben Gunn rushed into the clearing. The look on his face arrested our actions for pure, mortal terror was wrote there. Gibbering worse than a spider monkey robbed of its rations, he were!

"There's a dell jus' down below, Long John! Full o' bones and skulls stuck a-top on poles, there is!" blurted Ben all a-tremble.

After I calmed him with a gulp o' grog we all followed the quaking Carpenter back to a small hollow bordering the lake. Ben was reluctant to return and I had to keep prodding him as he crept along, hesitant and fearful, starting at every sound. The first thing I became aware of was that all the tiny noises, as combined to make a living silence in the forest, ceased. Birds stopped their twitter and the drone of insects dropped off. Cap'n Flint were fidgety and fluttered nervously upon my shoulder.

The four of us hove-to on top of a bank which sloped gently down into the Dell. Bordering the water's edge this Shady Nook was enclosed by curious, tortured looking trees. Some of the oakish, gnarled roots grew along the ground, twisted and arched like mummified serpents, while the foliage above was compact – thick as thatch. A great circle of charcoal and half burnt billets marked the hollow's centre with a brace o' blackened stakes set on either side of it. Scattered around were all manner o' human remains: thigh bones, pelvis bones and rib cages. But by far the most grisly sight were the leering skulls that grinned down from poles arranged in a Round Robin about the outer edge o' this Devil's kitchen. The poles resembled rainbows for colour and the skulls were daubed with red symbols, bedecked in feathers and wisps of human hair.

"Wot manner of graven image is that?" breathed Darby, pointing to a hideous idol backed against the lake. "I ain't never seen no Owley like that un a-fore!"

This huge Totem was made from wood and coloured clay. It had a carved mask for a face, brightly painted bearing the great hooked beak of a bird, and from its head flowed a long mane of hair, half white, half black with a pair of huge bison's horns jutting out on either side to mark the ears. A cloak of feathers fluttered from its shoulders and looped about the neck were strings of shells, bones, teeth and claws – centred by a brace o' boar's tusks.

"This here must be a heathen Holy Place," I remarked.

"Something tells me we ought to about-ship and budge under full sail," said Hands with a nervous glance at me.

"Let's do like Israel says an' bear away, 'Q'," begged Ben Gunn, wringing his musket. "If we gets took alive, they'll turn us into Long Pigs like them Coon Cannibals does to their captives in the Great South Sea!"

"Brace your back-bone and be calm, Ben. The situation ain't that black. Bill's party will be on their return by now, so we'll hang-fire and hold our ground. Besides, we needs the water, matey. I'd soon as die from a dart as from thirst at sea. Them savages who worshipped here are probably long gone, anyhow. They be nomads, mostly, and roam at will for hundreds o' miles," I replied to the cringing Carpenter by way of comfort.

Darby was the only one who ventured down into the Dell. He felt around among the ashes and examined some bones. "These ribs is still ripe, Long John!" bawled he.

M'Graw's shout disturbed a big, buzzard type bird that had been hid from us, standing at the water's edge behind the Idol. It uttered a harsh cry, flapping clear with a splash, and flew off across the lake squalling like a scalded cat. Ben jumped near clear out his skin. His Musket exploded and a brace of balls smashed the Totem's mask to bits, while the echoes o' the shot rumbled on and on. I were so startled I fell off me crutch and rolled down the bank, head over heels. Cap'n Flint fluttered from my shoulder with a squawk of alarm and sought a safer perch on one of the skulls: "Fire as yer guns bear!" screeched she and started preening herself.

"Sink you for an empty headed swabber, Benjamin Gunn!" I cried, struggling to clear the rib cage I ended up cuddling. "Them bleached bones has more brains than you! Only a lubber carries a carbine on full-cock! Yer might 'ave killed one o' us!"

"Sorry, Mister Silver, but I'm all in a clove-hitch, I am!" wailed he.

"The cat's out the bag now, if any Karankawas be hereabouts," said Israel, bringing me my hat and crutch.

"Maybe they mightn't have heard it," replied Darby as he set me on an even keel.

"Aye, they mightn't have – thems who be deaf or dead! Time for us to tack! Bear me a hand up this blasted bank!"

We repaired back to camp and a-fore One Bell was out, Billy arrived hot-foot at the head of a breathless, sweating Crew. They'd heard the shot and when I reported the reason for it, Ben received another flea in his ear along of a verbal drubbing.

"Someday, Chippie, someone'll maroon you out o' harm's way and make the world that much safer!" predicted the Mate and trooped off snorting with all hands in tow to view our gruesome find.

When they returned, Joe the Carib and Pop-Eye the Greek were deployed as Scouts. Our Carpenter changed with La Beck and went to keg carrying. The Frenchman was stationed up a tree with a spy-glass – not that he'd observe much among those tall, white topped savannas. Carver Lowe and the Mad Marine were removed from Escort Duty and placed at the wood's edge on picket. Swabs to be sure, but sharp-shooters second to none! Our role was that of vanguard now – Billy Bones commanding. Israel Hands led the second detail back to the beach laden with water tubs. They were barely ten minutes gone when La Beck came down the tree like he was on greased skids.

"*Mon Dieu*! Smoke, *messieurs*! Nor'-Nor'-east and East-south-east!" reported our look-out, wide-eyed and full of panic.

I hopped in the Mate's wake to the wood's edge and, keeping under cover, we observed the directions given. To the North-East a thick column of smoke rose up from a range of low hills. Briefly, it stopped rising. Cut off at the base, it started to fade and had all but dispersed when a big, white cloud rolled upwards. Two smaller ones followed, ending with another big blob before reverting to a single column again.

"They use blankets or buffalo hides to cause them signal rings," Billy informed us, clever cuss that he is.

"It ain't how they says it, but what they might be saying as interests me!" I retorted. "Especially if my Obituary be wrote there! Maybe Pop-Eye is a-reading them signs and will explain 'em when he reports in."

These circles of smoke, floating one below the other, could be seen clear and sharp for miles against the blue sky. The second pillar, situated in the East, gave prompt reply and half a dozen small cotton balls of smoke puffed up from somewhere among the swaying savannas.

"I calc'late that sister column to be near, if not on the coast itself," remarked Billy. "Take a bearing, Barbecue, and give me a guess at the range."

Stepping clear of cover for a better view, I sighted the compass. Billy joined me and trained his spy-glass on the low hills. M'Graw and La Beck crowded behind us, while Carver and Pike closed in upon our flanks.

"Them smaller signals is more south than east, Bill, which puts you just about right," confirmed I.

"How far?"

"Not more'n half a league at the most, I'd say."

"Too damned close for comfort," muttered the Mate, snapping his glass shut. "I 'ope the water detail don't run into a rupture."

His sentence was punctuated by two shots that 'cracked!' out from the cane-break. Me'n the Mate exchanged glances of shocked surprise. Then war-cries rent the air. The swaying savannas, eighty feet or so to our front, crashed together in confusion.

"*Voilá*!" cried the Froggie pointing.

Next moment Pop-Eye the Creek Indian burst into view with Joe the Carib close behind him. Billy drew his barkers, deftly sweeping back both cocks with the heel of each hand – right and left.

"Stand-by to repel boarders!" screech my Parrot, fluttering onto my shoulder as I unslung me Musketoon and came on aim.

Canes were wavering every-which-way now. Suddenly, those in the fore came crashing down and a score of hideous, half naked, huge Savages charged into the open. I'd never clapped eyes on Karankawa Indians before and hope to the Almighty I never suffer the sight of 'em again. Some wore just a single scalp-lock upon their pates, in the same manner as Genghis Khan's Mongol hordes did. Chiefs and renowned Warriors o' Rank had their hair down to their waists, all interbraided with bean-beads and feathers. Their supreme mark of manhood was the embossed designs carved into their living flesh. This barbaric form of tattooing must've been the ultimate in torture to endure; for after strips of flesh were sliced out to the required pattern, white and black wood ash was then rubbed into the gouges before the wounds were allowed to heal. The resulting scars were quite impressive works of art, but I lost little time in admiring this heathen artistry.

The Musketoon bucked against my shoulder and smoke blossomed about me as our gang let fly into the howling mass. An arrow struck the ground between the Mate and me; another flizzed past my head. Five of the Savages fell and the rest faltered. They possessed no firearms, nor any weapons pertaining to the White Man's world. I had a hurtful discovery later, that even their knives were of primitive manufacture – painstakingly chipped from flint. Whether they knew about gunpowder and 'thunder-sticks', I had no idea, but one point was plain – they weren't a-feared of either!

Pop-Eye reached us and flung hisself breathless onto the deck, wheezing like he was ninety; but Joe the Carib stopped and turned to fire at his pursuers. He were closer to the Karankawas than he was to us, so when he went down with a lance through his leg there was nought we could do to aid him. On seeing this the Cannibals surged forward. I fired both my big bored, Sea-Service Pistols, killing one and wounding another. The Mad Marine shot a third and Darby downed a fourth. But despite our bullets the Karankawas knocked the Carib senseless with a stone-headed club and bore him away into the cane-break, warbling their cries o' triumph.

"J.F. ain't goin' to care for Joe bein' took, yew mind! 'Tis like brothers they is!" said Darby, all fingers and thumbs as he hastily reloaded.

"I'll wager his pet cannibal ain't none too pleased right now either," chuckled Carver Lowe, ramming another load into his own musket.

"That shark-toother once told me that the taste o' white man's flesh made 'im sick. Good riddance, I say!" spat the Mad Marine. "He'll be a long time crossing the Styx when they start barbecuin' . . ."

"Belay your blabber, Pike!" retorted Billy Bones. "Prepare to fall back! You lead off, Long John! Darby! La Beck! Stand-by to bear the Quarter-Master a hand, should he need it! The rest of us will bring up astern!"

After we'd loaded and primed our pieces, I took off on my crutch in such haste it were a wonder my shoe-sole didn't smoulder wi' friction! I led back through the trees and out into the cane-break on the other side. The trail was well trampled now and I fairly bounced along on the carpet of crushed canes. But we hadn't travelled far before a great wail of despair sounded in our wake.

"Hark at that caterwauling, mates! They've tumbled to the Idol that Ben blasted, I reckon!"

My words were scarcely spoke when the tempo of the cries changed to high pitched shrieks o' hate and rage. The sound rolled nearer, then the trail in rear was suddenly choked by a crazed mob of Karankawas brandishing their weapons. That cold, clammy hand called 'FEAR', started to pull and twist my guts into knots.

"Stand fast and present!" bawled Billy, his face grey and drawn. "FIRE!"

Our volley of heavy bullets, combined with buck-shot, smacked into them at such close range we could hear the 'Whop!' of the lead striking soft flesh. A dozen went down but the rest came on, leaping over the slain. I scarcely had time to drop my Musketoon and draw my big bored barkers a-fore they fetched us. That howling mob looked like giant imps fresh from Hell!

"Form a round robin! Close in!" I cried and along of a desperate drag on the triggers, discharged right and left.

Billy, Pop Eye and Darby M'Graw sided around me as I hurled my empty pops into the very faces o' them frenzied fiends and drew my Hanger.

Now the worst crime a Buccaneer can commit within the Brotherhood, short of a foul stroke against a fellow Rover, is to leave him in dire danger. La Beck set the rot in, I reckon, when he cried: "*Sauve qui peut*!" and took off like a kicked cur. Carver Lowe and his confederate, Mad Corporal Pike, also took to their heels; but we had no time to curse those swabs for the Savages swept in and closed around us – an angry sea of hate-filled, fiendish faces.

It was Cut and Carve and Catch-as-Catch-Can! The Karankawas stood in awe of me. Amputation was unknown among Indians and I don't think they ever saw a one legged man before. I must have cut a strange sight, to be sure, poised there on one foot, leaning on a pole with an empty trouser leg alongside and a green parrot perched upon my shoulder.

"Avast you swabs! 'Ands off the rum!" screeched my old bird and the Savages sprang back in surprise as if I'd sprouted horns.

"Why don't they skewer us wi' arrows and be done with it?" grated Billy.

"Fresh meat us, matey Billum! They wants um us for sporty torture and um long turn over slow fire!" replied Pop-Eye in his Pidgin English.

The Karankawas prodded and jabbed at me with lances and knives, seeking a chance to club me unconscious. I swung my cutlass, slashing more'n one shaft in half. Pop-Eye, Darby and the mate were likewise close-hauled. The Creek Indian suddenly went down, stunned, and Darby was dragged struggling from our circle. Squawking like a chicken under the axe, he was!

"Back to back, Barbecue!" roared Bones standing astride Pop-Eye's body. He delivered a great swipe, splitting the white spotted face of a warrior bearing a shield and a huge club made from a buffalo's shoulder-blade.

A flint knife sliced across my crutch hand. I ups with me timber and cracked the savage between the legs, catching him in the very core of his root. That made his eyeballs water and roll, that did! But then in parrying a lance thrust, I lost balance and sprawled on me back. 'All's lost, Long John,' thought I as Cap'n Flint fluttered into the air, swearing blue fire. The Savages hesitated, recoiling from my screeching bird. And thems as hesitates is lost! – for the next moment a volley of musketry was cutting 'em down like corn before a scythe.

"'Tis Hands, by thunder! We be saved!" roared the Mate, wrestling with a brace of muscle-bound Karankawas. The pair of them were head and shoulders above Billy, but he brought 'em down. One Indian rolled clear, jumped to his feet and ran. The other only got to his knees before Bill's pistol butt stove in his skull.

The surviving Savages broke and beetled off into the canes. I gained my knee and beheld Salvation. There, advancing up the trail about a hundred yards away was Israel's crowd. As I hauled myself up on my crutch, a strangled cry of terror sounded astern of me.

"Barbecue! Help me, Matey! Don't let 'em doo for Old Darby!"

I swung about and saw the one eyed steward being dragged into the cane-break and certain doom by four Karankawas. I could have let him go, but being an Officer o' Rank, I were duty-bound and besides, Darby was one of the better breed of Buccaneers in our Crew. The way things turned out, I done myself a heap of good in saving Flint's foxy-faced, little servant! Fate, did I but know it, had dealt me another winning hand!

CHAPTER XXX

A FRENCH COWARD AND A COURAGEOUS CARIB!

I hopped forward, meaning to have a set-to with my cutlass, when I remembered the Pettijeans in my coat pockets. Sticking the hanger into the deck alongside my leg, I withdrew a double-barrelled barker, cocked, took careful aim and fired. One Savage spun and fell. Ere the smoke cleared I dropped a second, punching my bullet into the startled face that was painted half blue, half yellow.

The third Karankawa left his fellow floundering on the ground with Darby, the two of them tearing and clawing at each other like crazed beasts, and came at me brandishing a curved, wooden club set with shark's teeth. He were a big brute, tall, well muscled and covered in scar-tattoos. His hair was long and loose, coloured same as the Idol's, and backed by a fan-shaped spray of eagle's feathers. A white mask was painted about his eyes, bordered in black. Around his waist he wore a skirt of animal tails, interspaced with snake skins that still retained the heads and rattles. A necklace of sun-dried human fingers hung upon his chest. He was a sight that would make one of Dante's Demons appear like a cherub!

With no time to draw my second pistol, I flung the empty piece in his face. Club raised, he broke stride, momentarily off balance, and before he recovered I'd snatched up my cutlass and along of a desperate lunge, run him clean through just below the breast bone. Now unlike a dagger, dirk or poignard, a cutlass's function be solely for slashing. The narrow steel of a sword or rapier allows it to slide in and out, easy like, but the Red-Skin's guts and gristle anchored the broad blade of my hanger. When he fell, I was forced to let go the grip to save myself from being dragged down with him.

Darby was in dire straits. The fourth Savage were sat astride him, one hand gripping his hair, the other poised ready to plunge down with a flint dagger. I transferred my crutch to my right hand and threw it in the manner of a spear. Its brass-bound tip caught the Karankawa full force between the glims. His head shot back and the impact broke his neck with a report like a dry stick snapping.

Then Israel's crowd were swarming around us amid much shoulder slapping and mirth. Laugh? I could've cried with the relief I felt!

"We drubbed 'em, ship-mates!" came Merry's jubilant shout.

"That'll learn 'em to fool about with Flint's Flock, that will!" cackled Ben Gunn, cautiously touching a corpse with his toe.

"Did you mind that big buck I blowed away? Fired from the hip, I did, mark you that!" boasted Morgan, striking a pose with his musket as if he expected to have his portrait painted there and then.

"By thunder, Quarter-Master! Yer more dangerous with a piece o' timber, perched on one leg, than a score of cutlass bearing buccaneers stood on two!" exclaimed Job Anderson placing his foot upon the Karankawa's body and pulling my hanger free.

"Barbecue, I'd sooner be braced by yew than a pride o' lions in a tiff," declared Darby, pumping and wringing my hand. "I'll not forget I owes yew this day! Aye, an' every day here-after!"

"Them Cannibals ain't going t' forget it neither! Did you spot the smoke signals, Bill?" asked Israel gazing about him, then frowned. "Hello, where's Joe the Carib at?"

"Took, captured alive! The same as we comed near to being on account o' these lily-white livered swabs!" snarled the Mate, swinging round upon the three who had deserted us. "Lowe! La Beck! Pike! I'm putting you up a-fore the Captain for cowardice! It'll be a Company Trial for you brave bucks! Now let's get under way – double damned quick! Job, you and Bart form a bosun's chair to carry the Quarter-Master!" ordered Bones.

"Haul up the ladder, Jack, I'm in-board!" bawled my old Poll after being restored to her perch upon my shoulder.

We collected our weapons that lay scattered and reloaded; then with me in the van sitting athwart my crutch, supported by Job Anderson and Bartholomew the Portuguese, the crowd of us hurried down the trail, keeping a wary eye to port and starboard. My beam-ends were well bruised from the constant bouncing, but we reached the beach without mishap. Blind Pew, Black Dog and four Seamen had the long-boat ready launched. Stood waist deep in water, they were, holding the craft steady against the Gulf's swell. The raft rode at its mooring ropes close by.

"The Red-Skins cried off, mates! They won't be cooking this or any other crew – not after the drubbing we gave 'em!" cried one wag to the Bosun's Party in a feeble effort to appear bold.

Those were his last words above board. Halfway to the boat he died along with five more, cut down by a shower of arrows that came flizzing out from the canes like bolts from the blue. The howling horde that descended upon us seemed to have swelled in numbers, being close on a hundred strong. Our crowd fired and fled. Racing into the water, some surged towards the boat, others the raft. Several threw aside their weapons and started swimming. A dozen Karankawas were killed in that first mad rush, but the bulk of 'em splashed into the sea where a general mêlée ensued.

"What means this, mates! Are we close-hauled?" cried our Bosun above the clash of arms and the cries of men. He stood like a Trojan at the long-boat's bows, holding the painter.

"Near broached-to and swamped! Climb aboard, Pew!" yelled Black Dog and promptly followed his own advice.

Being in the van, I was one of the first into the boat. Job and Bart bundled me onto a thwart and sprang over the gunnel themselves. The hand to hand fighting was at its height: clubs swinging, cutlasses flashing, men floundering, splashing, crying and dying. I had just fired me musket and was scrambling astern, when I see La Beck commit the ultimate crime of cowardice.

Blind Pew had one leg over the gunnel, La Beck was behind him when a Karankawa with club up raised reached for the Frenchman. Quick as a flash, this flotsam from France grabbed the Bosun and heaved him head first into the Savage's arms. The Cannibal dropped his club and seizing Pew's throat in both hands, pushed him beneath the boiling sea. I was clawing for a pistol when Pew's hand shot from the surface clutching a dirk, which he buried to the hilt in the Red-Man's belly. The Savage screamed as the Bosun expertly jammed down on the handle, twisting the blade to rupture his entrails, before surging up in a welter o' pink foam to push the dying Karankawa clear. Israel Hands pulled him aboard, spluttering and spewing salt-water. No one had seen the Frenchman's foul act, save me. Pressing matters of moment prevented me from making a coil of it then and there.

On board *Walrus* the Crew were already straining at the capstan bars, winching the raft in. Those of our Company who weren't on it or in the long-boat, were past caring. The sea around us ran red and was choked with the bobbing bodies of Seamen and Savage alike, at last in harmony, rising and falling on the ocean's swell. Death eventually reduces Kings to the level of Common Men!

Flint's Gunners couldn't bring cannon to bear against the Cannibals, for we were directly in the line o' fire. Our oarsmen struck out with their long sweeps, beating off the few Karankawas who had followed us into deeper water. Near wading up to their necks, they were, in a last ditch attempt to kill a few more of us. Billy was the last man to clamber aboard the long-boat.

"Give way together! Two-Six, heave!" I cried, helping the Mate to haul hisself dripping into the stern-sheets. His hat was gone, his coat torn and minus a left cuff. Embedded in the back of the same shoulder was the stub of a broken arrow shaft.

"Thunder!" gasped he. "An' to think I once had the chance t' clerk in a Corn-Exchange for five pound a year!"

The Karankawas returned to the beach, where they commenced firing arrows in our wake. Few shafts fetched us in the long-boat and those that did, missed. But two of the five Buccaneers that survived aboard the slower moving raft were slightly wounded. I was about to breathe my first sigh of relief, since setting foot on that accursed shore, when a new sound pricked up my ears. Then came Morgan's terrified cry of alarm:

"Cannibal canoes, look you!" shrieked the Welshman, pointing a trembling finger to port.

The rowers stopped and each man sat as if mesmerised. Bearing down upon us from the larboard side were three long Periaguas, each craft crammed with upwards of half a hundred Karankawas. The noise given off by these huge canoes was caused by the bow-wave surging through a series of holes bored in the cut-water. Along of each thrust from the broad, diamond-shaped paddles there came a sound as sinister as ever I heard – a steady: 'Whoomph! Whoomph! Whoomph!'

"Don't sit there like so many shirking lubbers! Pull for your lives!" cried Pew from up for'ard, his ear cocked towards the canoes.

Our oarsmen needed no second goading from the Blind Bosun. They set-to with a will and we fair skimmed along the surface, going like Spanish clappers we were until Ben Gun missed his stroke. Hauling on his sweep, gibbering with fear, our bungling Carpenter swept empty air with his oar-blade instead o' scooping the sea. He fell back into Israel's lap. The Gunner's rowing was shot, which in turn ruptured the entire rhythm of the sea-boat's crew. Oars clashed and splashed every-which-way, some up, some down, with spray flying in all directions. To keep us bow-on to *Walrus* I had the helm hard over, first one way, then t'other. Swinging on the blessed tiller-bar, I were, like a demented monkey!

"Shrivel my Soul! I've sensed better seamanship from a bunch o' drunks manning a bum-boat!" raged Pew, struggling to fit his own oar back in its row-lock amid the confusion. "What wet knee'd ninny arrested the rowing?"

"Blasted Ben Gunn – who else!" retorted Merry.

"He's done for the lot of us, he has!" snarled Morgan.

"Chuck the swab overboard!" cried Black Dog.

"Don't ditch poor Ben Gunn, mates! Not Old Ben!" pleaded our Carpenter, cringing between Israel's knees and clinging to his leg for dear life.

"Belay this blabber!" roared the Mate. "Pull for the platform, we'll make our stand there! No hope of reaching *Walrus* now!"

There was no way out for us, short of being granted the power to fly. Resigned to my fate, I looked to the raft. Only five hands were left on board and of these, M'Graw and one other were *hors de combat*, suffering from minor arrow wounds. Carver Lowe, Pike the Mad Marine, and Pop-Eye, their guns useless along of wet powder, stood with their backs towards us, cutlasses drawn, facing the on-coming canoes. As we got under way again, I noticed that the raft was no longer being hauled in by *Walrus*. The capstan cable was slack and swung idle, occasionally smacking the sea's swell.

"Why have they belayed winching in the keg carrier?" I asked aloud of no one in particular.

My question was answered by the crash and roar of *Walrus's* whole starboard battery. The ship disappeared behind a rolling bank o' white smoke that billowed upwards, obscuring all but the upper masts and rigging. Our sea-boat's Crew hove-to and craned their necks around towards the canoes. And what a sight to behold, mates! We watched while a mixture of ball, bar and grape-shot tore the three craft to kindling. One canoe was knocked halfway clear of the water with its painted Bird's Head Totem on the prow rearing up like a stricken sea-serpent. Amid this maelstrom of spray, splinters and iron were the mangled remains of the man-eaters. Some of them were blown into the air, whirling every-which-way same as chaff in a high wind.

Us sixteen survivors cheered ourselves hoarse. Ben Gunn cut more capers than a Merry Andrew. Standing upon a thwart he tried to dance the Horn-Pipe and promptly fell overboard, but nobody minded him.

When the smoke drifted away all that remained of the Karankawa Fleet was a flotsom of splinters, paddles and Cannibal carcasses encircled by a great patch of red water. Some savages survived, mind, and were now striking out with strong strokes for the shore. We were clambering up *Walrus's* gangway cleats when a shark pack swept in from the sea, drawn by the scent of the earlier carnage as we bolted for the boat. The sea-wolves busied themselves tearing at the dead and various bits of bodies. Several swimmers got butchered along o' this Feeding Frenzy, but most reached shore in safety. None of us aboard *Walrus* saw much of this performance. Grimmer events soon had us crowding the bulwarks with our attention rooted on the barbaric spectacle that took place upon the blood-stained, sandy beach.

Flint stood on the Quarter-Deck alongside some of the grinning, smoke blackened Gunners who had saved our bacon. His pale blue eyes pierced each of us in turn as we came aboard to the plaudits o' the Ship's Company.

"Rough run-ashore, Bill," remarked he dryly. "And a mighty high price to pay for water with nine men gone below."

"That ain't the worst on it, Cap'n . . ." began Bones, but Flint, glancing around at the faces of us survivors who stood about him in a half circle, suddenly seized the Mate's lapel, making him wince along of the arrow head embedded in his shoulder.

"Where's Carijo?" demanded the Buccaneer, eyes bulging, his countenance bloating to a bluish purple. "Where be ma brother at?" roared he.

"There were nought we could do in aid of him, Jim – he got took," returned the Mate, staring cool and level into the twitching, ferocious face.

"Alive?" croaked Flint.

"Aye, Sir. He suffered a spear in the leg. The swabs overhauled him and dragged 'im off a-fore . . ."

"Them savages is holding high-jinx upon the beach, Cap'n!" reported Port Tack. "By thunder, there's a bunch o' naked Amazons an' they got the Carib!" cried he, near ramming the spy-glass through his glim.

Flint reached the Cooper's Mate in a brace of shakes and tore the telescope from his hands, adjusting it to his own eye. There was a mad rush to the rail. Israel snatched my glass from the binnacle. I grabbed it back and clumped my way alongside Billy Bones, elbowing the Crew aside in company o' curses. My 'Bring 'em Nearer' showed a spectacle that brought bitter bile into my throat and set my hands to trembling that much, I had to steady the glass against the main-shrouds.

Joe the Carib stood stripped and spread-eagled between two stakes that had been sunk in the sand. His body was stretched tight as a drum. Around him were a dozen or so squaws, naked save for animal-skin skirts and necklaces of shells and claws loped upon their bosoms. They taunted him at first, pricking his flesh with flint knives and waving the blades before his face, while the Warriors jumped about jeering and yelling at us, waving their weapons in defiance. Some of 'em, to give the ultimate in insults, bent over to present their bums at us and patted their buttocks.

Carijo remained impassive, staring straight ahead. Then these fiendish females began their ritual o' slow torture. Taking turns they slowly dragged the tips of their knives down the entire length of his body, extracting every last ounce of agony from the twitching muscles. Strung up there like a crucified Dacoit, Joe never so much as blinked, while they carved him slice for slice and his red essence dripped to stain the sand beneath him. One o' these harlots from Hell, perhaps put off by his fixed, stony stare, suddenly jabbed up with her knife and put his eyes out!

"God's Blood! Who could imagine such a magnitude of wanton cruelty inflicted by a foul horde of female furies!" exclaimed the Doctor aghast.

"Tis the way of most Savages. The women do the butchering on captives, while their men-folk watch," replied Billy rolling his quid.

"Damn my soul!" bellowed Flint, sounding like a sick bull. "Pike! Lowe! Ye both has the reputation for sharp-shooting! Prove it the noo and deliver me ma brother from his slow demise! The rest o' ye gawking swabs, load all artillery with Langrage and stand ye by!"

"Our Pieces needs drying out, along of water fouled powder, Cap'n," replied Lowe with just a slight, sly trace of inward satisfaction.

"Allardyce! Fetch a brace o' Brown Besses from ma cabin! Lively noo, ye yellow haired loon!" snarled Flint and swung back to view the horror on the beach.

Our Crews were all a pully-hauly on the guns. Panic and fear was their goad, for Flint's mood were more dangerous than a coiled Diamond Back. As Carver and the Mad Marine primed their pieces, I saw the look that passed between them. Neither bore any love for Carijo and since it would be about their mark to place their bullets in his belly, instead of his brain, I decided to ensure the Carib got killed clean. They paid me no mind when I clumped across the deck and took station between them. Both sat crouched upon a cannon with their gun-barrels a-top the bulwarks. I can recall the markings on the metal of Pike's piece to this same day. The breech was stamped: 'POCOCK, C.3 – N.3', and the Lock-Plate had a Crown with G.R. below it, along of the name: 'WILSON 3 – 17'. "Ship-Mates," I said softly as they cheeked their stocks to sight along the barrel. "If Joe ain't dead after your smoke clears, both you bright sparks will be – *Comprende*?"

In answer to their startled glances I lifted the flaps on my coat pockets, casual like, and showed 'em the butts of my Pettijeans. Pike blinked, licking dry lips. Lowe swallowed hard several times and came on aim.

"Dinna dither, damn your eyes – SHOOT!" roared Flint.

Both Brown Besses exploded as one piece. The smoke billowed, eddied and drifted clear. I raised my glass and saw that Joe the Carib's head was hanging upon his chest with two, neat holes in his for'ed. A great cry o' rage reached us from across the water. Flint suddenly slumped down against the bulwarks.

"*Factum est*, James," said Flash Dan supporting him.

"Fire," croaked the Captain. "Blow those sons and bitches of Satan back to Hades where they belong." And with a long sigh, he slumped senseless into the Doctor's arms.

"STARBOARD BATTERY, STAND-BY!" I bellowed, taking up Flint's order as he was half carried, half dragged back to his cabin by the Doctor and Pop-Eye. Clumping my way clear, I yelled: "FIRE!"

The deck heaved beneath me as the guns smashed back into their breechings. For a few moments the rolling bank of smoke concealed everything. When at last it started to disperse and I was able to scan the beach through the tattered streamers with my glass, not a Savage was to be seen standing. Nothing had withstood that withering blast of bolts, bars, nails, broken bottles, bits of clipped lead and bullets. This discharge of scrap-iron had not only plowed up the beach and everything on it, but had cut a great, gaping swathe through the cane-break.

Of Carijo's torture stakes, only one jagged stump remained – a mute witness to the Carib's passing. As to the Karankawas, closely packed as they were, the carnage was utter and complete with just an occasional arm or leg rising briefly here and there only to flop down again. The breakers of the Gulf surged up that blood-soaked beach a foaming white and rolled back a vivid crimson. By the time the anchor was catted and we were under way, stern on to that shattered, accursed shore, the water was a fiery red for two hundred yards out, reflected in the rays of the sinking sun, and dotted with the black fins of marauding sharks – darting every-which-way in a frenzy.

PEECE SEVEN

MUTINY!

CHAPTER XXXI

BLIND PEW'S DUEL!

Flint ranted and raved that night. Soaked to the gills in booze and drugs, he stormed between decks, cutlass drawn, calling the Carib's name. The Crew scurried hither and thither like frightened rats to keep out of his way. Us Officers stalked in his wake: Me on my crutch; Pew tapping with his stick; Darby limping, favouring a woundy leg; Billy nursing his left arm in a sling; and Flash Dan carrying a tankard of rum spiked along of laudanum. When we finally persuaded the Captain to drink it out and helped him stagger back to the Great Cabin, he was put to bed where the Doctor opened a vein. The bleeding done us all a service! Flint was at last quiet and *Walrus* dozed fitfully 'til dawn.

The horror of Carijo's dying had darkened all else. Not until two days later was Flint fit enough to face the defaulters, brought before him by Billy. He sat slumped behind the desk in his great carved chair with the entire Crew arranged around him. There were dark, puffy pouches beneath his eyes and his face was that horrible shade o' blue which was now part and parcel of him. The Mate was seated on the Captain's right; I were sat to larboard alongside Pew. Stood facing us was Carver Lowe, Pike the Mad Marine and the Froggie, Jean-Baptiste La Beck. All three had been found Guilty by the Company's vote and were now awaiting the final verdict as to their fate.

"Grave charges, these," began Flint in his Summary. "Cowardice in time of Engagement would normally carry but one sentence – Death! But we be so under-manned, I kinna afford to lose even three sorry dogs such as ye. I hereby tip ye the 'Black-Spot', as in duty bound. Now pick up your Summonses and read what's wrote there," concluded the Captain pushing forward three squares of paper, the size of a cob, with the upper side marked by an ink-blot.

Lowe was the first to take his slip from the desk. His face flushed darkly when he read the small, neat print on the back of the paper: "To forfeit all shares of Prizes on this voyage!" exploded he. "That ain't punishment, 'tis robbery!"

"Curb your tongue to the Cap'n or I'll cut it out!" spat Blind Pew leaning forward on his Stick.

Pike and La Beck snatched up their slips, which read the same. The Mad Marine said nothing, but his dark, hooded eyes conveyed his feelings well enough as he screwed the paper into a ball and tossed it back on the desk with a nonchalant flick of his thumb. La Beck had the look of a sick man who had just swallowed olive oil. He weren't slow off the mark in making his excuses. His mouth started clacking like a pair o' castanets!

"*Mon Capitaine*!" exclaimed he, spreading wide his hands in open plea. "Harsh treatment indeed for one so loyal. Have I not pledged mon sword and mon soul to the service of this Company? Am I to lose thousands of francs for refusing to face impossible odds?"

"Ye could have lost yore life or suffered to be marooned on some lonely key!" snapped Flint. "Small mercies dinna be a major holding among my Company – be thankful!"

"*Sacré bleu*! I thought perhaps a fine of fifty francs . . ."

"Belay all your clap-trap!" thundered I, clumping my crutch upon the deck. "You be an insult to all Frenchmen who ever trod wood between wind and water! Hanging's too good for your sort, after your brisk performance in boarding the sea-boat!"

"*Mon Dieu*! I . . . I know not what you mean, mon . . . mon Quarter-Master!" stammered La Beck turning pale as tallow.

"Nor dinna the rest o' us," growled Flint glaring at me. "Explain yo'rself, John Silver! What mean ye by these wild words?"

"Ask Pew what befell him when clambering aboard the long-boat!" replied I, staring at La Beck and watching the fear creep into his eyes.

"Me?" inquired the Bosun in sneering surprise. "I only recall being hauled out the boat by a Red-Skin who tried to sink me. But eight inches of cold steel in his belly was all he got for his pains. I pressed home my point, you might say," grinned Pew. His smile were as warm and friendly as that of a Beak in Bow Street passing sentence.

"You was hauled out the boat, to be sure, and flung into the arms of a Savage by that swab there!" I cried, pointing a denouncing finger at La Beck. "That blasted Froggie near sank you to save his own skin!"

"LIES! LIES!" shrieked the Frenchman, spittle flying from his lips.

"Do you wish to have it out with me?" I roared and sprang up heaving on my crutch. "So be it! You avoided the dry blows last time, but you'll not sneak from this bout! When next we heave-to bordering a desolate beach, you'll face me and fight as a Gentleman o' Fortune should! By the living powers, if I don't ram your teeth and forked-tongue down your gullet on the end o' a pistol ball, my name ain't John Samuel Silver!"

"Hang-fire, Barbecue! Mine, matey, mine! The swab belongs to me!" cried Blind Pew, clawing and plucking at my coat.

"Avast!" Flint's voice cracked like the cat as his huge fist crashed upon the desk with such force that the heavy, silver ink-pot pounced and the quills jumped from their holder. "Do I still command this here Company or have I been deposed without the formality of being informed? Sit ye doon, Quarter-Master; likewise yoreself, Bosun!" snapped the Captain and turned to La Beck with eyes hard as agate and just as glittery.

"Silence from the Fo'c'sle!" bawled Bones swinging about in his chair and the murmurings of the Crew, grouped behind him, ceased in a second.

"La Beck," resumed Flint in a soft voice, but with a furrowed brow and a face like thunder, "I have fought yore fellow countrymen and never met a-one who disgraced either his name or the Flag of France – until now! Ye be a sore within a scab, an affront to every honest thief afloat. My Quarter-Master dinna be in the habit of telling galley yarns, so yore fate shall be this: Ye'll be set doon on some lonely shore and there-at be marooned, along of a pistol with one load, a gourd of water . . ."

"Asking your pardon, Sir," interrupted Pew politely. "Might I make so bold as to humbly beg for a retrenchment of this snivelling swab's sentence that's just been handed him?"

A gasp of pure amazement came from the Company and a ripple o' murmurs buzzed about the cabin, like the lazy drone of bees on a summer's day. Was this, the Bosun of *Walrus*, asking Mercy for the man who tried to Murder him most Foul? I gawked at Pew in disbelief – we all did! There he sat, mates, straining forward in his seat, his head cocked towards Flint, his stick held lightly in his left hand, a pipe poised in the right, and with the most horrible leer on his face I'd ever seen.

"Pew," said Flint gently, plainly as puzzled as the rest of us. "Do my lugs deceive me or be it that ye are asking clemency for this cur?"

"No, no," replied our Bosun brightening, perking up. "I only ask the chance to seek satisfaction in the normal way. Retaliation is my Right, as in Articles so stated – is it not?"

"You mean a duel?" exploded Billy Bones.

"Look here, Pew!" exclaimed the Captain as a wave of excited chatter surged around the Great Cabin. "Ye canna challenge La Beck to a fight, not ye with pitch-plugs in place o' eyes – 'tis madness!"

"No," returned Pew grinning like a shark and looking twice as dangerous. "But if this skulk has the pluck of a weevil in a biscuit, maybe he can muster enough bottle to challenge me – a poor blind man!"

The whole Crew erupted with a roar and above the babel came such cries as: "Pew's popped his pipe!" "The Bosun's gone batty!" all interspliced along o' the Mate bawling for "Order!"

"Further more, ship-mates! Hear me now!" cried Pew, standing up and raising his arms for silence. "Further more, I say this: Should La Beck throw down his gauntlet and win, I ask that not only he be reclaimed by the Company, but given back his full share of the prize money – including my cut t'boot! What say you to that, Captain?"

No one moved; no one spoke; we hung in stays a-waiting on Flint's answer with baited breath. I for one, didn't believe my ears. Neither, by the following account, did the Captain.

"I ken I'm on drugs, along of a booze filled brain, but will someone give me a poke to prove I dinna be in dreamland hearing what Pew is a-saying," muttered Flint, wearily brushing a hand across his for'ed. He gazed at the grinning blind man for what seemed Eternity before he finally said: "'Tis yore life, Bosun. If Death be yore desire, along of a reward for the man who murthers thee – so be it!"

Pew near danced a jig with delight. "There now, Frenchman, your choice! Challenge me and win back your Blunt, plus mine, or suffer to be marooned to die like a dog – choose!"

"*Mon Dieu*, you are mad!" gasped La Beck in amazement, not believing his luck. "But I accept!"

"Then challenge me! Challenge me!" Pew hissed the words. He stood hunched, wringing his stick in both hands like it was to be a neck.

"I, Jean-Baptiste La Beck, do challenge Bosun Pew to an *'affaire d'honneur'!*" The Frenchman suddenly smiled, disclosing stained, crooked teeth when he added: "May God have Mercy on his Soul!"

"Amen to that!" said Pew and sat down beaming, happy as a city urchin in a country Squire's orchard.

The Mate noisily cleared his throat. "When we sight land and are hove-to off shore, the Quarter-Master will conduct the pair o' you to the beach with such seconds as you nom . . ."

"Stay a bit, Bill, stay a bit," broke in the Bosun. "Since I am the challenged party, the choice of when, where and how rests with me, now don't it?"

"Aye, Pew – it do," agreed Billy, exchanging baffled glances with Flint.

"Well then, I choose here and now aboard *Walrus*. The place: battened down in the hold with all glims snuffed. And how? Daggers in the dark!"

"But . . . but I will not be able to see," stammered La Beck turning pale.

"Oh, dear," sighed Pew, his grin growing wider than a Cheshire Cat's. "Too bad, ain't it. Looks to be as if you'll have to play Blind Man's Buff along o' me!"

All hands remained silent for a moment, while the significance of what the Bosun had said slowly sank in. Flint started to chuckle; someone sniggered; then the whole Crew roared out their mirth. Bellow followed bellow and the Cabin echoed to shades o' Bedlam. Even the Mad Marine held his sides, along of his wheezing whine. Through my tears I saw the Froggie stood there wearing a look on his face sicker than a Jew chomping pork. He weren't enjoying the jest one bit!

Lunch was gobbled down in a fever of haste and excitement – the duel being set to commence at four bells. Flint broke a golden rule and allowed the hands to make wagers on the outcome. As Quarter-Master, my duty was to officiate and ensure all were correct and above board. Along of the noon-day meal, La Beck was invited to Mess with Port Tack, Carver Lowe and that crowd. One oddity was when Flash Dan reported seeing the Cooper's Mate sneaking up from the hold shortly before 'Hands-to-Mess' was piped. For what purpose we none of us could fathom – then!

The appointed hour found us Officers, who were to officiate, grouped on the Orlop Deck in company of the two combatants. Apart from me, there was Flint, the Mate and the Doctor – in case only a wounding ensued from the clash. Knowing Pew's prowess with a knife, I'd wager a Guinea to a Groat there was more chance of a man walking on the moon!

I searched both parties, paying particular attention that La Beck hadn't secreted a tinder-box about his person with which to flash up a glim. Satisfied, I led the way into the hold, carefully hopping down each step with a lantern raised on high in my right hand. Pew followed, clutching my coat tail. Behind him came La Beck with Billy bringing up astern, holding another glim. While the Mate conducted the Frenchy for'ard to the cable-locker, I positioned the Bosun aft outside the Coffers Cave that housed three hundred thousand pounds and Flint's Serpent.

"Be sure and sink the swab, Pew. I got Five Guineas riding on you," I informed him, placing the Bosun's dagger in his hand. "Be lucky."

"Don't fret over your Blunt, Barbecue. It's as good as doubled itself already!" was Pew's parting shot.

After blowing out the glim in the tin-lined light room, alongside the magazine, I returned to the steps where Billy a-waited on me.

"I hope Pew knows what he's about," said the Mate as we ascended to the Orlop-Deck. "That blasted Froggie seems a mite too cock-sure o' hisself for my liking."

Flint and the Doctor stood ready with a cover, which they placed upon the coaming when we stepped through. We lit pipes, poured a goodly measure of rum and sat down to await the result. Flint placed his watch on a barrel between us with its gold-lid wide open.

"I'll wager ten Silver Riders there ain't no response from below within fifteen minutes from this point in time. Any takers?" asked the Captain, clicking the coins into a pile alongside his clock.

"Done!" replied Flash Dan matching the value with Dutch daalders.

"I'll cut a slice o' that, Cap'n!" I said and added three guineas to the stakes a-top the barrel.

Since there may be some of you Readers who reckon Blind Pew to be close-hauled, him having no eye-balls an' all, I'd best explain a little bit about blind people in general and Pew in particular. When a body loses its power o' sight, all other senses become enhanced: Touch, Smell and Hearing be intensified two-fold, far above the standard of us normal beings. Got that information from the Bosun hisself. Pew could hear the surf pounding on a lee-shore long before the leadsman in the chains. He could smell land, whereas the look-out in the Crow's Nest couldn't even see it with a spy-glass. As for movement, our Bosun was a sight quicker, sharper and more nimble on his pins than most able-bodies, once he knew where things were at. If any one was close-hauled groping about in the blackness of the hold, rest assured it weren't Pew – and you may lay to that, ship-mates!

It lacked but six minutes for Flint to win his wager with Flash Dan and me, when there came a crash and clatter from below. Billy gave a start, spilling his rum, and the Doctor broke the long stem on his clay-pipe against the bread-bin. A shout, sounding more like a roar of rage, was followed by a high, thin scream – then silence. I heard the shuffle of faltering foot-steps coming up the stairs. One rap echoed beneath the cover followed by two more, hesitant and slow.

Flint and Billy removed the hatch in a brace of shakes and we beheld the white, upturned features of La Beck. The Frenchman mounted the last few steps with a slow, measured tread. His knees were level along of the coaming when he paused, swaying, his stare fixed and glassy. He gave a sort of queer, rattling gasp and pitched forward upon his face. Sticking from between his shoulder-blades was the fluted pommel hilt of Blind Pew's dagger. Staring at the Frenchman's corpse we saw a hand come groping over the coaming, the blood-stained fingers fluttering along the edge.

"Holloa, mess-mates! Anybody 'ome?" called Pew and his head popped into view. The green shade that covered his glims was gone and the black pitch-plugs in place of his eyes, surrounded by the mangled flesh of his splinter scarred for'ed and cheeks, drove a chill through us all as we stood there in the gloom. "Come now! Will no one bear the Bosun a hand or do I have to sing for blasted assistance?" chided he irritably.

"Well fought, Pew," replied Flint, his voice husky, and guided the Bosun to a seat on the bread-bin.

"I could use a pipe and a noggin, by way of a bracer," replied Blind Pew. "It were a close-run thing, that took place down there, and I near came a cropper."

Flint fired up his own pipe and placed it in the Bosun's hand, while the Doctor poured him a drink.

"I'm so glad you didn't let the grass grow beneath your feet, Pew," grinned the Physician. "Your prompt action earned me a handsome profit this afternoon, don't you know."

"Swift was the word for it, Flash Dan. I had to budge an' act lively for there's been some Dutch trading down below," resumed Pew, puffing smoke and drawing it deep into his lungs. "I first sensed all weren't well when I heard that French fly-by-night fumbling with a lanthorn, which he unhooked from its becket on the Samson Post. I was near enough to hear his breathing and smell his fear by the time he'd lifted up the shutter. Stuck the swine afore he fired the glim or I'd be in his boots by now – cold as pork!"

"But he had no blasted tinder-box!" I exclaimed. "Searched the swab alow and aloft, I did! Shiver my timber if this don't beat all and cast a black light on me!"

"Hello, what's here?" Billy crouched down beside the body and after a slight tussle, took an oval, brass tin from the death grip of the Frenchman's stiffening fingers. Etched into the lid was a sea-fight scene between two Frigates with the name HMS *Diamond* below. When the Mate opened it, engraved on the reverse side in scrolls were the words:

ABLE SEAMAN
HARRY PAY
HIS
TINDER TIN

"Who in Hades is Harry Pay?" asked Flint scratching his chin. "Is he listed along o' this 'ere Company?"

"Aye, Sir, the swab's listed sure enough, but better known by another name," I said, feeling my face go tight as I glanced around me. "Him, it was, whom Dan here see sneaking up from the Hold!"

"Thunder!" exploded Billy. "Port Tack!"

"Port Tack as ever was!" I nodded.

"Boil my blood and fall on!" grated Flint, grinding those terrible teeth. "Harry Pay, is it? He'll 'Pay' right enough!"

In gazing at the engraving upon the lid, I cast an eye on the contents. The box contained steel and tinder, but no flint. "See here, the Striker be missing,"

I remarked, pointing.

"A minor matter," returned, Flash Dan, casually lifting a lantern. "The Froggie probably dropped it when Pew finished him. No doubt I shall find it down there alongside the light. Besides, the Bosun needs his eye-shade. We don't want all the Crew going overboard in viewing his beauty, now do we!" grinned he and started below.

There, for the moment, the matter rested.

CHAPTER XXXII

PORT TACK!

The Cooper's Mate was arrested, clapped in irons and stood trial that same afternoon. Flint appointed hisself Judge; Billy Bones was Prosecutor; and the Jury was drawn from the Fo'c'sle. Topping the stiffest yard to nothing, Port Tack nominated ME of all people to defend HIM! I conducted my Brief, along o' the Prisoner, in the privacy of the Mate's cabin, which we shared. Israel Hands was stationed outside the door, acting as Master-At-Arms. His assistants for this occasion were Morgan and Merry.

"Allardyce was in on it," the Welshman was saying to George. "Borrowed three guineas off me, he did, to bet ag'in the Bosun!"

On entering the Cabin, I said: "See here, 'Arry Pay, what's the game?" I removed my hat and sat down on Billy's sea-chest opposite him across the narrow table. "There ain't no love lost between us, to be sure, nor ever was! So why choose me to try and save your neck?"

"Because you're the best man in this 'ere Crew by a long shot. You be brisk and business like. Only brains can cut me loose from the rope that's as good as around my wind-pipe already. We've had our differences and clashed on occasion, but you ain't the kind of cove to let his feelings run rough shod o'er his sense o' dooty an' fair play – not you!" replied Port Tack with what I took to be open honesty.

And right he was, of course!

"Shiver my sides! You're either the biggest fool afloat or the shrewdest! I ain't quite decided on that score yet. But mark you this! Flattery don't wash with me!" I snapped, gazing intently into his face and trying to fathom if the truth were wrote there.

"Do I look lubber enough to try and daddle you with that?" cried he, chinking his gyve chains in spreading his hands as wide as the manacles allowed. "I'm no flattering fool nor shrewd neither, else I wouldn't be a-sat here sufferin' the Grand Order o' the Iron Garters! To be sure it were me as placed the tinder-tin in the glim. Bad luck on my part, Flash Dan see me leaving the 'old. I'm desperate, I am, and unless you comes up trumps for me, I'm dead! Mind you, Quarter-Master," he added, coiling his tongue into his cheek and looking sly, "if the Cap'n hangs me for planning the Bosun's down-fall, he'll have to hang half the fo'c'sle for conduct unbecoming! Swing one – swing all, I say!"

"The Mate has a cast-iron, open and shut case ag'in you, along of the Doctor's testimony. If I'm to do my best by you, then I have to know what's what from first to last. At present you've peached too much or too little – now talk!"

And talk he did!

The Cooper's Mate blabbed as only a man can who's Hell-Bent on saving his skin. By the time he'd finished, more than a third of the Crew were implicated in the plot to make easy pickings by betting on the Bosun's death. To solve this sour problem, Port Tack made many a helpful suggestion and Old Long John swallowed 'em hook, line and sinker. Fact was he used me for a mouthpiece to swing Flint around into doing exactly what were wanted. Moulded my thoughts like they was putty in his hands!

Leaving Port Tack under guard of Israel, I repaired to the Great Cabin and made a full report to Flint. He decided to adopt the plan put forward by me, along o' the ideas from the Cooper's Mate. To try and chastise all the conspirators would result in the whole Company falling together by the ears. This way at least some degree of discipline would be maintained. The hands were 'Piped Aft', along with the Prisoner who clinked and clattered his chains in between Morgan and Merry. When all was settled, Flint summed up, assessing the worth on what Harry Pay had said.

"Those of ye nominated for Jury Service may stand-down, seeing that the Prisoner sees fit to plead Guilty as Charged," began the Buccaneer.

Flint sat with a face of stone, glaring around the crowded cabin. His features were an iron mask that gradually grew bluer and more bloated. Suddenly, he smashed both fists upon the desk, exploding in rage as I reckoned he would.

"Boil my blood and fall on!" thundered he. "Three Court-Martials in one day and now this Conspiracy! The deeper I dive into this case, the murkier be the waters! For all o' ye who knew the Bosun to be up against marked cards when he went below, hear this! I either lead this Company on the course so stated in Articles, or I'll end it! Harry Pay stands here alone, convicted by his own tongue! Is there any man staunch enough to stand alongside him and share the blame? Ye who were brisk enough to place money down for sure profit on Blind Pew's death!"

Not a man answered; not a man moved.

Flint continued to glower at the Company, grinding his terrible teeth, his huge hands opening and closing into clenched fists upon the desk-top, while his eyes darted and flashed every-which-way like slithers o' steel.

"Sink my Soul, but yore a sick lot to look at, so ye are!" grated he finally. "And I've a sicker heart sailing alongside such a sad parcel o' dogs! Harry Pay, would ye care to name the names of them as were in the know, along o' wagers made against the Bosun?"

"No, Sir! 'Tain't my policy to peach ag'in my mates!" replied Port Tack, looking firm and proud.

"Some mess-mates!" spat back the Captain. "For my money I'd rather berth beside the muggers that bask on the mud-banks of the Hoogley. But so be it! Since none choose to side with ye, they shall have the punishing of ye. At Two Bells of tomorrow's fore-noon watch, ye will Run the Gauntlet – twice! One drubbing will be for yoreself and the second to receive the blows o' those skulking swabs who ain't got bottle enough to take their own stripes! March the Prisoner below, Master-At-Arms!" cried Flint and stood up sudden like, as if shot, flinging back his chair.

Hands, Morgan and Merry ushered their charge clanking from the Cabin as though their bums were a-fire. Flint came round his desk and stood facing the Crew. The tension was tighter than a Jew's purse-strings when asked for charity and the stench o' fear was strong enough to slice with a cutlass. Those nearest the Captain fell back a pace or two when he suddenly strode to the Mizen-Mast trunk and removed one of the huge bored, pintle blunderbusses from its niche in the rack. All eyes followed Flint's every move. Returning to the desk, he took a copper flask from a drawer and carefully primed the massive Migulet Lock. Snapping shut the frizzen to cover the pan, Flint slowly sat down. Two sharp, distinct clicks shattered the silence as he drew the Dog's Head back to full cock. With the butt firmly clamped under his arm, the Captain lowered the bell-shaped muzzle to cover the entire Crew.

"I shall count to six," said he very softly. "If any of ye hen-hearted swabs remain in my sights by the time I say seven, I'll trigger this piece and send ye t' Purgatory."

I swear to this same day that, Time, the Earth and the Hearts of the Fo'c'sle hands all stopped at that precise moment.

"ONE!" Flint's voice boomed out like the Clap of Doom.

The Great Cabin shuddered and shook under the impact of pounding feet. En masse, the Crew stampeded into the narrow doorway with Flint's count sounding out their death knell behind 'em. By the time he bawled "FIVE!" all that remained of our staunch Company were two crumpled, tricorne hats, one crushed sombrero, a broken clay-pipe, somebody's wipe and a single shoe. Sprawled amid this wreckage was a very bruised and battered Ben Gunn!

"Don't blow me away, Cap'n!" pleaded our Carpenter, going through his usual routine of grovelling when threatened as the Doctor helped him up. "I put all me money on Bosun Pew, I swears it!"

Flint lowered the Migulet's hammer onto half-cock and laid the piece on the desk. "Rest easy, Ben. It dinna be ye I'm at logger-heads with. Take ye a noggin of what ye fancy to compensate for your cuts and contusions. Do the Honours, Bill, we could all use a snort," said he wearily brushing a hand across his for'ed, his voice sounding tired.

Apart from the Mate and Ben Gunn, us Officers who remained in the Cabin consisted of Blind Pew, Black Dog, Darby M'Graw, Job Anderson, Doctor Hunter and Me. Sipping my drink in heavy silence, a thought crossed my mind. "By the bye, Flash Dan. Did you find that missing flint from Port Tack's tinder-tin?" I asked, pretending to make small talk.

"Indeed, John, I did," returned he, quizzing me along of an arched eyebrow. "The striker was laying beside the lamp, exactly where I said it would be. Why do you ask?"

"Ah, small matter, Doctor, small matter," I replied putting on my hat. "Time for a couple o' turns around the deck afore supper, I reckon." Draining my drink, I hobbled out leaving strange looks in my wake.

I had me much thinking to do, for there were a few facts that didn't quite ring true. Now the deeper you dips your toes into muddy waters, mates, the thicker be the sludge at the bottom of it. Some inner instinct warned me that I'd barely touched the surface o' this particular pool. All this conspiracy to win a few pound at Pew's expense pointed to stronger undercurrents leading to a deeper, blacker intrigue. But the 'What?' and the 'Why?' had my brain buzzing, 'till I thought it would pop!

At nine o'clock the following fore-noon, just as Two Bells were struck, the whole Crew assembled on the upper-deck. I divided them into their respective Watches, port and starboard, with a gangway between the twin ranks of about four feet. Each man was possessed of a length o' rope or a belt or in Pew's case, a thin rattan cane, which he swished, cutting the early morning air with evident relish of what it were required for.

"Be sure to give me good warning on when to strike!" reminded the Bosun to Black Dog, who stood alongside him armed with a stiff piece o' manilla.

Port Tack was brought up from the Brig. After his shackles were removed, Hands, Merry and Morgan took their place in the line along of the rest. The Cooper's Mate stripped off his shirt, disclosing a thickly matted, black thatch o' hair on his broad chest. His arms and shoulders were well muscled. Just as well considering the Crew, seventy-five in number, would inflict close on two hundred blows against his naked body. I noted with interest the faded, serrated scars on his back – a memento of RN vintage caused by the clawing embrace of the Cat. Here was yet another ex-tar who had forsaken King and Country to go a-roving on the Account.

"Prisoner passed fit for punishment, Sir!" reported Flash Dan to the Captain. Even chastisement was conducted 'Man-o'-War' fashion aboard Flint's Ship.

"Carry on, Quarter-Master!" ordered he and repaired to watch from the Poop-Deck in company of Billy Bones.

I turned with Port Tack to face the twin files of waiting men. Some were eager; others hesitant and unsure. A few like Ben Gunn were decidedly unhappy about inflicting corporal punishment on one of the toughest members in our Company.

"No striking about the head or below the belt!" I cried. "Should he go down, he's allowed to rise under the count o' ten before another blow be struck!" Turning to Port Tack, I said: "If you duck your napper and run like a hunted stag, some of 'em might miss their stroke. Go to it, 'Arry Pay!"

The Cooper's Mate laughed at me – laughed, he did, by thunder! Then folding his arms, he casually stepped between the first brace of Buccaneers. A rope's end 'Thwacked!' against his bare back raising a livid, white weal which turned fiery red as a strap repeated the punishment on his scarred skin. Port Tack never so much as flinched. This shell-backed ex-tar were as tough as Pusser's Cheese and, shipmates – that's TOUGH! To say he walked on slowly would be an understatement. He sauntered, passing blessed pleasantries whenever he came abreast of his cronies. When Ben Gunn delivered his half-hearted stroke, Port Tack paused and rebuked him. "Come, Chippy!" cried he. "I've known gnats to hit 'arder! 'Ave another go!"

The Crew began to guffaw as our Carpenter, wriggling with embarrassment and flashing beet-root red, tapped the Cooper's Mate a second time on the shoulder.

"Well struck, Ben! I almost felt that un!" jibed he and walked on.

Most of the Company were laughing fit to split. I took careful note of those who weren't, for it showed they didn't favour the Cooper's Mate. No more blows descended upon Pay's broad back, not until he drew abreast of Black Dog. The Bosun's Mate delivered a vicious swipe with his rope's end and cried: "Now Pew!"

Blind Pew's cane swished and struck, leaving a livid stripe upon a tattooed bicep bearing a flag and crossed cannons. The laughter quickly dropped off. Then, to the utter amazement of us all, Port Tack stopped yet again, this time level alongside the Blind Bosun and declared loudly: "Ship-mates! I never thought to feel the sting from mosquitoes this far out to sea!"

More boisterous laughter rippled along the ranks, interspliced with jeers aimed at the Bosun. "Gar!" shrieked he and began to belabour Port Tack with a flurry of blows. The Cooper's Mate stood solid as stone, arms folded, coolly taunting his antagonist to greater efforts. In a frenzy, Pew lashed out right and left, snarling like a demented dog. The merriment gave way to murmurs of disapproval. Port Tack's cronies stirred uneasily and their mood turned ugly, flaring into open threats against the Bosun. Carver Lowe gripped the hilt of his hanger, his knuckles bone-white, while beside him, The Mad Marine palmed a pair of pistols. I still shudder and come out in a cold sweat to think on what might have happened had the Bosun's cane not broke. Pew was spent anyway. He stood holding his side, panting and gasping for breath.

"Deary, deary me! You appear a mite puffed, matey! I should stand-down afore yer fall down!" mocked Port Tack and swaggered to the end o' the line amid wild cheers and applause. He turned, holding up his hands for silence. "Ship-mates! Fellow Rovers!" bellowed he. "My sentence was to Run the Gauntlet twice! Well, I walked it! Aye, and I'll pass between you again, bearing no malice to any man who chooses to give me more stripes!"

"Belay that kind o' talk, 'Arry! You've conducted yerself more'n any Gentleman o' Fortune present here could hope to match! God-damn me if I don't stand here and die in defence of you, for I love you like a true brother!" cried Carver Lowe as a good many of the swabs started cheering.

"I'll go second for that!" bawled Allardyce. "Why, I'll wager a pound to a pinch of snuff, Port Tack's taken blows enough for five times twenty!"

"'Specially from that Judas-haired swab with pitch blobs fer eyeballs and a pig-nut fer a brain!" shouted Pike the Mad Marine at the top of his voice. "Port Tack's the man fer me!"

"What say you, mess-mates?" chimed in Carver.

"Shrivel my . . ." began Blind Pew, clenched fists quivering with rage, but Black Dog pulled him clear as a great roar of assent came from two thirds of the Company.

Big Job Anderson and Me backed against the Poop, followed by the Bosun and his Mate, Hands, Morgan, Merry and a few more, while the majority surged around Port Tack and hoisted him high on their shoulders. His eyes caught mine and I saw the gleam of triumph in them. Realization hit me then, as heavy as the six tons o' shot we had aboard. In a flash I knew the score. The Cooper's Mate had swung the Company onto his side, leaving us Officers sat athwart a powder-keg along of a short fuse!

"AVAST YE MUTINOUS DOGS!"

We turned and beheld the Captain crouched over the serpent-headed swivel, one hand gripping the fish-tail handle on its cascabel, the other holding a smouldering fusee. Further along the Poop rail stood Billy with the huge butt of a pintled blunderbuss jammed against his shoulder, its bell-shaped muzzle angled down at those who crowded the deck.

"Scurry below, ye scurvy rats, afore I blow ye there in bits!" roared Flint sighting along the barrel, his face livid.

"Yer days o' blowing anybody any-place is numbered, Flint!" cried Carver Lowe stepping forward and shaking his fist. "There'll be votes cast a-plenty in the Fo'c'sle this fore-noon!" vowed he.

I saw Flint tense and flinch, as if physically struck. The swivel's muzzle dipped to cover Carver and his match hand started to move. I believe he intended to fire and would have done so, but for the timely intervention of Flash Dan – along with a few carefully chosen words of wisdom.

"Sir!" said he, raising a hand and moving directly in line of the gun's maw. "The whole Crew is out of salts! Port Tack's punishment has left us all badly flayed! Might I respectfully suggest that I take him below to the dispensary and review the damage, while the Company lay for'ard with a glass of grog to cool their coppers?"

Flint never moved nor spoke. He just stood staring, his blue tinged face twitching.

"By your leave, Captain!" The Doctor bowed and led Port Tack below.

The Crew slunk off. Some went by way of the aft hatch; others trooped for'ard to the Fo'c'sle. A small knot of Seamen remained, standing apart from the Duty Watch. Among those clustered around the two Battery Commanders, Morgan and Merry, were Ben Gunn, the Great Dane, Pop-Eye, Bartholomew the Portuguese and Shamus O'Brien.

"Asking your pardon, Sir," said George touching his forelock in salute. "These men have elected me Spokesman and want it known we are for you, from first to last – one an' all!"

Flint continued to stare, unseeing and unhearing, as I thought. Then the icy, blue eyes blinked and flashed. When he spoke it was in his normal, guttural growl. "Thank'e, Mister Merry. Take ye these staunch hands to the Tiller-Bar-Flat. Coxswain!" said he to Anderson. "Ye are in Command. Guard ye well the Gun-Room and suffer none to enter there, save my Officers."

"Aye, aye, Sir!" replied Job along of a salute and led his contingent below.

"Bill!" resumed Flint, descending the Poop steps still clutching the slow match. "Ward-Room meeting of all Officers – this minute!"

As I clumped into the Great Cabin astern of the First Mate, Blind Pew and the rest, a multitude o' thoughts clapped aboard my mind. I'd heard tell of men taking punishment and enjoying it too, would you believe! Perhaps Port Tack were one o' these odd people who liked pain. How and why this should be, I can't rightly fathom. Don't much care for it m'self – it hurts!

Along of us being seated and drinks served by one eyed Darby M'Graw, three points became crystal clear: first, most of the Company had gone overboard for Port Tack's bravado; second, us Officers were close-hauled and far from secure; And third, *Walrus* was on par with a fire-ship, ready to burst into flame at the drop of a cuss-word or cocked-hat!

Flint's philosophy regarding the rupture was to storm through the Fo'c'sle swinging a belaying pin, but I didn't hold with that.

"Speak soft, lay aft and allow tempers to cool. If we bide our time, this trouble may blow itself out. Them's my views. I ain't got much faith in 'em, mind! But it's either that or take on the entire Crew. And fifteen ag'in sixty ain't good odds!"

"Long John's in the right on it. 'Tain't the course I'd lay, mark you! Him as strikes first – that's my fancy! But we be too few t'risk a major mutiny," admitted Billy Bones with a snort of indignation.

CHAPTER XXXIII

A CRIPPLE GRAPPLES FOUR!

The first hint that our pussy-foot policy weren't going to pay-off came in the guise of drunken singing from the Fo'c'sle. It echoed through the Ship, backed by shouted taunts and threats aimed chiefly at Flint. Then when Black Dog went to 'Pipe-Up' the Watch below, to relieve the look-out and wheel, he returned almost immediately.

"Trouble, Cap'n! All stations be abandoned and none came in answer to my call!" reported he.

"Mutinous swabs!" snarled Pew and made to rise.

"Belay, Bosun, ye'd be in harm's way," said Flint, placing a restraining hand on his arm. "This situation needs tact, not more tension along of harsh words." His eyes flashed at me. "Barbecue, care ye for a sojourn to the Fo'c'sle and maybe fathom what's a-foot? They have nay hash with ye, so perchance they'll heed ye and reason."

"Aye, Sir," returned I rising, "if they don't slit my gizzard first!"

Flint's thick, scarred fore-finger stabbed out. "Tell the dogs this from me! Any harm befalls ye, I'll blow up the Ship! I can do it too, without setting boot beyond that there bulkhead! Convey to those curs I mean every last word, by thunder!"

"How, pray, do you propose such a feat, James?" asked Flash Dan, recently returned from attending to Port Tack. "A far cry here from the magazine – not that I wish to meet my Maker just yet."

But before Flint could answer, Billy flashed him a disapproving look and broke in with: "You want for me to accompany the Quarter-Master, Sir?"

"Nay, Bill! Yore temper be too much on par with mine!" replied Flint, rolling his quid of coca leaves and scowling.

"Bah!" spat the Bosun. "To sit here in stays, cowering from them mess o' swabs goes clean ag'in my grain! Lead me for'ard and give me the feel of a throat to place my knife-edge alongside – that's what I say!"

"They'd rip your brisket apart and turn your innards into tripe, Pew – you above any! If Long John can't lay 'em aboard with reason . . ." Israel Hands shrugged and left the sentence unfinished, looking at me. "Don't seem right for you to go it alone, Barbecue."

"Then feel free to come aboard, Gunner. You've nought to lose but your life!" I replied, expecting Hands to sink and remain silent.

Much to my surprise, Israel accepted. We disarmed ourselves, to show good intentions, and along of him opening the door, I clumped out onto the Quarter-Deck. A face was seen peering above the for'ard hatch coaming, but it disappeared before I'd taken two steps. The Fo'c'sle rang to the last verse of 'Fifteen Men', which gradually faded and dropped off altogether on the Sentinel reporting our presence.

"Leastways we won't arrive unannounced," I remarked dryly as we slowly made our way for'ard.

All was silent save for the creaking of the wheel, the helm having been lashed amidships. Only the Ship was singing now. Shrouds and rigging hummed softly as *Walrus* glided through tranquil waters. Sailing under a single jib and goose-wings, along of light airs, our speed held steady at two or three knots.

The Gunner and Me exchanged glances, the sun beating warm upon our backs. He swallowed and I took a deep breath, then descending the steps we entered the Fo'c'sle. I went in first. Smoke and the reek of rum, spliced with the stench of unwashed bodies, hit me like a hammer. Port Tack sat at the end of a mess-table with the Crew sprawled around him. Some were seated on the bow-chasers; others lounged against the bulkheads. All of them were facing me and Israel. Glared, they did, silent, sullen and angry.

"Holloa, Quarter-Master! Brisk fer business as ever was, I see!" greeted the Cooper's Mate with a leer.

"Maybe he's com'd to pay his respects!" sneered Pike the Mad Marine amid guffaws and sniggers.

"Carver, where's yer manners at? Give up the bread-bin so's the 'Q' can sit down and rest his brains!" ordered Port Tack, still smirking behind the hand that was rubbing his nasee nose.

The Fo'c'sle shook to the roar of laughter as Lowe vacated the biscuit barrel and dragged it across to where I was at. Brushing aside the skirts of my coat, I had my eyes on, Pay, when I went to rest my rump. Too late I realised my error. Unbalanced on a bent leg and with my weight off the crutch, I crashed to the deck flat upon my back, along of Lowe pulling the bin out from under me. The Company vapoured, howling and holding their sides or clinging to mess-mates in their mirth. I noted some, however, who weren't laughing. Old 'Sails' Lowether, for one, sat glum and silent, looking more worried than a sprat among a shoal o' mackerel!

Israel started forward to assist me, but was checked by Pike's cutlass point pressing his throat. The Mad Marine stood grinning: "Hang-fire, Gunner, hang-fire!" sneered he. "I seem to recall a sim'lar sit'ation when your one legged Yahoo clouted Carver with his pole!"

"Avast! Put up yer hanger, Pike! And you, Carver my Buck, belay them capers!" rebuked the Cooper's Mate. "Set Mister Silver on an even keel and seat 'im right an' proper like I said to."

Three brace of hands reached to help me rise. Pike, along of sheathing his hanger, made a fourth. Now no man alive treats me for a butt and comes off clean to boast about it afterwards. You may lay to that if ye believe not another word! My anger was red-hot, but controlled. Seizing my crutch I knocked the legs out from under one swab, smashed the tip o' my timber against the chin of a second, and gripping the lapels of Pike and Carver, I was hauled upright when the curs recoiled. Their surprise was still stamped upon their faces as I grabbed a handful of hair on each of them and cracked their heads together. The pair of them slumped to the deck, dazed.

Supporting myself against the barrel, I pointed at Port Tack. "Lay you to this!" I roared, stabbing with my fore-finger as if it were a sword – wishing like blue-blazes it were. "If Hands and Me don't report aft safe and sound, afore One Bell is up, Flint'll blow the boards out from under you and your rat-pack!"

That put a bung in their puncheon, that did! Along of me broaching aboard the bully boys, a great hush had fallen over the Fo'c'sle. I settled myself on the bread-bin, while Israel closed-up astern of me and passed me my crutch. Carver and Co shook off the helping hands and, on regaining their feet, stood glowering. If looks were daggers I'd be dead, I reckon, for I could feel the heat o' their silent hate boring into me.

"No one's a-crossing of you, John Silver, and none here intends you any harm," replied Port Tack, making the understatement of the year. "The hands is a little high spirited, seeing we had us an election and . . ."

"Elections, is it? So that's your game!" I snapped. "Well Flint wants to know what's what and why the ship was left to sail her blessed self!"

"An' so he shall!" returned the other just as hotly. "This Crew's tired of being hazed by a drug-crazed Captain – that's wot's wot! Rules is rules and we has rights, same as any other Rover Company! Well we ain't dancing the horn-pipe t' Flint's toon no more! A'ter we've held Council and a Vote of Confidence on who's to cap'n this 'ere crew, I'll report aft at the head of a depytation!"

The outburst left Port Tack blowing hard. He sat scowling at me with wild eyes for a moment, then gazing beyond my mug he jerked his head. I sensed rather than saw some half a dozen bodies leave the Fo's'cle, along of the draft from the door behind me. Around us the Crew murmured in agreement, nodding their heads and clacking like a bunch o' washerwomen.

"That be tellin' 'im, 'Arry!" voiced some wag from well back out of harm's way.

"You're cutting out to be quite a Leading Hand among the Company, what with this morning's performance. The Crew'll be eating out o' your palm and calling you Cap'n next, I shouldn't wonder." I said, thinking hard. Pay's next remark nearly exploded my brain.

"*Sic itur ad astra*," grinned the Cooper's Mate.

"And learned in Latin too, by thunder! Seems Flash Dan has doctored your brain along of your body, eh?"

"Ah, he has a pleasant way with him, has Flash Dan," replied Port Tack looking sly.

I casually glanced about me and noticed the Company was missing several prominent faces, the Mad Marine and Carver Lowe amongst them. "You appear to have lost some mates. Decided t' turn-to, have they?" I asked. "Or maybe they has need o' medical attention!"

"They'll be on the Orlop-Deck, guardin' the 'old. Flint's loony enough to try anything. But lay to this, John Silver! If he tries for the magazine, there'll be a noo face in Hell – double quick!" promised Pay.

"Flint wouldn't blow hisself away, along of the treasure. 'Tis a bit o' bluff on his part, I reckon," stated, Port Tack's yellow haired side-kick, puffing smoke towards a centre beam.

"Allardyce, you ain't much the man for thinking nor ever was, but think on this – one and all!" cried I raising my voice. "Has Flint ever bluffed or backed when steering a set course? And regards guarding the magazine – why, he can pull the bung on this old bucket wi'out leaving his cabin!"

"How so?" demanded Port Tack. "I knows for a fact he ain't got powder stowed there, not enough to rupture the stern at any rate!"

"I don't know how, but this I does know. If any of your gang goes off half-cocked, we'll all be dividing the Blunt in company of Davy Jones! Believe that if nothing else!" I said hotly, heaving myself up on my crutch. "Now I'll take your intentions to the Cap'n and tell him to expect a social call around supper time!"

With that, Hands opened the door for me and I clumped out – Israel slamming the wood shut. We exchanged glances, both blowing a long sigh of relief. For a second or two there was silence behind us, then the Fo'c'sle became a babel of sound that even the thick bulkhead couldn't stem. They were making hard time o' their discussions, being as they only had one brain between ten!

"Sounds like a Washerwomen's Convention, it do!" grinned the Gunner, voicing my earlier thoughts.

"Excepting the chief scrubber were missing from that little meeting," I said as we went aft.

"I don't fathom you, Long John," returned he, eyeing me with a puzzled expression. "Can't you be more plain?"

"All in good time, my lad, all in good time." And with that I lifted the latch and we entered the Great Cabin.

I made a full report to Flint. He sat in his shirt-sleeves, smoking in silence, the long tails of his black head scarf trailing over one shoulder. Occasionally his gold earrings flashed, reflecting the light of the single glim we used to fire-up our pipes. Darby M'Graw, Blind Pew, Black Dog, Billy Bones and the Doctor were also in attendance, along of Me'n Hands.

"So!" said the Captain, draining his great silver goblet and holding it out for Darby to replenish with neat rum. "The numbskulls think I'd step doon in place of one o' them swabs, do they? Fall on! Of all the fools afloat, I have a double dividend trying to set me high and dry. Well, on their own heads be it! If I have to sink 'em one by one and sail the ship with fifteen instead of seventy-five, I'll do it, by thunder! And there's an end to it!"

"Not quite, Sir! There be a few shreds as needs clewing-up," I said indicating to the Steward for a refill. "Some shark's been heaving a deep sea lead in murky waters and the tallow that be smeared on the base of it has brought up a score o' bits and pieces from the bottom of these hum-drum, but serious soundings!"

I got up and fired me pipe from the glim, along of a fresh load of baccy, and began clumping athwart the Cabin.

"Thunder, Barbecue! Belay prancing aboot as if acting the blasted play, while we hangs here on tenterhooks! Anchor yore arse and out with it!" urged Flint, his blue-tinged face twitching.

"First Point!" began I, stopping to starboard and facing my audience. "Port Tack takes the blame for trying to short change the Bosun, along of leaving La Beck the means to light his way in the Hold!

"Second Point! By refusing to peach on mates and showing how pistol proof he is in taking a drubbing for most o' the Company, he gets the backing of the whole Crew – 'cept for a staunch handful!

"Third Point! Now he proposes to take over without a blow being struck or a shot fired!" I puffed smoke and inhaled, blowing out a grey cloud. "So what do it all add up to?"

"The swab planned it!" barked Billy Bones.

"Aye, from first to last, shrivel my Soul!" snarled Blind Pew. "I'd like to take his eyes out!"

"Planned it? Port Tack? Him as first earned his bread pinching pennies from errand boys running between Leather Lane and Bow Common? Bilge!" I retorted. "Our friend 'Arry Pay couldn't organise a cock-fight in a blessed barn-yard – you may lay to that!"

"By the powers . . ." began Flint, his face turning from blue to purple.

"So what are you implying, John?" interrupted Flash Dan sharply, but cool and concise as ever.

"I'm saying there be a brighter mind behind the Cooper's Mate's mouthings. He ain't got brains enough to form a grain o' bird-shot in a fowling piece, let alone manage Mutiny – not 'im! Which brings us full Round Robin back t' the first point – the red herring as was laid in the hold!"

My pipe having gone out, I stuck the stem through a button-hole on my red coat and took up my drink. Glass in hand, I began clumping back and forth across the Cabin again.

"Blind Pew were never meant to get killed – him as died was the doomed party!" resumed I. "Think ye on this. When the Bosun clapped aboard La Beck, guided by the racket of his fumblings with the glim, do 'e suppose the Frenchy dropped the striker, carefully closed the tinder-box, then clutching it in his hand, staggered top-side to die all tickety-boo at our feet – along o' Pew's poignard buried t' the hilt in his back? La Beck gripped the box like it was his Mother's hand when Pew delivered him his death blow – THE BLASTED TINDER-TIN WERE NEVER OPENED!"

"Stab me and fall on!" exclaimed Flint. "If this don't beat all for cold, calculating, double dealings I'll give up booze! By thunder, Barbecue, ye'll be a candidate for the Bow Street Runners yet!"

"But see here, Barbecue! If Port Tack didn't do the planning on it – who did? asked Billy Bones, the broken veins in his fleshy nose glowing like the embers of a beacon fire.

"*Ecce Homo*!" came the soft reply.

CHAPTER XXXIV

DEVILS NEVER DIE!

We all turned to face the Doctor. Barring me'n Flint, most were none the wiser by his remark. He stood quite still behind the backgammon table near the stern-sheets, on which I'd placed my pistols and cutlass, along of Hand's hanger and barker.

"Echo Omo?" repeated Blind Pew, getting it wrong as he screwed up his evil face in bewilderment. "Who in Hades might he be? I don't recall a member o' this Crew as bears a tag such as that un!"

Now I ain't no Scholar, not I, but I remember enough from my Bible reading days, as a boy mind, to know that it were Pontius Pilate's exclamation on Jesus being brought alongside him for judgement.

"Behold the man, indeed," I said eyeing the Doctor with cold disdain. "I knowed Flash Dan was part and parcel o' this conspiracy, when first he admitted to finding Port Tack's flint in the hold. La Beck were never meant to find the striker. He was cold pork before he started below!"

"How thoughtless of me," replied the Doctor with a sad smirk.

The silence was such that you'd have heard a pin drop in that Cabin, along of my statement. Then everyone exploded at once, save for Flint. He remained staring at Flash Dan as if stunned – a man mesmerised with his mind in a turmoil.

"Shiver my . . . By the powers . . . I'll . . . I'll . . ." spluttered the Mate, words failing him.

"Carve the swab!" cried Pew.

"Cut the cur down!" raged Black Dog.

"Tain't possible – not Flash Dan!" gasped One Eyed Darby in disbelief.

"Sink the Saw-Bones!" thundered Hands.

"SILENCE!"

Flint's voice boomed out with the force of an erupting volcano. Slowly he stood up and I saw that his fingers were all a-tremble, while his face became that horrible shade of blue.

"Daniel Hunter, I'd have placed my last peece of eight on yore loyalty. But now the best ye can hope for, from me, is to choke quickly when I hoist ye aloft to the main-yard, along o' yore black-hearted treachery," said the Captain. He spoke quietly, but his voice sounded hoarse and it grated like an old rusty lock.

"Speaking of treachery, I have a little tale to tell on that score," remarked Flash Dan, cool and steady. "It concerns the Captain of the good ship *Naiad* and what befell her and the Crew!"

Flint's hand snaked out, knocking over his silver goblet in his haste to grab one of the cannon-barrelled Queen Annes that lay on his desk. He gripped the barker's rum-soaked butt and froze, for Flash Dan had been a sight quicker. Snatching up my twin Pettijeans, he swept back the cocks and covered the Captain before we could blink.

"James!" warned he. "Sit down and leave the pops alone!"

I involuntary started forward, as if pushed, and so did the Mate. Flash Dan's left hand moved a fraction and we hove to under the menacing black 'O's of the twin muzzles.

"Don't be a Silly-Billy! And kindly keep your hand away from the pistol concealed in your sling! As for you, John; I spent considerable time and skill in saving your life by cutting off your leg. It would be a great pity and much to my chagrin were I compelled to reverse the role and end it by blowing off your head!" beamed he in his best bedroom manner.

I see him yet stood there smiling, hands steady as rocks in holding my guns; his smooth, boyish face alight and alive with the corners of his eyes crinkled into crow's-feet, along of the sparkling blue laughter that was in them. You couldn't hate a man like Daniel Hunter, not in a month of Sundays, and I still thinks of him with much affection.

The Mate sat down snorting through his fleshy nose, but I remained standing. "Doctor, there be one small point you've overlooked," I said and slowly hopped towards him. "Along of carrying pistols around in my pockets, I leave the pans unprimed. That way I don't run the risk o' losing vital parts of my person." I stopped in front of him and watched the expression freeze upon his face. Gradually it faded into a blank mask. The eyes lost their light of laughter and became cunning and calculating.

"Don't compel me to call your bluff, John! For I shall do so and if you are wrong, you'll be a long time dead," returned the Doctor, his blue eyes like chips of ice between narrowed lids.

"To be sure," I replied swallowing hard and hoping like Hades he hadn't shaken the pieces too much in snatching them up. "Fire away!"

Stood eye-ball to eye-ball, we was, not three feet apart, when there came a sharp, crisp click as he triggered the pistol in his right hand. A second click sounded. We both broke our gaze and looked at the larboard gun. Flash Dan snapped first one lock, then t'other. The black flints clamped in the jaws of the Dog's Head struck the frizzens, knocking 'em back as sparks showered into empty pans.

Without further ado, the Doctor handed both barkers to me. "*Pax vobiscum*, John," said he along of a wan smile.

"Ah-ha, ha!" cried Flint jubilantly jumping to his feet, a Queen Anne cocked in each great fist. "What a brisk hand ye be, Barbecue! A smarter trump were never laid, by thunder! Now stand ye aside! I aim ta blow yon swab clean through the stern-sheet windys!"

"*Dies Non*, eh James!" retorted Flash Dan. He stood proud and completely unafraid, gazing steady into Flint's mad eyes.

"Ye have a Judge! Aye, along of Jury an' Executioner – ME! Stand aside, Silver!" roared Flint yet again.

I held my ground. Closing all four frizzens I half-cocked the hammers and turning each pistol upon its side, first larboard then starboard, banged the butts against my timber leg. My Pettijeans were self-priming, you see, and the large vents in the breeches allowed powder to trickle into the pan when treated in this manner. Hence my sweat in confronting the Doctor, after he grabbed them, in case they were shook up. It would have been Lights Out for Old Long John!

Full of confidence with both pistols primed and cocked, I raised my head to meet Flint's enraged, startled gaze. Small wonder he was well vexed and boggle-eyed; for along of lounging on my crutch, I held the pops at hip level with both brace o' barrels aimed dead-centre on his guts.

"Flint!" snapped I, cool and self possessed. "For years I've kept me weather-eye on you. I'm a trusting soul up to a point – short of a flash-point! You be a man of many dark secrets, this I know, along o' the Mate and dear old foxy-faced Darby, who be stood there looking like he's seeking a hidey-hole t' dive into. Your past doings ain't my concern, but the past has a way o' repeating itself along of the present, same as in History, and I for one wants to hear what became of the *Naiad* and her Crew! When Phineas McGinty lay a-dying he started t' speak of her, but you hushed his yap real quick! And I mind yet the look the good Doctor here flashed our Captain on that occasion! What about it, shipmates? Bosun? Black Dog? And you, Israel! Ain't you h'interested in what befell your predecessor?"

"There stands a man who betrayed his mates!" cried Flint, his blue face flushing darker. "Would ye believe him above yore Captain?"

"Afore we can disbelieve him, we first has to hear him, Sir!" replied Hands with a logic that was rare for him.

"Speak your piece, Saw-Bones, and be done with it!" spat Pew from where he sat hunched, clutching his stick in both hands.

Flint swallowed hard. He glanced at Billy, then back to me. Slowly he started to sink into his seat. I never saw a man turn so old and sick, all in a moment. His face just seemed to cave in, along of his legs giving way, for he sat down with a bump. Billy nervously fingered the sling that supported his left arm, gazing at his boots, while Darby's one-eyed, glum look suggested he'd lost two guineas and found tuppence.

"You has our undivided attention, Doctor – to be sure!" I said without turning, still keeping Flint covered.

"Many, many years ago, when I was learning the seedier, coarser side of my chosen profession as an Assistant Surgeon on board HMS *Scarborough*, stationed at Barbuda, we plucked a sole survivor from the sea," began Flash Dan. "It was off the coast of Saint Christopher. The man was clinging to a portion of top-mast, to which a fragment of the cross-trees was still attached. This poor wretch, near wasted away with starvation and half mad with thirst, was mere skin and bone. Adding to his misery and want, a pistol ball lay embedded in his breast. I had the care of him, but he was beyond all human help. Wounded, delirious and dying, nobody paid heed to his rantings and ravings – save me. He lingered for half a day and well into the night, but before he died I managed to piece together the gist of his rambling story."

The Doctor paused to fire his pipe. At that point the Mate pitched in with: "Nobody minds the rantings of a raving man along o' him near holding hands with Davy Jones. They ain't no more binding than a ballard book!"

"This Body did!" continued our Master-Surgeon, eyeing the Mate with a ghost of a smile on his lips. "He was, by his own admission, a common Pirate who belonged to a very uncommon Crew. His ship was the *Naiad*, captained by a Buccaneer whose reputation was notorious even in that distant day. The policy of this Captain was to bury accumulated treasure. Having just performed this practice, after making a great purchase, they were celebrating in their usual style when the ship blew apart."

"What were this cove called?" asked One Eyed Darby, looking more sly than Reynard.

"My patient? Pickard by name, an Ex RN Rating, known to his mates as Bill. He was up for'ard, performing his ablutions, when he found himself hurled off the heads into the sea. He wasn't the only one caught with his trousers down, so to speak. Barring him the whole Crew perished – or so he assumed. Imagine his surprise, while clinging to the cross-trees, when a long-boat came gliding by in the dusk. Aboard it he beheld the Captain, his Steward, the First Mate and the one armed Quarter-Master. In response to his call for aid, bullets were his only reply, one of which caught him in the chest. The long-boat hoisted a lug-sail and bore away. My man died cursing the name of Captain Flint!"

"That dinna be the full story! 'Tis only the 'full and by' on it of what ye are saying!" cried the blue faced Buccaneer starting up. "They were plotting a Mutiny ag'in me – the same as like ye have done! Not content with their fair share, the swabs wanted to nail ours! Ain't that the way of it, Darby? Tell 'em, Bill!"

"Aye, tell me, BILL!" The cabin fair shook to my bellow, for Flint's past practices were crystal clear now – plain as print. "I mind what you told me'n Hands all them years ago! Retired to set up Gentlemen in earnest – you said! Rolling in guineas – you said! Small wonder Johnson couldn't include Flint's Crew in *A General History of the Pyrates*! None o' the lubbers was never met with on account of being paid-off along o' praiseworthy words from the Poop and a quick match to the magazine!"

"Was that to be our reward for loyal service, *Captain* – our bones left to bleach alongside coral?" hissed Blind Pew and I saw his hand slide beneath his sea-cloak for to feel the deadly dagger that lay concealed there.

"NO! NO! NO!" thundered Flint, striking his fist upon the desk with each strong denial. "I never intended the such for yore Fate! Ye be the best bunch of Officers I ever shipped aboard! Pistol proof to a man, ye be worth gold-dust to me in slitting Spaniards – gold-dust and diamonds I tell ye!"

"Ah, and a blessed bag o' margaritas thrown in for a booster, I shouldn't wonder!" I replied, feeling sour enough to spit tacks. "See here, Flash Dan!" I said half turning, but with my weather eye on Flint. "How come you didn't confide your fears to me?"

"Because I didn't know if you were included in the select circle of survivors. I thought to wait and see if I was invited," replied he. "I intended a bloodless coup. Once in control of the ship with the Crew under my direct command, I would have raised the matter discreetly without fear of reprisal."

"So now we can expect the whole Company down around our ears, them thinking we was the ones who intended turning 'em off!" grumbled Black Dog.

"I never conveyed my suspicions to a soul!" cried the Doctor. "Faith! Had I done so they would have slaughtered you all to a man – regardless of my influence or intervention!"

"So what might your excuse have been to cause this Crew t' mutiny in accordance to your plan?" asked Billy Bones, speaking as if with a mouthful of broken glass, crunching each word along of grinding his teeth. He was fuming and would have flung hisself on the Doctor, then and there, if not for the presence of me and my pops.

"Excuse?" smiled Flash Dan. "Captain Flint has already answered that question – all three hundred thousand pounds worth! Greed gave them the reason, added wealth was the incentive. I merely planted the seeds. Port Tack was to be Captain, sharing joint command with me. Carver Lowe opted for First Mate; Allardyce QM; and Pike as Bosun."

Billy looked set to have apoplexy on the spot.

"And the rest of us?" snapped Flint with his usual fierceness. "What of this present ward-room?"

"That would have depended upon how you answered my accusations," returned the Doctor evenly. "But to put our distrusts and differences in ordinary, for the moment. There have been rumbles and grumbles of discontent from the Fo'c'sle for months. Port Tack and Carver Lowe are like a canker among this Crew. That pair of bad uns know no bounds. The rest of the Company are mere wolves and follow the lion who roars loudest. For my money, I think our happy Band of Rovers are near ready to 'part the bear-skin' between them!"

Before any of us could reply, there came a click and Wun Hung Lo crept into the Cabin without waiting on the formality of permission. The Cook's smooth yellow features, bearing a wispy beard and drooping moustache, were usually void of expression. But now as he shuffled over to Flint, slipping his hands into the long, loose sleeves of his black smock, his oval face appeared marred with all the worries in the world. I un-cocked my guns and put them in my pockets. The present danger was past – more fool me for not thinking on the future.

"Claptain Flint," began the Chinaman breathlessly, giving a nervous glance towards the door. "I bling velly bad tidings. All foc's'y men makee much tlouble for you. I thinkee maybe they come to . . ."

Clattering footsteps from beyond the Cabin door cut him short, while three, short, hard raps upon it made him recoil in terror. It opened and Allardyce entered: "Fo'c'sle Depytation for t' see the Cap'n!" said he stepping to one side, and Port Tack trooped in at the head of Carver Lowe, along of Pike the Mad Marine. There were two more besides them, both shifty-eyed cronies of the Cooper's Mate. So far as I could see, none were armed. No hangers hung at their sides and their open coats revealed no knives or barkers tucked in their belts.

"Come aboard, 'Captain' Pay!" cried Flint sloshing rum into his goblet. "Brought yore 'First Mate', the 'QM', and 'Bosun' Pike too, I see! Will ye be acquiring 'Yore' cabin before or after we've partook o' belly-ballast, being as 'tis supper-time?"

"So! Someone's blabbed, eh? Peached like Silver's Parrot!" said Port Tack, giving the Chinaman a withering look. "Scram, yer slant-eyed, nosy, yellow hided Heathen!" snapped he.

Wun Hung Lo fled from the Cabin, scurrying out of the door whimpering with fear.

"Avast!" snarled Flint, eyes flashing. "I gives the orders, both inside and outside this 'ere cabin!"

"Small odds it now," resumed the Cooper's Mate glaring back at the Buccaneer, cool and calm. "Fo'c'sle carried the motion to a man, save for the swabs holed-up in the Gunner's Room. Threatened to let some lead into us if we showed face in them quarters. But they'll soon come alongside when they see how the cards is set. Here be our verdict on you!"

So saying, Port Tack slapped a bit of paper down on the desk in front of Flint. It was roughly cut to the size of a crown piece with its upper surface bearing a smeared circle of gun-powder – the all too familiar, dreaded Black Spot.

Flint picked it up and turned it over: "DEPOSED!" gasped he in mock surprise. "And the lubber who wrote it even got the spelling right. By the Powers! If this ain't enough to cause a hoar frost in Hell – sink my Soul!"

"Yer sunk, sure enough!" sneered the Mad Marine.

"Jest away, Flint, but yer game ain't worth the candle – not now! You has t' step down, along o' being laid aside, and another elected in your stead," added Carver Lowe with a leer.

Flint eyed him steady: "'Tis *Captain* Flint," said he in a voice as soft as a Serpent's hiss, but far more menacing. "And since I weren't elected to this office in the first place, I can hardly be deposed in the second. If there's any stepping doon to be done, the onus belongs among ye mess o' swabs."

I were stood alongside the Doctor at the stern-sheets; Black Dog and Pew sat on a tiger-skin covered chest to starboard, while Israel Hands lounged against the larboard side of the Mizen-Mast. Billy Bones and Darby were on a bench with their backs against the port bulk-head. Flint's desk and great carved chair was on the same side, positioned at an angle so's to command a clear view of the door and the whole Cabin. The six Pirates stood shoulder to shoulder, aligned facing him.

"Be that yer final word?" grated Port Tack.

"Every last letter, by thunder!" spat Flint, raising the goblet to his lips.

"Then Amen to it!" cried the Cooper's Mate. "SINK 'IM, LADS!"

Trickery was Port Tack's stock-in-trade, but the black-hearted treachery that was performed at that precise moment left us breathless and belayed. Acting like a row of puppets pulled by the same string, the six Pirates drew a brace of pistols from behind their belts, concealed under their coats. Smoke lanced with flame mushroomed from six muzzles, half obscuring the assassins, as each man discharged his starboard piece into the seated figure of Flint – Point Blank! I saw at least two bullets splinter the chair's back, bursting out with a smoky, red spatter where they passed clean through him. One ball sent the goblet spinning across the Cabin, before plowing a deep furrow along his left temple. The big Buccaneer shuddered and shook under the impact of the six heavy bullets, reeling like a punch-drunk prize-fighter receiving invisible blows. Then he slumped athwart his seat, gripping the arms on the chair, his knuckles gleaming bone-white.

"Stand-fast!" roared Port Tack, wreathed in smoke. "Him that moves first shall get served the same!"

Blind Pew had half risen, only to be pulled down again by the mutilated left hand of Black Dog. "Have they done for him? Has the Cap'n croaked?" asked the Bosun, his voice shrill.

"Aye, aye! Blown t'purgatory like that much chopped pork!" returned Black Dog in awe.

The rest of us stayed stationary, as if nailed to the spot. Stunned, we was, and speechless.

The Mate sat like a statue, mouth agape in disbelief, then he turned to the Doctor: "The Devil rot you, Dan Hunter! I'll see you in Hell alongside the Cap'n for this day's work!" vowed he.

"I swear on my mother's grave, I had no hand nor knowledge of these foul doings," returned Flash Dan, clearly as bad shook as what we were.

Flint's head had flopped towards me, twisted back upon his shoulders. Twin rivulets of blood coursed across his face. One rolled over the bridge of his battered nose, the other trickled down his cheek to drip off his chin. With teeth bared, locked together in a dreadful leer, his eyes were wide open and looking sideways at those who had shot him. Terrible to behold was the tell-tale light of life that still burned in them!

"This 'ere Crew's under noo management, along o' the Cap'n poppin' his buttons – sudden like, heh, heh," cackled the Cooper's Mate. While his cronies kept us covered, he swaggered round the desk and bent close to Flint's frozen face. "Arskin' yer pardon, Sir!" mocked he with a sneer and salute, "but seeing as you've stepped down, would it be in order fer yer steward, by way of Celebration, t' pour me'n my mates a . . ."

What happened next has since passed into Pirate folk-lore. Flint's hands flew up and caught Pay by the throat. He gave a startled cry of terror, dropped both barkers and clawed at the fingers that were strangling him. Flint lunged from his seat. Still holding Pay's wind-pipe in one huge hand, he seized the Mutineer's belt and lifting him bodily above his head, hurled him with a cry of rage clear across the desk. Port Tack collided with Carver Lowe who discharged his remaining pistol prematurely, exploding a decanter on the desk. Both men cannoned into the Welsh dresser, backed against the bulkhead, and fell to the deck with crockery crashing about them. Flint's best porcelain it were too – priceless and irreplaceable, according to Darby.

"God preserve us!" cried Flash Dan aghast. "The man's not mortal!"

One of Port Tack's cronies, near blubbering with fright and trembling like a blancmange, snapped a shot at Flint. The ball missed him by a mile, thunking into the bulkhead alongside the Mate and M'Graw. Darby dived onto the deck, but Billy's hand snaked inside his sling. Moments later his own barker flared and bellowed, spewing smoke. Hot lead slammed into the Pirate with a loud "Whop!" He screamed, spun and fell clutching his chest.

As for myself, I was in a right royal clove-hitch. The hammers having snagged on the hem inside my pocket, I was struggling to draw a pistol, along of keeping balance, when the Doctor snatched up Hand's barker from the backgammon table and punched a bullet into Pike, winging him in the bicep. The Mad Marine staggered and dropped one of his bull-dogs. He cursed, clamping the hand that held his second piece tight against his upper-arm.

Streaming shards of broken china, Port Track and Carver Lowe rushed from the Cabin closely followed by Allardyce and the Mad Marine. I managed to free my pistol in time to give 'em a parting shot. But because of poor visibility, due to the swirling smoke, all I achieved, along of shooting at shadows, was to smash another of the Captain's prized plates.

The sixth Buccaneer, a tall squint-eyed swab with a red bandanna tied about his head, dropped his guns.

"Quarter, Cap'n! I wanted no part o' these foul doin's – I swear it!" pleaded he, holding out both hands.

His reply came from Pew. Guided by the quavering voice, the Bosun whipped out his dagger and sent it flashing through the smoke. The man gave a gargling gasp and collapsed with the Bosun's long blade buried in his throat.

"Bull's Eye, Pew!" cried Black Dog.

"Shiver my liver and fall on," grated Flint through clenched teeth. He stood glaring down at his crockery, swaying a bit to be sure, but standing none the less alive after soaking up six heavy bullets. "How, think ye, am I to replace my blasted china – short o' going to Canton!"

CHAPTER XXXV

FIFTEEN MEN!

There came a tramping of running feet and Anderson rushed into the smoke filled Cabin. Behind him was Morgan, Merry and the Great Dane – all of them bristling with weapons. They hove-to and gaped at the bloodied, swaying figure of Jim Flint in awe.

"We . . . we heard shootin', Cap'n . . ." began the Coxun, his voice trailing off into an awkward silence.

"Aye, and ye'll hear a damn-sight more afore this night departs. I dinna take kindly to being used for a blasted butts!" came the Captain's hissed reply. "Ain't left the Gun-room undefended, have ye?"

"No, Sir! There's Ben Gunn and Shamus O'Brien a-guardin' on it with Bart and Pop-Eye – all stood to arms, so they is, see!" chipped in Morgan.

"Boil my blood and fall on! Ben and O'Brien would probably blow their own fool heads off if it came to repelling boarders! They're both poor Musketeers when it comes ta handling bintooks! Bill! Ye willna be up ta much in rat-catching, along of yore woundy wing. Take ye the Bosun, Black Dog and Job here, in company of the Quarter-Master, to keep shop below. Send Pop-Eye and the Portuguese top-side for replacement," ordered Flint wheezing for breath.

We were taken all a-back, sudden like, by a high, thin, keening scream that rebounded through the Ship from for'ard – cutting into our nerves same as a knife. I'd heard and seen enough men sent below to recognise a death-cry in the offering.

"Thunder!" exclaimed George Merry. "Some swab's sunk the Cook by the sound of it! I 'ope the supper don't burn!"

Flint swore a blasphemous oath, his face going tight. "I'll take for his price!" vowed he, leaning on the desk for support. "Nobody could knock-up a chicken chow mein like Wun Hung Lo."

"Cap'n! I has a score to settle along of Carver Lowe – personal like! Guarding the Gun-room ain't on the cards for me!" I said hobbling forward, grim with determination.

"Be it on yore own head, Barbecue," he replied, eyeing me with what I thought to be a flicker of fear. A strange look, to be sure, coming from Flint. But there again, he'd had a trying day!

"What of this turncoat, Cap'n?" asked Billy, glowering at the Doctor who still stood beside the backgammon table with Israel's empty pistol in his hand.

"This turncoat had best remove yours, Jim, and plug those shot-holes before you bleed to death," answered Flash Dan for hisself. "We are fouled, you and I. Better to sign Articles in a mutual peace – for the moment."

"Aye, I'm leaking worse than a sprung stave on a cooper's cask. If yore skill saves me, I'll set ye safe ashore with any as chooses to share yore company," replied the Captain and sat down wearily in his splintered chair. "Be about yore business, Bill. I shall attend the Mutineers after Doctor's done attending me."

While Morgan and Merry went below for the Doctor's medical case, Flash Dan and Darby stripped off Flint's blood-soaked, close fitting body-coat and shirt. The Captain sat quiet and silent, munching a cud of coca leaves. His broad chest and shoulders bore masses of the blue, Carib tattoos branded in the skin. There were four wounds and a big bruise on his body. Three of them looked bad, but the fourth, shiver my sides, should have been fatal! We all stood boggle-eyed, staring at the hole with a thin rillet of blood leaking from dead-centre of Flint's heart!

"Who are you?" whispered Flash Dan, gazing at the battered, blue-tinged face in awe and not without a little fear. "What are you?"

I could sense everybody present felt the same flesh-creeping dread – confronted by something bordering on sorcery. Flint suddenly flashed his pointed teeth in a leering grin. Then he roared with laughter that ended in a bad bout of coughing.

The Doctor peered closer, placing a hand over the wound, then moved it along. "Dear God!" exclaimed he, straightening in disbelief and surprise. "Your heart is on the wrong side! It should lay to the left of your breast-bone, yet I feel it beating on the right!"

So, despite his internals being a bit jumbled, Flint was a mortal man after all! Relief flooded all our faces as the Doctor, assisted by Darby, got busy. One bullet had seared his scalp, coming to within a hair's breadth of blowing out his brains. The two balls that lay embedded high in his left shoulder were quickly and skilfully removed by means of a probe and pen-knife. The fourth was deflected by a rib, rolling around his body just beneath the skin to emerge out at his back. A fifth had flattened itself against the gold watch in his waistcoat pocket, ruining the clock and leaving a bruise the size of a cricket-ball. But the sixth bullet, in passing clean through the spot where his heart should have been, touched no vital organ. And that, mates, is how the Legend came about – Flint had no heart!

Once his wounds were plugged and bound, Flint donned a clean, white shirt, slipped into his black top-coat and drawing his great clam-hilted cutlass, turned to us who stood in awe of his immense vitality: "Be ye For or Against me?" asked he and without waiting on a reply, strode purposely from the Cabin. Hushed to a man, we all followed in the wake of his bloodied foot-prints.

As I clumped out along with the rest, a sense of foreboding crept over me. Here's for why. You mind Flint's Song: 'Fifteen Men?' Well Fifteen was the number o' Buccaneers in that ballad and excluding Flash Dan, Fifteen strong were we. What worried me was how many of us would still be above board when all was settled. If only one survived to lay hands on our hoarded blunt, I vowed, then and there, Long John Silver would be that Genteel!

Flint took a speaking trumpet from beside the binnacle and raised it to his mouth: "Hear ye this!" roared he. "No Bullets but those moulded in Hell, along of the Devil's own hand, can ever do for me! If ye lay aft, one by one, and surrender yore arms – I'll hound ye no further! But any as dinna comply will be cut doon like chopped pork! Those who tried to sink me shall be tried for Attempted Murther! Ye have five minutes, starting from this same moment!"

At first, not so much as a finger stirred up for'ard in response to Flint's Ultimatum; then shadows began gliding towards us from the Fo'c'sle. Old 'Sails' Lowther was in the van.

"I ever wus fer you, Sir," said he on coming abreast of the Captain. "All this treachery were none of our doin'. Me'n some mates wants put ashore at the first sight o' land, askin' yer pardon, Sir," concluded the Sail-Maker and placed his weapons on the after hatch-grating that had been closed to guard against surprise attack from below.

"We be yours to a man, Cap'n!" said another following suit, touching his forelock in salute.

"Honoured I am, to be sure!" snapped Flint. He coughed, spitting out red saliva between the Buccaneer's boots.

The whole Crew stank of fear and eyed Flint in awe, as if he were some ogre or yahoo. One by one they surrendered and were mustered on the Poop by Darby M'Graw. We Officers stood bunched by the wheel, watchful and silent. When Darby delivered his final tally to the Captain, it was found that only six Mutineers were missing as remained alive: Port Tack; Pike the Mad Marine; Carver Lowe; Allardyce and two other unsavoury characters. The first was a Manikin from the Main of Africa, Jacko by name, but known to one and all as

'The Poisoned Dwarf'. The second was an evil, scar-faced Turk, a native of the Barbary coast, called 'Ahmed the Moor'. Both of them were close confederates of the Cooper's Mate.

"I want these swabs alive if possible, but dead if necessary," said Flint. "Doctor, and you, Darby, keep ye yore weather-eye on oor re-mustered Crew and guard oor backs! Long John, take ye Bart, Pop-Eye and Israel. After we clear the Fo'c'sle, search below decks – all before the beam. I'll seek 'em aft – follow me!"

With Blind Pew, Black Dog, Billy Bones, Ben Gunn, Shamus O'Brien and Job Anderson guarding the gun-room, along of Flash Dan and One Eyed Darby watching the Poop, it left only eight of us to hunt out the remaining Mutineers. Under Flint's direction were Morgan, Merry and the Great Dane.

Information from the Crew told us only two were holed-up in the Fo'c'sle, the Poisoned Dwarf and Ahmed the Moor. We proceeded for'ard with much caution, my gang covering the larboard side – Flint's to starboard. The Captain walked slower now, his breath rasping, coming in short, sharp jerks. I saw his face beaded in sweat, glistening in the light of the newly risen full moon.

A red tongue o' flame suddenly stabbed out at us from between the stanchions a-top the Fo'c'sle-head. Bartholomew the Portuguese, who was slightly in front of me, gave a cry and fell to the deck, mortal wounded. I fired at the flash. Hands, Flint and Tom Morgan also returned fire, aiming at the puff of smoke. Next instant a figure rose up, staggered, and tumbled over the stanchion rails. A turban rolled across the deck as a ball-butted Migulet pistol clattered onto the boards, its silver muzzle bands glinting in the moonlight. Sprawled between our two gangs lay Ahmed the Moor – riddled by four bullets.

"Damnation seize my soul!" swore Flint, for in the same moment a small figure scurried from the deep shadow beneath the Fo'c'sle steps.

"Beware, Jacko!" cried the Great Dane and made a grab for the Manikin, only to recoil with a cry of agony.

The Poisoned Dwarf leapt into the fore-mast, starboard shrouds and scampered aloft. Swung up the ratlings like a blessed monkey, so he did. The Great Dane stood swaying, cursing and clutching at a bleeding stab in his side, his big blond head craned towards the fleeing fugitive. I fired, exchanged Pettijeans, and emptied both barrels. Flint fired. George Merry fired. We parted ratling ropes and splintered the main-spar, but didn't hit the midget. He moved too fast and on gaining the fighting-top platform, he was lost to our view.

"Kapitan! I vill go for him and slit der swab into Schnitzels, same as he do on me!" vowed the Big Norseman. Clamping a great knife between his strong, white teeth, he painfully started up the shrouds after Jacko.

Now the Poisoned Dwarf, although small, was the liveliest top-man I ever saw. This Manikin from the African Main was black as a tar-bucket, bald as a cannon-ball and solid muscle from pate to pumps. He used to do what we called 'Sail-Walking', treading down the billowing canvas so the hands could haul it in and clew it up easier – and him holding onto thin air! I've seen him swing all over the tops, from Fore-Mast to Mizen and back again. Why he didn't choose to escape from the Great Dane, beats me. Maybe he reckoned to settle him. Instead, he climbed to the Fore-Top-Gallant and walked out on the spar. Then he crouched, bobbing up and down gibbering like a gibbon, while waiting for the slower moving Norseman.

My neck ached from looking up. We all held our breath as the Dane edged along the yard towards the Dwarf. Suddenly Jacko sprang. I saw the glint of knives as they closed and struck, each stabbing the other. The Great Dane, who never had much to say at any time, seized the Dwarf and holding him tight, fell soundlessly off the spar into the sea. We rushed to starboard and gazed astern, but they never surfaced in this world.

"You could say, 'There goes the Long and the Short of it!'" I said, tongue in cheek; but I was truly sorry to see the Great Dane take his last, long dive down to Davy Jones – him being a staunch hand an' all!

"I reckon the Dane received his death hurt along o' that first thrust," remarked Flint, rolling his cud of coca leaves. "Time to sound out what be in store for us below-decks."

With some apprehension we went below, Flint's Gang turning aft – mine moving for'ard. Pop-Eye led off, holding his lance flush to his fore-arm ready for an instant throw. Hands brought up astern, his pistol at the ready. Our ear-drums were straining fit to split, but the only sounds to be heard was the sighing of the sea whispering along *Walrus*'s hull and the creaking of her timbers.

"Pop-Eye," said I to the Creek Indian. "Wouldn't you find it more fitting to exchange that there harpoon for a barker or cutlass? Ain't exactly the ideal weapon for close-quarters, now is it?"

"Ah, Long Johnny. Lance always loaded, never hang-fire. Shoot further than 'from Wood to Black-Skin', not like cutlash," returned he grinning. As he glanced back at me the feathers braided into his scalp-lock fluttered in a down-draft of air.

Those were the last words he spoke above board. He took two steps into the galley, when a faint scuffle sounded from within the gloom and we froze. Pop-Eye drew back his arm and flung the iron that had been intimate with many a mighty monster's great heart. A pistol flared and bellowed in the darkness as the lance left his hand. The Creek followed it, falling full length upon the deck. In the glow cast by a single lantern, I saw that Pop-Eye's big glims were upturned towards his brows – sightless with a bullet-hole between them!

I quickly hove-to, hopping behind one of Cook's coppers. Israel crowded in behind me. We waited. Nothing moved, although we could hear the soft splash of what sounded like dripping water. Our only light came from the smouldering billets within the grate of the big, brick stove and the glim swinging amidships. Set upon the hob was a large cauldron of simmering stew, its beefy smell now spiked with powder-smoke and a sickly, sweeter odour that I couldn't quite put my finger on.

"Maybe they has budged?" breathed Israel in my ear.

"Would you fancy to go and see?" I hissed back and the Gunner pulled a face, saying no more.

Arm in arm with great caution I unhooked the glim from its becket with the tip o' my crutch, being careful to keep the light away from me and the line of fire. Still nothing. I extended the lantern, slowly weaving it to and fro. The light flooded over the far bulkhead and there stood Pike the Mad Marine with his chin upon his breast, his feet splayed, the smoking barker still in his dead hand. Transfixed to the timber, he was, held upright by the shaft of Pop-Eye's lance that had smashed through the centre of his chest.

"Here's luck!" said Hands, peering at Pike. "Pity the Savage didn't remain above board to see his flipper stroke."

"Tread easy, Israel," I warned as he stepped out. "Pike follows Carver about like a pet dog. He ain't far away, I reckon."

The Gunner took the glim from the tip o' my timber and moved forward. I hobbled after him. We didn't see the second body on the other side of the stove, not until Israel bumped into it and sprang back with a cry of terror. He held the glim up for closer inspection. Wun Hung Lo swung slowly from side to side, suspended by his pig-tail tied to a becket in the beam. Teeth bared, the Cook grinned down at us hideously, his eyes glassy and with his throat cut from ear to ear.

"Poor old China. He's smoked his last pipe of opium, he has," remarked Hands after recovering from near kissing the corpse.

"See here, Israel," I said pointing to the wide pool of blood beneath the Chinee's dangling feet, source of the dripping sound we had heard and the sickly stench that was mixed with the smell of the stew. "Carver got careless when he walked through this mess of his own making."

We followed the bloodied foot-prints down the hatch that led to the cable-flat. This part o' Ship was well lit, seeing it was the for'ard end of the Lower-Gun-Deck where the majority of the Crew messed. The bows were fenced in by a partition about four feet high. This area, known as 'The Manger', served a two-fold purpose. First, to act as a run-off for water gushing through the hawse-holes in rough weather or drawn in by the dripping cable when the anchors were weighed; and secondly, as a place to keep livestock for fresh rations at sea – pigs, goats and poultry. At the moment it should have housed nothing more than junk and shot-torn canvas, bits of which were used by the Sail-Maker for patching. But the bloodied boot marks that ended at the partition told another story.

"To every Pig his Place! And every Dog has his Day! Well you've seen the best o' yours, Lowe you swab, so step out here – lively!" I cried levelling my Pettijean pistol.

Carver slowly arose, glaring at me. His piggy, pale eyes seemed lidless, same as a snake's, and were unblinkingly fixed on my gun. As I hobbled forward the muzzle wavered. Lowe's hand came up with a flash of steel. In the same tick of time, Israel stepped across my path to cover Carver from the larboard side and took the knife in his shoulder that was in line of my chest. The gunner gave a cry, dropped the glim and staggered against a cannon's cascabel, gripping his hurt. I triggered my piece, both barrels, but in the heat and haste of that first action top-side, I had committed a raw OD's trick of Failing to Reload!

Carver's surprise and dismay disappeared in a moment. He vaulted the partition with his hanger drawn. "See you, Silver!" snarled he. "I'm a-going t' carve yer open and strangle yer along o' yer own gristle!"

I flung the empty pistol at him, which bounced off his broad chest. He minded the bruising blow no more'n the fluttering of a moth. Clawing at the hilt of my own cutlass, I was barely able to parry his first murderous slash for he closed on me in a second.

"By the powers! Long have I awaited this moment!" I cried in defiance. "I put you down twice, Lowe, and a third time'll make it final on your slate – by thunder!"

"Come now, Cripple!" taunted he, our blades hissing and kissing, poking and parrying. "I'll 'ave yer tangled in yer own tripes a-fore I works up a sweat!"

Israel had slumped beside the gun. I tried to keep my back against the breech, but so fierce was Carver's attack, I was compelled to give ground. Having driven me out onto the open deck, Lowe suddenly spun about to the helpless, grey-faced gunner and plucked the dagger from his shoulder. Israel screamed and fainted clean away, along of the pain and shock. Double-armed, the ex Bullock was twice as dangerous. Grinning fiendishly, he came at me with a will.

"You be the swab who sliced one o' my 'Earrings' half through, en route to Sarasota, when I were near swept overboard!" I snapped, parrying another savage swipe.

"Aye, yer would 'ave gone below that day were it not fer the meddling o' Merry and M'Graw!" returned he with a sneer. "But t'night's as good a time to put you under Davy Jones's Lock!"

He thrust his blade and ripped my shirt, inflicting a painful scratch across my ribs. I, in turn, delivered a slight stab to his thigh which slowed him up some. Seizing chance by the scruff, along with perfect timing, I suddenly swung my crutch and sent his cutlass spinning from his hand. In hopping backwards to maintain balance my heel struck the thick messenger rope, that was used to haul up the anchor, and I fell flat on my back. Recovering his surprise, Carver came at me with a yell of triumph and a mighty leap – dagger held high. Still gripping my cutlass flush to my side, a simple flick o' the wrist brought the tip up and Carver landed smack on top of it. He sat astride me gasping, gaping at me in disbelief, his chest pressed against the guard with my blood-smeared blade protruding from the back of his ragged Red-Coat.

"Damn . . . yer . . . Silver," wheezed he in a whisper.

"Carver, I reckon I've settled you!" I said and heaved the swab off me as his eyes glazed, turning into those of a corpse.

Morgan and Merry were suddenly alongside, hauling me on to an even keel. I turned to be confronted by a grinning Flint, and there, helping my moaning gunner to his feet was Allardyce – above all people!

"Well struck, Long John my lad," said the Captain eyeing Lowe. "He'll be doing his carving in Hell from here on oot!"

"How come that swab ain't in irons?" I asked, noting the fear that flickered across Allardyce's face.

"He turned 'King's Evidence', in a manner of speaking," smirked Flint, "and showed me where Port Tack had gone to ground. Hid hisself away in a bread-bin, bless his black heart!"

The Captain then went on to explain how a great roll of sheet lead had been placed on the lid, imprisoning the Cooper's Mate, while Ben Gunn was summoned to nail the top down. Air holes were also bored in the barrel to save him from suffocating. Flint had bizarre plans for Mister Pay. He reserved Allardyce for a jest too, but of course I never knew of his true ending until years later back on Treasure Island.

We all repaired to the Great Cabin for a much needed caulker, where Israel's stab was dressed by the Doctor. The wound, although deep, weren't dangerous. I was sat with a glass of brandy awaiting my turn to have my scored ribs attended to, watching the sunrise, while reflecting that our 'Fifteen Men' were now reduced to 'Twelve', when Flint spoke:

"Night passes and the evil things depart," said he in a tired voice, filling the buckled goblet that had deflected the bullet from his brain.

"Aye, Sir," I agreed. "But the Beauty of a Golden Dawn can also herald Disaster and Death!"

PEECE EIGHT

SKELETON ISLAND!

CHAPTER XXXVI

MAROONED!

Port Tack was kept confined in the bread-bin for three days without food, but was allowed any amount of water that he wanted. This latter life-stay was administered by means of the Cooper's Mate sucking on the nozzle of a leather bag inserted through an air-hole. For added discomfort, Flint ordered each Crew member to collect ten cockroaches apiece, which were then channelled into the bin through a paper funnel. Ben Gunn, his jailer, took special delight in this practice, along of Bone-Head O'Brien. Port Tack at first cursed, then pleaded and finally broke, sobbing for Mercy. After three nights of enduring these loathsome, creepy crawling horrors, Harry Pay was a gibbering, blubbering wreck. And the stench from that barrel was on par with Black Dog's socks!

Old Ebenezer Lowether got granted his request to be set ashore with three mates at the first sight of land, which happened to be an island off Cape Florida. I had the handling of setting him safe on *terra firma* in the long-boat. We left them fire-arms, powder and shot, together with three kegs of water, salt pork and biscuits. Their Island was lush in vegetation, which housed wild-life, so they wouldn't have starved. Halfway back to the Ship I reckon they had a change of heart, because we saw them run up and down the beach waving their arms and hollering. But wind and tide wait for no man and so we left 'em there, knelt upon the sand, their hands raised in supplication, calling on us for Mercy or cursing us to Damnation. Maybe they were rescued, same as Selkirk was, or perhaps their bones is bleaching yet on that distant, lonely shore.

Came the Day of Reckoning for Port Tack, *Walrus* dropped anchor in the very midst of the Dry Tortugas. Grim and barren Islands they be too, with hardly enough life-support for the crabs and sea-birds that abound there. When released from the barrel, the Cooper's Mate couldn't stand. His clothes were foul and he stank worse than a disturbed skunk. He was tried and found guilty in ten minutes. Allardyce was pardoned – for the moment!

"I have a special fate for ye, Harry Pay, to be witnessed by the entire Ship's

Company," concluded Flint.

When all was said and done the Crew were ferried ashore in our two remaining ship's-boats. As in duty bound, being Quarter-Master, I came off last in charge of the prisoner with Hands acting the Master-At-Arms, along of Morgan, Merry and Big Job Anderson as escort. Once on the beach Flint bade the Company to sit crossed-legged upon the sand, just above the high-water mark. That lonely, barren caye were like being at the end of the Earth, surrounded by sea and sky, with thousands of birds circling above us, screaming their rage at being disturbed from their domain.

"Pick ye five mates!" ordered Flint to Allardyce and motioned Black Dog forward bearing a brace of spades. "Now dig me a hole," said he, pointing to a spot on the weed-lined water mark.

Taking it in turns, Allardyce and his five mates, all former cronies of the Cooper's Mate, began digging into the soft, white sand. Each spadeful contained bits of powdery coral, shards of broken shells, tiny ones still intact, and a fine, grey grit – the result from a million years of pounding seas. While they worked with the sweat streaming off 'em, hundreds of small crabs scurried away in all directions from their thrusting spades.

An icy dread settled over the Company as they sat watching these preparations take place. My blood runs cold, to this same moment, in thinking on the fate that Flint had dreamed up for the doomed man. Port Tack hisself stared with the sweat rolling down his face in rivulets. He was silent enough at first, until the full manner of his ending hit home in his slow brain. Then, wide-eyed in terror, he started to shriek and rave, twisting and turning, struggling against the cords that bound him. And who wouldn't on the realisation he was to be BURIED ALIVE!

The true way of it wasn't that simple. When the hole was completed, Flint measured it for depth. He had some sand replaced and stamped down. Only then did he seem satisfied and ordered Port Tack to be lowered into it. Screaming and struggling, Harry Pay was interned by his former friends. How he raved and swore, begged and pleaded – all to no avail. On the hole being filled in, stamped and packed tight around him, the former Cooper's Mate was buried, sure enough, but only up to his neck. Eye-balls bulging, he twisted his head every-which-way in an effort to get free. Frothing at the mouth, I reckon he weren't far short o' becoming insane!

"Captain Flint, I protest this barbarity!" exploded Flash Dan, white with anger and revoltion.

"Why?" asked Flint mildly amused. "If ye be concerned over his being lonely, I can order another hole dug, Doctor!" This last sentence was hissed in Flash Dan's face. Then our demented Leader swung about to face the rest of the

Crew. "There be the swab who tried to sink me full o' shot-holes! Any as feels sympathy and wants to join 'im, just breathe the word!" roared he.

Not a man-jack among them so much as murmured. They sat like statues as if their tight faces were hewn from stone.

"Look ye to the tide!" continued Flint, his battered, blue tinged features ablaze with fiendish glee. "Ere an hour's out this cur will be spitting crabs and salt-water, along o' the birdies pecking his eye-balls!"

"Leastways with his buttocks deep sunk in sand, his brains won't suffer sun-stroke," drawled Billy Bones dryly.

Flash Dan, who had walked some little way off in disgust, returned and confronted Flint. He held a small, silver pannikin and a brandy flask. "Would it be too much to allow that poor, doomed creature a final drink to help him face the end?" he asked.

"Aye, Doctor, do yore duty. He be sick enough for yore services by the look on him!" sneered Flint. "Mayhap humanity might erect a monument in yore image, one fine day!"

"I think not, especially when it becomes known I played a major part in the saving of YOU!" retorted the Doctor and turning on his heel, he went over to squat beside the blubbering Cooper's Mate.

Flint stood speechless, flushing in rage, his face twitching.

"Here my man, drink this!" said Flash Dan, supporting the back of Pay's head in one hand and placing the pannikin to his parched lips. "Down with it in a single draught!" ordered he sternly.

Port Tack obeyed to the letter. The Doctor got up and stood clear as Pay began to gasp. His eyes bulged, his breath rasping in his throat. Convulsions tore at the body buried beneath the sand. Then there came a deep rattling sound, similar to a gargle; his glims glazed, his mouth went slack, along of a lolling tongue, and Harry Pay was beyond all vengeance.

"Boil my blood and fall on! Ye have pushed Port Tack across the Bar and wi'oot my blasted permission! What did ye give the swab?" raged Flint.

"Compassion and mercy," replied Flash Dan, cool and quiet with a cocked eyebrow. "Combined with a tincture of the late Carib's poison."

"By thunder! Ye've crossed me for the last time, Daniel Hunter!" cried the Captain and brought his great, curved cutlass hissing from its shark's skin sheath.

Flint would have split the Doctor, who was unarmed, from Pate to Pelvis, then and there, if not for me. I swung my crutch, catching him on the wrist, and knocked the hanger out his hand. He stood gaping at me, rubbing his wrist-bone. Then to the amazement of all, he sank to his knees and began beating both fists upon the sand. Raving, he was, cursing, swearing and crying.

While Darby did his best to console the Captain, Billy faced me – solid and hard-set like granite: "Some day, John Silver, someone'll take that timber off you and ram it down your gullet!" threatened he, his glims all a-glitter.

"So ho! And who might the man be to do that small service – YOU?" I snapped in hot return, moving nearer the Mate and thrusting my face close to his fleshy, broken veined mug. "Care you to try blowing me up?"

Billy winced and backed down. "I only got one good arm," he mumbled lamely.

"An' I only got one good leg, so on that score I reckon we be even! But one leg, timber leg, or no blasted legs, I'd match any four o' you swabs any day! Come to me with a cutlass or barker – him that doubts it!" I roared, glaring about me.

"Easy, Long John," soothed Anderson. "None here's a-crossin' you, shipmate. You've a stauncher standing among this Company more'n you know."

Billy and Darby assisted Flint back to one boat; I hobbled along with Flash Dan, Blind Pew, Black Dog and Job Anderson to the other. From that day forth, Flint's Flock started to scatter. All those who had sailed in the *Walrus* when we escaped from Porto Bello, banded themselves around me, save for Billy Bones and One Eyed Darby M'Graw. Only the Treasure held us together, mind; but until we finally split the bearskin, nothing was ever the same again.

As I sat in the stern-sheets being rowed out to *Walrus*, my last glimpse of that accursed Caye was of Port Tack's lifeless face staring blankly from the sand – crawling with tiny crabs. Nearby, some birds had landed and were strutting around with their razor-sharp beaks agape, panting in the heat, each with its bright, beady eyes fixed on the head of Harry Pay. That summed up our Crew, I reckon, scavengers watching and a-waiting on the pickings!

Flint stayed confined to his cabin until we anchored off Tortuga – the town situated on the North-West coast of Hispaniola. The top part of the Island was French owned, while the lower half were ruled by Spain. During the trip the Captain raved bad, the worst I ever heard him. Sometimes drunk, sometimes drugged, but more often than not ranting along of being both. Billy, Darby and the Doctor attended him. It was Flash Dan's skill that kept him semi-sane and saved him from floundering altogether. Better had he poisoned the maniac, same as he done on Port Tack. After our arrival at Tortuga, Flint sunk into that strange, tortured, twilight world of the insane. He only ever emerged but thrice to be the complete man: once, shortly after leaving Tortuga; again at Skeleton Island; and finally on the day he died. However, all soundings to their proper depth of place!

Some days before we dropped our hook at the French buccaneering base, I had me the first of two conversations that proved to be of more value than gold dust, since the information saved all our lives later – thems that mattered anyway. I was standing my Watch, one moonlit night, when Darby M'Graw staggered to me. Dead drunk, he was, bearing a cup of piping hot coffee heavily spiked with rum.

"Thank'e, Darby and right welcome," said I. "But hadn't you best seek your berth, ship-mate?"

"Long John, I ain't forgot I owes yew my life," began he, swaying slightly, but slurring not a word. "One good turn deserves another, so hear me now, matey. J.F. be a-feared o' yew, for there ain't no other man alive who ever faced him down once and lived to tell on it – let alone twice! When Flash Dan leaves this Company, go with 'im, John. *Walrus* is doomed – along of any as remains aboard."

"You've either said too much or not enough, Darby. How can Flint destroy the ship without blowing hisself up and from his own cabin as I recall?"

The foxy-faced little Steward put his arm around my shoulder and tapped his nose knowingly with a forefinger, winking at me with his one remaining, beady, bright eye: "J.F. has a fuse leading from the Great Cabin itself, direct to the magazine. It be hid beneath a loose board, along-side where the Mizen is stepped, under the zebra rug. Once lit, yew has five minutes, matey, then – Boom!" concluded M'Graw with a hiccup.

"What of Flint, Bones and yourself, eh? How do you abandon ship on such short notice?" I asked.

"Ah," replied the Steward with another knowing tap on his nose. "Comes the day o' doom, J.F. gives some excuse for the Chaloupe to be towed astern. Along of him ordering a deal more grog for all hands than their heads can carry, when they's full seas over, we pulls in the painter, loads rations and water through the stern-sheet windy, fires the fusee and away to a calm haven for awhile."

"The same as was done aboard the *Naiad*?" I pumped the question with a sideways squint at the Steward.

"Aye, mate!" sniggered he. "An' the same as were done aboard the Old *Revenge* afore her! Flint's first ship, the *Hastings*, went the same way!"

"What of the Treasure? Flint wouldn't send that down to lie under Davy Jones's Lock and the long-boat won't hold a tenth of it!"

"J.F.'ll bury it – same as he ever done," returned Darby. "Why, from our purchase o' past years, what with Flint's share, Bill's share, Old Phineas's share and mine, along of this latest hoard, there'll be around Seven Hundred Thousand Pound catched on Skeleton Island. Then there's the arms and bar-silver buried in the sand-hills!"

"By the powers!" That sheer amount of money fair took my breath away.

"I'll stove-in any plan to bury the Blunt that's aboard here!" I replied grimly. "You may lay to that, by thunder!"

"Ah, Barbecue. J.F. will find a way. He ain't failed yet, matey. Take my advice – cut and run while yew can," said the foxy little Steward and with that he tottered back to his berth amid a bout o' hiccups.

Here was food for thought, indeed, as I sipped my scalding toddy. I was now ahead of Flint, thanks to Darby. Knowing what he planned to do gave me a chance to spike his intentions – nip 'em in the bud, so to speak. But the turn of events proved far different from what any of us reckoned on – either for Me or the Captain!

My second windfall regarding information came from Flash Dan hisself. On the evening we were anchored in the Road off Tortuga, I was sat alone in the Cabin I shared with Billy, the Mate being in attendance of Flint, when there came a tap at the door and the Doctor slipped in.

"Well, John," said he seating hisself on Bill's sea-chest that had the initial 'B' burnt into the lid, and placing his cocked hat on the small table between us, "the parting of the ways, I fear, come gun-fire."

"Sorry you be a-going, Dan," I replied, pouring him a goodly measure from my personal brandy bottle. "It won't be the same aboard *Walrus* without you. We've sailed a good few leagues together, you and I."

"Then come with me, Quarter-Master," said he, bending far forward and speaking sharp but soft. "I shall have a third of the Company in tow tomorrow morning – join us, do!"

I eyed him steady. "I'll not turn my back on all the Blunt as be stashed below. I'd never sleep o' nights for the haunting memory of it. I intend to reap my cut – come Hell or High Water!"

"John," began the Doctor sipping his booze. "I intend to have it all! But mark this: should Flint fail to surrender it except by fire and sword, if you survive the fight, whether you are for or against me, you shall receive your fair share, I promise, upon my Honour!"

"How d'you reckon to take it, start another Mutiny?" I asked in some surprise, firing my pipe. "Our gang far outnumbers yours and Flint won't make you a parting present of it – you may lay to that, my lad!"

Flash Dan smiled. "Did you know Black Bart's Flag-ship is docked at the quay?"

"Roberts? Aye, Israel made mention on it."

"It is my intention to team up with him," continued the Doctor. "If a hoard of three hundred thousand pounds don't set his taste buds to tingling – nothing will! He also has a ship for consort with around three hundred men to call on under command. Too much of a match even for *Walrus*!"

"By the powers, Doctor! If Flint knowed what you was at, you wouldn't leave this 'ere ship alive!" I said puffing smoke at the deck-head.

"Listen, John. When my crowd are ferried ashore tomorrow, inside of an hour every tavern in Tortuga will know what *Walrus* carries in her hold. Bill Bones will cut-and-run the minute we disembark, small good may it do him. Those who remain on board here can't sail forever. And as for Captain Flint?" Flash Dan paused to drain his brandy before dropping a bomb-shell in my lap. "He is dying!"

"DYING?" exploded I, near blowing my pipe-cap off. "Thunder! So the six bullets he soaked up have done for him after all!"

"Not a bit of it. Drink and drugs will be the cause of his demise. The rum is rotting his bowels and the drugs his brain!"

"Do'e know he be bound for Davy Jones?"

The Doctor shook his head. "No, I neglected to inform him. But if he isn't dead within six weeks, I shall abandon medicine and take up a tinker's trade." Flash Dan got to his feet and stood gazing down at me, fingering his hat. "What say you, John. Will you accompany me on the morrow?" he asked, more serious than ever I saw him.

"Thank'e kindly, Dan, but I reckon I'll hang-fire awhile."

He nodded, pausing with his hand upon the latch. "One word of warning, old friend. Flint has a phial of the Carib's poison – the same as I gave to Port Tack. A single drop could kill an elephant. Think what the lot would do dumped in a butt of drinking water. Take care, 'Captain Silver!'" smiled he and was gone – the door clicking softly shut behind him.

That were the way of it, ship-mates. In the morning we shook hands and I saw him off into the bum-boat that ferried him ashore, amid a fleet of the same small craft carrying those who were also leaving. Safely out in the Road, some shook their fists, others yelled insults. Flint weren't present, but Billy was. The Mate stood sullen and spoke not a word – snorting through his broken veined, fleshy blue nose. I mind yet the last sight but one of him who had saved my life: standing in the stern-sheets resplendent in his crimson coat, his wig white as snow, raising his hat in silent farewell from where it rested upon his gartered, bent knee. To my dying day I'll always harbour fond thoughts of Doctor Daniel Hunter, Master Surgeon – him whom we called: 'Flash Dan'!

CHAPTER XXXVII

FLINT'S LAST FLING!

The Doctor was right, of course. Before the bum-boats had beached, Billy's commands set the Bosun's pipes trilling and we made ready for sea. Worked like Negro stevedores, our Crew did, but ere the anchor was weighed and catted there was too much activity ashore for my peace of mind. Men were rushing hither and thither or stood clustered together in groups upon the quay, pointing out towards us.

"It's sink or swim for us now, Billy my Buck! Reckon you ought to see the Cap'n and get us a course for Savannah, if you ask me," I remarked all condescending like, after lowering my spy-glass.

"The Captain ain't to be disturbed, so we'll run before the wind until I says different! Besides, I ain't asking you, John Silver!" snapped the Mate, glaring at me with blood-shot, bleary eyes.

"Billy, how old might you be?" I asked, slowly clumping closer until we confronted each other face to face.

"Fifty and eight! What odds it?" growled he, the scar on his right cheek flushing an angry red.

"If you wants to reach fifty and nine speak civil to me in future! Got that, 'Mister Mate'!" I retorted slamming my glass shut.

Bones's fleshy nose turned even bluer, while the rest of his ugly mug went white. I left him blowing in his bristles and hobbled aft to keep Anderson and Merry company, stationed at the wheel. Our tiff was soon laid aside when Morgan's warning cry fan-fared a bigger trouble.

"There's craft of all kinds standing t'wards us! An' the *Royal Fortune* is unfurling canvas too – look you!"

Following the mad scramble for the starboard side, I saw all manner o' small boats putting out from Port. That Fleet consisted of anything as could float. There were Canoes and Piriaguas; Long-Boats and Bum-Boats; Ketches, Sloops and Schooners. The whole mass bore an army of Buccaneers bristling with weapons. Good order and discipline had gone by the board, for every man-jack in Tortuga was set to nail our Treasure – and some swabs still maintain there be 'Honour Among Thieves', shiver my sides! Some of the bigger craft ran down the smaller vessels, spilling men every-which-way into the sea. Armed to the teeth, as they were, most of them sank like stones. Good riddance, I say!

Tortuga Roads soon resembled the aftermath of a major Fleet Action with flotsam floating everywhere. Crowding on all canvas, alow and aloft, we steadily drew away from them barring two of the tall ships – Black Bart's *Royal Fortune* and her nimble Consort, *Ranger.* As for the Mate and Me? We had to lay aside our differences and combine for the common good – namely ours! It were a case of 'Die dog or bury the hatchet' and Billy knew it!

"We shall come about, Mister Bones, and get the wind of Roberts – rot him!" snapped a familiar, broken voice from astern of us.

We turned to find ourselves confronted by Flint.

The Captain stood feet astride, straight and solid with his hands clasped behind him beneath his coat, the long tails of his black head-scarf streaming past his face, while the back brim of his sombrero was blown flush to the crown by the wind. He appeared much the same as ever, save for his features. They were mottled, mauve and blue – the thin, bloodless lips and nasee tinged purple. Beneath the pale, watery blue eyes hung flaps of dark puffy skin, like folds in a sea-cloak, for most of the meat had long gone from Flint's face. Gaunt, he was now, a ghost of his former self. Even his clothes looked to be cast-offs from a bigger man.

"Aye, aye, Sir! We'll do Roberts down and daddle 'im yet!" declared the Mate, flashing a look in my direction that as good as included me in his statement.

"Quarter-Master Silver!" cried the Captain. "Care ye to con my ship and bring us safe from harm's way?"

"Aye, Sir!" I roared – my eyes locked on Billy's. "Stand-by to come about!"

"Close-up the larboard battery, Bill! Black Bart shall receive a little broadside to remember us by!" bellowed Flint.

Ah, ship-mates, it was quite like old times. But as it turned out, this togetherness was the last in a long line of many. We swept down on the *Royal Fortune*, sweet as a gull, taking her completely by surprise. George Merry's guns bucked and rolled, giving Roberts plenty to think about. Caught short, his Helmsman got hisself in a clove-hitch and near collided with their consort, but *Ranger* veered just in time – worse luck! Some shots came back at us, mind, only much too late for we were already clear. Black Bart was so prodigiously a-feared of sinking us that his Gunners aimed too high in a vain effort to bring our sticks by the board or rupture our sails and rigging. Apart from a few severed cords and holes in the canvas, small was the damage sustained by us. I never knowed it then, but that broadside heralded the swan-song of *Walrus* in regards to battle. Our old war-horse never spat ball or belched smoke and flame again!

In bearing away I trained my spy-glass on Roberts's Flag-Ship. Flying from the Mizen-Peek was his famous Ancient. This Banner of black silk portrayed a skeleton bearing an hour-glass in one hand and crossed bones in the other. Alongside this Death's Head was a dart or spear, beneath which lay a heart dripping three drops o' blood. A pennant of the same black silk streamed from the main-mast. Up for'ard, fluttering on the jack-staff, was another Black Flag with a man printed on it. This effigy of Roberts held a flaming sword and each of his feet were planted on a skull. One was marked: A.B.H. and the other: A.M.H., signifying – 'A BARBADIAN'S HEAD' and 'A MARTINICAN'S HEAD' – on account of so enraged was Roberts by the Governors of those Islands at their attempts to have him took to be gibbeted alive!

Through the battle smoke, two red-coated figures standing on the Poop caught my eye. The taller man, swarthy faced and wearing a great gold-chain around his neck, could only be Bartholomew Roberts hisself. Beside him, laughing and waving his hat, same as ever he done, stood Flash Dan!

"Sir!" said I handing my glass to Flint and pointing. "There be an old ship-mate of ours alongside Black Bart!"

The Captain took one look and the fire went out of his eyes all in a moment. Wordlessly, he thrust the spy-glass back at me and tottered off back to his Cabin. When Billy drank in the same sight he let go an oath, damning all Doctors for 'Swabs'!

Well now, ship-mates, the long and the short of it were this: in going about we was spotted by several other tall-ships, which immediately altered course and gave chase. *Royal Fortune* and *Ranger* soon took the van, leading a Pirate flotilla of eleven sail that were strung out astern of us from horizon to horizon, abaft our beam. These sea-wolves pursued the *Walrus* down through the windward passage, situated between Cuba and Hispaniola, and out into the North Sea. That night, Flint tried every trick in the book to shake 'em off, along of a few that weren't, but the morning showed sails still on our stern.

The thorn in our side was *Royal Fortune's* Consort, the nimble *Ranger*. She could have fetched us easily, but being small and lightly armed she was no match for our teeth. Instead, she showed her stern lanthorns and stuck doggedly to our wake all through the dark hours. The slower moving Brigs, Schooners and Snows simply followed where the Sloop's dancing stern lights led them. Ironic, it was, that the Royal Navy delivered us!

We were sailing South-East by East, and all the hands were dead weary with little or no sleep after suffering three days of non-stop duty-watch and stand-by, when at least two divisions appeared off our larboard bow. *Walrus* stood on, beating-up towards them, only veering at the last minute. I myself pulled a fast one. Our port lids being closed, we presented no threat to the Men-o'-War. I ran-up British Colours and ordered the Crew to wave and cheer. Hollered ourselves hoarse, we did. The Pirate Fleet scattered like ducks before a punt-gun with the R.N. in hot pursuit – God bless 'em!

Walrus continued on her merry way rejoicing, down through the Little Antilles, past Margarita, where the best pearls come from, and sailed round between Tobago and Trinidad. It was off the coast o' this latter island that we sighted our first top-sail for some time, but she immediately went about and put back into Port o' Spain. By and large, after nearly three weary weeks at sea, we arrived off the mouth of the Orinoco River and dropped our hook in the haven of Captain Kidd's anchorage at Skeleton Island. Only then did Flint emerge, the first time in over a fortnight, and confronted the Crew with a call for a Fo'c'sle Council. He was more gaunt than ever, his mottled features drawn and tired.

"Hear ye this!" began he, with us Officers stationed alongside him on the Poop. "Oor position be far from secure! Sanctuary today, aye, but what of when we put to sea again?"

Addressing the Crew mustered below on the Quarter-Deck, Flint gripped the rail before him, rolling his eyes to all quarters. To my mind, those once huge hands were so wasted and gnarled, his fingers now resembled the talons of some giant, extinct bird o' prey. And his sunken, mottled blue-tinged face was ghastly enough to frighten his own Mother. I tell you, mates, I've seen better colour on corpses that have been swinging in chains and sun-drying for a month or more!

"No word carries more weight nor spreads faster than the cry of GOLD!" thundered the Captain. "By the time we leave here, every Freebooter and Buccaneer will be hunting our hides! There's a month of sailing between us and safety in Savannah – fifteen hundred miles of sea more dangerous than if we cruised up the Thames to Execution Dock! Time and distance enough to be clapped aboard and the Blunt lost, thinks ye! Well I have Treasure of my own stashed here already! I've bar-silver and arms by the ton! And money to the tune of four hundred thousand pounds!"

The excited murmuring among the Crew swelled in volume with everybody yapping at once. Hungry dogs, one and all, with greed gleaming in their eyes. Flint held up his gnarled hands for silence.

"Aye, my lads! Enough wealth to refit King George's Navy – and pay the wages of every jack-tar in it for a full year! That's what be buried among those there hills!" cried Flint pointing towards the towering peak of the spy-glass.

While he spoke I watched the effect of his words upon the Crew and saw he had them all to a man. Magnetic was Flint in the role of orator, speaking with fire and gusto – the same as ever he done. Apart from Billy and Darby, only I knew what he was at, but thought it best to keep my own Council for the moment.

That was my First Mistake!

"What I propose, along of yore permission, be this!" continued the blue faced Buccaneer. "I'll take six of ye ashore and bury the Blunt right alongside mine for safety! Then we'll strike out for Savannah, fit oot a Consort and return here to collect the lot – arms, bar-silver, my own fist and the Sarasota haul! Ye be a brisk bunch, the boldest set of blades I ever sailed with, despite oor wee differences in the past! And for a booster, I say this t'ye: I'll divide share for share, including mine own Rhino, with every Rover that comes back to help collect it! What say ye to that, my lads?"

Of course the lubbers vapoured like colliers given a half-holiday. Their cheering sent hundreds of wild ducks quacking into the air from the Fen at the far end of our anchorage – a whirling black cloud, circling and swooping in the rays of the sinking sun. Flint's past practices were forgotten in a twinkling, along of his new policy. Ben Gunn started to dance the horn-pipe; and Blind Pew stood grinning like a stoat in a hen-house. Even Israel Hands looked about ready to bend down and kiss the Captain's boots!

"But Kapitan, vhy don't we take zer monies back to Savannah now? If ve all *schnell* ve can dig up der silver an' udder treasure much quick, yah?" asked Herman the German.

More wild cheering and those poor blessed marsh-birds didn't know if they were on wing-tips or toes – coming or going.

"In the first place, Dutchy, *Walrus* couldn't burthen all as be buried here – the fruits from twenty years of privateering! Secondly, we only have seventy-five men to guard it! When we return I shall have three hundred hands for protection!" explained Flint, flicking his tongue over dry lips and looking crafty.

"Hell, Cap'n," drawled a big, balding, hare-lipped man called Keach. "The more hands we hire, the less Dinero there'll be for the rest of us come share-out time!"

A grumble of agreement arose from the Company. I saw Flint's face tighten and start to twitch in anger over this, the first threat to his carefully laid plans. He eyed the buckskin-clad ruffian who was born and bred in Savannah, and replied shrewdly.

"Stacy, my son," returned the Buccaneer, speaking soft and leaning forward, resting his forearms upon the rail, "if I were to bring five hundred men, ye'd still clew-up richer than the wealthiest Lord as sits in Parliament. To business!" said he, slapping both hands against the guard-rail and straightening up. "Allardyce, ye be a brisk, clever fellow as ever held a bucket for to swab the lower-deck! Step ye up here a moment!"

Smirking to his mates the yellow-headed, long boned accomplice of the late Harry Pay swaggered onto the Poop, hitching up his hanger. Flint placed a claw-like hand upon his shoulder and addressed the Crew.

"Ye all ken Allardyce!" boomed he. "Now I nominates his yellow napper of hair to be my beacon, so to speak, a pointer to where the jolly dollars will be buried! Ye have the importance of a compass, my lad!"

Flint suddenly roared with laughter, his gruesome mouth agape, and patted Allardyce on the back. The silly lubber laughed along with him and all the Company joined in.

"Pick ye the same five mates, Mister Allardyce, who helped ye plant Port Tack!" cried the Captain. "For they'll assist ye to bury oor fist along of the Quarter-Master!" And again his harsh, grating cackle rang out, only this time it were directed at – ME!

'Thunder!' I thought. 'Here be a king-sized twist in my tail!' Close-hauled with other pressing matters of moment, I'd clean forgot that as QM, my duty was to ensure the Blunt were safely handled – all fair and square with no rip-offs. Now it was my turn to think quick and act cool as clumping forward I addressed the Captain.

"Hang fire a moment, Cap'n Flint! Reckon you this to be good policy? This 'ere Crew ain't exactly renowned for its honesty, now is it! What's to stop some swabs from sneaking off in Savannah, seizing a ship and doubling back to claim the whole lot for 'emselves?"

That outburst were my Second Mistake!

Murmurs of discontent rippled among the Company below us, while Flint eyed me with a glittery gleam like the cold stare of his Serpent. Before the Crew had a chance to think for themselves, Flint swung them all to his own favour and put my influence in irons at a single stroke!

"Why, Quarter-Master!" exclaimed he. "These bold blades below me here elected ye for QM because they trusts ye! Am I to understand that Long John Silver don't trust them?"

The murmuring erupted into open anger: "Who's ta say you won't cut-and-run ta be first t' break-bulk, Silver!" bawled some wag, concealed out of sight at the back.

"Avast!" snarled Blind Pew. "Order below decks!"

"Avast yourself, Bosun! The man has a right to air his views, this being a Fo'c'sle Council!" countermanded the Mate.

Pew's head swivelled towards the sound of Billy's voice. He stood hunched up, hugging his stick, his green-shaded, scarred face working in a horrible fashion with his small teeth agape like those of a cornered weasel. "Bah!" he spat. "Discipline's gone by the board and this Crew along with it!"

"Hear me now!" I cried, raising my right hand. "Be this how you want these affairs finally conducted?"

The great roar of assent that greeted my question near blowed me off the Poop. Their faces told me any more talk would be a waste o' breath.

"On your own heads be it then!" I thundered and storming down the steps, clumped my way below for I had me much hard thinking to do.

For a starter I didn't fancy going ashore with Flint. It would take several days of heavy humping to haul all the Treasure inland and bury it where he directed. During that time I'd need to eat, drink and sleep. And you Readers will recall Flash Dan's warning about the Captain having a phial of Joe the Carib's poison, don't you? Then there were the five mates of Allardyce – every one a close confederate of the late Port Tack. They bore no love for Long John. So apart from running the risk of being poisoned by Flint, there was also a good chance one of them would stove in my skull as I slept or stick a knife in my back. Full and by, the Devil's Books weren't stacked too tickety-boo for old Barbecue. Came the morning, I feigned illness.

"This 'ere stump o' mine is giving me merry hell, Cap'n," was my excuse from where I remained in my hammock when the Mate came in and announced 'His Nips'.

Flint eyed me shrewdly, playing the deep game himself. "Small odds it, Allardyce can double in yore role," replied he and went out slamming the door. I sensed a chilling ring to those words that smacked of the grave.

"SEA-BOAT'S CREW CLOSE-UP!" came the Bosun's guttural cry.

I stayed in my berth for the most of the morning with strict instructions for Israel Hands to let me know the minute Flint cast-off in transporting the last of the Treasure ashore. Near Six Bells in the afternoon, it were, before the final cry of: "AWAY SEA-BOAT'S CREW!" sounded and the Gunner came for me. In company of him, I clumped top-side.

"You got better quick!" growled Billy Bones, breaking off from watching Flint, who was seated in the stern-sheets of the long-boat, steering, while the six Seamen pulled for the beach.

"Aye, the air's a sight sweeter and more breathable now!" I retorted glaring at the Mate, but he held his peace. Turning his back on me, he walked away.

"'Ope Allardyce don't lose my knife," bemoaned Morgan. "Keeps its edge like a razor, it do. Best Toledo steel it is, see!"

"Allardyce borrowed your knife, did he, Tom?" I remarked along of a cocked eyebrow. "Wonder what he intended cutting?"

"Aye, came and asked me for a lend o' it last night, he did!"

Now I tell you, mates: I felt sicker than an OD weathering his first storm at sea in watching that Blunt being off-loaded on the beach. I felt in my bones that all that money was slowly but surely slipping away from me. Each of the six, strong, heavy boxes had been built special by Ben Gunn and the name *Walrus* branded into the lids with a hot-iron.

I know I've made mention before that a Quarter-Master aboard a Privateer be a powerful personage, but only in as much that the Crew agree. Had I contested the Captain in hard line, open conflict, chances were that I'd have been voted down and deposed. So for the moment, matters would have to remain as they were without me rocking the boat. "*Alea jacta est*!" as the Good Doctor would've said: "The Die is Cast!"

For nigh on a week we stood off – waiting. None were allowed ashore under pain of death. Then one morning with the rays of the rising sun shooting up from behind the spy-glass, a single pistol shot cracked out flatly. Echoing against the crags it rumbled on and on like thunder in the crisp, clear air. The wild ducks in the fen took flight, whirling into the sunrise with a great humming of fluttery wings. The Crew closed-up top-side in one mad rush. They remained there gaping towards the shore, watchful and alert.

Along of Flint's signal we saw the Chaloupe come gliding towards us from the gloom of the tree on the shore-line. The Captain sat on the centre thwart strongly pulling on the sweeps, his head bound in a blue scarf instead of the customary black, and he was – Alone! Speculation among the hands was rife:

"Flint's left 'em to guard it!" stated one.

"Maybe they ain't finished buryin' it and run out o' rum!" said a second.

"'Ope theys ain't stole it and done a bunk!" voiced a third idiot fearfully with the brains of a brass buddha.

Jabbering like washerwomen, they were. I glanced at Billy, but the Mate never so much as batted an eyeball. This turn of events was new to everybody except Him, Darby and Me. When the Captain clambered aboard his face was mottled and mortal white, to be sure, but he was humming happily to hisself for all that.

"Since 'tis my responsibility, where be the Treasure at, Cap'n?" I demanded, clumping forward to confront him.

"Ah," sneered he, "ye can go ashore if you like, Quarter-Master, and stay, but as for the Ship, she'll beat-up for more, by thunder!"

"That ain't the plan, Sir!" said George Merry.

"Tut, tut," returned Flint, bearing his awful teeth in a gruesome grin. "It is now and there dinna be a damn thing ye can do about it!"

"Where's Allardyce? Still owes me money, he does!" wailed Morgan.

"More to the point!" cried Keach the Savannah colonial, elbowing his way through the Crew that crowded around the Captain. "Why ain't my brother James come back?"

"He's under hatches with the other four swabs that tried to cross me! But Allardyce still be above board, heh . . . heh . . . heh," cackled Flint and then threw back his head and roared with laughter.

Keach's beard bristled and his eyes blazed in anger. Bellowing with rage he flung hisself on Flint, seizing his throat in both big hands. The Crew scattered like quail before Squire's gun, save for Keach's mate, 'Sneaky' Al, who tried to trip the Captain while they wrestled. But Billy stepped in and cracked his skull with a belaying pin.

"Avast all o' yew! I'll blast one an' all if any tries to interfere!" threatened One-Eyed Darby from a-top of the Poop. The little Steward was crouched behind the serpent-headed swivel with a slow match smoking in his hand.

I lost little time in clumping clear. Backed against the bulkhead below the Poop, I was safe enough if Darby let go his load. I wasn't alone, mind. Most of my Gang closed up and crowded in beside me.

A month ago Flint could have crushed Keach, same as squeezing a swab, but his giant strength was failing, along of his health, and his activities on the Treasure Island had left him weaker. On the other hand, although Keach was fit, he had been laid-low by a bout of Yellow Jack. So pound for pound I reckon they were about even. Keach seemed to be making a good job of throttling Flint. The Captain was as close-hauled as ever I saw him with his face turning bluer than the bandanna knotted about his head.

They swayed and stumbled back and forth across the deck, each with his hands locked upon the other's throat. When they came up short against the port bulwark, close to the main-chains, Flint forced Keach's head back, cupping the heel of his left hand beneath the bearded chin, and snatching a belaying pin from its becket, dealt him a sickening smack alongside his temple. Captain Kidd done the same thing on a mutinous Gunner Moore back in 1697 aboard the *Adventure Galley*, except Kidd clobbered him with a bucket! Before Keach had a chance to slump senseless upon the deck, Flint heaved him overboard where he sank like a stone amid a swirl of blood-stained water.

"Kill me if ye can," croaked the Captain, gripping the shrouds for support while holding his throat. "Or if ye dare. Sink me and ye've seen the last of Seven Hundred Thousand Pounds, for I'm the only one left alive as knows the place. 'Tis all in here," said he, tapping the blue scarf that bound his bald head. "Mark ye this. If I goes below, then the secret of where the Blunt be buried dies along o' me!"

Under the menacing serpent-mouthed black 'O' of Darby's gun muzzle the Crew, true to their colours, cringed and did nothing. Not that they could do much except risk getting blown to Purgatory. One and all they retreated to the Fo'c'sle, growling and grumbling like the beaten dogs they were. And that, mates, concluded Flint's last fight; for his next bout of dry blows were to be with the fearful fantasies locked within his own black conscience – along of the Great Reaper swinging his scythe!

CHAPTER XXXVIII

BILLY BOWLS OUT!

Walrus crowded on all canvas and we left Skeleton Island before noon. After Billy and Flint repaired to the Great Cabin, I went up on the Poop and stood alone. As I watched the three hills slowly submerge into the horizon's haze astern, I wondered under what circumstances I'd see the flat topped spy-glass again – if ever. Some deep down, inner sixth sense told me that my Buccaneering days were almost shot and the time was coming close to 'Cut-and-Run'!

When I visited the Fo'c'sle in company of all Officers, save for the Mate, the Crew came crying and bleating to me like Lost Sheep: "Wot we gunna do, Barbecue?" "Show us the way, Long John!"

Aye, they were mine to a Man from that moment on, but it was a case of slamming the Stable Door after the Horse had Bolted – or in this instance, the Treasure!

"Let's take Flint prisoner and sweat the swab!" said Merry glancing about him for support.

"Aye, George, we can cut that Diawl's ears and nose off for starters, see!" suggested Morgan eagerly, his Welsh blood running hot. "That'll make 'im blab, mark you!"

"If six blasted bullets don't slow him down none, what chance have we got to clap him in irons – thems of us still left standing after the set-to, that is!" voiced Anderson, his sarcasm as cutting as a cutlass.

"Job's in the right of it, Tom! Flint suffered three years o' Spanish torture and never broke. He would spit in your eye and die laughing afore he'd blab where the Blunt was at. Besides, Flash Dan once told me that them coca leaves he chews act like a kind of caulker on the nerves – dulls the senses to pain, they do!" returned I.

"What's to be done, Long John? Are we to lose a King's Ransom through want of Resolution?" grated Pew, grinding his teeth, looking more vexed than a Knight of Old with a flea locked under his armour.

"Steer steady and hang-fire for the moment, Bosun," I replied. "I'll deliver Flint an ultimatum. Either he sticks by his Word, rigs out a consort and returns for the treasure, or we'll about-ship, sail back t' Skeleton Island and take it apart, stone by stone, hill by hill and find that Fortune if it takes ten years! And I'll tell 'im this: while we're scrabbling in the dirt, him an Darby an' Bones can spend their last days buried up to their blasted necks in it – same as was done on Port Tack. Their brains can broil in the sun without benefit o' poison to ease their plight! That's what I'll say, by thunder!" I concluded venomously.

They cheered me from the Fo'c'sle and continued vapouring as I clumped my way aft to the Great Cabin. The door was bolted and barred.

"Who's there?" came the Mate's gruff voice in response to me clouting a panel with my crutch.

"Me, Billy! Old Barbecue, come for to speak with his 'Dear Captain'!"

"He ain't t' be disturbed! Helm hard-a-lee, John Silver and bear away!"

"He'll be a sight more disturbed if I puts the helm up and orders, 'About Ship' back to Skeleton Island, where you'll both blister an' sun-dry! Open up!" I cried, feeling my temper shoot to the peek.

When Billy opened the door he held one of his silver mounted, Brescian pistols in his hand, the muzzle aimed slap-bang centre o' my belly.

"Put up your piece or cut loose your dog, Bones!" I hissed. "But without me to hold the Crew in check, you'll be blowing bubbles long before we beach back on the Treasure Island!"

Wordlessly, Billy slid the Snaphaunce back in his belt. Following this wise move, as I clumped past him into the Cabin, he closed the door and shot the bolt home behind me. Darby was clearing dirty pewter platters from the desk. I saw from the scraps left on the plates that they had food cached in the Cabin: jerked beef, salt pork, ship's biscuit and some pickles. The little Steward looked just as sly and foxy with one eye as he had with two.

"Here's the Quarter-Master comed to have a quiet word, Sir," said he, gently shaking Flint's shoulder.

The Captain sat with his eyes closed, slumped in his great carved chair, methodically chewing coca leaves like a cow do her cud. He held a small-bowled, long, thin stemmed ivory pipe which gave forth a wisp of yellow smoke and the sickly sweet, nauseating smell of opium. Darby shook him again, murmuring: "Capt'in, Capt'in Flint, Sir. The QM be here."

Slowly his lids fluttered open and he viewed me with bleary, deep sunk, hooded eyes. "Ah, Barbecue, Barbecue," breathed he.

Hitching my stern, stump side onto the table, I leaned across it resting upon an elbow and began to carefully explain, word for word, what the Crew wanted of him. When I'd finished he eyed me for a moment through his drooping lids, then pulled the big, brass-bound Bible towards him and placed his bony hand on it.

"I . . . Vow . . . to . . . ye, . . . John Silver, . . . I . . . shall . . . fulfil . . . my . . . first . . . Intention . . . – Ye . . . has . . . my . . . Oath . . . and . . . my . . . Honour, . . . sworn . . . upon . . . this . . . Sacred Book.' Flint spoke his Pledge slowly and concisely as if reading a lesson. "Leave me now, for 'tis near my dream-time and dear Nester beckons. Ah, my sweet hen," sighed he, fumbling with the opium pipe, trying to find his mouth.

It was Darby who finally guided the stem to his mauve lips as I made ready to leave. He drew in the vapours from the 'Flower of Forgetfulness', sucking on the nozzle like a babby do the pap. His lids fluttered, drooping lower and lower until they closed. I left him there dreaming of his Wife and Yesterday – safe, for the moment, from the horrors that would plague him Tomorrow.

Jim Flint's Word was so much chaff in the wind and about as worthless. Mind you, he was sincere! I knew only too well what he meant by 'First Intention'. I knew that when the time was ripe, he'd blow *Walrus* out from under us – along of abandoning in the sea-boat with Billy and One Eyed Darby. That same evening, I took a glim and descended into the hold. I went warily for Samson was out hunting rats and I didn't want to end my days crushed to death by those silky coils. It took me a time of searching around outside the magazine until I located the fusee leading down from Flint's Cabin. Cunningly concealed it were too!

The quick-match was composed of three cotton strands, twisted and spliced into one length, which extended for thirty feet or more. For fast burning it was first dipped in a boiling solution of white wine vinegar, saltpetre and mealed powder, then rolled in more mealed powder, moistened with spirits of wine. It led down from below the floor-boards of the Great Cabin, past the double planks of the Gun-Room beneath it, and ran along the right angle of a centre beam with tacks to hold the cord in place every few yards. The fusee fetched the magazine through the roof, supported by means of being twisted around a looped coil of old rope that hung from several spare spars becketed below the Deck-Head. If you weren't looking for it, you'd never have seen it!

Along of breaking out a ladder, propping it against the locker-wall and hauling myself up it, two seconds work with a jack-knife made me feel a whole sight safer. My exultation was short-lived when the mass of ropes, suspended on the spar above me, suddenly moved and dropped three feet lower. Looped alongside my shoulder with his forked tongue flickering and his red eyes glowing like dull coals in a grate, hung Samson. The snake hissed and crooked its huge head into a murderous coil, ready to butt me. No man ever descended a ladder faster, short o' falling – you may lay to that! I grabbed the glim, ups with me crutch and took off out the hold quicker than a Quaker fleeing from a fight or foul language!

I didn't peach Flint's plan to the rest of the Company nor the fact I'd made it safe below decks – not even to my gang. They'd know the long and the short of it soon enough. My reasons were three-fold: Firstly, I saw no sense in making the Crew more bloody-minded and alarming them with the news that they were afloat on a bomb-vessel ready to blow. Secondly, there were too many loose tongues aboard to make for strict confidence. And Thirdly, if any high cards were to be sneaked up sleeves, Long John Silver's cuff would be crammed full of all the aces by thunder!

Walrus didn't follow the normal trade routes in sailing back to Savannah. Our aim was to avoid other ships, be they Prizes or Privateers – those above any! Two look-outs were posted in the cross-trees from dawn to dusk and if any top-sails were sighted, the Order was to 'Bear Away'. From Skeleton Island we beat-up out into the Atlantic, giving the Antilles a wide berth to leeward off our larboard beam. The sailing of the Ship was left to Me and Job Anderson with Billy supplying the courses obtained from, and set, by Flint. The Buccaneer was half-mad, to be sure, but a Navigator second to none!

One problem plagued me to such a degree, I lost sleep and grew thin over the worry of it. What if Flint was to die or become a permanent piece of 'Bedlam Bait' – what price the Treasure then? So on the day that Billy decided to cut loose from our cramped quarters and bunk-up in the Great Cabin, along of helping Darby to cool Flint's increased ravings, I broached him with the subject when he came to collect his sea-chest. The Mate was reluctant to talk at first. He just sat blowing through his nose, glaring down at his boots, until I hammered home a few hard facts.

"See here, Billy, 'tis as much for your benefit as it is for mine! Flint's got the death-haul on him already; even Blind Pew can sense the man's decline and decay. Flash Dan hisself told me he'd be under Davy Jones's lock inside o' six weeks!" The Mate jerked his head up at this and met my gaze with a startled look. "You didn't know that, did you? No, well, it don't much matter none. The point is, if Flint croaks, then the Crew will be looking at you to lead 'em t' where the Blunt's buried."

"But I don't know where it's at, Barbecue – I swear!" blurted Billy with a worried frown creasing his fleshy face.

"D'you think they'll take your word for it? Nay, matey, not from old Flint's Number One! By the powers, Billy! I'll go down on my knee and give thanks to the Almighty that I ain't in your boots when he goes below! You'll suffer worse torture than Guy Fawkes ever done, along o' lashes, slow-matches, hot-irons and maybe a needle or two under the nails – not t' mention Pew's woolding cord!"

Billy's countenance changed to the pallor of old putty, a dirty shade of grey, save for the scar. My outburst on all the possible pleasantries in store for him had the beads of sweat popping out his pores faster'n maggots from toasting cheese. I almost felt a faint twinge o' sympathy, seeing the Mate all a-tremble. Then I near hugged myself in watching him squirm as I delivered my *coup de grâce.*

"Oh, they'll believe you, Bill – eventually! But where will it leave you? In a right Royal mess, along of an invitation to either dance the yard-arm jig or take a walk along the Black Plank, blindfolded and bound with either the sharks or Davy Jones a-waiting on you at the end of it! Depending, of course, on how hungry the fishes are or how fast you sink!"

Billy's iron will and reserve finally cracked: "Flint made a Map!" he confessed, dabbing at the sickly sheen on his face with a large, blue polka-dotted handkerchief. "All with bearings and written directions so simple a child might find the place, 'appen he could read a compass."

"Where's the Chart at?" I cried, feeling my eyeballs burn.

"Flint put wax seals on it, along o' my thimble, and keeps it in a calf-skin wallet taped ag'in his chest."

"His sea-chest?"

"Thunder no, his tattooed chest! None could lift it off 'im, not even asleep. The slightest tug 'ud bring him top-side, pronto," explained the Mate. "And he holds them Queen Anne's, tight gripped an' ready cocked in each hand!"

"You'n me'll have to sign Articles over this matter, Bill. Glue your weather-eye on Flint's chest, along of scratching my back with information, and I'll keep the Crew off yours – agreed?" I asked, lifting my hand and half extending it towards him.

"Done!" said Billy and we shook on it, pumping hands like long lost brothers. But ere we arrived safe home at Savannah, the swab tried to poison me!

Flint's final bout of insanity came as we cruised up the coast of Georgia, performed in front of the entire Crew. Eight Bells was just striking the bewitching hour and the Watch below was preparing to relieve the look-out and wheel, when Flint suddenly rushed onto the Quarter-Deck. He was brandishing the great, clam-shell hilted cutlass, clad in a white night-shirt and sea-boots with a chamber-pot stuck on his head. Wild-eyed and dishevelled, he were, unshaven, twitching, drooling at the mouth – his face the colour of a decaying corpse on a gibbet.

"Crowd on all canvas!" he cried. "The swabs are swimming up astern of me! Scots wha hae wi' Wallace bled! Crowd on all canvas!" he repeated.

"Swimming is it they are, Sir!" exclaimed Morgan from beside the wheel, afore I could get a word out. "Who?"

"Them!" hissed the demented Buccaneer glancing fearfully behind him. Then with his eyes starting from his head, he pointed his cutlass up at the Poop and shrieked: "THEEEMMM!" in a long drawn out cry.

Billy came blustering from the Cabin. Barefoot, he was, wearing open-kneed leather breeks with his shirt wide to the waist and the tails flapping. Darby followed behind him, padding along like a trained dog, dressed only in cotton undervest and drawers. The Watch Below were top-side now with Israel Hands at their head, him being my relief as Duty Officer. Crowding in rear and still stumbling through the aft and for'ard hatches came the rest of the Ship's Company, bleary-eyed and all a-grumble over lost sleep.

"First rate Captain's Keeper you turned out to be!" I growled, directing my sarcasm at Billy, but with a wary eye on Flint who had backed against the Bulwark brandishing his blade. "Thought you stood watch and stand-by, along with the Steward?"

"Darby dozed off when I were cat-napping forty winks and the Cap'n slipped his cable afore we could catch him," replied the Mate, looking sour and glaring at the one-eyed little Steward who stood shivering.

"Suppose he jumped overboard, along o' being moonstruck! Where'd our Blunt be then?" voiced Israel Hands.

"Aye, him having the Chart anchored to his chest!" added Pew; for I'd held no secret about Flint having made a Map. The more eyes on Mister William Bones, the better for all concerned – especially ME!

Flint shook his fist and snarled defiance towards the Poop, aiming his aggression at something only he could see: "Rot ye – one and all!" he roared. "What right have ye to plague me? Ye whose heart I devoured and whose head hangs shrivelled in my cabin! Did ye not cause the death of Her who was so Dear? And ye, o Caballero! Was it not ma Carib brothers who barbecued and partook of yore flesh first? I see the crook-backed manikin stands among ye – him whom ma Serpent swallowed! Why come ye here with a multitude of men long dead? Those of ye who swung at ma yard-arm or perished by the plank, along o' them's I blew to Davy Jones, ye all died b'yore own foul, treacherous folly! Begone from ma Ship, I say! Swim ye back across the Styx and return to yore own Place!"

"Cap'n, you'd be better off in your berth, Sir, tucked up tight with a nice noggin of hot rum toddy, by way of a caulker," I soothed.

My words fell on deaf ears, my voice no more than a croak, for the air had turned chilly cold in a single whisper of wind. Flint weren't a sight for the squeamish at any time, but as he pressed back against the bulwarks, Sheer terror stamped itself upon his mottled mug. The whole Crew backed oars, mortal feared to a man! I never saw a face to match Flint's, afore or since, nor sensed a bigger foreboding that walked aboard *Walrus* that night!

"No, no!" shrieked Flint extending the fore and little fingers on his left hand, curling the others into his palm as he thrust his arm out in this Medieval Sign to ward off evil. "Come ye no nearer me!"

Now I ain't windy by any manner o' means, but when it comes to Spirits it pays to be cautious. I've heard tell they only allows themselves to be seen by those they haunts. It didn't take much to conjure up in my mind's eye what Flint, in his imagination, was seeing for real. Coming off the Poop were a host of dead men who for years had hung about his neck like millstones: the Headless Grandee; the Cannibalised Caballero; the Hunch-Backed Spanish Captain, in company of the Friars and all those he had done unto Death. The list was endless!

"Stay sway, Allardyce! I left ye wide-eyed and sightless, pointing at the Pole Star! Begone back t' yore Caye, Port Tack! Hands off me, Keach!" raved Flint and drawing back his cutlass, sent it spinning towards the Poop steps.

The heavy blade struck the hand-rail, slicing off a huge splinter, then went whirling out to sea. Turning end over end, horizontally, along of the moonlight sparkling and flashing on the silver clam-shell guard, Flint's hanger reminded me of a Mamuque I once saw flying over the Indian Ocean. 'How many skulls had that steel split asunder?' I wondered as it fell into the sea with a silent splash.

Flint was cringing beside the bulwarks now, blubbering and frothing at the mouth with fright, while slapping away the imaginary hands that were reaching for him. My own mind began playing tricks on me: were those gliding shadows caused by clouds scudding across the Moon or the moving Spirits of dead men? Was that the creaking of the Ship's timbers or the slow, shuffling footsteps of things unseen? And the murmurings I could hear – wind in the rigging or the sighing souls of the damned?

With a strangled cry that came from the very bowels of his being, Flint pitched forward senseless upon the deck – the chamber-pot smashing into smithereens. Billy and Darby bore him away to the cabin, each as pale as the other. I returned to my own berth and drank out a full gill of brandy before hitting my hammock; even then I kept the glim burning!

On the day before we docked at Savannah I was sat in my cabin, waiting on the evening meal, when there came a knock on the door and Billy entered bearing my 'Solomon Grundy', along of a tankard o' Rumfustian. Behind him strutted Sir Francis, the Ship's cat, sniffing at my savoury victuals with his tail stood to attention.

"Thought I'd bring your belly ballast aft, Barbecue and save the Cook a journey, seeing as I'm about to relieve the Watch-Keeper," said the Mate setting down the turtle-shell tray.

"Why, thank'e Bill. 'Tain't every Quarter-Master as gets the First Mate for a flunkey!"

Surprised weren't the word for it. I see Billy's face go tight at my gentle jibe and, snorting through his nose, he departed slamming the door. I thought no more of it for the moment. 'Sir Francis' jumped upon the table and sat patient, a-waiting his cut of my rations.

Now that old cat were special, mess-mates, having been aboard *Walrus* since we first stole out o' Porto Bello all them years ago. And as for bravery? Why, he never missed an action, mates. In time of engagement, instead of seeking safety below, he'd sit between the Poop stanchions and view us Officers and Gunners on the upper-deck with what I always thought to be a critical eye! Named in honour of 'Sir Francis Drake', him as went Privateering for the Virgin Queen, that there Pussy was entitled to anything aboard Ship whenever he so desired. He messed for'ard with the men, mostly, but had dined along of Captain Flint hisself on many occasions.

"Enemy in sight!" squawked my Old Poll from the safety of her perch. "Stand-by to repel boarders!"

But the cat paid the parrot no mind. I scooped his share into a little dish and poured him some Rumfustian into a bowl, to wet his pipe, for he liked a nip, did Sir Francis. He were lapping the beverage as I reached about for the Tobasco. Cap'n Flint suddenly became all a-flutter, her harsh cry of alarm spinning me round, and there lay the cat flat on his back with all four puds in the air. Stiff as a poker and dead as a door nail – shiver my timber!

'Thunder!' thought I. 'Some swab's poisoned poor Pussy! What sort of Seaman 'ud do down a dumb animal?' Then with a jolt that shook me to my very bearings, I realised the intended victim was ME! It didn't take long to fathom who was at the bottom of it – Billy Bones, first and last! I laid Sir Francis in my hammock, curled like he was asleep, then smoked a pipe and reflected on the situation. And who says it don't pay to be kind to God's creatures!

Ditching the stew along with the drink, in case that were doctored too, I took my tankard and platter and quietly hobbled out onto the Quarter-Deck. Billy was stood with his back to me, bouncing up and down on the balls of his feet, humming to hisself, the same as he ever done when he were well pleased. I closed up behind him, striking my crutch upon the deck with my last step. The Mate spun about like he was shot. His face went white and his nose glowed blue, while his eyes near popped out from his head.

"B-Barbecue!" stammered he.

"Barbecue to be sure, Bill! Why, who was you expecting, the blessed Holy Ghost, maybe?" I chuckled pleasantly. "That supper were so good, I'm off to give Cook my compliments and get some more. 'Specially that Rumfustian. Had a bigger bite to it than a shark!"

Still chuckling I clumped for'ard, leaving a very frightened, confused and bewildered First Mate astern. For days afterwards I caught him viewing me as if I'd sprouted two horns and a tail. As for the cat, I put it about that he'd died in his sleep from old age. We buried him in the morning with Full Honours, parcelled in sailcloth along of a brace o' swivel balls, as befitted a brisk Member of the Brotherhood. Had I told the truth regarding Sir Francis's end, the Crew would have sunk Billy beside him, I reckon. More's the pity I didn't, for if I'd been in possession o' ten toes I'd have kicked myself later!

My reunion with beloved Charlotte Eleanor more than compensated for all the hardships suffered at sea – aye, and ashore! Pretty as a picture, she was, being a bit plumper but looking more tasty than plum-duff. I learned from her that Joan Fuller had married and was now gone to keep a tavern in Bridgetown, Barbados. The Governor was also absent, summoned to New York on the King's business. Snug in the private parlour of The Rover's Rest, I could afford to let go my guard and relax, for Flint had refused to leave *Walrus* and Billy, of course, remained aboard with him. Winter wasn't far off and I settled down to enjoy these last, golden days of Indian Summer, thankful to be safe home from the sea.

Flint pacified the irate, discontented Crew by paying them from his own pocket; or rather I paid 'em with money given me by the Mate: "Tell the swabs we'll set sail back to Treasure Island, soon as the Cap'n feels better, along o' finding his sea-legs again!" was what Billy said to me. But in less than forty-eight hours after stepping ashore, I was once more clumping my way down to the quay where *Walrus* lay berthed. Beside me was a very excited Tom Morgan, for I had been summoned by Flint hisself.

"He's calling for you, Long John, so he is, see; in between raging for rum and singing. Maybe he is ready t' return to Skeleton Island and get the Treasure. The Mate says for you to shake out all reefs and come quick!" explained the Welshman breathlessly.

I mind that day of days like no other. Sunday, it was, and nearing the end of September when this freak heat-wave set Savannah to sweltering. The sweat was pouring off me ere I'd hobbled fifty paces. I heard Flint long before I reached *Walrus*. The stern-sheet windows were wide open and he was singing 'Fifteen Men', with all his old fire and gusto. As I clumped up the gang-way he fetched the last verse:

"And all for Gold and Silver Plate;
Yo-ho-ho and a Bottle of Rum!
Doubloons and Moidores and Peeces of Eight;
Yo-ho-ho and a Bottle of Rum!"

Darby ushered me in past Blind Pew, Black Dog, Israel Hands and a host of others. All those who crowded the door were ordered to wait outside. One glance at Flint told me the end had come. His face was blue, his lips black and his eyes looked to be on Fire. So emaciated was he, that he could no longer stand without assistance.

"Welcome, Long John, my lad!" cried the Captain from where he lay in his hammock, fully clothed. "Darby! Rum for my Quarter-Master and top me up while ye be aboot it!"

The Steward complied, draining the dregs from the crystal decanter into Flint's buckled silver goblet: "Rum's all out, Sir," said he.

"Then below wi' ye and re-supply!" bawled the Buccaneer, eyeballs bulging, while his face turned a deep purple.

Poor Darby took off with the speed of someone looking for a water-butt, along of his bum being ablaze! Flint forced hisself to sit up. For a brief moment he eyed me and the Mate, each in turn, cool and steady. Then reaching inside his shirt, he drew out a sweat-stained calf-skin wallet.

"Here be my Fist!" said he, holding it up. "Many a man lost his life in the amassing of it. Many would sell their Souls to possess it. Aye, and unless I am bad mistook aboot this Brotherhood, there'll be a sight more blood spilt in the seeking and the reaping of it. Take it, Bill. 'Tis up ta ye, along of Barbecue, to make and mend among the Crew," gasped Flint and drinking out his rum at a single swallow, fell back breathless.

"Shouldn't I hold it, Sir? Me being Quarter-Master makes it my responsibility – as in Article Bound!" I said, glaring at Billy while feeling the sweat trickle down my face.

"I'm Second in Command! It stays with me!" snapped the Mate, stepping back a pace and stuffing the packet in his pocket.

I reckon we would have comed to blows then and there had not Flint, who lay breathing hard and fast, gazing into his empty goblet, suddenly raised hisself up again and bellowed at the top of his voice:

"Darby M'Graw! Darby M'Graw! God-damn ye! Fetch aft the rum, Darby!"

A gurgling gasp preceded a deep, throaty rattle; then along of a violent shudder, he fell back into his hammock. The motion set it to swinging. His hand holding the goblet flopped over the side. Slowly, his claw-like fingers relaxed their hold and the cup tinkled onto the deck, rolling to rest against the

Mizen step. Flint's glims were wide open, but the light of life had left them – the Flower of the Freebooters lay there withered and dead!

Billy leaned over the body and closed those glassy eyes, placing penny pieces upon the lids. Darby came creeping in, leaving the door wide open. A half-dozen frightened faces peered through as the Steward slowly put the full decanter down on the desk, realising that the man whom he had served for a quarter of a century would never drink it. On reaching the hammock along of hesitating steps, he dropped to his knees and took the Buccaneer's lifeless hand in both of his.

"Oh, Capt'in, Capt'in, is yew really gone below?" whispered M'Graw with the hot tears rolling down his grubby cheek from his one remaining eye.

The Mate motioned those at the door to enter: "Come! Pay your last respects to the greatest Pirate as ever was or will be!" he said and crossing to the stern-sheets, stood gazing out the window – lost in a multitude of his own thoughts.

One by one the Crew came in, Black Dog leading Blind Pew. They removed their hats, those who wore them, and gathered gaping in silence around the gaudy, Indian hammock that held the mortal remains of James Flint.

"Me'n J.F. was together from the first, ever since he saved me from bein' rolled by two toughs, while drunk ashore in Maracaibo. Twenty-five years through thick and thin – fair weather'n foul," sniffed the one-eyed little Steward, blinking back his tears.

"Touching to be sure," I murmured, hobbling alongside Billy. "But now about this 'ere Chart!"

The Mate eyed me, cool and shrewd: "Seeing as we none of us trusts the other, here's wot I'll do. You give me the remains o' this day to put Flint all Ship-Shape-and-Bristol-Fashion, ready for planting, and come Two Bells of the First Watch, send your Missus down to me. I'll cut the map in half and she can choose which piece she brings back," whispered he.

"Thunder!" hissed I in return. "You think me fool enough to fall for that? What's t' stop you from making a copy o' my half?"

"See here, Barbecue," began Billy looking agitated. Withdrawing the wallet, he took out the Chart. "It's still fastened along o' the Wax Seals that Flint put on it. Which ever piece your Missus takes'll have a Seal on it, but one half's no good without t'other. We both of us have to be present t' benefit and won't open our respective bits until we hoves-to, safe in Cap'n Kidd's anchorage at Treasure Island – agreed?"

"So be it! 'Til nine o'clock then," I replied and hobbled home – far from happy. Storm clouds were gathering on the horizon to seaward, but in more ways than one!

The weather broke at sunset and along of a high wind the rain came driving down in a solid sheet, while thunder rumbled and flashed, cannonading the clouds. "God's Guns," as Flint used to say.

Although the storm was still strong, at the appointed hour my staunch Charlotte braved the elements and went on her errand. I sat waiting in the parlour, occasionally clumping into the tap-room to fetch rum for my guests – having Blind Pew, Black Dog, Morgan, Merry, Job Anderson and Israel Hands boarded under my roof. Paying guests, mind! The tension among that Company was so tight you could've plucked it like a lute and played a blessed toon – the Death March would've been appropriate! I smoked non stop; Israel fidgeted as if cooty with fleas; Black Dog kept snapping segments off his long pipe stem; while Pew bit his nails, puffed out clouds o' smoke, took a drink and went back to biting his nails.

When Charlotte returned she was wet through, but beaming good natured as ever. While she went top-side t' the bedroom to change, I were near crushed to death by the Company who crowded me close to inspect the paper she had given me. It looked to be in order, the wax seal bearing the dotted imprint of a thimble. The parchment was passed from hand to hand. All of 'em wanted a feel of it and by the look on their faces, the lubbers half expected the Treasure to fall in their blessed laps. Then it were placed in Pew's long, sensitive talons. Almost immediately I saw him give a start and go tense.

"Flint carried this about his person, didn't he?" barked the Bosun, fingering the Seal.

"Aye, that he did. Confined in a wallet, it were," I replied, feeling my innards flutter and go tight.

"If that be the case, then these rough and pointed edges would have flaked off and worn smooth!" snapped Pew. "Open it!"

I tore it out his hands, my own all a-tremble as I cracked the wax and unfolded it. We all of us stared dumbfounded. The paper was blank except for a scrawled, tottery single line o' writing:

Suck Eggs John Silver

"Well?" demanded Pew irritably, thumping my floor with his stick.

"The swab's Dutch-Traded me! By the powers! Bones he is by name and bones is all he'll be b'the time I get done doing 'im!" I raged, ripping the paper to bits.

"To the Ship!" bawled Hands.

"Get me my cloak!" cried Pew and there was a mad scramble for hats, coats and cutlasses. We were still getting in each other's way when Ben Gunn rushed in, wild-eyed, breathless and soaked to the skin.

"Come quick, Quarter-Master! Darby and the Mate is fallen t'gether b' the ears! Locked in the Great Cabin, they be, and there's blue murder going on an' we none o' us can get in!" gabbled the Carpenter, wringing his hands and hopping from one foot to the other.

We sorted ourselves out and stampeded down to the dock. I ordered the Able-Bodies on a-head and clumped astern with Pew holding onto the square tails of my coat. Such was my haste, I fell twice, slipping in the muddy street that resembled a river more than a road. The second time I brought Pew down on top o' me. Deafened by thunder and dazed by lightning, along of the rain in my glims, I were almost as blind as the Bosun. On reaching *Walrus* the both of us were wet, cold and covered in mud. All was quiet, save for our gang hammering on the Great Cabin door.

"There ain't no answer from inside, Sir!" said George Merry.

"Don't stand there squalling along of polite knocks!" snarled Pew. "Down with the blasted door!"

"Fetch for'ard fer a pole-axe!" cried Israel.

"Stand aside!" ordered Anderson and there stood our big Coxun with the serpent-headed swivel gun cradled in his arms.

Two hefty thumps from this make-shift battering ram and the door-post splintered, then the bolt within gave way on the third stroke and the door flew open with a 'Crash!' We surged in and stopped. The Cabin was a wreck: chairs thrown over, books and papers scattered; even the desk was swept clean with the crystal decanters and glasses smashed upon the floor. Flint was in his hammock, the same as when last I'd seen him with penny pieces on his eyes. Also sprawled on his back close by was Darby. He lay on the zebra-skin rug, which now, in addition to the black and white stripes, bore heavy blood-stains.

"He be still alive, Long John!" informed George Merry cradling the Steward's head in the crook of his arm.

M'Graw's single glim fluttered open as I bent over him and saw the great bleeding stab in his side. "What means this mayhem, Darby? Where's Bones?"

"Ah, Quarter-Master. Yew is too much adrift, mate. I . . . I clapped aboard the swab . . . ransackin' the cabin an' robbin' the Capt'in of his money. We . . . we had a hot five minutes an' . . . an' he settled me. Bill's done a bunk into . . . a yawl as was berthed below . . . the windy. Abandon . . . ship, Barbecue for he . . . he lit the Fusee . . . as leads . . . to . . . the . . . magaseeeen," sighed Darby and died.

Then, it was, I noticed the board laying beside the Mizen-Mast step with a wisp of smoke spiralling up from the hole in the floor!

"Run for yer lives, the ship's about to blow!" shrieked Hands from beside me, wide-eyed and white faced with terror.

"Avast!" snarled Pew. "Any who abandons here can kiss his share of the Blunt good-bye! Save the Ship! Down to the hold, you shirking dogs and snuff that blasted match!"

There came a mad scramble to clear the Cabin. Every man-jack had the fear of death stamped upon his face, along of being blown to Kingdom Come at any moment, but their fear of the Blind Bosun over-rode this minor matter. Pew's presence was so forceful, his bearing so dominating, that the Crew obeyed him without question nor hesitation. Discipline, is what they calls it! One and all they clattered down between decks to the hold, leaving me and the Bosun alone in company of Flint and Dead Darby M'Graw. I started to chuckle, then laughed loud and long!

CHAPTER XXXIX

WALRUS GOES WEST!

Pew faced me, looking puzzled, his head cocked to one side: "There be a goodly chance you'll die laughing, Long John, if they don't dampen that fusee in time!" reminded he grimly.

"You've put 'em all in a blue funk over nought, Pew. I snipped that quick match before we docked in Savannah!"

I then explained on how Darby told me about the secret fusee and what I'd done to doctor it. Pew was delighted and a little more than relieved. Together we clumped and tapped our way below. I for one wanted to watch the antics of that party o' panic-stricken Officers. They didn't disappoint me neither!

The quick match, spluttering and smoking, had burned for half its length along the deck-head. Not one of the lubbers thought to find where the fusee entered the magazine. Instead, they were running around below the burning cord like headless chickens. Merry was stood on Job Anderson's broad shoulders, trying to reach the fusee by flapping a jacket up at the beam, while five feet away lay the very ladder I had used. Israel Hands and Black Dog were scooping buckets of bilge water and tossing them towards the deck-head, soaking everybody including themselves. Topping the stiffest yard to nothing were the combined brains of Ireland and Wales. O'Brien and Morgan were running in and out of the magazine locker with armfuls of cartridges in a vain effort to empty it afore the fusee fetched the powder. But the prize chuckle-head in this drama was Ben Gunn. He was jumping in the air, waving his arms as if trying to fly, and blowing at the flaming match with all his breath along of each leap.

"By the powers, Pew! I ain't seen a sight such as this since Old Farmer Casey's cows escaped into a wheat-field back in my younker days!"

I'd no sooner spoke when the fusee spluttered down towards the magazine. The Crew scattered, diving behind thick tiers of cable, save for the main two idiots o' this saga. O'Brien knelt behind the Kelson, his back-side poking upwards, and hugged his head with his arms. And Ben Gunn, sink me for an

Old Sinner, closed his eyes and stuck both forefingers in his ears.

"'Tis a wonder they don't meet in the middle of your head, Benjamin Gunn!" I roared as the flame reached the fusee's end and fizzled out.

Heads popped up or peered from behind cover and soon me'n Pew were surrounded by a bunch of bewildered, frightened men who hadn't quite fathomed the fact that they were still above board and breathing.

"Shrivel my Soul!" snarled Pew. "Lucky for you we got Barbecue, to do the thinking for us! If not for him, we'd be pork and in pieces by now!"

"Hark you all and hear this!" I said glaring about me. "First and foremost we have to summon all hands and search Savannah alow and aloft, room by room if need be, 'til we track down Mister William Bones!"

"Oi knows where he's at, Sur!" stated O'Brien with a salute. "Oi m'self an' Ben took his sea-chest aboard the Sloop *Rebecca* around T'ree Bells back, so we did!"

"YOU WHAT?" cried the Bosun and Me, both in the same breath.

"Oi, Sur, to be sure!" beamed this bone-headed, Irish bog-hopper, along of another salute.

"Top-side, all hands!" I yelled and started clumping up the steps, dot-and-dash fashion, in a high fever of haste.

"The *Rebecca* be berthed upstream on t'other side of the river, Long John," panted Pew from behind me.

"Billy took the Yawl, so we'll have t' launch the Chaloupe!" added Israel. "There won't be no water-men abroad this time o' night for us to pipe a bum-boat alongside!"

We tumbled out onto the Quarter-Deck. It had stopped raining and the storm was passing on with the moon scoffing the wind, as they say. It sighed through the rigging like a lament, sounding lost and lonely. Low, fleecy clouds were racing towards the sea, but they had company. Being borne down river on the ebb, I saw the stern of a Sloop. A quick grab of my glass confirmed my worst fears. The light of her lanthorns showed me the name set amid the gingerbread on the taffarel: *Rebecca*.

The blood pounded through my brain, making my head whirl, as I watched the whereabouts of a King's Ransom slip further and further away from me. Snapping the spy-glass shut, I twisted about on my timber leg. I could feel the ferociousness that was stamped upon my face, making the skin burn, and those nearest me drew back in alarm.

"Come you 'ere, Benjamin Gunn!" I snarled, passing the spy-glass to Black Dog. And when the Carpenter came cringing abreast of me, I seized his throat in my right hand. "Where for be the *Rebecca* bound?" I roared, forcing him onto his knees.

"I don't rightly know, Mister Silver," croaked poor Ben. His eyes bulged and his face turned purple, for my fingers were a point short of throttling him. "The Mate said he were a-goin' to recruit fresh hands," gurgled he with his eyes rolling up into his head.

"With his blasted sea-chest?" I bellowed, feeling my own eye-balls bulging. "You an' O'Brien has 'till cock-crow to report *Rebecca's* destination t' me aboard the Rover's Rest! Failing that, I'll set the pair o' ye t' swinging on the Main-Yard a-fore the sun's an hour old!" cried I and flung the Carpenter into the arms of O'Brien.

How I never sunk them pair o' swabs, then and there, just shows to what degree I were master of my self control, now don't it? Wish I had done – mind! After colliding with the rank Irelander, those two dullards hot-footed it across the deck and disappeared down the gang-board in a twinkling. I motioned the Company to follow me and we repaired to below the Great Cabin into the Gunner's quarters. I recall yet the notice tacked to a support post:

'RULES OF THE GUN-ROOM'

RULE ONE:	The GUNNER is ALWAYS RIGHT!
RULE TWO:	If This Ain't The Case, Then RULE ONE Will Apply!
RULE THREE:	Should Any ROVER Be In Doubt Regardin' RULES ONE And TWO: 'KEEP YER TRAP SHUT!'

Such was the Philosophy of Israel Hands.

We fired up our pipes and everybody helped hisself to a noggin of rum from the Gunner's private keg. I seated myself behind the mess-table hanging between the brace of stern-chasers, and took stock of the present company I was lumbered with. At the start of the mutiny the staunch hands had numbered fifteen men, like in Flint's song. We were now reduced to nine, including myself. Barring Ben Gunn and Shamus O'Brien, who didn't count for much anyway, nor never did, seated around me were: Blind Pew; Black Dog; George Merry; Job Anderson; Tom Morgan; and Israel Hands. Here then, was all that remained from Flint's original 'Flying Forty'!

"I don't fathom you, Barbecue," began the Bosun. "Bill's bowled hisself out with our map and here's us sat a-suppin' rum like it was Sunday. We should pipe 'All Hands!' Sound the Hue and Cry an' let's set sail after the swab – that's my vote!"

"Pew, in the first place it is Sunday!" I replied puffing smoke. "In the second place, we wouldn't get too far without rations and water. And for number three, we don't know where the *Rebecca*'s bound. We could chase all over the ocean for ten years and never meet her more. No, mate. This situation calls for careful planning – *Festina lente*, as Flash Dan would say."

"What in Hades do that mean?" asked Black Dog scowling.

"Hasten slowly," came my soft answer. "Something which your sort ain't accustomed to doing. Rush here, rush there, a drink o' rum today and go hang tomorrow! What price the Jolly Dollars then?"

"Long John's right," said Job Anderson. "We won't go far wrong following the course set by our Quarter-Master – that's for sure!"

"Go on, Barbecue! You tell us wot's wot, see!" urged Morgan.

"Supposin' Bones talked *Rebecca*'s Cap'n into sailing for the Treasure? There's a double broadside for starters an' us hung here in stays!" grumbled Merry glowering about him.

"George! If I were to put a double broadside in your ear, I'd still miss your brain – it being that small!" I retorted.

"Stay a bit, Barbecue! Let's not launch off on a war o' words and wit!" cried Pew, thumping his stick upon the deck.

"I'd never do such a thing, Bos'n, not with poor George only 'half' prepared – Listen! Billy wouldn't trust his own Mother with knowledge o' that Treasure, let alone a Shipful o' strangers – thunder no! Here's what he'll do, most like. He'll make for some port of commerce, New York, Boston or maybe even England. Wherever *Rebecca*'s bound it won't be a Buccaneering base – you may lay to that! Once safe ashore, he'll seek out a snug berth and stay low 'til all risk o' pursuit be passed. Then he'll fathom out how to collect the Blunt. Knowing Mister William Bones, as I do, he won't be sharing it with nobody!"

"But where do us starting looking for the swab?" hissed Blind Pew and began tearing at his finger-nails with his teeth.

"Wherever the *Rebecca* first docks," I replied and took a good pull of rum, for my pipe were well parched with so much talking.

"She could put-in to half a dozen ports, Long John, all of 'em hostile to us. *Walrus* is too well known, by name and reputation in any road, to follow up in. We'd be in irons afore we could belch and sharing a date with Jack Ketch on Execution Dock!" exclaimed Hands.

"Ah, Israel, you're a sharp lad, to be sure!" I nodded and smiled, took a couple of puffs and continued. "But Long John's way ahead o' you on that score. This old war-horse has got to go West – likewise the Crew!"

"Capital!" cried Pew. "The more blunt for us come share-out! We don't owe them mutinous dogs a damn doit nohow!"

"How d'you figure to get rid of a whole Ship then, along of the Company? There be more o' them than there is of us, see, mark you," reminded the Welshman, squinting through the smoke haze.

"Same way Flint planned on doing it – a quick match to a full magazine with us laying off in the long-boat."

"You mean they is to be blowed up?" scowled George Merry. "I got me two good mates among them as be berthed ashore! Saved my life at Sarasota, now surely that's worth something to . . ."

"Staunch hands?" I asked, interrupting.

"Aye, Johnny and Dirk be pistol proof enough," returned Merry with a nod.

"Then we'll include 'em in the Company, if there ain't no objections," I said, giving all my gang an enquiring glance.

"That Dirk, be a bit of a shirker, but he's bold enough in a set-to," admitted Black Dog, putting a grog-glass into Pew's groping hand.

"So be it then. But mark you this, George Merry!" I warned, jabbing at him with my pipe. "Don't breathe a word to 'em until I say! Mates have a habit o' telling mates, who tell mates! Afore you know it, we'd be the ones under hatches! Your mouth is apt to be a mite slack at times and flap more'n my left trouser leg in a high wind!"

"I'll not peach the plan to a soul, Long John – I swear!" vowed Merry.

"Woe to him who does!" snarled Pew. "For his tongue'll flap free enough in two halves – along of me slitting it!"

In the dim, smoky light of the Gun-Room, George looked to turn green.

"Why bother sending them below board, John? Be easier and a sight safer to leave 'em laid aside in Savannah, wouldn't it?" enquired Anderson tamping down his tobacco with a musket ball.

"Easier, aye! Safer, no! I don't want a bunch of has-been Buccaneers following up in my wake, unlooked for like Pirates at Prayer! We can't afford loose-ends in this deep game. Loose-ends have a way o' terminating into hangman's nooses with the necks of those who make the mistakes being stretched in 'em!" I glared about me. "Any more questions?"

"Aye," drawled Israel looking shrewd. "I inspected the match as remains a-top the magazine. There be less than six feet left."

"So?"

"So who'd be fool enough to fire a fast fuse that short?"

There came a clattering on the stairs that led down from the aft hatchway and O'Brien stood beaming his gappy-toothed grin at us. "Yerzz good Lady Wife told me Oi mought find yerzz still 'ere, Quarter-Master!" he boomed. "The *Rebecca* be bound for Bristol!"

"Well done, Shamus my son!" cried I, slapping my knee in delight. "Pour the man a noggin! There now, Gunner, I reckon that puts paid to your last question!"

We all roared with laughter and the rank Irelander joined in our mirth. He didn't know the joke was on him, for I had big plans concerning our friend

O'Brien. Little did I dream that a dullard such as he would be capable of causing a back-flash, where all of us were to fall head-first into the grave and barely have time to jump out again afore it was filled in! We were still enjoying a goodly giggle, when there came a crash and a thump from above in Flint's Cabin. Our sniggering broke off quicker than if our throats had been cut!

"Wha . . . what was that then?" faltered Morgan, turning whiter than a dove.

"Some swab's skulking around in Flint's Quarters, that's what!" I cried. "Top-side, all hands, and lively!"

We tumbled up the steps onto the Quarter-Deck and hove-to. There, kneeling alongside the wheel with his hands clasped in prayer and his head tilted towards Heaven, was Ben Gunn blubbering silent mouthings at the Almighty.

"Save me, Mister Silver!" wailed he wrapping his skinny arms around my leg. "I only went in the Cabin for a bit o' Flint's Parmesan cheese, as I know he keeps there in that Ming pot on the dresser! Just about to lift the lid, I was, when he jumps out his hammic and sits on the floor a-lookin' at me!"

"Come now, Ben, Flint's dead!" I snapped, feeling my blood run cold. "Black Dog, take Israel and Tom for a look-see!"

"I ain't setting foot inside that Cabin, not for all the gold in Castille!" replied the Bosun's Mate stepping back a pace.

"Nor me neither, not nohow, Long John!" voiced Morgan. "It ain't wise to cross a Spirit – isn't it?"

"'Specially Flint's," said Israel all solemn and for the first and last time in his life I saw the Gunner cross hisself.

"Thunder! One word from this 'ere cretin of a Carpenter and you're ready to go-about an' run at the drop of a hat! Well by the living or dead powers, whichever the case may be, I've faced Flint down twice alive an' I'll face him down in death!" I glared about me, gripping my trusty timber tight enough to crack a walnut, then clumped into the passage-way that led to the Cabin.

Now I confess, approaching the stove-in door on my own, my leg turned to jelly and I could feel my tarred queue sticking out from the nape o' my neck – straight as a jack-staff. I had to keep my teeth tight clenched to stop 'em from sounding like castanets. Then with a deep breath, I mustered every last ounce of courage I possessed and entered.

My heart misfired and the sweat popped out of every pore. Flint was there upon the floor, sure enough, staring straight at me. Sat with his hands still folded across his chest, he was, for all the world same as a blue-faced Buddha! I half turned, ready for to flee, but in hesitating I saw what were amiss. During Darby's set-to with Billy, the hammock rope, secured to the bulkhead, had been near cut through. When it parted, in swinging back against the Mizen, to which the other end was tied, Flint was dumped upon the deck and propped against the musket rack. Staring he was to be sure, the penny pieces having fallen from his eyes, but dead as chivalry and stiff as a plank – along of what Flash Dan used to call *rigor mortis*. My expelled breath o' relief left me more lightheaded than too much rum and you may lay to it!

I summoned my staunch Crew, condemning the Carpenter for a fool and the rest for rank cowards. Ben Gunn I set to repairing the door, while the others interned Flint in his hammock. Handled him like he was possessed o' the plague, they did. The hammock were then lashed up and there he lay, swinging above board in a gaudy cocoon. Darby M'Graw was wrapped in the zebra-skin rug and served the same, his canvas bed being at right angles to Flint's. When all was carried out to my satisfaction, I locked the door and hobbled home in company of my lodgers. Wet and weary I was to, but my Charlotte soon had me tucked up snug along of a clean, flannel night-shirt, secure under the eiderdown with a nice hot toddy.

News of the Captain's death and Darby's murder spread faster than a secret among washer-women. The town's people being God-fearing, suspicious folk, soon learned our whole history from the blabbing mouth of Ben Gunn. I sent word out for the Carpenter, but he was missing from *Walrus* together with his sea-bag. We found ourselves shunned, the married members of our Crew declining the company of former ship-mates. Then Blind Pew was stoned by a mob of jeering children. In consequence, the Bosun's flailing stick struck and badly concussed a young boy. All Savannah showed bare-faced hostility. Charlotte was refused service at market and when rocks started crashing through the Rover's Rest windows at the dead o' night, I knew it were high time to cut and run!

I sold the Inn for a quarter of its true value. The swab of a Merchant knew I were close-hauled and on the verge of cutting my cable. That same fore-noon we all berthed aboard *Walrus* and made ready for sea. Close to sailing, we were, and I was stood on the quarter-deck discussing some minor problem with Job Anderson, when a Schooner bound for the South Sea trade came gliding past.

"Thunder!" exclaimed the Coxun pointing. "Look'e there, Long John!"

I swung about and there, standing just abaft the Traders' midships was – Ben Gunn! He hauled hisself up on the bulwarks and cupped both hands to his mouth. "Goodly-bye, 'Mister' Silver, you silly, stork-legged old lubber! Lost your Carpenter, thinks you, and right you are, says I! Hope your timber leg gets woodworm, along o' dry-rot!" cried he. Then the swab stuck his thumbs alongside his temples, twinkling his fingers at me, and poked out his tongue.

"By the Powers, Gunn! It'll be a Black Day for you when next we meet!" I roared in reply, burning up with rage.

But the Schooner had already carried the Carpenter out of ear-shot and out of my life – or so I supposed. Little did I imagine that along of our next meeting, my forementioned 'Black Day' was to be all mine! You wouldn't credit a lubber such as Ben having the last laugh on the likes of Old Long John, now would you? Ah, well he did too, but that be a different story!

We sailed for Boston, keeping the shore-line in view. The course was straightforward and navigation wasn't difficult, seeing as Flint's maps were of the best – made by the great Herman Moll hisself. My excuse to the Crew was that I'd arranged to meet a consort there; also, Charlotte needed to be placed ashore in company of the Bosun, Black Dog and Job Anderson who were to journey into Town with her and make arrangements to re-supply *Walrus*.

In the dimness of a false dawn, *Walrus* hove-to off the coast about two miles from Boston harbour, since we couldn't sail into port, not aboard Flint's old war-horse. After Charlotte and Pew's Party were safe landed with all their traps and mine, including Cap'n Flint in her cage, we cruised ten miles off the coast, finally dropping anchor at dusk. Still in company of our dead Captain and his faithful Steward, I spent a busy two hours with paper and pen, seated at Flint's desk, for I'd promised the Crew a surprise come sunset – and how!

At the appointed time, Israel piped: 'All Hands Aft' for Captain Silver's address – the trusting Souls having elected me their Leader.

"My Lads!" said I from my station on the Poop, using Flint's old phrase. "You've been patient with me in sailing under sealed orders, so to speak, and borne all this secrecy in true Brotherhood fashion! When Billy Bones cut and ran with Flint's Fist, I told you not to worry! Trust old Barbecue, I said, and trust me you did! Well, now it be my turn! The Mate's map ain't worth tu'pence, for I switched papers afore he fled! Here's the true Treasure Chart!" I cried, waving aloft my efforts of earlier in the day.

They cheered and applauded me to a man, while I glanced down on 'em, beaming my good intentions. One and all were looking up with reverence in their eyes – made me feel like the Blessed Pope, they did!

"And now, ship-mates!" I continued. "To show my prodigious faith in this 'ere Company, just send the youngest member among you up here!"

There was much muttering in discussing this, until finally a thin, gawky, spotty-faced youth were hussled to the fore, grinning like he'd just been voted Cap'n. "Here he is, Sir!" bawled the Lad's usher. "Young Joshua Grotty, a point short o' eighteen!"

"Step you up here, my son!" I ordered and Israel delivered him, blushing like a bride. "Whether we become rich as princes or end our days sponging for grog like paupers, depends upon you, younker – Guard it along o' your life!" I said and presented him with the worthless Chart. His eyes near popped out his head, to be sure!

"But enough talk! This calls for a celebration! Break out the rum and drink a toast to success – all hands!"

By the row that greeted my words, I'd have wagered ten guineas that their vapouring fetched Boston Harbour. The next few hours were pure bedlam aboard *Walrus*. They drank and danced the hornpipe and roared out bawdy songs. Young Grotty was treated like Royalty with every Member fawning over him, wanting to see the Map. They fondled it and studied it, pouring over my fake instructions as to where Flint's Fist lay. Soon, the paper was grubbier than Black Dog's wipe, bearing the finger marks of every Fo'c'sle Hand aboard. I passed among them, exchanging pleasantries here and a drink there, but spitting most of the offered rum back into the cup. For what I was about to embark on needed a clear head – and you may lay to that, mates!

Around nine of the clock, before everybody became full seas over, I put the first phase of my plan into operation. When I casually remarked to a group of revellers that I was worried about a possible loose googing that housed the rudder pintles, and would they oblige me by lowering the long-boat so's Mister Merry might check it, they near fell over themselves to comply.

Close to the 'Bewitching Hour' with my crowd all gathered in the Great Cabin, along of George Merry's two mates, Dirk and Johnny, I took a final tour of inspection. Bodies were flaked out everywhere, snoring fit to split. The whole Ship stank of rum. Young Grotty was fast asleep in the Fo'c'sle, clutching the useless chart to his chest. A group of hardened Rovers still kept him company, drinking while discussing on how they intended spending their forthcoming wealth. I took a drink, wished 'em 'Good-Night' and hobbled aft. On the way I pulled the haliard that released Flint's Pennant and sent the twelve foot banner of red silk bearing the name of 'NESTER' streaming from the Main-Mast-Head for the last time. Then I hoisted the spare Jolly Roger to flutter from the Mizen Peek. I had Flint's original Ancient in custody of Charlotte, packed in my sea-chest. With all flags flying, the stage was now set for *Walrus*'s final scene upon the high seas!

"Listen close, Shamus my Buck," I said taking the Irelander to one side. "Gunner Hands has showed you where the fusee is at and here's Flint's own flasher with which to light it. When you get a-top the ladder against the locker, count to fifty. You can count, can't you?"

"Aye, Sur, Oi can, but . . ."

"Good! Fire the fusee on reaching fifty and by the time you reports back here, we'll be a-waiting ready in the long-boat. Fifty, mind! Now off you go and look lively – time is short, matey!"

"Not arf as short as that damned match," chuckled Hands after O'Brien had darted through the door.

We wasted not a moment. The sea-chests being already loaded, Morgan and Merry clambered through the stern-sheet window into the long-boat first, ready to assist in bearing me aboard. I gave Flint one final salute:

"Sleep tight, Cap'n, for if ever a rough hand came to his Eternal Port, it were you," I said and slid over the sill.

Dirk followed me, along of Johnny. Israel were last to leave the Cabin. The Gunner had barely turned to untie the painter, when O'Brien's bulk blocked out the light. He was through the window in a twinkling with a cherry: "All's set, Quarter-Master, Sur! Oi fiored 'er up an' she be a splutterin' foine!"

My mind went numb for what seemed Eternity, then jolted into action. There was no time to scold or summarise O'Brien's mistake. We had less than two minutes to draw clear of *Walrus* or share her fate.

"Out oars!" I cried, my voice shrill. "Cast off! Push clear, lively you lubbers! Pull for yer lives! Steady, STEADY! Give way – TOGETHER! Two-six HEAVE! Two-six, HEAVE!"

Under my direction with me at the tiller, we drew away from *Walrus* sweating worse than heretics on a bonfire and sick with fear. Apart from me calling the stroke and steering, no one breathed a word. Our combined efforts sent the long-boat skimming across the surface. Calm, it was, with just a trace of a swell rolling in from the mighty Atlantic. Above us the moon hung in the star-studied sky, bright as a midnight sun. Its beams reflected on the sea, which sparkled and glittered like it were strewn with jewels. Bathed in this brilliance, *Walrus* appeared similar to the Dutchman's ghost-ship – shimmering in the eerie, white light.

We were two hundred yards away, I reckon, when *Walrus* seemed to leap out of the water and a great pillar of flame shot up from amidships, which arrested our rowing. The blast fetched us with a roar, fanning our faces in a warm wind. *Walrus* reared like a live thing; then our Tusked Totem plunged down into the briny and a great wall of billowing foam tumbled towards us. Caught in the surge of this miniature tidal wave, the Chaloupe was carried along on its crest for maybe another hundred yards. It raced on and left us tossing about in the wake of its swell.

Walrus went down by her head, her flaming rigging hissing into the surging sea amid clouds of steam. But she still retained her sticks. The stern reared up out of the water and started to spin. Flint's Red Banner streamed from the Main-Mast, turning in sweeping circles as the stern spun faster and faster in the vortex of its own making. The pennant dragged around the lip of the whirlpool like a streak o' blood and was sucked from sight. I felt the long-boat being pulled towards its parent ship and for one awful moment I had visions of us drawn down into the void o' Doom!

The light was still glowing in the Great Cabin when the water rushed in and extinguished it. My last memory of Flint's war-horse was of the Mizen Peek trailing Jolly Roger. The flag spun faster and faster, sinking lower and lower, then it disappeared down this hole in the ocean. We were being swept towards it, as if caught in a mill-race, when the water suddenly collapsed in upon itself and the greatest Shroud on Earth rolled on, as it did since the dawn of time, leaving us bobbing about like an empty bottle.

And there's the finish of it, thinks you, but no, mates. *Walrus* had one last violent card to play before all was done. We were sat in silence, trying to muster our thoughts, when a triangular shaped head broke the surface, swimming among the wreckage roughly a pistol-shot away.

"A turtle, by thunder!" cried the man Dirk, along of the light being tricky.

"Shark ho!" exclaimed Hands in the same breath, pointing.

I felt a twinge in my stump, for sweeping in was my old adversary from the deep – him whom I hadn't clapped eyes on since the day I lost my leg. Aye, ship-mates, 'twere Clipped Fin. The shark made a bee-line for the turtle, then veered and dived. Once more the sea bubbled and boiled. A great multi-coloured coil arched up, thick as a messenger rope gleaming like a rainbow, and splashed down. Next moment the shark shot out of the water, his huge jaws clamped on one of the thick coils that was looped around his body. No mistaking that triangular head for a turtle's now.

"SAMSON!" we roared – one and all.

Flint's serpent had his teeth buried in the big fish's gills. Together they fell back with a mighty splash and sank from sight. The sea became calm, soothing into a gentle swell again. That was the last I ever see of Samson or Clipped Fin.

"By the Powers," I whispered. "Don't that beat all."

Along of getting my breath, I turned to the Irelander who was still sat spellbound. "You was supposed to count fifty afore lighting that fusee," I croaked, for my pipe was parched and my voice sounded like a rusty gate-hinge swinging in the wind.

"Aye, Sur, but Oi tried t' tell yerz. Oi can only count in TENS! Ten, Twenty, T'irty," blurted he.

For better or worse, fair or foul, we were stuck with Bone-Head O'Brien. He never learned the true nature of what we intended for him, not until Israel Hands told him some years later during an argument they had aboard the *Hispaniola*. O'Brien and the Gunner ruptured into a Royal set-to, which proved fatal for one of 'em. But there again, that be part and parcel of another tale.

We hoisted the lug-sail, broke out the rum and bore away from *Walrus*'s final resting place where she guarded James Flint and Darby M'Graw in Davy

Jones's domain. But ere we sailed, Tom Morgan scooped up a white, sodden square that was floating on the surface. It was Young Grotty's ink-smeared, tattered chart.

The sun was just peeking above the horizon of the sea when, with me at the tiller and a stiff breeze behind us, I sailed the long-boat into Boston Harbour whistling 'Lillibullero'!

CHAPTER XL

THE QUEST FOR FLINT'S FIST!

Well, ship-mates, we mustered as planned, joining up with Charlotte, Blind Pew, Black Dog and Job Anderson. Now you'll agree, I'm sure, that all gathered together we cut rather an unsavoury sight, barring my wife, of course. She, above any, was still pretty as a picture. But a good looking Negress couldn't compensate for the way we presented ourselves to the general public: Me with one leg; Pew with no eyes; and Black Dog missing two talons on his left hand. A gang such as ours travelling together would be bound to cause comment, and the last thing we wanted was to draw attention to ourselves. So along of donning the cloak of respectability to pass undetected, we decided it safer to separate and re-group in Bristol.

I had a little over three thousand pounds banked in Boston, plus the five hundred I'd got for The Rover's Rest. Blind Pew was worth twelve hundred; and Israel Hand's purse contained one hundred and fifty. Apart from a few guineas scattered among them, the rest were flat-stoney-broke. So it was agreed that those with money would finance those who hadn't – to be paid back in full in due course, mind!

Tom Morgan, George Merry and Shamus O'Brien signed on a Merchantman, bound for Town-Side. Pew and Black Dog paid their way to London Pool. Israel Hands and Job Anderson took ship to Portsmouth via Holland; while Me and the Missus had us a sort of holiday, sailing first to Kingston, Jamaica, and finally docking at Falmouth. Black Dog had a wife in Bristol and it was at his house we were to rendezvous.

Posing as a merchant dealing in Margaritas, of which I had a few, Me and the Missus sailed from Boston along of a sad note. Everywhere, stuck up on bill-boards, were big, black-lettered broadsheets proclaiming:

THE TRYALS OF THE PYRATES
Taken by his Majesty's Ship *Swallow*, begun at Cape-Corso-Castle, on the Coast of Africa, March the 28th, 17-

ACQUITTED:		74
EXECUTED:		52
RESPITED:		2
TO SERVITUDE:		20
TO THE MARSHALSEA;		17
KILLED	(in the *Ranger*:	10
"	(in the *Royal Fortune*:	3
DIED	(in the passage to Cape Corso:	15
"	(afterwards in the Castle:	4
NEGROS	in both ships:	70

TOTAL:		267

I forked out a half-penny and bought a more detailed Account. The gist of it were this: HMS *Swallow* had engaged Bartholomew Roberts and after a fierce fight in which Black Bart was killed by a grape-shot striking him in the throat, the RN Fourth-Rater captured both the *Royal Fortune* and *Ranger*, along of a hundred and eighty-four prisoners. The names of those Executed for Piracy leapt out of the paper at me, their faces flashing before my eyes: Valentine Ashplant; Thomas Armstrong (an RN deserter executed aboard HMS *Weymouth*); Bunce; Burtson; Philip Bill; Crow; Clement; Coleman; Davies; Fernon; Giles; Goss; Harper; Hardy; Haws; Hynde; Richard Harris; Robert Hays; Daniel Harding alias Hunter, Barber-Surgeon. There it were, mates! So died 'Flash Dan', swinging and a-sun-drying on the Guinea Coast, a far cry from his native Croomsbury in Somersetshire that he so loved to talk about with a wistful gleam in his eye.

Well, to cut a long story short; we arrived safe at Falmouth and took coach to Bristol where we berthed at the Old Anchor Inn. Near froze to death, I did during that journey, for there ain't nothing more cruel than an English Winter – and me having lived in the Tropics these past twenty-five years agone! Pew and Black Dog were already in-board at the latter's house, as were Morgan, Merry and O'Brien. Anderson and Hands reported in a week later. I was fortunate enough to purchase a nice little Inn down by the Docks, which I had painted and done out, renaming it: 'The Spy-Glass'. My private parlour became our 'Ward-Room', in a manner of speaking, and it was from here that I plotted our future courses in the quest for Flint's Fist.

Now I reckoned it wouldn't be too hard to track down an old, blustery, cantankerous Seaman with a sabre cut on his right cheek, along of the mighty pleasant way he had when far gone in rum. My Gang scattered to all points of the compass in their search for Mister William Bones, Esq. O'Brien, it was, who first brought news concerning the whereabouts of the Mate. A pot-boy in the Ship informed him that he remembered such a man catching the mail coach one morning, close to nine months ago. When asked if he was sure, the lad replied:

"Yes, Mister, 'cos I dropped 'is big box wiv the letter 'B' burned in the top off me barrow and 'e clipped me round the ear! An' I got no tip!"

That was Billy, right enough!

I personally spent a small fortune in plying drinks to every coachman that ever rode the Royal Mail out of Bristol and eventually came up with a trump. One of them recalled my 'Dear Old Ship-Mate' and having set him down at the Royal George, in a hamlet thirty miles or so along the coast, known as 'Black Hill Cove'. I sent Black Dog to spy out the Inn and late the following night his son tumbled me from my bed, near banging the front door down off his hinges.

"Me Da's at 'ome with an 'ole in his shoulder. Says for you to hop round a bit lively. Says he clapped aboard Bill Bones and near got killed!" so this ragged, snotty-nosed, gangling brat informed me.

I flew through the town to his hovel and was seated in the parlour afore an hour was chimed. Blind Pew was present, the Bosun having lodged there. Black Dog was sat with his left shoulder swathed in bandages, his dark complexion now turned to the colour of tallow. His wife was a tall, skinny, bird-like creature with large teeth that matched her eyes – green they was! While she hovered about me, pouring a goodly go of brandy, I listened to Black Dog's tale o' woe.

"The swab ain't berthed at the Royal George, Long John, but across the Cove at an isolated Inn called the Admiral Benbow. I broached him to about the Map and we ended having dry-blows. Threatened to peach on the lot o' us. 'Swing one, swing all,' says he. If it hadn't been for the Inn sign as hung above the door, he'd have split me down to the teeth!"

"Was there much company present?" I asked, my fingers twitching for a feel of the Mate's throat.

"No, all I see were a young boy. The Innkeeper's sick a-bed and there's only the younker, along of his mother. Hawkins is the name, so I were informed at the Royal George."

"We shall have to look alive and budge, pronto," said Pew, "afore Bill shakes out another reef and alters course, along 'o setting sail again."

Budge we did!

After mustering my crew in the morning, I hired us a Lugger and we set sail down the Severn on the ebb. Black Dog came with us, for he knew the land-Marks of Black Hill Cove and we had no Chart to help in locating 'Kitt's Hole'. We hugged the Coast, sailing slowly, with Job Anderson acting as leadsman up for'ard. The chance of surviving a shipwreck in those icy waters would be slim indeed.

The light was already failing when we hove-to and dropped our hook in Kitt's Hole. I sent Dirk and Johnny ashore to find out if our quarry was still berthed at the Admiral Benbow. They were only newly arrived, having been fog-bound off Cape Cod and near wrecked in the Azores before docking at Bristol. They returned sometime after dark with news both good and bad. Billy was still in residence, sure enough. My Scouts reported hearing him singing Flint's old favorite, 'Fifteen Men', at the top of his voice and far gone in rum. The bad news was that Hawkins the inn-keeper had Crossed-the-Bar the previous evening and in consequence there was much coming and going of neighbours. Dirk and Johnny also learned, at the Royal George, that the funeral was to be held on the morrow.

The next day was even busier, along of Hawkins being laid under hatches, and since we'd been spotted by some yokel snooping about up on the cliff, I decided to put to sea so's not to cause undue alarm. Our luck was held tighter in stays when the wind veered and we couldn't beat-up back to Kitt's Hole until the following afternoon. Cold, frosty and foggy, it was too, and with us running low on rum!

Determined to make Billy sweat blood, I decided to tip him the dreaded, 'Black Spot' in accordance to Flint's Old Articles. But here I hit another hitch. No way could I climb up out of the dingle. The wooded hollow of Kitt's Hole was steep, along of loose shale and earth – wet and slippery. And the rest of those chicken-hearted swabs who called 'emselves 'Gentlemen o' Fortune' refused point-blank to confront the Mate – save for Blind Pew. He was staunch, was our Bosun, you can't deny him that, mates! Off he went with Anderson to set him on the right road and we waited.

He returned to the plaudits of us all!

"Pew, I reckon you got bottle enough to face down the Devil hisself!" was my remark.

"Did he threaten you, Bos'n?" asked Merry all agog.

"What did he say, Pew?" cried Black Dog.

"Not a blasted word – not one! I got hold of the Younker and forced him to lead me in and march straight up to, Bill. Near twisted that calf's arm off in making plain my point," added Pew with a cackle in relishing the pain he had inflicted upon Young Hawkins – cruel I calls it!

"Billy thinks he has 'til ten o'clock," I said. "But I intends to turn the screws on that swab, all the way to the blasted stops! Pew, have you bottle enough to venture there again and demand that Chart in exchange for his life?"

"Aye, Barbecue! I could smell his fear when last I faced him!"

"Take the gang, but keep 'em out o' sight from the Tavern. If Bill don't cough up the Chart, then pipe: 'All Hands' and lay him aboard. Give him a go of your woolding cord. Oh for ten toes, by thunder!" I cried and cursed myself for the helpless cripple I were.

Waiting is always the worst part of anything, whether it be a visit to a tooth-puller or to have a tankard re-filled in a crowded pot-house where the serving wenches are slow. And so it were with me, ship-mates. I didn't even have my Old Poll aboard to pass a few sentences o' Tom-Fool sea-talk. I smoked, drank rum and clumped around the deck. Sat upon the hatch-cover, I was, filling my fourth pipe while watching the moon's beams dancing on the water, when a pistol cracked loud and clear in the crisp night air.

I jumped as if shot and swept the cliff top with my spy-glass. Soon the bobbing heads and shoulders of two men running hard hove into view. They disappeared in a twinkling, descending into the trees, and I heard them slithering and sliding in the loose shale as they came pell-mell down the steep slope of the Dell. Three more heads came over the crest of the cliff followed by an avalanche o' shale and stones. All five landed on the beach in a bunch, tumbled into the row-boat and sped towards me, the two sets of sweeps rising and falling in a flurry of spray – the broad blades flashing in the moonlight. Nine men went ashore! Thunder, where were the other four?

"Blasted Revenooers!" gasped Black Dog, being the first to climb aboard. "One o' them Riding Officers trampled Pew below, Long John – he's pork!"

"Bill's dead too!" added Hands.

"Bill and the Bosun under hatches! What fool killed the Mate? And the Map? What of the Chart?" I cried, seizing a fistful of Black Dog's jacket.

I was cut short by five mounted men topping the cliff's crest. The riders dismounted and started to lead their horses down the treacherous slope into the dingle. Why they didn't leave their nags top-side beats me. Customs were mainly brawn more than brains anyway!

"George! Tom! Hoist the spanker! Job, take the tiller! Black Dog, cut the cable! Israel, grab that musket!"

My commands were obeyed without comment, for we were close-hauled by the Customs Men – thinking us smugglers. The Lugger's fore and aft sail caught the quartering wind and we began to make headway as the Revenue Officers reached the shore, emerging into open ground.

"Lugger ahoay! Heave-to in the King's name!" came the cry from the beach.

Cupping a hand against my mouth, I yelled a reply: "Keep out the moonlight or take hot lead in the Devil's name!"

Along of my warning, Israel triggered his piece and sent a ball spinning towards the beach. I don't think he hit anybody, but they looked lively and retreated into the shadow of the trees. Shortly afterwards we doubled the point and were lost to view.

As soon as it was safe, I 'Cleared-Lower-Decks'. Billy, it appeared, had died of apoplexy, while Blind Pew fell victim to his own foul temper. The Inn was found abandoned with the front door wide open. This was after Pew had tried to deliver the 'Black Spot', but felt the door barred from within. My gang ransacked the deserted tavern, alow and aloft, but Bill's sea-chest had been turned out already. This news sent Pew round the bend and he vented his rage on his mates, lashing out with his stick – right and left. He was still thrashing about in the road when the Riding Officers came galloping over the hill. Everybody scattered leaving the Bosun to die like a dog in the dirt, trampled under the hooves of the horse he accidentally ran into. Black Dog saw it all. Dirk and Johnny cut across country, while O'Brien followed the coast road back to Bristol. They all reported in at the Spy-Glass next day. As to the Chart, Flint's Fist was now in possession of the people who owned the inn, either the boy or his mother. All we got for our pains and the loss of Pew was the Mate's money bag, containing £20 15*s*. 4½*d*., plus a bit of silver from the till. On top of all that, I had to pay the Lugger's owner £3 8*s*. 6*d*. for the loss of his anchor! One way or the other, it looked like we had seen the last of Flint's Fist!

But fate works in mysterious ways, mates. Less than a fortnight later the tavern talk in Bristol was – TREASURE! It came to my ear that a certain Squire Trelawney had purchased a Ship, the *Hispaniola*, and along of her being fitted out, he was seeking a Crew. The Squire was a loose talker, to be sure, blabbing about Flint's Fist to one and all. His agent, Isaac Blandly by name, was well known to me and I pumped him for all the information I could concerning John Trelawney.

Now it was the Squire's habit to take an early morning stroll down to the Docks before breakfast, so with a meeting in mind, I spruced myself up. Standing before the mirror with Charlotte fussing and brushing my fine red coat a sobering thought suddenly struck me: I was fifty! It was nearly two years since Flint had died in Savannah, Billy had done a bunk and the *Walrus* went West. My beefy face were a little redder, a little more lined, my blond hair thinner, and I noticed Charlotte's curly thatch was sprinkled with salt and pepper. Where would it all end, I wondered, with old age just around the corner, as I hobbled off to make a memorable date with my own destiny!

"Top o' the morning to'e, Sir! And a rare, fine one it is too for this time of year!" I greeted to a tall, square-shouldered man around my own height with thick, black eyebrows and a ruddy face.

John Trelawney broke off from watching a ship being made ready for sea and viewed me from head to foot with an air of interest. "Good morning to you, Sir. I take it I am addressing a Seaman by the . . . er . . . ah, cut-of-your-jib?" replied he, rolling the sea-phrase around his mouth like it were a humbug.

"To be sure, Sir, or I was until a-losing of my leg while serving under the immortal Hawke," returned I, removing my hat and looking pious. "But God Bless King George, I say, and another broadside for Old England – ha, ha!"

"My man!" boomed the Squire, beaming at me in a manner that caused me a little alarm, for I thought he were about to embrace and kiss me. "It is old salts such as your good self, who have kept this country Sovereign of the Seas for so long! I would deem it an Honour – an Honour and a Privilege to shake you by the hand! Squire John Trelawney, Sir, at your Service!" cried he, extending a broad palm.

"John Silver, Sir – and very much for yours!" I replied and we shook hands heartily.

The Squire engaged me on the spot for Ship's Cook, and took my advice in all matters pertaining to recruiting a Crew. Like leading a bull by the ring in its nose, so it were! I got him to employ all my gang: Job Anderson as Boatswain and Israel Hands got hisself signed on for Coxswain, under my guidance. In short, Flint's entire flock – all of 'em left alive, that is, barring Black Dog. Since his true colours had been revealed for those of a common Pirate, he was to escort my Missus to a safe little hideaway abroad after she'd sold the Spy-Glass. And as for Batty Ben Gunn, only God or the Devil knew where he had gone!

'Tis said that the Devil looks after his Own. Well he were certainly rolling the dice and stacking the books in my favour, at long last. Aye, everything was coming Long John's way; then one bright morning, Young Jim Hawkins came my way. But that saga be recorded by a far more mightier pen than mine. Yes, Shipmates, there ain't much left in the telling of this tale. You'll have to shake out another reef and seek another star to steer by, namely *Treasure Island*!

We've covered a few thousand leagues together, you and I, since being Pressed into this story, but before I close this 'ere log, I'd like one final word: I wants it known to one and all that never, not once, did I ever say: "HA-HA, JIM LAD!"

'AMEN!'

GLOSSARY

A Cripple Grapples Four	see *Treasure Island*, Chapter X
AB	able seaman
Account (on the)	piracy on the high seas
Act of Grace	royal pardon
Affaire d'Honneur	duel
Ague	acute fever
Alcaide	governor (Spanish)
Alligator-pear	avocado pear
Ancient	flag
Appeal to the little stick	use force
Apollyon	angel of destruction (Rev. IX 11)
Aqua-vitae	brandy
Argus	giant with a hundred eyes (Gk Mythology)
Ars longa vita brevis	art is long, life short
Athwart-ships	from side to side
Aut vincere aut mori	victory or death
Baksheesh	alms (something for nothing)
Banshee	female spirit, Irish
Bar (the)	'crossing the bar', dying.
Barbecue	Long John Silver's nickname
Barbary coast	North Africa
Barbuda	Barbados
Barca-longa	large Spanish fishing boat
Barker	pistol
Barracouta	Ferocious tropical fish of the pike family

Beak	magistrate
Bearskin	*See* split the bearskin
Becketed	slung by a looped rope
Bedlamite	lunatic
Belay the last pipe	cancel the last order
Bewitching hour	midnight
Billy Bones's sea-shells	see *Treasure Island* Chapter IV
Bintook	musket
Black Bart	Bartholomew Roberts, a pirate captain
Black Cayman	South American alligator
Black Jack	pirate flag
Blowing big guns	heavy gale
Blunt	money
Bombay buccaneer	naval defence of the East India Company
Book of Books	the Bible
Books	playing-cards
Bottle	courage
Bow-chasers	forward facing cannon
Bow Street Runners	the first detectives
Breaching whale	surfacing whale
Break bulk and lose ballast	be sick
Break bulk	pilfer from cargo
Brig (the)	place of detention on ship (US)
Brig	brigantine; a 2-masted merchant ship
Bring 'em closer	spy glass
Bring to book	bring to account
Brisk hand	staunch fellow
Broach-to	in danger of capsizing
Bucks	Indian warriors
Bulldog	short barrelled, heavy bore pistol
Bullocks	marines (a term used prior to 'Jollies' when they became 'Royal Marines' in 1802
Cable	200 yards length
Camino Real	Royal Road
Cannibal coast	now part of Texas coast
Careen	clean a ship's hull
Cascabel	projection at end of cannon

Cat's paw	slight breeze
Catch as catch can	no holds barred
Chaloupe	long-boat
Cheese down	to coil (ropes)
Chika	Indian corn-beer
Chiki	Seminole summer sleeping house
Chippy	carpenter
Clear lower decks	muster ship's company to give out information
Cloacina, the Temple of	lavatory
Clotpoll	fool
Cob	blob of silver weighed and stamped for minting into coin
Coca	Peruvian shrub, source of cocaine
Cockfords	London club
Coil	fuss, argument or fight
Collier	ship that carries coal
Comadreja (el)	The Weasel (Spanish)
Company (the)	Ship's Company; the crew
Common chest	public property
Comprende?	understand (Spanish)
Coquette	flirtatious woman (Spanish)
Coromandel	coast of south-east India
Coup de grâce	final blow
Cowkiller	buccaneer
Crossing the Styx	dying
Crow	crow bar
Crusher	master-at-arms
Dab-hand	someone good at doing something
Dab-toe	sailor R.N.
Dacoit	bandit, Burma and India
Daddle	cheat
Dago	insulting term for man of Spanish, Italian or Portuguese origin
Dagon	god of the Philistines, half man, half fish
Dart	arrow
DD	discharged, dead (RN term)
Dead eye	circular block of wood with one or three holes in it

Dead marine	empty bottle
Dei gratia, de mortuis nil nisi bonum	by the Grace of God, say nothing but good about the dead (Latin)
Devil's books	playing cards
Devil's sea	Bermuda triangle
Diamond-back	rattlesnake
Diawl	devil (Welsh)
Dies non	day when judges do not sit
Dinero	money (Spanish)
Dog's head	hammer of a pistol or musket
Doing a duck	capsizing
Doit	small Dutch coin, worth half a farthing, valueless
Double-headed angel	chain shot
Doubloon	Spanish gold coin
Drubbing	good hiding
Dry blows (trading)	fighting without profit
Ducks and drakes	a game: skimming flat pebbles across water
Duppy	ghost
Dutch-trade (to)	to cheat
El Animoso	The spirited one – Philip V of Spain
Elephant and Castle	The name by which Londoners referred to King George's two huge German mistresses
Execution dock	Wapping Old Stairs, London
Factory	trading post
Factum est	it is done (Latin)
Faked	coiled
Fall together by the ears	to fight
Fathom	nautical measure, six feet
Fer-de-Lance	yellow viper of tropical America
First bell	half past twelve (or the first half hour of any watch
First Rate ship-o'-the line	three decker, ship of a hundred guns
Flash packet	girl friend
Flasher	tinder-box

Flipper stroke	the killing lance was plunged into a harpooned whale behind the flipper
Flower of forgetfulness	poppy
Flux	dysentery
Flyer	success
F'o'c'sle	forecastle: front part of ship
Foot pad	highwayman on foot
Fortuna favet fatuis	fortune favours fools
Four bells	first two hours of the watch
Frapping	rope used for lashing other ropes together to increase the tension
French leave	desertion
From wood to black-skin	To within touching distance (whaler's term)
Full and by	condition of a ship held as close to the wind as possible with her sails full
Full seas over	dead drunk
Furicano	hurricane (Spanish)
Galley-yarn	rumour
Game not worth the candle	not worth doing
Gammon (to)	hoax
Gibbeted alive	hung in chains until dead, then left to decay
Gingerbread	gilded scrollwork
Goose-wing	one of the lower corners of a ship's mainsail or foresail when the middle part is furled up to the yard
Grace	act of grace; pardon
Grampus	spouting whale
Great gun	£20,000
Great South Sea	South Pacific
Greenwich	naval hospital
Greetin'	crying (Scottish)
Groat	an English silver coin, worth fourpence
Grog	rum and water
Gun-fire	cannon fired an hour before sun-rise, declaring harbour open

Halberd	axe-like weapon with steel spike, mounted on long shaft
Handspec	long handled lever
Hanger	cutlass, sword
Heads	lavatories (situated on the Beak-head)
High-Toby	high road: 'to take the H-T' to become a highwayman
Hispaniola	now divided between Haiti and the Dominican Republic
Hogshead	large cask holding 52½ imperial gallons
Holy-stone	sandstone block 'the size of a bible', used to scour and whiten ships' decks
Hooghly	Indian river that flows through Calcutta
Hunraken	Carib storm god: origin of 'hurricane'
Ill office	harm
In toto	entirely (Latin)
In vino veritas	in wine the truth comes out (Latin)
Jack Ketch	notorious hangman
Jerked meat	strips of sun-dried meat
Jesuit powder	quinine
Jetsam	goods thrown from a ship and washed up on shore
John Company	East India Company
Johnny and Dirk	see *Treasure Island* Ch. V
Johnston, Captain Charles	pseudonym of Daniel Defoe
Joint	hand or foot
Judas haired	red haired; Judas Iscariot was said to have had red hair
Junk	a) old ropes b) pork
Ken	know (Scottish)
Kelson, keelson	ship's inner keel
Kill-devil	rum
Knee	L-shaped timber
La mer	the sea (French)
Larboard	old term for port, or left hand side
Lateen	triangular sail

League	three nautical miles
Letter of Marque or Mart	privateering commission
Leviathan	whale
Light pair of heels	clean hull
Linguister	interpreter
Little bit dead	native jargon meaning wounded
Locker	magazine or shot locker
Logged	recorded in ship's log book
Long pig	South sea island cannibal name for white captive
Long twelve	12-pounder cannon
Loon	fool
Lung fever	tuberculosis
Madre de Dios	mother of God (Spanish)
Main-hot	as in Spanish Main
Make a mend	time off
Magellan, Ferdinand	Portuguese navigator, first captain to circumnavigate the globe
Malabar coast	West coast of India to Bombay
Mamuque	UFO
Margaritas	pearls, named for the island where the best pearls come from
Manger	pen up for'ard where livestock is kept
Marled	bound with marline
Marline	light rope
Mast headed (to be)	minor punishment in which a man is sent to the top of the main-mast to sit for several hours
Master	sailing master, navigator. In Long John's case, only to sail the ship
Match	prepared cord for firing a gun
Mawmar	drain of the bilge pump
Mealed	finely ground
Me illumina, Domine	Enlighten me, Lord (Latin)
Merry Andrew	drunk sailor
Miller, Andrew	The Andrew, a term meaning the Royal Navy, named after a notorious press-gang officer

Moidore	Portuguese gold coin worth about 27 shillings
Mon dieu	my God (French)
Moses boat	flat, broad-bottomed boat for carrying casks
Mosquito Coast	east coast of Nicaragua
Mugger	Indian crocodile, lying in wait for victims, hence modern street robber
Nantucket sleigh ride	being towed by a harpooned whale
Nasee	smashed nose
Neaters	neat rum
Newmarket	The home of British horse racing
New Spain	Mexico
New Granada	Colombia
Ninny	fool
North Sea	here, the Caribbean
O'Brien, Shamus	see *Treasure Island*, Ch. XXV
OD	ordinary seaman
Oggin	sea
Old Roger	also Jolly Roger: pirate flag
Old stander	long term buccaneer
One bell	same as 'First bell'
Orca	killer whale
Ordinary (in)	laid up, put aside
Orinoco	Venezuelan river
Owley	idol
Palm Key	Florida
Palmetto	palm fronds
Palsy	paralysis
Pax vobiscum	peace be with you (Latin)
Peek (from) to keel	from top to bottom
Perros	dogs (Spanish)
Peruvian bark	quinine
Petty tally	store of comforts for sick men
Picaroons	pirates
Piccaninny	small negro child
Pintle	bolt on which the rudder turns

Piragua	dug out canoe
Pistol proof	brave, daring
Pistol shot away	about 25 yards
Plata	silver
PO	Petty Officer, RN
Poignard	dagger for the left hand
Point of honour	flogging
Pole-axe	long handled battle-axe
Pooping	a huge wave breaking astern
Port o'Spain	see *Treasure Island* Ch. VI
Potting shed	conservatory
Preventers	supporting ropes
Quarter	mercy
Quarters	action stations
Queen Anne	bell-barreled pistol
Queen's coat (to wear the)	served in the army of Queen Anne
Quill driver's cramp	writer's cramp
Quirt	short whip
Quis custodiet ipsos custodes?	who will guard the guards themselves (Latin)
Quoin	wedge for raising a cannon
Real	Spanish coin of eight reals. A 'real' is one 'bit' – could be cut into eight pieces for small change
Redshanks	indentured servant
Red tape	ship's papers
Reynard	fox
Rhino	money
Rider	Spanish cash stamped with a mounted knight
Riggers	men in charge of the ropes
Rio Grande	great river (Spanish)
Roads	sheltered off-shore anchorage
Rolled	attacked and robbed
Round robins	circles
Rovers	pirates
Rudder googings	rudder supports
Rumfustian	mixture of beer, gin and sherry, heavily spiced

Run-ashore	night on the town
Sacré Bleu	Sacred Blue
Sail	ships
St Christopher	St Kitts
Salt-box	long, cylindrical leather case for carrying a powder charge up to the guns from the magazine
Salve	hail (Latin)
Samson post	support post beneath hatchway
Sauve qui peut	save himself who can (French)
Schnell	quickly (German)
Seas, 'at the seas'	buccaneering
Sea-lawyer	one who professes to know everything
Selkirk, Alexander	Robinson Crusoe
Sewed	touching the bottom
Sheet-anchor	an anchor for emergency: added security
Shellback	scarred by excessive flogging
Shooting a line ashore	bragging
Shot	cannon ball, bullet
Sic itur ad astra	such is the way to the stars (Virgil)
Sinite parvulos ad me venire	suffer little children to come to me (Latin)
Six bells	third hour of any watch
Slip moorings	to die
Snotties	midshipmen
Snow	large two-masted merchant ship
Soloman Grundy	salmagundi; dish with many ingredients
Sons of Adam (like the)	stark naked
South Seas	South Pacific
Spanish coquette	enticing woman
Spanish Lake	the Caribbean
Sparks	diamonds
Split the bearskin	divide spoils and/or split up company
Spoilt cargo	worthless
Square number	cushy job
Starter	a length of rope knotted at one end, used by the Bosun's Mates to gee-up the crew

Standing rigging	fixed ropes
Stern-chasers	two cannons jutting from the stern
Stick	mast
Stink pot	smoke bomb
Strike ones colours	surrender
Sweat (to)	torture
Sweeps	oars
Swinging the lamp	telling stories
Styx	river of the Underworld over which Charon ferried the souls of the dead
Tank	the ocean
Tartar; catch a t. by the ears	take on more than one can handle
Throw out one's ballast	be sick
Timoneer	helmsman (French)
Tiburon	killer fish
Torta	large Spanish silver ingot
Totem	figurehead or emblem of worship
Town-Side	Liverpool
Traps	luggage
Truck	gun carriage wheel
Tuck	sword
Turn-to	start work
Turnip man	George III (Farmer George)
Twist. Plugs o' twist	chewing tobacco
Two cables' length	four hundred yards
Union Flag	Union Jack
Vapour	to shout
Vino. In vino veritas	in wine is truth, when people are drunk they are indiscreet
Virgin Queen	Elizabeth I of England
Voodoo	sorcery in the West Indies
Ward-room	officer's mess
Warp (to)	tow
Water ship (to)	take on fresh water
White (the)	squadron of the Royal Navy; there were three: red, white and blue

White doves nesting with blackbirds	pertaining to intermarriage
Will-o'-the wisp	marsh light
Wipe	handkerchief
Writing his will	dying
Yahoo	brute in human form
Yawl	ship's small boat
Yellow Jack	yellow fever
Younker	young lad

SOME VERY GOOD BOOKS

The Spanish Main	(
The Men-of-War	(
The Frigates	(The Seafarers: Time-Life Books
Fighting Sail	(
The Pirates	(
David Mitchell	Pirates
John Gilbert	Pirates and Buccaneers
Daniel Defoe	A General History of the Pyrates
William Falconer, 1780	Falconer's Marine Dictionary
Peter Kemp	The Oxford Companion to Ships and the Sea
Cyril Hamshere	The British in the Caribbean
Captain A. A. Bestic	Kicking Canvas
James Choyce	The Log of a Jack Tar 1790s to the 1820s
Alexander Kent	The Richard Bolitho Stories
C. S. Forrester	The Hornblower Stories
Alexander Fullerton	The Thunder and the Flame (The Story of the Epic Sea-Fight between Sir Richard Grenville's *Revenge* and fifty-three Spanish ships)
Jeffrey Iverson	More Lives Than One . . ? (The Bloxham Tapes)
Jacques-Yves Cousteau and Philippe Diole	Diving for Sunken Treasure
Howard Linecar	Coins – Coin Collecting
Samuel Carter III	How to Sail
Robert Abels	

(Catalog No.32. New York) Antique Firearms and Edged Weapons
Golden State Arms, Inc. 1958 World's Guns and Other Weapons
Collins National Dictionary
Collins English Gem Dictionary
Oldham's Concise English Dictionary
Roget's Thesaurus of English Words and Phrases
The Book of Books – The Holy Bible
And Last but not Least, R.L.S.'s Immortal

TREASURE ISLAND!